Praise for the novels of

Lora Leigh

"Leigh draws readers into her stories and takes them on a sensual roller coaster." —*Love Romances & More*

"Leigh writes wonderfully straightforward and emotional stories with characters that jump off the page." —*The Road to Romance*

"Fraught with tension from the first page to the last . . . A love story of the deepest kind with a very emotional and sensual base. Combine all these elements together and [you're] guaranteed an intriguing story that will have you glued to the edge of your seat." —*Fallen Angel Reviews*

"Blistering sexuality and eroticism . . . Bursting with passion and drama . . . Enthralls and excites from beginning to end." —*Romance Reviews Today*

"A scorcher with sex scenes that blister the pages." —*A Romance Review*

"Thrilling . . . Explosive . . . A perfect blend of sexual tension and suspense." —*Sensual Romance Reviews*

"An emotional read." —*The Best Reviews*

"Hot sex, snappy dialogue, and kick-butt action add up to outstanding entertainment." —*Romantic Times* (top pick)

"Ms. Leigh is one of my favorite authors because she creates new worlds that I want to visit and would move to if only I could." —*Erotic-Escapades*

"The writing of Lora Leigh continues to amaze me . . . Electrically charged, erotic, and just a sinfully good read!" —*JoyfullyReviewed.com*

"Wow . . . The lovemaking is scorching." —*Just Erotic Romance Reviews*

Nauti Deceptions

Lora Leigh

BERKLEY SENSATION, NEW YORK

THE BERKLEY PUBLISHING GROUP
Published by the Penguin Group
Penguin Group (USA) Inc.
375 Hudson Street, New York, New York 10014, USA

Penguin Group (Canada), 90 Eglinton Avenue East, Suite 700, Toronto, Ontario M4P 2Y3, Canada
(a division of Pearson Penguin Canada Inc.)
Penguin Books Ltd., 80 Strand, London WC2R 0RL, England
Penguin Group Ireland, 25 St. Stephen's Green, Dublin 2, Ireland (a division of Penguin Books Ltd.)
Penguin Group (Australia), 250 Camberwell Road, Camberwell, Victoria 3124, Australia
(a division of Pearson Australia Group Pty. Ltd.)
Penguin Books India Pvt. Ltd., 11 Community Centre, Panchsheel Park, New Delhi—110 017, India
Penguin Group (NZ), 67 Apollo Drive, Rosedale, North Shore 0632, New Zealand
(a division of Pearson New Zealand Ltd.)
Penguin Books (South Africa) (Pty.) Ltd., 24 Sturdee Avenue, Rosebank, Johannesburg 2196,
South Africa

Penguin Books Ltd., Registered Offices: 80 Strand, London WC2R 0RL, England

This book is an original publication of The Berkley Publishing Group.

PRINTING HISTORY
Berkley Sensation trade paperback edition / February 2010

Library of Congress Cataloging-in-Publication Data

Leigh, Lora.
    Nauti deceptions / Lora Leigh.
        p. cm.
    ISBN 978-0-425-232552
    1. Women teachers—Fiction. 2. Sex scandals—Fiction. 3. Kentucky—Fiction. I. Title.
    PS3612.E357N383 2010
    813'.6—dc22   2009042379

PRINTED IN THE UNITED STATES OF AMERICA

10 9 8 7 6 5 4 3 2 1

For Sharon,
for watching my back and always watching over me.
For being more than a friend. And for putting up
with all my eccentricities.
For Cory, for taking the time, and trying to be patient.
For my children, Bret and Holly.
Thanks for loving me, for accepting me,
and for being not just my children,
but also my friends.
And for Ryan, because you'll make a good
baby daddy.

PROLOGUE

Four years ago

Now, how had she known the day was just going to suck? Caitlyn Lena Rogue Walker watched as Principal Thompson entered the classroom after her freshmen students had left for the day. Hot on his heels were the self-righteous Nadine Grace and her bully of a brother, Dayle Mackay.

She knew what was coming. Somehow they'd found a way to punish her for coming to a student's defense the month before. She had been waiting for the shoe to drop, and she had a feeling that when it fell, it was going to be an earthquake in her little life.

At least she didn't have to worry about it happening any longer.

Maybe she should have heeded her father's advice about coming here to his hometown to teach. He had wanted her to stay in Boston; he'd wanted her to be a lawyer rather than a teacher. Or better yet, the wife of a lawyer. Being a lawyer or the wife of a lawyer didn't suit Caitlyn Rogue though. Neither did the name Lena—her friends and family knew better than to call her Lena if they wanted her to respond. She wanted to teach, and she wanted to teach in the picturesque little town her father had told her so many tales of.

Perhaps she should have heeded the tales he had told her of Dayle Mackay and Nadine Grace though, as well as his warnings to make certain she stayed off their radar. But staying off their radar hadn't been as easy as she had thought it would be.

And as her father had warned her, they would target her simply because she was a Walker. Nadine Grace and Dayle Mackay had tried to destroy her father when he was younger, and it seemed they were more than determined to destroy her.

She had lived in Somerset for one short year. Long enough to know she loved it here. Long enough to plant a few quick roots, to dream, and to meet the county's beyond-sexy sheriff.

The schoolteacher and the sheriff. What a fantasy. Because within months, she learned that her father hadn't been exaggerating about Dayle and Nadine. At the end of the school term the year before, she'd been forced to enter their radar to defend one of her students against Nadine's accusations that he had cheated on an exam that she had overseen as a member of the Board of Education. Caitlyn knew the boy hadn't cheated, just as she knew that no defense would help her now.

As her gaze met the two, she could feel her stomach tightening in warning as her heart began to pound a heavy, sluggish beat.

Brother and sister resembled each other in too many ways. The same black hair, the same squared features. Nadine was built smaller, and her eyes were hazel rather than green. Dayle Mackay was taller, with thicker black hair and forest green eyes. He would have been handsome if the evil that was a part of his soul didn't reflect in his eyes.

Neither Dayle nor Nadine spoke as they entered the room with the principal. Rogue remained in her seat, watching them cautiously as Nadine moved forward and slapped a small stack of pictures down in front of her.

A glimpse of the first one was enough to know exactly how Dayle and Nadine intended to destroy her.

Caitlyn stared down at them, feeling shame, mortification, but mostly defeat. She had never known defeat until she stared down at the pictures that she knew she could never refute. Not because she hadn't done it, but because she had been unable to stop it.

Fanning the pictures out slowly, she had to bite back a cry that tightened her chest and had her hands shaking. She had somehow known that one night that she couldn't fully remember had been a setup. She had sensed it then, she knew it now, and the rage and pain festered in her chest like a wound she wondered would ever heal.

Rogue swallowed back the bile that rose in her throat and ordered herself not to react, not to show pain, fear, or anger. She had her pride and she would be damned if she would let these two know how much they were hurting her. How much they were stealing from her.

"As you can see, Ms. Walker, there's no way we can allow you to remain within the educational system," Principal Thompson informed her in a tone laced with chilling morality. "Such actions cannot be condoned."

No, they couldn't be, Caitlyn would be the first to agree with him. If she had done it voluntarily.

The pictures showed her half undressed, her skirt raised well above her thighs, her legs spread for the male between them. Higher, her blouse was undone; a female, her long hair obscuring her face, obviously caressed Caitlyn's bare breasts with her lips.

Caitlyn blinked down at the photos. There was no fighting them, though she knew, whatever had happened that night, she hadn't had sex. When she had awakened in the unfamiliar hotel room, the first thing she had done was schedule an emergency appointment with her doctor. But the school board wouldn't care about that. No more than they would care about the blood tests that had shown that whatever happened, she hadn't gone into it willingly. Rogue had been drugged and betrayed.

She was still a virgin, but she would be branded as a whore.

She could fight it. She could call her parents. Nadine Grace and Dayle Mackay had no idea how powerful her parents were now, how eloquently they could seduce a jury, how enraged they would be if she ever let them know what had happened here. Brianna and Calvin Walker would descend upon this county like wraiths from hell with all the powerful Bostonian wealth they had amassed behind them.

Her grandparents, the Evansworths, were icons in Boston. Her mother's parents would destroy Grace and Mackay without a thought.

But her father had warned her, and she had promised him she was a big girl, and that just like her brother and sister, she would carve out her own future, and she would succeed. She had promised him that there was nothing this county could do to destroy her.

She was going to teach, marry, and raise babies in the mountains. That was her dream. And her dream was crumbling beneath her feet. She felt her world shifting on its axis, felt the shame and the rage building inside her until she wondered if her head would explode with it.

Nadine sniffed. "You have a week to leave and we'll not resort to putting the pictures on the Internet."

She stared back at the pinched-face bitch that so hated her student Shane Mayes simply because he was the sheriff's son, and the sheriff refused to kowtow to her or her brother. It was rumored Sheriff Zeke Mayes kowtowed to no man, or woman.

"I really don't give a fuck where you put them." It wouldn't do her any good, Nadine would do as she wished anyway. "I'm not leaving Somerset."

"My dear Ms. Walker, your employment here . . ." the principal began.

"Is obviously at an end." Caitlyn smiled tightly as she picked up the photos and shoved them in her case. "I'll clear my desk this evening, Mr. Thompson."

"You'll leave town," Dayle Mackay stated, his voice like ice.

The man was a viper. His son, the town's bad boy, had a heart of gold. But this man, he was black, evil. It was in his eyes, in his face. It was almost enough to send a shiver down her spine. But she didn't shiver, her spine straightened and pure Walker arrogance and stubborn pride kicked in. Her father had once warned her that her pride would be the death of her.

"Go to hell, Mackay." She could barely speak. Fury was ripping through her, tearing at her.

"Your reputation will be less than nothing by the time we finish with you, Caitlyn." Nadine's tight-lipped, superior smile looked like a wolf's curl of the lip. Anticipatory. Ready to strike. "You don't want to stay here."

"No, you don't want me to stay because you're terrified that if one person stands up to your viciousness, then others will," she stated calmly. "I'm doing more than standing up to you, Nadine, I'm warning you now, you can't hurt me."

Nadine's smile was cold. "Your position within the school system has been terminated, Ms. Walker, and your standing in this county will be history." Her tone assured Rogue she felt she had done the damage she wanted to do.

Caitlyn forced herself to laugh. Her father had taught her how to be strong; her mother had taught her how to be a lady. But her grandmother, ah, her grandmother had taught her how to be a bitch and made Caitlyn enjoy every lesson.

Bess Evansworth was a force of nature and a law unto herself. And Caitlyn had been her favorite. She had always allowed Caitlyn to tag along with her and her cronies to their luncheons and teas. And Caitlyn had learned.

"Put them on the Internet." Caitlyn's smile was all teeth. "I dare you. Better yet, mail a set to my grandparents. Their address is easy to find. Evansworth. Taite and Bessamine Evansworth, Boston. I'm sure my grandmother will get a tickle out of it. Though, Daddy might return to Somerset." She shrugged as though she didn't care. "You could take your chances."

She shoved the few possessions from her desk into her bag. She didn't have much. They hadn't really given her time to settle in. She could fight the school board, but who really wanted to? She'd come here with dreams, and over the past months she had learned how ineffectual those dreams were in these mountains.

Somerset was beautiful, inspiring, and filled with dark, poisonous little creatures just waiting to strike. She had sensed that during the first few months here. She knew it the moment she had met these two, and now she felt their swift, sharp attack.

The pictures were in her purse, but she knew that meant so very little. Simply that she had her own copies. Damn them.

"Staying here will serve no purpose," Dayle Mackay snorted. "You're not wanted, you little bitch, any more than your ignorant father was wanted or any of the Walker clan. The lot of you are nothing but white trash, whores, and drug-guzzling bastards."

Oh, one day, he'd pay for that one. They would both pay for that one.

"Oh well, far be it for me to prove you wrong," she replied mockingly. "Do whatever the hell you want with the pictures. But."

She paused as she picked up the oversized bag at her side. "Be watching for me. When you least expect it." She looked between the two. "When you very least expect it, I'll be there. And it won't be trumped-up photos that are used to break either one of you. It will be the truth."

She left the school, and she left her dreams behind her. She put her dreams behind her, and she refused to call her parents. This was her life, and the thought of dragging them into the mess she had allowed to develop made her cringe.

It was her fault. She should have done as her father warned her and let his friends, who managed the bar he still owned in town, know who she was when she went there, rather than hiding from them. It wouldn't have happened then, because they would have watched out for her.

The problem was, she hadn't wanted anyone to watch out for her. She had been too confident that she could watch out for herself. She was an adult. She was able to defend herself. In the arrogance of youth she had convinced herself that nothing or no one could touch her.

She had entered that bar as confident and arrogant as any young woman that had just turned twenty-one, watched the excitement and fun with a sense of anticipation. And she had let herself be betrayed and nearly used. She had made that mistake. It was no one's fault but her own. She would live with it.

She wasn't about to leave Pulaski County though. As she drove home, she stared out at the mountains, watched the sun blaze full and bright as it began its descent in the evening sky, and she knew she couldn't leave.

She had been raised in the city, but these mountains, they were a part of her. From the moment she had entered them, she had known she had come home, and she'd known she never wanted to be anywhere else.

But now, she knew an adjustment would have to be made.

Her eyes narrowed, her jaw clenched. Damn Nadine Grace and Dayle Mackay. She wasn't going to be run out of town. She wouldn't be defeated like that. They had won this round, and those pictures would probably be on the Internet within hours. But that didn't mean they had beaten her.

Her hands clenched on the steering wheel as she drew in a hard, deep breath. Her father had always called her his little rogue. He would smile fondly when she dressed in her "good girl" clothes as he called them, and his eyes would always twinkle as though he knew something she didn't.

"You're as wild as the wind," he would tell her, and she had always denied it.

But now, she could feel that part of herself burning beneath the surface of the "good girl." The dreams of teaching had always held her back. A teacher had to be circumspect. She had to be careful. But Caitlyn Rogue Walker was no longer a teacher. She no longer had to worry about being circumspect. She didn't have to worry about protecting a job she didn't have.

She flipped on the car's turn signal and took the road that headed to the little bar outside of town. It had begun there—somehow, her drink had been spiked there that night—and if her father knew what had happened, he would burn it to the ground. Unfortunately, she had loved being in that damned bar.

She had sat in the corner, watched, devoured the atmosphere and had longed to be something more than a "good girl" while she had been there.

There was an apartment overhead. The manager, Jonesy, was a good friend of her father's, as were the bouncers that worked there. She only had to walk in, announce who she was, and take over ownership.

Had her father somehow sensed her dreams would go awry

here more than he had told her? Because he had offered her the bar. Told her that when she got tired of playing the political games that filled the educational system that she could always run the bar. And his eyes had been filled with knowledge, as though he had known the wildness inside his daughter would eventually be drawn free.

Her reputation had been destroyed because of whatever had happened there the one night she hadn't been cautious enough. Now it was time to remake that reputation.

Rogue was young, but she was pragmatic. She was bitter now, and she knew that bitterness would fester until Nadine Grace and Dayle Mackay had paid for what they had done. But she wasn't going to let it destroy her. She wouldn't give them the satisfaction of destroying her.

She smiled in anticipation, in anger. Nadine Grace and Dayle Mackay had no idea what they had done. They had destroyed Caitlyn Walker, but nothing or no one could destroy the Rogue she intended to become.

One week later

Sheriff Ezekiel Mayes eased from his current lover's bed and moved through the bedroom to the shower. The widow he was currently seeing slept on, oblivious to his absence as he showered and dressed.

It would be the last night he spent with her, he knew. Zeke insisted on privacy in his relationships. He didn't publicly date; he didn't claim any woman. There was no room in his life, his heart, or his secrets for such a woman. And she was steadily pushing for more. He knew if he didn't break it off now, then it would only become a mess he didn't want to face.

He didn't want ties. He didn't want the complications that came from claiming any woman as his own. He didn't want the danger he knew a woman of his could face. He was walking a thin line and he knew it; he wouldn't make his balance more precarious by taking a lover that could become a weakness. Calvin Walker's daughter was definitely a weakness, simply because of her affiliation with the Walkers and others' hatred for them. The job he had set for himself demanded a fragile balance at the moment. Maintaining that balance would be impossible if he gave in to the needs clawing at his gut right now for one innocent little schoolteacher.

As he moved from the bathroom Mina rolled over and blinked back at him sleepily. Slumberous, dark eyes flickered over him as a pout pursed her full, sensual lips.

"It's not even dawn yet," she muttered, obviously less than pleased to find him leaving.

She should have expected it. He always left before dawn.

"I need to get into the office early," he told her. And he did, but it could have waited.

Mina Harlow was a generous, warm lover, but she wanted a relationship, and Zeke wasn't ready to complicate his life to that extent. He hid enough of himself the way it was, he wasn't interested in hiding it on a regular basis.

"Whatever." She stretched beneath the blankets before eyeing him with a glimmer of amusement. "Oh, I forgot to tell you. That little schoolteacher that looks at you with stars in her eyes, Miss Walker. The school board fired her last week."

He didn't want to hear this particular piece of gossip again. He sure as hell didn't want to hear the satisfaction in Mina's tone at the fact that the little schoolteacher had been hurt. Mina was gloating over it, simply because Caitlyn hadn't hid her interest in him.

This was bullshit. Catty, snide, and hurtful. He'd thought better of Mina at one time.

"I don't like gossip, Mina," he reminded her.

She gave a soft little laugh. "Come on, Zeke, it's all over town and now it's hit the Internet. Pictures of her in the cutest little threesome with another couple. Who would have guessed she had it in her."

Zeke wouldn't have, and he still didn't believe it. He'd heard about the pictures more than he wanted to. He refused to look at them.

"Miss Goody Two Shoes got caught having her fun," Mina said smoothly. "I can't believe she thought she could get away with playing like that here. She should have known better."

Zeke's lips thinned as he sat at the bottom of the bed and pulled his boots on. Dammit, he didn't need to hear this again. He could feel that edge of burning anger in his gut, the one that warned him he was letting a woman get too close.

Caitlyn Rogue Walker was nothing to him, he told himself. He couldn't let her become something to him, either. She was too damned innocent, no matter what those photos might show. Not to mention too damned young.

"Too bad the cameraperson didn't take a few more." Mina yawned then. "Miss Walker wasn't even fully undressed, but she was definitely getting ready to have a good time."

His jaw bunched. The innocent Miss Walker had pissed off the wrong people, and Zeke felt responsible for that. Hell, this was just what he needed. He had steered clear of her for the express purpose of making certain she was never targeted for any reason because of him, and she had ended up as a target because of his son instead.

She had caught the attention of two of the town's worst inhabitants. A brother and sister who delighted in destroying anyone they could. She had caught their attention by defending his son at school.

He felt responsible. It was his son, and despite his knowledge that she had been set up, he still hadn't managed to find a way to punish those who had hurt her or to tamp down his growing interest in a woman he had no business touching.

He could feel the curling knot of anger, a hint of territorial possessiveness where the teacher was concerned and squelched it immediately. Miss Walker was too young, too innocent. She wasn't a woman that would accept a sex-only relationship, nor was she a woman Zeke would be able to hide the darker core of his sexuality with, as he did other women. Women such as Mina. Women who touched only his body, never his heart. Miss Walker had the potential to touch the inner man, and he refused to give her the chance.

He'd failed to protect one woman in his life already; he wouldn't make that mistake again.

"She's Calvin Walker's daughter, you know," Mina continued. "Hell, I thought he was dead. What's he doing with a daughter? Damned Walkers have never been worth crap, so it shouldn't be surprising."

Zeke rose to his feet and turned back to her. "I'm heading out, Mina. Take care."

This relationship was over. He could barely manage civility now. Mina had always seemed like a kindhearted woman. She had a ready smile, compassionate hazel eyes, a gentle face. And a mean streak a mile wide. He'd learned that over the past few months. When it came to other women, younger women, anyone she considered a threat to what she might want at the time, she turned viperous.

"And you're not coming back." Her expression lost its amusement now. "Did you think I didn't know your attention was waning, Zeke?"

"We had an understanding, Mina." He'd made certain of it before the relationship began.

She sat up in the bed, unashamedly naked, her short brown hair mussed attractively around her face.

"Your attention hasn't been worth shit since you met that girl," she accused him snidely. "You go through the motions, but I don't doubt you're thinking of her when you're fucking me."

His brow lifted. "Jealousy doesn't become you, Mina, and it's not a part of what we had. In this case, you're wrong. There's nothing between me and Miss Walker."

And there never could be. She was too young, too tender. Zeke didn't mess with women whose innocence lit their eyes like stars in the sky. Caitlyn Walker was the forever kind, and Zeke simply didn't have that to give her. Forever required the truth, it required parts of himself being revealed, and he'd learned at a young age that the truth wasn't always acceptable.

"There's nothing between the two of you because you're a closemouthed bastard intent on making certain you never give so much as an ounce of yourself," she snapped. "What's wrong, Zeke, can't anyone match the memory of that paragon you were married to? Or did you simply spend too much time in Los Angeles partying with all the gay boys?"

Zeke stared back at her silently. Prejudice in the mountains was still alive and thriving; he'd known that before he came home.

"Good-bye, Mina."

He turned and left the room. He'd be damned if he'd let himself be drawn into an argument with her, especially one she could use against him at any time in the future.

Zeke had a lot friends that still lived in L.A., and yeah, a few of them were gay. He and his past wife, Elaina, hadn't felt that sense of prejudice that thrived here. He didn't give a damn what a man or woman's sexual preference was. He hadn't cared then, and he didn't care now.

As he left Mina's little house outside town, he reminded himself that he was here to do a job, not to make friends or to find another wife. He'd been born and bred in these mountains; he knew every cliff and hollow, every breath of breeze and sigh of the wind. And he'd missed it like hell when he'd been forced to leave. Not that he'd had a choice at the time. It was leave with his mother or face the further destruction of his soul.

At fourteen, his life had changed forever. One moment in time had cursed him and had caused his parents' divorce. Moving to L.A. with his mother and meeting Elaina, the woman he'd married, had changed it further. At seventeen he'd become a father himself, and through the years he had learned the hard way that he couldn't run from his past. It had found him, and his wife had died because of it.

He was back in Kentucky because of it. Because he was tired of running, tired of fighting to forget what couldn't be forgotten.

Damn, he loved these mountains though, he thought as he started his truck and pulled out of Mina's back drive. The sun was rising over the peaks of pine, oak, and elm that filled the rolling hills. There was a mist in the air that drifted off the nearby lake, and the scent of summer filled his senses.

The vision of Rogue—he just couldn't see her as Caitlyn—filled his head, no matter how hard he tried to push it back. He was thirty-two years old, a grown man next to her tender twenty-one. She was so damned tiny she made a man second think his own strength and so damned innocent that all a man could think about was being the one to teach her how to sin.

Someone else would have to teach her, he thought, if someone hadn't already. He was staying just as far away from that land mine as possible. She would be the one woman that would tempt him. If he dared to touch her, if he even considered taking her, he'd never be able to give her only a part of himself. And because of that, he could never have her. There wasn't enough left of him to give, sometimes he felt as though he had never completely found himself and never would until the demons of his past were destroyed.

Securing that end wouldn't be easy, he had known that from the beginning. Navigating the waters of deceit could come with a very high price. It was hard enough protecting his young son from it; he couldn't deal with protecting a woman as well.

Vanquishing those enemies meant doing the job alone. And until one little schoolteacher with violet eyes, he hadn't minded paying the price.

ONE

Present day

Sheriff Zeke Mayes stepped into the squalid mobile home and grimaced at the scent of blood and death that filled it. The rusted metal of the mobile home outside gave only a hint of the depressing interior. No more than twelve by forty, the tiny home was littered with refuse, old dishes, old food, stale whisky and tobacco, and congealing blood and brain matter scattered across the walls and threadbare, dingy carpets.

Old beer, food, and vomit stains spotted the floors where used newspapers, dishes, and dirty clothes hadn't been thrown. It was a damned mess. And right in the middle of it was the bigger mess.

"Hell." He stepped farther in, careful to steer well clear of the body laid out on the floor. "Get forensics in here, Gene, and call the coroner."

Deputy Gene Maynard looked around the room with a confused frown. From the gun still clenched in one of the dead men's hands to the brain matter splattered around the floor.

"Forensics? Hell, Zeke, this ain't no homicide. These boys done done themselves in," he spat in disgust. "You pull forensics out here and Alex Jansen is gonna piss down his leg for you tying up his boys that way."

Zeke turned and stared at the deputy. Some days, Gene liked to think he knew Zeke's job better than Zeke did. Zeke stared back at him silently, daring him not to do as he was told. It would be a simple matter at this point to suspend him. Hell, it might speed things up, even if it would garner more suspicion than Zeke needed.

Gene sighed, gave a quick nod of his dark-haired head, then left the trailer and loped back to the cruiser he'd arrived in to make the call. Zeke turned back and stared at the mess once again. Yeah, it looked like just what it could have been. One brother killing the other, then killing himself, but maybe that was the problem, it looked too much like it. And the Walker boys might have been trouble more often than not, but this just didn't sit right in his gut. It resembled too closely several other unsolved crimes over the past ten years and pinched his gut with warning.

Hell, he hadn't expected this when he'd answered the call earlier from the sister of these two men, asking if the sheriff would check up on them. Lisa Walker was stuck in Louisville looking after their grandmother in the hospital and needed some things from the old woman's house. She was trying to get hold of Joe or Jaime to bring them to her and the phone here had stayed busy through the weekend.

Zeke stared around the room, found the phone by the recliner, and narrowed his eyes at the old-fashioned base. The receiver was off the hook, barely showing beneath the newspaper laying over it.

Joe and Jaime Walker weren't exactly scions of the community. They were irritants sometimes, normally harmless, fun-loving country boys. Joe worked at a lube and oil in town and Jaime worked whenever the mood hit him, wherever he could get a job at the time. And for the past few years they'd been supplying Zeke with information pertinent to a group of homeland terrorists that had been disbanded the year before.

This wasn't a murder-suicide, and Zeke knew it; he could feel it.

Jaime was sprawled in a dilapidated easy chair in front of the silent television set, a neat little hole in the center of his head. Dark hair feathered over his brow and framed his handsome face. Once bright, laughing blue eyes were blank and cold in death, but his expression seemed surprised.

His muscular arms rested on the chair, blood stained his white T-shirt. He was still dressed in jeans and boots; he hadn't settled in for the night, perhaps preparing to leave later.

The television was turned off. Zeke stared at it, then at the television remote laying on the floor by the recliner. There was a half-empty bottle of beer there, too.

Joe Walker was crumbled to the floor, the back of his head blown to bits. His face was in profile, and horror seemed to crease it.

He, too, was dressed in well-pressed jeans and a white shirt, boots on his feet. The boys had meant to go out, Zeke thought. They were dressed for a Saturday night on the town.

They hadn't made it out last night though. For some reason, it appeared one brother had killed the other, then himself. Gray matter and blood stained the floor and walls and the reek of death was stifling.

Son of a bitch.

"They finally offed each other." Gene stepped back into the doorway and stared at the wasted corpses. "They were fighting at the Walker bar just outside of town Thursday night over some woman. Rogue had a few of the bouncers toss them out and send them on their way."

Zeke turned to stare at the deputy coolly. "Does offing each other fit either man's personality, Gene?"

It looked as though Joe had stepped inside, closed the door, and shot his brother, then himself. A murder-suicide. Simple and not really unusual. It happened, too damned often. But that wasn't what had happened here.

"Looks to me like ole Joe finally had enough of Jaime stealing his women." Gene sighed and shook his head. "Those boys never did amount to much despite Calvin Walker tryin' to send them through school. They graduated but never did do much else, did they?"

Zeke held his tongue there. He didn't know what Calvin Walker had done for his distant cousins any more than he knew why the hell he left his daughter, Rogue, to suffer in that damned bar outside of town. It wasn't any of his business, either, Zeke told himself, other than asking the necessary questions to close this case.

He stared around again and shook his head. Hell, Joe and Jaime had been tight. Fraternal twins rather than identical, but still, damned close in looks and with each other. The girls loved them. Young, old, or married, it didn't make a difference. The Walker twins were laid-back, easygoing, laughing, and as thick as thieves. Poke at one brother and you might as well poke at the other. And yes, they were known to fight over their women, but never in a serious way.

This just didn't make sense.

"Forensics is pulling up, coroner is behind him. Looks like the new chief of police is here to oversee how you're usin' his boys," Gene announced mockingly as Zeke stepped toward the open door and moved to the rickety front porch before heading toward the driveway.

Alex Jansen pulled in behind the forensic team and the coroner. The new chief of police was ex-military and damned sharp.

Zeke held up his hand, stopping the forensic team as Alex strode toward him. There was still the slightest limp in Alex's stride from a wound received during a mission in the Special Forces before he took over the job of chief of police, but the limp was growing less noticeable.

Dressed in a short-sleeved dark blue shirt, jeans, and boots, Alex looked like exactly what he was. An animal prowling in a man's body.

"Zeke." Alex extended his hand, his gray eyes concerned. "We got problems out here?"

"Seems I might have." Zeke pushed his hat back on his head as he stared around the sunlit meadow the Walker mobile home sat within. "Walk in here with me. I need another set of eyes. We go as far as the door and that should be enough to keep from messing up your boys' area."

Alex nodded and followed behind him as Zeke led the way back to the trailer and then stood aside as Alex stepped into the doorway. Zeke didn't talk. Instead, he stood by the doorway, staring at the scene again.

"Immaculate," Alex murmured, and Zeke knew Alex wasn't talking about the state of the habitation but rather the scene of the death itself. "No apparent hesitation on the shooter's part. Walked in, aimed, and shot. Jaime didn't fight, and neither did Joe." He turned to Zeke. "Any sign of drugs?"

Zeke shrugged. "I'm leaving that call up to your boys and the coroner. I'm ordering an autopsy just to be sure. The rest." He just shook his head. "Doesn't feel right, Alex."

Alex stared around again, his arms crossing over his chest, eyes narrowed. "No," he finally said slowly, carefully. "It doesn't feel right, but sometimes, it doesn't."

And there wasn't a damned thing you could do about it, either, Zeke finished silently. It wouldn't be the first time someone had died in this county and the answers weren't there, and it wouldn't be the last. But this one was closer, it was more personal, despite the distance he tried to keep between himself and Rogue Walker, cousin to the two dead twins.

He moved back as Alex stepped outside and stared around the overgrown clearing. The Walkers' home sat in a small valley surrounded by oak, pine, elm, and dogwood. It was the end of April and spring was making itself known with a vengeance. It was already seventy, the sun beating down with blazing strength and heating the land around them.

"Let's get out of the way then." Alex sighed as they moved from the porch. "Forensics will do their job, see if they can get any answers for you."

Zeke almost breathed a sigh of relief. Alex's predecessor would cry and moan for weeks when he had to loan out the forensics team to the county.

"Thanks for the loan, Alex," he stated, watching his own words, his own responses. Alex knew the same thing Zeke did. This was a murder, straight and simple, committed by a particular man, in a very particular manner.

"Need any help with this?" Alex asked as they moved back to the parked vehicles.

Zeke shook his head, aware of Gene trailing them now.

"Not yet. I'll keep you up-to-date on it though. Gene said there was rumor the boys were fighting at the bar the other night. I'll head out there later and talk to Rogue."

Alex paused and stared back at Zeke, amusement suddenly gleaming in his eyes. "She's helping Janey at the restaurant," he informed Zeke then. "Haven't you been picking her up lately?"

Zeke lifted his hand and rubbed at the back of his neck. Rogue

was a sore spot with him; it was one of the reasons he hated finding Joe and Jaime as he had. Those boys were favorites of hers, and
damned if someone wasn't going to start wondering if Zeke was
spending precious county money because of the rumors that were
drifting through town that the sheriff and the bar owner were sniffing around each other.

"Not lately," he finally admitted. "The warmer nights, she's
been riding her Harley in." That didn't mean he didn't check up on
the leather-wearing, motorcycle-riding hellion as often as he found
time to do so.

Hell, he hated admitting that he missed those late-night calls,
just as he came off duty, requesting a ride from the restaurant
where she was helping Alex's lover back to the bar she owned. The
woman was a managerial whiz kid, yet she had come here as a high
school mathematics teacher five years before.

She was an enigma to him. She messed his head up every
damned chance she had, and he wasn't a man that liked having
to question parts of himself that he had never questioned before.
He'd made a decision before he returned to Kentucky, and now he
had no choice but to stick with it. Until this was finished, there was
no time for the emotions Rogue Walker inspired in him. There
was no time for love.

And what the hell was he doing thinking about love? He was
eleven years older than the spritely little hellion and ages older in
experience. The last thing he needed was to allow his heart to get
mixed up in the roller-coaster ride he'd have with her.

"Let me know if you need any help then." Alex nodded. "Rogue
works tonight and then the next two afternoons at the restaurant if
you're wondering about her schedule."

A mocking smile tilted Alex's lips as Zeke stared back at him
silently. He didn't have a damned word to say to that.

When Janey had opened the restaurant to six nights rather than four, Rogue had signed on to help her with it until she could find a dependable manager.

Alex chuckled, moved to his car, and slid inside before putting the vehicle in gear and driving off. Turning, Zeke surveyed the vehicles in the meadow and watched as his deputy loped back to him.

"Coroner is ready to collect the bodies and forensics is ready to release them. You ready?" There was the slightest sarcasm to Gene's voice.

"Tone down the sarcasm, Gene, you're pissing me off," Zeke told him. "If you have a problem with how I run my office, then say so up front."

Gene's lips tightened as he glared back at Zeke. "You're turning into an asshole, Zeke," he accused him. "You're throwing away good taxpayer money on a cut-and-dried case of murder-suicide. You act like those Walkers are scions of the county and you have proof of murder."

"They're citizens of this county, and they paid their tax dollars," Zeke informed him. "I figure we can allot a certain amount of it on making certain what happened here; what do you think?"

Gene was one twitch of the lip shy of a sneer. "Well, you obviously don't need me here wasting my time, too. I'll head back to the office while you oversee this."

"You'll head out on patrol," Zeke told him softly. "I have this to take care of. File your report before you go off duty, and I'll check it over when I come in later."

Gene's blue eyes glittered for the barest second with calculation. "Gonna go question that Walker girl? She's family to this rat trash, Zeke."

"Another word and you're going to regret it," Zeke snapped. "Haul your ass out of here and get on patrol. I don't need your advice or your opinion on the Walkers or this investigation."

"Murder-suicide doesn't constitute an investigation," Gene argued, his face flushing beneath the hot spring sunlight. "Son of a bitch, Zeke. Just 'cause you have a thing for Rogue Walker don't mean her family ain't still gutter shit."

A thing for Rogue Walker. There it was, that knowledge that obviously someone had mistaken his friendship with Rogue for something more than what it was. Simple friendship, he told himself.

So why the hell was he forcing himself to hold back, to keep from curling his fists and plowing them into his deputy's sneering face?

"You need to take a few days off," Zeke said carefully. "Several actually. Until you can rein in your mouth, Gene. I'll file the papers when I get back to the office. Maybe, in a few days, we can discuss your problems with how I run my department and my life and whether or not you can keep your damned nose out of it."

Otherwise, the man was going to be sporting a broken nose. Before he could follow through with that thought, Zeke strode away from his deputy and headed to the trailer, where the coroner was having the bodies removed.

It was a damned shame, Zeke thought. Those two boys, as wild as they were, weren't the murder-suicide type. For the most part, Walkers were just ornery. Not lazy so much as fun loving and laid-back. They played hard, worked as much as they had to, and had fun. They weren't troublemakers, and they weren't violent. But they were valuable sources on a silent investigation that was still ongoing. And they had been murdered.

"Sheriff." The coroner, Jay Adams, nodded as Zeke stepped up to him. "I'll autopsy, just to be sure drugs didn't play a part, but it looks pretty conclusive in there."

Jay was middle-aged with a full shock of bright gray hair and thick gray brows. His weathered face was creased with laugh lines and his hazel eyes were somber. He'd been coroner as long as Zeke had been sheriff, and he was damned good at his job.

"I appreciate it, Jay." Zeke nodded as he watched the assistants load the bodies into the coroner's hearse.

"Think we need to pull in the coroner's investigator from the city?" Jay asked then. "We could transport to their facilities. I could get you more information."

Zeke crossed his arms over his chest and rubbed at his jaw for long moments before nodding. "I'll clear it through the chief." Alex wouldn't argue the decision; he knew as well as Zeke did what they were looking at. "Transport to their facilities and see what we can get."

"Your gut is working on this one, huh?" Jay grunted. "Hate it when it does that, Zeke. Means we're gonna end up squabbling with city hall. You know how they like to mess with things."

"Yeah, I know," Zeke breathed out roughly, wishing he could trust Jay, that he could discuss his suspicions with the older man. "But like you said, my gut is burning, Jay, and I don't like it."

"Eh. That looked a little suspicious to me anyway." Jay suddenly grinned. "Hell, you know a body just ain't gonna sit there when someone jumps in the room with a gun. And you know, between here and town, I'm sure I'll consider the fact that something doesn't look right about those wounds. They can't naysay me like they can you."

Favor given, favor owed. "You got it, Jay." He clapped the other man on the shoulder. "Let me know how I can return the favor. I'll be waiting on your report."

"I'll try to be quick about it," Jay drawled. "Helps though when the city coroner happens to be your daughter, huh?"

"That doesn't hurt a bit," Zeke agreed with a small chuckle before turning his attention back to the mobile home.

He'd wait until forensics cleared out before going through it himself and feeling the area. Not just investigating it, but feeling it, just to be certain it was the work of the same man that had committed countless other murders in the county over the past twenty-odd years.

Maybe it was him more than the case that had him reluctant to leave and begin the investigation, he thought as the forensics team began to file out. This case meant going to Rogue when he hadn't seen her in over a month, hell, nearly two months. Not since the warmer spring air had descended on the mountains and she had started riding the Harley to the restaurant. And he hated admitting that he missed those few nights a week he had been driving her back to the bar each night. Missed her teasing and her laughter when he had no right to it.

He wasn't looking forward to telling her about Joe and Jaime. He didn't like lying to Rogue, and he had no choice but to hide certain information from her. Information such as the fact that her cousins had been gathering information for him and Homeland Security special agent Timothy Cranston. Information such as the fact that he knew to the soles of his feet that the boys had been murdered by the same man that had killed Zeke's wife and his father. The same man that Homeland Security has been searching for since the arrest and deaths of Dayle Mackay and Nadine Grace.

The man known only as the exterminator. The backbone of the Freedom League. A man that killed without conscience, without mercy, and without a trace.

TWO

Murder-suicide?

It wasn't possible.

Rogue sat in a back corner of her bar, stared at the dancers, the drinkers, the bikers, and the good ole country boys and girls that filled the establishment she simply called the Bar. That was what it was. Just a bar. A dance hall. A place to drink. It was the place Nadine Grace and Dayle Mackay's lackey had drugged her drink almost five years before.

The pieces she had put together over the years suggested the couple in the photos had helped her home. So nice of them. Then they proceeded to let Nadine and Dayle into her home where those pictures had been taken.

She had identified the couple within a year. Her father's friend Jonesy had quietly taken care of making certain that particular couple never came to Somerset again. Something about a drug buy that the police had received a tip on, and a hell of a long sentence for both of them. But her father hadn't found out, as far as Rogue knew. Of course, Jonesy, her father's friend and then Rogue's, had promised her he would make sure her father didn't know. How he had managed it, she didn't know. She was just thankful he had.

And the Bar was home now. She owned it. Her father had owned it before her, his last tie to the county that had seen him as nothing but white trash. They saw her as something even less, she sometimes thought. Like they saw the rest of the Walker clan, like Joe and Jaime.

Running a scarlet fingernail around the lip of the whisky glass in front of her, she tried to beat down the knowledge that here, in this county, the name Walker was, as her father had warned her, well less than sterling. Shiftless was one description. Thieves and gutter trash was another. But Rogue knew her family. Family like Joe and Jaime. They had been filled with laughter, charm. They had a sense of fun inside them that didn't correlate to the nine-to-five lifestyle others held so highly.

Jaime was steady in his friendships, his laughter. He liked to get drunk and raise a little hell on Saturday nights, and he loved women. Joe had been just like him. Neither of the two men had a cruel or mean bone in their bodies. They weren't conniving and they had never stolen a thing in their lives.

And now, they were gone.

She had been at the hospital when their sister, Lisa, had told Grandmother Walker that the boys were dead. A light had gone out in the old woman's eyes.

"Hey, Rogue."

Her head lifted at the sound of her bartender's voice at her side. Lifting her gaze, she met Jonesy's compassionate look.

Jonesy eased his burly body into the seat beside her, his hazel eyes somber as he watched her.

She liked Danny "Jonesy" Jones. A biker with a heart of gold, a mean-assed temper, and a head like a brick. An accident had cut back on his cycling and given him a limp, but he was still as tough and as no-nonsense as he had been when she first met him five years ago.

"Kent watching the bar?" She looked over to the long teak counter filled with customers.

"Kent and that new girl, Lea. She's a good 'tender."

Rogue nodded. Lifting her shot glass she tossed back the aged whisky, let her lashes flutter at the burn, then placed the glass back on the scarred table.

"Got a call," he told her then. "Alex Jansen's fiancée. Said to tell you the sheriff is heading this way. She's worried 'bout you. Asked that you call her tonight."

See, that was the problem with friends, they wanted to know every damned thing. Where your head was, where it was going, what you were thinking, and what you were feeling. She'd made the mistake of making friends with Janey Mackay and her sister-in-law, Chaya, last year. Big mistake. Never mess with Mackays, she reminded herself.

"I'll call her back later." She shrugged.

"Sheriff will be here soon." His thick forearms crossed on top of the table. "Zeke ain't no man's fool, Rogue. Or no woman's. If he's askin' questions, then something's wrong."

She shook her head at that. "No. He's just making sure. He's anal like that, Jonesy."

She poured herself another drink, sipped at the liquid this time, and stared into the full dance floor. Normally, she would have been out there herself, dancing, laughing, pretending. Always pretending.

"They were good boys, Rogue." He patted her hand awkwardly and scowled down at her. "You did your best for them, girl, even when I told you they were gonna come to a bad end with all their womanizing. You can't ask more than that from yourself. Whatever happened up there with them, it's not on your shoulders."

Maybe she hadn't done enough. Joe and Jaime with their laughter and their devil-may-care attitudes. Maybe she had missed something, been too busy, too self-involved to see something that could have saved them.

She couldn't figure it out. She just couldn't make it make sense. That was why she was sitting here at a dark table staring into the smoky atmosphere of her bar rather than scandalizing the county as a hostess at the most exclusive and notorious restaurant in the town, Mackay's. She was here instead, hiding, hiding from the false condolences and the questions she knew she would receive elsewhere.

She was a Walker. White trash, gutter-guzzling sleaze was but one of the nicer descriptions she'd heard. She'd laughed in public over it, sometimes; she shed tears in private and wondered why the hell she stayed.

Pulaski County wasn't the center of the universe, she had told herself countless nights. She could return to Boston, teach anywhere she wanted to teach, and escape the mountain-bred hypocrisy and cruelties she had known here. But even in Boston, she had never fit in.

And Boston didn't have Sheriff Zeke Mayes.

God, she was such a fool. If any man had ever proven he had no intention of touching her, then it was Sheriff Mayes. He stared at her sometimes as though the very thought of being around her was horrifying. And then there were times, times his brown eyes had darkened further, his lashes had lowered, and she could see the hunger he thought he was hiding from her.

There were times she wanted to crawl into him and just lay against him. Nights she dreamed of being wrapped in those strong, muscular arms. And there were nights she actually faced the truth that even if it ever happened, it would never last. And she wondered which was worse. Never having? Or having and losing?

"You're worryin' me, girl," Jonesy finally said with a sigh. "Sittin' around drinkin' and reflectin' ain't your way. Remember that? You don't mope and feel sorry for yourself; we taught you better than that, remember?"

Her lips tilted. "They." The little mountain bikers' club that didn't even have a name. Thirteen overgrown teenagers in men's and women's bodies who had known her father at one time or another rallied around her and taught the too-soft little schoolteacher how to be the rogue she had been named for.

They had been regulars at the bar. They had seen the couple she had left with that night, and they had helped her plot her vengeance against them. They had sheltered her for the first year beneath their protection, and they had taught her how to be tough. How to fight. How to laugh at the insults, and how to grow up.

"I'm fine, Jonesy," she promised him. "Just a little mellow."

She sipped at the whisky. She didn't drink it often. It took a certain mood, a certain anger to allow her to enjoy liquor. She was a beer girl, until the anger overflowed her control and she had to face more than she wanted to face.

"A little too mellow to be facing that sheriff." Jonesy pulled the whisky bottle out of her reach with a temperamental scowl. "You never face your enemy weak, girl. I taught you better than that."

"Zeke's not my enemy." But she didn't reach for the bottle again.

Zeke wasn't her enemy, but he was her weakness. He made everything inside her weak, made her ache and heat, and made her wish for things that she knew she couldn't have.

"Sheriff Mayes is gonna break your heart," Jonesy warned her with a hint of anger. "Pull yourself up here now. He's gonna be here soon, and you don't want to see him while you're feeling sorry for yourself and missin' those boys."

She shook her head, almost smiling. That was Jonesy. Never let them see you bleed. And she was bleeding. She could feel it, from a wound inside her heart that she couldn't seem to close.

She shook her head. "Joe wouldn't shoot Jaime," she said softly. "Neither of those boys would have ever hurt each other, Jonesy, let alone anyone else."

"If there's something more involved, then I have no doubt Sheriff Mayes will find it, girl," he grumbled, his voice becoming more fierce. "Come on, Rogue. He'll be here any minute. Pull yourself out of this or you're gonna hate yourself in the morning. You know how you always end up kicking yourself whenever you let Mayes see you weak."

She was always weak around Zeke. It was a fact of life. Like taxes and breathing.

"Go tend the bar, Jonesy." She sighed. "I'll be fine."

Jonesy stared at her for long, silent moments. Rogue could feel his worry and his anger. Jonesy always worried about her, and it always managed to piss him off. And tonight after he closed up, he'd probably call her father, and her parents would worry then, too. If she wasn't careful, her father would end up on her doorstep and then talk about stirring up some stink. The closest he'd come to Somerset since leaving it so long ago was Louisville. She always met him there. God help her if he ever actually came here.

Jonesy rose to his feet. His heavy hand gripped her shoulder for a second in a tender hold before he heaved out a hard breath and moved through the crowd, back to his bar.

Zeke was coming, and she was weak. He would be here soon, and she felt lost and alone and uncertain. She hated feeling that way; she avoided him at all costs when she felt that way, because she wanted nothing more than to curl against his broad chest and make all the darkness that seemed to surround her go away.

As though he could do that.

She finished the whisky in the glass, capped the bottle, and motioned to the waitress to take it away before rising to her feet.

Four-inch heels were like a second skin to her feet. Vivid red to match the scalloped lace edges of the scarlet camisole she wore beneath her black sleeveless leather vest. It was paired with a short leather skirt that showed off her legs and flashed her upper thighs. Flipping back the riotous red gold curls that flowed over her shoulder, she drew in a hard breath and made her way across the bar to the door that led back to the kitchens and the steps to her upstairs apartment.

She wasn't facing Zeke while the customers of the Bar watched on. Jonesy would direct him upstairs.

Would he come in uniform, she wondered? Or in those thigh-hugging jeans and loose shirts that always made her mouth water? She wanted to strip him so damned badly she could barely breathe for the need when he was out of uniform.

She didn't want to even consider what he did to her when he was in uniform. She tried to ignore the wicked little urges she had then, because it was a hell of a lot worse than without the uniform.

Maybe it had something to do with those handcuffs hanging on the side of his belt, she thought mockingly as she made her way up the stairs to her apartment. Yeah, had to be those handcuffs. She had some interesting fantasies where those were concerned.

Unlocking her apartment, she pushed it open and stepped inside. The lights were on. She left them on because she didn't like the dark. She and her friend Janey Mackay were a lot alike in that regard. The dark was a lonely place to be for Rogue.

The large, open living room and kitchen greeted her. Spotlessly clean, because she really didn't spend much time in her so-called home. The dark brown leather couch and chairs were comfortable; the scarred coffee table was an antique she hadn't had time to refinish. Or perhaps just hadn't made time. There was something about those scars of time on it that appealed to her.

The double doors into her bedroom were open, a low light on her bed stand shining into the room. And it was quiet. So quiet.

Maybe she needed a cat. A cat would at least meow at her when she came in, or so Janey had assured her.

Shaking her head, she paced over to the tall, wide windows and drew a curtain back enough to stare into the parking lot below. Just in time to watch Zeke Mayes pull into the lot in the full-sized farm pickup he drove when he wasn't on duty.

Hell. He was going to be in civilian clothes.

She watched closely as he parked, opened the door, and stepped out beneath one of the bright lights shining overhead. Her mouth watered.

A long-sleeved white button-up shirt was tucked into snug jeans. She thought he might be wearing boots. There was the glint of his badge on the pocket of his jeans. He wore it like that sometimes, and she thought it was the sexiest damned thing she had ever seen.

She wondered where his handcuffs were.

Her fingers clenched on the material of the curtains as she felt herself heat at the sight of him. She might be a virgin, but she knew all the signs of arousal and a night that was most likely going to involve toys of some sort.

Her clit was swollen, the bare folds of her sex felt flushed and damp. Her nipples were peaking beneath the camisole and vest, and she could feel that nervous little flutter attacking her stomach and thighs. Just the sight of him was enough to sensitize her body.

It was lust. Lust was a powerful force, she reminded herself. It couldn't have anything to do with the need to just curl into his arms and rest there. That was weakness, not lust. It was loneliness. She had separated herself from most friendships, she hadn't allowed herself a lover because she couldn't have the lover she wanted. So comfort wasn't something she knew a lot about. But it was something she missed more often than not.

Running her hands down the sides of her skirt, Rogue pulled back from the window and drew in a deep, hard breath. She could almost feel him moving closer. Through the bar, his shoulders brushing against the women who would crowd closer, just to feel the heat and hardness of his corded, muscular body.

She closed her eyes, remembering the feel of him herself. The way his body seemed to wrap around her when he almost, just almost brushed against her. Zeke always made certain he didn't actually touch her unless he had no choice.

The jarring ring of the phone had her eyes jerking open. Frowning, she pulled the cell phone from the clip at her side and flipped it open after checking the number.

"Yeah, Jonesy?"

"Sheriff wants to talk to you," he growled. "You in?"

Her lips almost twitched at his protectiveness. "Yes, Jonesy. Send him on up."

Jonesy grunted and she could almost see the wrinkles in his brow as he frowned.

Flipping the phone closed, she laid it on the table by the couch and moved to the door. She opened it, pulled it wide, and moved back to the kitchen for a bottle of water. Something to do with herself as she waited. To calm herself, to settle her vulnerabilities until she could reestablish her shields.

Joe and Jaime's deaths had thrown her. It had left her drifting, uncertain, questioning too many things in her life. The twins were two of the few people she had allowed herself to care for in the past years. She kept most people at a distance simply so they couldn't hurt her, so they couldn't be used against her to hurt her. It was easier that way. Easier on her heart and on her life.

Damn, she hadn't realized how much she had let herself care about people until today.

"Leaving your door open like this could be dangerous." Zeke's dark voice filled the room as she reached inside the fridge for the bottle of water.

She paused, closed her eyes, and took in a deep, hard breath before clenching the water and pulling back. She turned to face him, letting the fridge door close as her eyes met his.

They were eagle fierce in his sun-darkened face. His dark brown hair was cut short, almost military short. There was the lightest sprinkling of gray at his temples. It was sexy.

Those damned jeans molded to his thighs. The fabric of his shirt was just a little loose but did nothing to hide the power of his broad chest and shoulders. And yes, he was wearing boots. Scarred work boots. The kind that just made a man's legs look strong and sturdy.

"I knew you were coming up." She shrugged. "Close the door behind you."

He stood there, staring at her.

"Unless you're scared to be alone here with me." She moved slowly through the kitchen area to the living room. "Afraid your reputation will suffer, Sheriff?"

His lips quirked. Rogue watched as his arm reached out, his fingers gripped the doorknob, and he closed the door slowly. A second later, those lean fingers flipped the locks in place without his gaze ever leaving hers.

"So brave." She pretended to shiver. "You're living dangerously this week."

He stared back at her the way he usually did unless she pushed him. As though he were on the edge of being bored with her. Damn him. She didn't bore him. She made him hard. He was filling those damned jeans out in ways she knew they weren't meant to be filled. That was not boredom.

"You heard about Joe and Jaime," he stated as he moved farther into the room. "I tried to find time to come out and tell you myself, but I was tied up with forensics and city hall."

"Not a problem." She shrugged as she twisted the cap off the water. "I'm sure I heard about it before the coroner ever had the bodies loaded and ready to go. Your deputy likes to run his mouth, Sheriff. Seems he thinks trailer trash like the Walkers don't warrant a forensics team. Bad blood showing and all that. Why should the city waste its money on two men that just got what they deserved."

His lips thinned. Anger perhaps. Irritation definitely as he strode to where she stood. "Sit down, Rogue. I'll deal with my deputy and city hall. Until then, I'd like to figure out what the hell happened with Joe and Jaime."

She sat down on the couch and would have laughed in mocking amusement when he took the chair beside her, except the disappointment went too deep. She would have felt his warmth if he had sat on the couch. And she felt cold inside. For some reason, she felt lost. As though she had traveled too far and too long from some vision of security and now found herself deep in unfamiliar territory.

"I'm sorry about Joe and Jaime, Rogue." Zeke sighed then, rubbing his hand over the back of his neck. "I know those boys were closer to you than most folks knew. That's why I need to talk to you. See if you can help me figure out what happened."

Rogue slid the high heels from her feet and folded her legs beneath her. No sense in worrying about whether or not her legs looked nice in front of Zeke right now. He was keeping his gaze firmly on her face. Besides, feeling sexy and being reminded of why he was here didn't go hand in hand.

"Joe wouldn't have killed Jaime," she told him with a firm shake of her head. "Joe and Jaime were too close, Zeke. They might have fought over a woman every now and then, or anything else, but they would have never hurt each other. Not for anything."

"What about drugs?" He leaned forward and stared back at her in demand. A demand for the truth, as though she would lie to him.

"They didn't have the money for drugs," she told him. "A little pot every now and then, sure. But not the hard stuff. They didn't touch hard drugs."

"But they did smoke pot?" he asked.

"Probably." She lifted her shoulders. "I never saw them do it, but I assumed they did from a few jokes they've made over the years. I never saw any evidence of it though. The most I've seen was a few too many beers and a little brawl here and there over a girl. They usually made a few swings at each other, started laughing, and then headed home with the girl together. They were like that. Nothing was serious for too long."

"What about enemies?" Zeke asked. "Did they have any you'd believe would want to hurt them?"

She stared back at him heavily. "I can't think of a single enemy those two boys had. For all their womanizing, they were well liked. I never knew of anyone wanting to hurt them. And why ask that question if it's a cut-and-dried murder-suicide as your deputy believes?"

She watched Zeke suspiciously now. Why the questions if he believed Joe had murdered Jaime, then killed himself?

"There was a murder, no matter what happened or why," Zeke told her. "I need to figure out the what and the why to close this case, Rogue. I don't like questions left dangling."

"Then you have a hell of a question going on there," she told him. "Because I'm telling you, Joe wouldn't hurt Jaime. He was the oldest twin. He was more protective toward Jaime. No one hurt Jaime that Joe didn't come running."

He still watched her closely, that somber gaze moving over her face, almost to her neck. For a second, she had a feeling that he would have looked lower, but he didn't. He kept his gaze on her face, and that pissed her off.

He was sitting here questioning her over her cousins' deaths, deaths he had to suspect couldn't have played out as it was made to look. He could have come to question her at any time, but he came late, after he was off duty, in plainclothes, and aroused.

Unlike him, she'd had no problem looking below his neck. Or his waist. She sure as hell had no problem looking below his belt.

"Look, Zeke, I can't tell you anything you obviously don't know already," she told him. "I know Joe or Jaime—neither one would have hurt the other. Whatever happened up there is bogus. It was a setup and I can't figure out why, because Joe and Jaime were a threat to no one."

"We thought you were a threat to no one last year when you were attacked as well," he reminded her. "It wasn't what you knew on Mackay and Grace that landed you in the hospital, Rogue, it was what they were afraid you knew. What could Joe have been afraid of that would have made him kill his brother and himself?"

Last year she had managed to get herself twisted into a Homeland Security investigation into Nadine Grace and Dayle Mackay. As he'd said, it wasn't what she had known but what Grace and Mackay thought she might have known that had been the problem. When the investigator, Dayle's son's lover, Chaya Dane, had questioned her, it had drawn Rogue within their sights once more.

She'd spent a week in the hospital, bruised, with a cracked rib and a bruised skull, but she'd come out of it alive.

"Someone else killed Joe and Jaime," she told him. "Get that in your head, Zeke. Someone set that scene up. Because I know to the soles of my feet neither of those boys would have hurt the other. It wasn't in them."

His jaw flexed, and his gaze jerked to her feet where they rested at the side of her body, then back to her face. How interesting.

God, he made her mad. Never more mad though than he was making her tonight. He was almost foaming at the mouth to touch her, as desperate for it as she was, and still, he denied both of them.

He nodded. "I'll keep checking things out," he told her. "But unless forensics or the coroner comes up with something, then murder-suicide is what we're looking at. And it damn sure looks as though Joe killed Jaime and then himself."

Her lips twisted mockingly. "Yeah, and there are pictures on the Internet that make me look like a world-class slut," she reminded him. "Trust me, looks are incredibly deceiving."

His gaze darkened, though it never moved from her. Sometimes, she wondered exactly what was going on behind that fierce gaze. Hawklike light brown eyes that seemed to reflect shadows of emotions that she could never really decipher.

"I've never seen the pictures," he finally said, surprising her.

Rogue's brow lifted. "Really? You must be the only man in the county that hasn't managed to find them."

Zeke wasn't a man to lie, about anything.

"I never went looking for them," he told her. "I didn't want to see them, Rogue, because they didn't matter between you and me."

THREE

Of course they didn't. Those pictures, one way or the other, would never change the fact that he might want her, but he had no intention of touching her.

She'd tested that theory over the winter. All the rides she'd requested after the long hours she had put in at the Mackay restaurant. The nights she had invited him up for a drink or tried to linger in his vehicle to talk, to flirt. She'd given up. She'd let it go. She wasn't begging him.

She unfolded herself from the couch, reached down, and picked up her shoes before staring down at him.

"Do you have any further questions, Zeke? It's late, I need a drink, and I was looking forward to a bubble bath. Honestly, I don't know what else I could tell you about Joe and Jaime that you don't already know. Or think you know."

And she couldn't handle being in the same room with him tonight. She wasn't as strong as she had been in the winter. Perhaps those winter months had weakened her. Hoping against hope each night that she had flirted her way into his car that something, anything, would come of it. Only to have her hopes dashed time and again.

"You're throwing me out?" He tilted his head and looked up at her, his gaze flashing with a heat she was afraid to delve too deeply into. "After weeks of trying to get me up here to your apartment, you're not even offering me a beer?"

"No. I'm not. Good night, Zeke. Lock the door on your way out."

She turned and walked to the open bedroom door. She could feel his gaze on her, felt him watching her, his eyes burning into her. Suddenly, her skirt was too short, the vest flashed too much skin at her midriff and back. She felt exposed, vulnerable. She felt weak.

"Hell of a change, Rogue. You tried to seduce me half the winter. What happened?"

She stopped and turned around slowly to see him standing, cocky, assured, confident.

"I gave up," she replied shortly. "As you said, I *tried* to seduce you. You weren't willing. I don't beg. End of story."

His expression tightened, a muscle jumping at his jaw as his gaze raked over her then.

"You're too damned young," he finally berated her, and perhaps himself as well, she thought. Or he was trying to convince himself.

"I'm too damned tired to play games." It was all she could do to keep her shoulders straight and to fight back the tears. "Joe and Jaime were family. This has hit me rather hard, and as you see"— she lifted her arms wide to encompass the empty apartment—"it's just me and the bubble bath for comfort. I don't need to add games to tonight's stress if you don't mind."

Zeke watched Rogue closely. He saw it then. That shadow in

those deep violet eyes that had held his attention. A shadow he had never seen before. Loneliness. Loss. He knew that feeling. And in the past five years whenever it struck, it was Rogue that came to mind. Her smile, the promise of passion in her eyes, the need to touch her, the certainty that she could calm the beast that raged inside him.

Damn her. She'd managed to worm her way into his life, there was no doubt of that. He'd missed her in the past few weeks since she had started riding her Harley to the restaurant rather than calling him and bumming a ride. Hell, he'd more than missed it. It was as though something were suddenly missing from his life. There was an emptiness where those hours lay now, a sense of waiting.

"Why don't you have a lover, Rogue?" He looked around the apartment. To his knowledge, as long as she had lived in Somerset, Rogue had never had a lover.

He didn't count the pictures that had ended up on the Internet. He'd investigated that himself, and though he could never find proof, there was enough suspicion to prove to him that Rogue had been used somehow. Rumor was Nadine Grace and Dayle Mackay had targeted her when she had defended Zeke's son over a test at school. Nadine had never liked Shane because Zeke had refused to walk the same path his father had walked. Thad Mayes had held the position of sheriff for years, and through that time he had protected Dayle Mackay and the Freedom League's collective asses. He hadn't just protected them, he had been part of them. Zeke refused to follow that path, and Nadine had finally found a way to strike back, through Shane.

A month after standing up for his son, Rogue had left the bar with a strange couple. She hadn't been well known then; no one had thought to question her when she left. And then Rogue had been out of a job in the school system and the pictures had shown up on the Internet.

Oh, Zeke knew how Grace and Mackay had worked, he thought

as he found himself moving across the room, his gaze drifting, again, to the scalloped lace that peeked over her leather vest.

Bra or camisole? he wondered. Probably one of those short little camisole things. Scarlet red and flirty. Just like the shoes she carried in her hand.

"You didn't answer me, Rogue," he reminded her. "Why don't you have a lover?"

And he wasn't certain he wanted to hear the answer to that question. The same reason perhaps that he didn't have a lover. Because he couldn't have Rogue.

"Does it matter why?" She stood still, determined as he moved to her, stopping within a breath of touching distance.

He stared down at her, feeling things he knew he had no right to feel. Things he knew he shouldn't feel, not for this spritely little woman-child that was much too young for him.

He was playing a dangerous game tonight and he knew it. But he needed a taste of her. Just enough to hold him over, to dampen the lust raging through him.

"Don't play games with me, Zeke," she breathed out wearily. "Honestly, I don't have time for them. I don't have the strength for them right now."

"Have I ever played games with you, Rogue?" he asked, reaching out to touch her cheek, knowing, damn, he knew this was a mistake. The worst mistake he could possibly make right now. Because he couldn't follow through. He couldn't have her and revenge. It wasn't possible.

She didn't answer him. He could have used one of her smart remarks right now. Something to remind himself that she was way too young. Twenty-six, even if it was almost twenty-seven, was too far from thirty-seven years old. Eleven years. Two years less than that which separated Alex Jansen and his fiancée, Janey Mackay, Zeke thought. But just because Alex could handle it didn't mean

Zeke could. Hell, his son, Shane, was nineteen. He was closer to Rogue's age than Zeke was.

"You don't play games," she whispered, her expression softening, transforming, turning sensual, tempting.

Damn, the things he wanted to do to her. The ways he wanted to do them. He was here to question her about her cousins' deaths; instead, he found himself relishing the softness of her cheek. Skin like satin and silk combined. And as he looked, he realized it was all but devoid of makeup.

She looked like a temptress with those violet eyes though. Those long, riotous red gold curls flowing around her, making a man wonder what it would be like to be bound within them.

"This is a bad idea." He sighed, lowering his head and allowing his rougher cheek to brush against hers. "Tell me to leave."

"Leave," she breathed as she softened against him.

He almost laughed. Damn her, she could make him laugh when no one else could. "That wasn't an order, Rogue."

"Oh. It was supposed to be an order?" A little, knowing smile tugged at her lips.

Oh yeah, she knew he wanted her until he ached with it. And she wanted. She wanted with the same hunger. He could see it in her eyes.

Her shoes dropped to the carpet, the light thud barely registering in his head. Hell, he could barely hear anything over the race of his own pulse and the thunder of lust in his veins.

He let his lips skim her cheek. The need for her threatened to erode his control and his senses.

"I'm leaving," he told her. "This is too damned dangerous."

"Of course it is." One small hand clenched on his upper arm. The fingers of the other were pressing against his stomach. She could feel his abs flexing; he could feel the warmth of her through the material of his shirt.

His cock pressed imperatively against his jeans. The hard throb was making him crazy. It had made him crazy all evening. How much hell was one man supposed to endure before the hunger overrode control? he wondered. And what was it about this one woman that threatened his control?

He let his lips brush against the curls at the side of her face. They were soft, fragrant. Like silk that smelled of dawn. He wanted to crush them between his fingers, hold her in place, and eat her up with kiss after kiss. He wanted to taste those lush, sensual lips. He wanted to feel her tongue against his, hell, he wanted all of her.

"You're teasing me." Her voice was weak, a hint of need quivering within it as she shifted closer to him. "Don't tease me, Zeke. Kiss me, or let me go."

"You're supposed to tell me to leave," he reminded her.

"Kiss me or leave. Do one or the other."

"Kissing you would be a very bad idea." So why wasn't he stepping back? Why wasn't he letting her go? Instead, he was moving closer, one arm curling around her back as he gripped her jaw with his hand and lifted her head.

"Or one of your better ideas," she retorted breathlessly.

He didn't give himself a chance to think, and he should have. He should have considered the consequences, and he damned sure should have considered the spark that blazed between them even when they weren't touching.

He should have considered it, because each time he did, he knew better than to draw closer to the fire. He knew better than to let his hunger get the best of him. But he didn't consider.

He brushed his lips over hers as they parted. Light as a whisper, he let himself feel her lips. He came back for a taste. The barest taste of that full lower lip, and it was ambrosia. Nectar. It was the sweetest taste of flesh that he swore he had ever known. If he wasn't mistaken, there was the lightest flavor of his favorite drink that lingered there. The slightest hint of the dark, potent whisky he preferred.

"Zeke," she whispered his name against his lips. "Please. Don't tease."

She didn't whimper, she didn't beg. It was a demand given in the tone of a woman who accepted that the tease might be all she would receive.

But the man wasn't teasing. Zeke didn't tease. He was almost as helpless in the grip of the sensuality weaving around them as she was in his hold. He lifted her closer, notching the hard width of his cock against her as he turned and pressed her into the wall, his lips parting, his tongue pressing between hers, his need controlling every objection his head was listing as he allowed himself to sink into her kiss.

Her arms were around his neck. Her legs lifted until her knees rode his hips, and hell, he was lost. He was barely aware of the fact that he was jerking her skirt over her hips. Short-assed skirt. It tempted him. Teased him. Made his hands itch to jerk it up and see what she was wearing beneath.

Feeling what she was wearing worked, too. Or not feeling it. All he could find was the thinnest scrap of material running between the cheeks of her ass, a tiny triangle covering the hairless folds of her pussy.

He was doomed. He was going to hell. He was going to be flayed by the whips of guilt and remorse the second he managed to pull his lips from hers. So why the hell should he bother now? He could keep kissing her, kissing her until the guilt and remorse were burned away to cinders beneath the hunger that blazed out of control.

Because Rogue tasted as wild as her name, as free as sunshine. She was the promise of an eternal flame, the illusion of something he knew didn't exist. The illusion of true emotion. Because in this kiss there was more than pleasure. There was the darkness he held within him rising to the fore, and the fantasies he knew he had no business considering with this woman tempting his mind.

"Damn you!" He muttered the curse against her lips, because he couldn't get enough. He couldn't taste enough of her, couldn't kiss her deep enough, wild enough. He couldn't press his jeans-covered dick tightly enough between her thighs, he couldn't feel her heat close enough. They were both damned. Because he couldn't stop. Because the feel of her, the sweetness of her was too much. She kissed like a dream, and God knew, he had given up on dreams years before.

"Damn me?" Rogue gasped, breathless, nearly panting as flaming little fingers of sensation raced over her body.

Her lips were swollen; she could feel their tenderness as his kisses moved from her lips to her jaw, to her neck. His lips caressed; he might have nipped with his teeth. She was certain he had. But oh God, his tongue. He was licking over her neck as though taking greedy, tiny tastes of her flesh. And between her thighs. His fingers were between her thighs, tucked beneath her rear as her knees gripped his hips, caressing, feathering over the silk triangle of the thong she wore. Caressing the damp material as her juices eased from her sex.

She could feel how slick she was, how wet. Her flesh was swollen, her clit throbbing. Her pulse raced, adding to the sensitivity of her flesh, the ache of need between her thighs.

Moaning his name, her head fell back against the wall, her eyes closing as she felt his lips at the top of her breasts, above the scalloped edge of her camisole top. The top button of her vest eased open.

"This is insane." The words sounded torn from him.

Insane? It was the most pleasure she had ever known in her life.

"Damn. Rogue. This has to stop."

She kept her eyes closed, her hands on his head, holding his lips right where they were, brushing between her breasts. The feel of them, like rough velvet stroking her, was a heady sensation.

She was going to have to let him go. She knew it. She could feel it. She was going to have to let him walk away and spend the night alone. Again. Without him. Without the comfort she needed, without the man she needed to hold on to.

She fought the tightening in her chest, her throat. The tears that wanted to fill her eyes and she held back, trapped inside her heart.

"So stop." Her head fell forward, her lips pressing against his forehead, her fingers still gripping his neck. "All you have to do is stop."

And kill her. And take away something she hadn't known she was missing until now. She hadn't known how good it could be, how hot it could be. She hadn't known how his touch could send pleasure tearing not just through her body, but deeper, to that untouched core of her. To that part of her that had always held back, that had always remained aloof.

She wasn't aloof with Zeke. She wanted to beg. She wanted to plead with him not to stop, not to take the warmth away from her. Not to steal his touch when she had waited so damned long for it.

A second later, he was easing back from her. Rogue forced her knees to unclamp, forced herself to find her footing as he slowly, so slowly released her, then stepped back from her.

"Did you get all you wanted?" She resorted to sarcasm to keep from crying. "If so, as I said before, you know where the door is."

She turned, almost stumbled actually, to get away from him and find the relative comfort of her bedroom, her big bathtub, heated bubbles that in no way would replace his touch.

"I'm too old for you, Rogue; you know that as well as I do."

A second later she found herself pulled against his chest, her back flush against him, absorbing his heat and his anger.

She shook her head slowly. "It's not the age, Zeke," she said softly. "That's your excuse. Why don't you just admit it? Your reputation can't afford me, and we both know it."

Silence filled the air between them. She felt his fingers tighten at her hips, his chest expand behind her.

"You think I won't fuck you because you could hurt my reputation?" There was an edge of mockery to his voice that was cutting. "Oh, Rogue, sweetheart, you have no damned idea how wrong you are. I won't fuck you, baby, because I know what no one else knows. I know exactly why a relationship with me would destroy both of us."

"Oh really?" She didn't see destruction. She saw the need, the aching, dark loneliness that no one else could help ease. A hunger that only Zeke could fulfill. That she had always known only Zeke could fulfill. "And what is it that you think you know?"

"I know, Caitlyn Rogue, how very innocent you are next to me and what I know I'll end up taking from you. You're not a woman who will let a man fuck her for the emotionless pleasure of it. You're not a woman who could ever give what I need easily. And you're not a woman a man can walk away from without regrets. You're too young for those regrets. And I'm too damned old to want to see them strapped on you. Think about that. Remember that. Because the next time you invite me to your bed, you just might find more there than you expected."

If he expected her to take veiled threats and innuendo as an excuse, then he'd better be thinking on that one again.

She tossed him an angry little snarl as she jerked out of his arms.

"What, Zeke, do you like to get frisky with your handcuffs?" she snapped, turning on him and nearly bursting into flames at the look on his face. "Do you like to play the big, bad sheriff when you fuck your women?"

His lips quirked with an edge of amusement that she simply didn't appreciate. Almost a smile as those predatory brown eyes roved over the loosened front of the leather vest.

"Me getting frisky with the handcuffs would be the least of your problems," he growled back at her, and she almost believed him.

She pretended to shiver. "Should I whimper and beg for mercy?"

"Probably." There was a grunt of laughter. "One thing is for damned sure, you'd end up spanked. Does that smart mouth of yours ever stop?"

"Only when I'm kissing cowardly sheriffs with more excuses than handcuffs." She smiled tightly. "Go home, Zeke. I'm tired of playing with you tonight. I tell you what, the next time I'm in the mood for a little slap and tickle I'll give you a call. Seems that's all you're willing to put out at any given time."

Oh, she was pissed. She glared back at him, seeing the amusement, the careful watchfulness he displayed. He thought he could walk into her home and just play the big, bad dominant lover throwing out his little warnings? Who the hell was he this week? The dom from hell? Bullshit. She'd heard how the sheriff liked to fuck for years. All night. Hard and heavy. He was like a stallion ready to mount and ride at any given time, one widow had drawled drunkenly during a pity party of epic proportions when her studly sheriff had stopped coming to her bed. Rogue was tired of hearing the damned tales from women drowning their sorrows in her whisky.

"Smart-ass." His voice lowered, deepened. "That one was free, sweetheart; keep it up and I'll start running a tab for you. And I do collect."

She pretended to shiver. "I'm shaking in my shoes."

He looked at the shoes on the floor, then back at her feet before his lips tightened and he gave his head a hard shake.

"I'm getting the hell out of here," he told her. "If I hear anything about the twins, I'll let you know."

"Just send one of your little deputies," she ordered furiously. "I've decided I don't like playing with you after all, Zeke. I think it's time for me to consider other potential buddies."

He stopped.

Zeke could feel the blood exploding in his head at her angry little threat, and the fact that she just might be serious. Was she serious? He stared into her eyes, keeping his eyes narrowed as he gauged her expression.

Yep, she just might be serious.

"I wouldn't jump into anything if I were you," he warned her. He tried to keep the warning light, but he failed miserably. He knew what he sounded like. Like a man warning his woman back from a boundary she was getting ready to cross.

He couldn't have her, but he'd be damned if he was going to stand aside and watch some other bastard take her now that he'd had a taste of her.

That thought froze him as effectively as Rogue's warning had. Hell, he was losing his fucking mind.

"Fuck it," he suddenly snarled. "None of my damned business."

"None of your damned business," she agreed, evidently angrier now than she was to begin with.

Zeke watched the flush that mounted her cheeks, the glitter of battle in her violet eyes and almost, just almost wondered at the dominant spark that seemed to trigger a cascade of lust in his gut.

Damn her. She wasn't supposed to challenge him. Get pissed, yeah. Challenge him? Hell no. It was the one thing he'd fought to keep from happening over the years. Rogue challenging him wasn't something either of them wanted to test right now. Not while the taste of her lips lingered against his, while he could still feel the slick, silken juices from her pussy against his fingertips.

"Be careful, little girl," he told her gently. "Challenging a big dog is a hell of a lot different than those little Chihuahuas you run with sometimes. They bark at the wind and tuck their tails between their asses and run when I growl back. Remember that. And you better consider that there's a reason for it. I'm not a lapdog you can curl up with, pet and stroke a few times, and consider it a done deal. You're a baby next to me, Rogue. It's not the years between us that hold me back; it's the fact that you and I both know there's things about me you don't want to tempt. Otherwise, you wouldn't be so damned determined to push me."

Her brow jerked up. A perfect little sarcastic arch.

"I'll be sure to have nightmares tonight," she drawled. "Lock up when you leave, Sheriff. I've had enough of the deep, dark warnings and dominant male bullshit. I'll let you know when I'm ready for more."

She sauntered past him, and he let her go. He had to force his fingers not to curl into fists to hold back the urge to reach out for her. He had to force himself not to follow her when the bedroom door closed.

Hell, he had to force himself to leave her apartment. To stride across the room, turn the lock on her door, and step outside before pulling it shut behind him. Forcing himself down the stairs and through the bar was even harder.

Because he knew what she was doing. She wasn't in a damned bubble bath. He felt her gaze the minute he stepped from the bar. She was up there watching him, the same as he had watched her enter the bar countless times. And he wondered if she was remembering the dark promise of that kiss they had shared, because he knew he sure as hell wouldn't be forgetting it.

The kiss itself was a challenge. He should have known the minute she began battling for his taste, pressing for more, for a deeper caress, a harder taste, that he was in deep trouble where that woman was concerned.

He should have known Rogue wouldn't listen to a warning, that she wouldn't see reason. She was young, impulsive, wild as the wind. Too young. Son of a bitch. He jerked his truck door open and lifted himself into the seat before slamming it closed. He wanted to ram his fists into something; he wanted to howl at the fucking moon, race back inside and show her how a man hungered, how a man took his woman, and exactly how a man expected a response.

She had no business playing games with him. No damned business pushing his buttons and leaving him with a dick so damned hard that if he did manage to get it to relax, then the bastard was still tender, still ready for action. He hadn't been this damned ready for sex in more years than he wanted to count.

The woman worked his cock quicker than old man Parsons swore Viagra worked his. This was a damned mess, and he was beginning to lose not just his control but also his common sense.

She was, quite simply, too damned young for what he hungered for.

FOUR

Rogue woke the next morning with a headache. Gremlins from hell were digging into her brain with dull little pickaxes right behind her eyeballs. She'd known when she lay down to sleep the night before that rest wouldn't follow her into that dark void of unconsciousness. Dreams had instead. The same dreams that had tormented her for years.

Those damned pictures. That fateful night that had begun the emergence of the woman she hadn't known resided inside her.

David and Amy Kerring. They had been strangers in town, but Caitlyn Rogue Walker hadn't exactly been well known in her father's bar. She hadn't told anyone her relationship; she liked to watch, to listen, with no one knowing who she was. That night, David and Amy had been friendly. Rogue hadn't particularly liked them, but damn, she had been so dumb. She had turned her back on them only moments, but it was long enough for them to spike her drink.

The next thing she had known she had woken in a strange bed, half dressed, reasonably certain she hadn't been raped, but she had known something had happened.

Nadine Grace and Dayle Mackay had happened. They had been there, and her nightmares proved it. Nadine had giggled and laughed like a schoolgirl as Dayle Mackay snapped the pictures that had been used to humiliate her ever since.

Never let them see you sweat, bleed, or cry, her grandmother had once told her. Rogue had kept her head high, but it hadn't been easy. Staring Zeke Mayes in the eye after those pictures hit the Internet had been even harder.

Now, today, four years later, she found that bravado was second nature, pissing people off came easily, and pretending to be the wild, vivacious Rogue was like a second skin now. Unfortunately, the illusion was only skin-deep. The wild, sexually aware, teasing, motorcycle-riding hellion was just that, a game, a joke on the county and the people that had turned on her. Beneath the skin Caitlyn still lurked, waiting, watching, and fantasizing about a man she couldn't have.

So what did she do after the best kiss of her life? Did she have incredibly erotic dreams of getting him out of uniform and devouring his hot, hard body? Of course not; she had nightmares.

And she also had a job outside of lounging around the bar. She'd skipped out on Janey the night before, but she couldn't skip out today or tomorrow. The lunch-crowd days were murder, and the bookkeeping at the end of the day looked like something a cyclone had blown in if Rogue didn't get a hand on it quickly.

Not that Janey couldn't handle the paperwork; it was just that Rogue was better at it and she knew it. And she hated having to figure out Janey's system when she called demanding help. It was a hell of a lot easier when it was Rogue's system.

April was being especially nice when she stepped out the back door of the bar that afternoon. The early afternoon sunlight was pouring down and warming the mountains with unseasonably heated days. Perfect days for the motorcycle ride to the restaurant. The nights were colder, though, and far less hospitable, but endurable.

She missed the nights Zeke had picked her up after he went off duty at night. The sheriff's four-by-four Tahoe had been toasty warm and smelled of Zeke. That rich, dark male scent mixed with a hint of aftershave.

Straddling the Harley, Rogue gave herself a mental shake, turned on the ignition, and kicked back the stand before pulling out of the back lot of the bar and heading toward Somerset.

The Bar was only a few miles out of town, but the drive to the Mackay restaurant was nearly a half hour. By the time she pulled into the back lot there the chill wind had sliced through her leather riding chaps and heavy jacket. Her face felt frozen, and she wasn't looking forward to the ride home that night.

Damn, if she kept this up, she was going to have to pull that ugly sedan out of the garage where she kept it stored and start driving it again. Wouldn't that just leave her reputation as the bad-girl biker in the dust. Her dignity, too, because that sedan was damned ugly.

Kicking the stand in place, she pulled the key from the ignition, tucked it into her front pocket, and dismounted in one smooth move before pulling the small leather backpack she carried from a saddlebag.

Janey was in the office as Rogue strode in. The other woman was sitting nice and cozy and warm in her lover's arms where he sat in the large leather chair behind the desk.

"Chief of police caught lazing on the job," Rogue reported tongue-in-cheek. "Sources close to the owner of the Mackay Restaurant and Café report that said chief definitely knows how to make use of a leather office chair. Pictures below."

Janey rolled her eyes as Alex grunted, though his gray eyes were lit with amusement.

"Sources close to Rogue Walker are also well aware of a certain sheriff's late-night visit," he stated, though his gaze turned somber. "Has he learned anything yet?"

Rogue shook her head as she loosened the buckles to her chaps and slid them from her jeans-clad legs. "Nothing that I know of and I've ignored the phone this morning, so the gossip hasn't exactly made it to me yet."

"The gossip we can definitely do without," Janey stated, her dark green eyes sparking with anger.

Janey had endured enough gossip since her father's death. Dayle Mackay had been a maggot and his sister, Nadine Grace, had been even worse. Sometimes Rogue thought it rather ironic, the friendship she had developed with the other woman, considering her history with Janey's father and aunt.

"Have you heard anything further?" She watched Alex as he lifted Janey to her feet, then rose from the chair.

The man was definite eye candy. She got a nice slow look, then arched her brow at Janey's frown as her lips twitched in amusement. It was a game. Rogue couldn't help it. Alex always just almost blushed, and Janey always bristled. Rogue laughed.

"I haven't heard anything further," Alex growled. "Stop trying to embarrass me, Rogue. It's not going to happen."

Rogue shrugged. "Hey, a girl needs some excitement in her life, ya know."

Janey leaned back against the table set close to the wall and arched her brows at Rogue's comment. "I guess that's why Zeke called Alex no more than five minutes before you arrived. To add excitement to your life?"

Rogue glared back at her. "Yeah. Right. If he lets my life get any more exciting, I might not be able to handle it."

"Uh-huh," Alex murmured. "Explains the beard burn under your jaw."

Rogue's hand flashed to the incriminating mark, and she felt the heat flood her face. Dammit. She knew she had covered that with makeup.

He laughed in response. "Good makeup job, but I watch Janey try to hide the marks too damned often not to know what you're hiding there. Tell him to shave before he comes around next time."

At that, he dropped a quick kiss on his fiancée's lips and strode from the office as Rogue plopped onto the couch facing Janey's desk.

"I hate him," she muttered as she flashed Janey a mocking glare.

Janey laughed as she took a seat beside Rogue on the couch. "Yeah, he has that effect on people sometimes."

Janey tilted her head to look beneath Rogue's jaw again as Rogue narrowed her eyes and stared back at her broodingly.

"It's just beard burn," Rogue muttered. "It will go away soon."

"What is it about the men around here that they just can't get past marking their women?" Janey asked then.

Rogue snorted. "I've seen the marks you leave on Alex, Janey. I swear I think you're trying to have him for a midnight snack."

Janey's lips pursed with a wicked little smile. "Sometimes."

Rogue shook her head as a feeling of loss swept through her. She was jealous of her friend. Janey had with Alex what Rogue had only dreamed of having with Zeke in the past five years.

Why the hell was she so focused on this single man to the point that no other would do? What was it about Zeke Mayes and his total reluctance to touch her that kept her dangling on that ever-present string of attraction to him? Whatever it was, it was going to have to stop.

"I'm not his woman anyway." She shrugged as she rose from the couch, picked up her pack, and headed for the door that led into the restaurant itself. "According to him, why, little ole me is much too young for his big, bad sheriffy ass. Seems he wants more of a woman than it appears I am."

She tossed Janey a careless smile, but it hurt. No, it didn't just hurt, it pissed her off. She could have had a dozen lovers in the past five years. She didn't have to sleep alone. She didn't have to drift through the days waiting to see one man above all others.

She wasn't ugly. No one would have to put a bag over her head to fuck her.

Rogue jerked open the door and closed it behind her before taking a deep, cleansing breath. She had work to do. Three days a week she was the manager, and it just so happened that she had to pick the three hardest days of the week.

That meant she had a lot of work to do. First off was dressing for the role. She moved to the small employee's lounge at the back and the dressing room there. The waiters and waitresses had uniforms, but Rogue dressed as she pleased. She dressed to draw attention and send tongues wagging. Janey swore that half the clientele showed up just to see what Rogue would wear next. Tonight, she was in a wild mood. Wild, but subtle. Subtle meant everything when it came to a particular mood, she thought with a tight little smile as she pulled the well-pressed clothing from within her pack.

The schoolgirl's checkered skirt was short but demure. It covered her ass. That was modest, but this one actually went a few inches lower and covered the tops of her thighs as well. The pleats were full and, if she turned a certain way, would flare out enticingly. With it, she wore a see-through white blouse, a shimmering gray camisole, and beneath that, a lacy black bra. Stockings and gray stilettos finished the outfit.

An hour later the curls that cascaded around her face were pulled up to the crown of her head and secured with a thin scarf that trailed behind her head. Makeup, a quick application of bronze lipstick, and she looked subtly enticing, sexy, and wicked.

And she knew exactly who would see her looking just young, fresh, and eager to be debauched. She almost laughed at the term her mother had once used. That was exactly how she looked, and Sheriff Zeke Mayes just happened to have a reservation for dinner with his son and his aunt, Lucinda Mayes-Downes, his father's sister.

Lucinda Mayes-Downes was no one's fool, and that old woman was as rowdy as any Rogue had ever known. Shane Mayes, Zeke's son, was a crackerjack. The kid was going to be a heartbreaker when he was older, if he ever managed to get hold of that penchant to fight at any given opportunity.

She shook her head, took her hands, and mussed her hair invitingly, then pursed her lips and blew a kiss toward the mirror before giving a light, anticipatory laugh and heading out to the dining room. To work.

Damn, how had she managed to let Janey convince her to actually work?

Zeke had a feeling when he met his aunt Lucinda and son in the parking lot of the restaurant that the evening wasn't going to go nearly as planned. Once a month he was roped into taking his aunt and son out to eat. A family thing, Lucinda liked to call it. It was more along the lines of an excuse to drive from Louisville where Shane was now attending college and staying in her guest room. An excuse to get nosy, to point out the fact that he was only growing older by the day and that it was time to settle down and give Shane a brother or sister.

Thankfully, Shane didn't seem quite so enthusiastic about the brother/sister part. He found quite a bit of amusement in listening to his great-aunt gently berate Zeke though.

Hell, it if wasn't the Mackays driving him crazy with their shenanigans, then it was Shane and Lucinda. How the hell was a man supposed to consider an affair, let alone a relationship, when his aunt seemed to have an earful of gossip, about him, each time he saw her?

"You're late, Zeke." Lucinda stepped out of the cherry red Mustang she owned, a new one, a bright smile on her face as Shane pushed himself from the passenger seat.

His son didn't look happy. Evidently his doting aunt had refused to allow him to drive her new baby.

"By five minutes, Lucy," he grumbled. "You're lucky I made it at all."

Lucinda's smile only brightened. "Of course you made it. Otherwise I would have had to start making calls, tracking you down, and pulling you out of the arms of whatever little widow you'd found to amuse yourself with. Funny, I haven't heard about any widows lately though."

He shot her a warning look. Not that Lucinda paid much attention to his warnings.

As he neared, she hooked her arm around his, the fine silk of her conservative blue blouse sliding against the cotton shirt he wore. Black slacks and conservative pumps completed her outfit.

Her once-black hair was now dark silver, styled to frame her face and add a touch of youthfulness to it. Her dark brown eyes sparkled with warmth, and a touch of impish mischief. No one could accuse Lucinda of hiding her playfulness under a barrel. The woman fairly shouted "good times" with that grin of hers.

"So, nephew, how is your love life?" she asked as he opened the door for her, casted her a baleful glance.

Because he was more than aware of the hostess who had glanced up and more than obviously caught his aunt's question.

"It's still none of your business," he told her as Shane snorted behind her.

"That's never stopped her, Dad," his son told him. "And before you try to lie to her, she's been on the phone for the past two days discussing you with her cronies here in Somerset."

"Friends, Shane," Lucinda reminded him with a long-suffering look. "I've told you, they're friends, not cronies."

"Children, we're in public," Zeke reminded them, ignoring his aunt's pinch to his arm as she restrained her laughter.

"Sheriff Mayes," Rogue's voice slid through the teasing. "It's good to see you and your family again."

God, her voice did things to him. He couldn't describe exactly what it did, but every cell in his body seemed to be drawn to the sound of her. The sight of her.

He nearly swallowed his damned tongue as she stepped from behind the reservation desk and motioned the hostess to her.

"Tabitha will take care of you tonight." She smiled back at them.

"Tabitha will do no such thing." Lucy moved in front of Zeke. "Young lady, it's been too long since I've seen you. You can take us to our table and say hello to me for a moment." She caught Rogue's hands and let her gaze go over the younger woman. Hell, Zeke couldn't take his eyes off her.

"Naughty Rogue." Lucinda's smile was pure devilry. "That outfit is to die for."

Rogue's brows lifted as she accepted Lucinda's light kiss to the cheek and held on to her fingers.

"I thought it particularly appropriate, for my age." Rogue widened her eyes, and Zeke had to give her credit for never looking his way. The woman could deliver a blow with precise, well-aimed precision.

He was thankful he managed to control his wince.

"For your age, huh?" Lucinda drawled. "That little hickey you're trying so hard to hide under your jaw doesn't seem near as age appropriate."

Zeke's gaze sliced to her jaw. He saw her face flush, and her gaze jerked from his face as Lucinda suddenly looked between the two of them. Shane gave an odd little choke behind him.

"Yes, well," Rogue cleared her throat. "More like a bit of beard burn. Occupational hazard with some men. I'll show you to your table now."

Her smile was a little tighter as she turned from them, but damn, the view was good. Shit, he shouldn't be looking. He jerked his gaze from the rounded globes of her ass beneath that flippy little skirt to his son. Only to see Shane's eyes trained in the same exact area.

"Hey, brat," he growled. "Look up."

Shane jerked his head up, blushed, and laughed, then to Zeke's surprise murmured back, "Shave next time."

Hell. He should have known better than to think Lucinda didn't know where he was last night. No matter the excuse he gave, no matter the reasons why he had been in Rogue's apartment, she had turned up with beard burn the next day.

Beard burn, his ass. Yeah, he might have scratched her with his evening stubble, but he also remembered the little bite of her he had taken in the same place.

"Rogue dear, you need to come to Louisville for lunch," Lucinda was saying as Rogue led them to their table. "We could have a girls' day out. Go shopping."

Wild violet eyes turned on Zeke as Lucinda turned her back on

Rogue. Zeke wanted to smile, hell, he wanted to laugh. She looked horrified at the prospect.

"We could gossip," Lucinda stated smugly as she glanced at Zeke. "Girl talk."

"I'll have to check my calendar, Lucinda," she answered, though Zeke swore she looked a little pale at the invitation. "Janey keeps me pretty busy."

"Well, I could have a talk with Janey." Lucinda stared up at her victim complacently. "You could even bring her with you. I never got a chance to get to know that girl. Her brother though, now he was a wild one. Somerset lost a fine bachelor when he married that agent of his."

"Yes, I definitely agree," Rogue agreed hurriedly. "I'll send Janey out to you as soon as possible. You can discuss it with her. Though Alex does keep her fairly busy."

Hell. Wrong statement, Zeke thought as he took his seat and saw the satisfaction on Lucinda's face.

"Yes, a good man will keep you very busy," Lucinda agreed. "Tell me, Rogue, who was the brute that left that charming little mark beneath your jaw?" She tapped her chin thoughtfully. "I hadn't heard you were dating, dear."

"I'm not." Rogue cleared her throat. "It was an accident with my curling iron." She twirled a curl nervously as she lied with zero guilt and a charming smile. "Nature isn't always perfect. If you'll excuse me now, Tabitha needs help."

Rogue escaped, leaving Zeke to stare across the table at his aunt while Shane fought to hold back his laugher.

"I'm going to assume you have a reason for torturing Rogue," he stated.

Lucinda's eyes widened. "I wasn't torturing Rogue, dear. I was merely chatting." She looked to Shane. "Was I torturing the child?"

Shane shifted in his seat, glared at his father, and cleared his throat. "Maybe some," he finally admitted, before Zeke received another of the boy's accusing stares. "Maybe you should torture the guy that left the mark."

Lucinda sighed. "If only I could learn for certain who did such a thing," she said calmly. "Why, I called everyone I knew since first learning of it this morning. Didn't you hear me on the cell phone, dear?"

"I did." Shane ran his hand over his shortened dark brown hair. "Hours' worth, Aunt Lucinda."

"Exactly." Lucinda sighed. "And the only man that she's even been known to speak with for longer than a few minutes was your father." She turned innocent eyes on Zeke. "You talked to her last night about her cousins' deaths, didn't you?"

"Yes." Zeke answered cautiously. Damn Lucinda, she was like a shark on the scent of blood.

"Did she mention who she was dating?" Supreme innocence filled his aunt's face. The look was frightening.

"Nope, and I didn't ask her."

He'd simply more or less ordered her not to consider dating anyone. He couldn't conceive the thought of Rogue in another man's bed. In the years she had been in Somerset, there had always been talk, especially after those pictures surfaced, but nothing serious.

"Not that I'm sure it matters." Lucinda shrugged.

"Meaning?" Zeke was nearly pushing the words past his lips now. What the hell was Lucinda up to? Hell, she was dangerous. He should introduce her to that Homeland Security special agent, Timothy Cranston; Aunt Lucinda could teach him a thing or two about interrogation.

"Wrong question," Shane muttered as Lucinda smiled again. That smile was known to make grown men whimper.

"Well, after those horrible pictures." She sighed. "Well, a man has to be careful, doesn't he?"

Zeke drew in a long, careful breath as Tabitha moved toward them. The waitress carried menus, and behind her one of the young waiters was bearing ice water.

"Aunt Lucinda," he said softly. "We don't want to continue this conversation."

"Oh." Her eyes widened. "Of course not, dear. Is she a very good friend of yours as well now?"

Friend. No, he had never called Rogue a friend. A fantasy. A temptation. The one thing he couldn't have and wanted more than his next breath. They were more than friends. They weren't lovers. He couldn't allow himself to step that close to her.

"Enough." He stared back at her as Tabitha moved closer.

Lucinda sighed. Shane made that odd choking sound again as Zeke sliced his gaze to him. His son had his head down, his lips tight, but if Zeke wasn't mistaken, that tight line threatened to turn to a smile. When Shane knew what the hell Lucinda was up to, and Zeke didn't, it was time to worry.

But a part of him was fairly certain he knew exactly what Lucinda was up to. No one had seen a mark on Rogue's neck before his visit last night, now, this morning, it was there, and obviously it had been seen by one of Lucinda's gossip buddies.

He was going to have to be more careful with Rogue's silken skin, he thought. It was tender, so damned sweet, and obviously he wasn't nearly as careful with her as he had been with lovers in the past. Because Zeke knew better than to leave a mark. He knew better than to leave any proof that he had spent the night with a woman, that any woman held his attention. Especially considering the fact that Lucinda butted her nose into so much as the hint that Zeke could be involved with anyone.

She believed the only way he was going to be happy would be if he remarried. Despite her own unmarried state, Lucinda wasn't happy unless everyone around her was enjoying connubial bliss.

As his father had once said, after Lucinda's husband's death, she had become damned strange. Fun. But strange as hell.

Silence filled the table as the waiter set water before them and Tabitha handed them their menus with her cheery little spiel on the chef's specials. She took their drink orders, then moved away with a promise to return shortly for their dinner orders.

"She's a pretty little girl, Shane," Lucinda piped up. "You could do worse."

"No, I couldn't," Shane muttered. "She's older than I am."

"So?"

"I have a girlfriend," Shane argued.

"So?" Lucinda pressed again.

Shane looked to Zeke with that inborn desperate plea of a son to his father to save him from drowning. Zeke stared back at him silently. The little brat had left him floundering on his own beneath Lucinda's less-than-gentle regard. Zeke would be damned if he'd save his kid now. Let him see how it felt.

"His girlfriend is barely seventeen, Zeke. Tell Shane that's too young."

"That's too young, Shane." Zeke wished Tabitha would get back with the whisky he'd ordered.

"Is not," Shane stated with a long-suffering sigh. "It's just two years. It could be worse."

Zeke stared back at him.

Lucinda tilted her head quizzically. "How could it be worse, dear?"

Shane's lips twitched. "It could be eleven years."

FIVE

He should stay away.

Zeke parked his pickup at the back of the bar, wondering why he bothered. There was no way to hide the vehicle, and everyone that knew him knew what he drove off-hours.

He shouldn't be here.

Flexing his hands, he reminded himself that he was just here to check up on her, make sure everything was okay. Her Harley was still at the restaurant. She'd hired a cab to return home after closing rather than calling him.

Striding to the back door he hit the intercom button and waited. He could have gone through the front and right up her stairs, but damn if he wanted to listen to more of Lucinda's questions tomorrow.

The locks on the door clicked, a second later the panel was pulled open and Rogue stood before him, still dressed in that short, checkered skirt and heels, and the thin camisole she had worn under the long-sleeved blouse earlier.

"What do you want, Zeke?" she asked, her voice low, wary.

She looked good enough to eat.

He was going to at least taste.

He didn't answer her. Catching the edge of the door he pushed
inside before wrapping the fingers of his other hand around her
wrist. He closed the door, locked it, then looked back at the open
office door and the light inside the room.

"Working?" He stared down at her as he felt the slow slide of
his control eroding into the dust.

"Does it matter?" Her lips twisted mockingly. "Ready for another slap and tickle, are you?"

He ignored the accusation; instead, he moved toward the room,
holding her wrist firmly and drawing her with him.

Stepping inside, he came to a hard stop, his eyes narrowing at
the sight of the man lounging back on the couch that sat against
the wall.

Cranston was short, portly, his brown hair thinning, his expression as innocent and as unthreatening as a child's. It was a damned
good thing Zeke knew just how devious and cunning the Homeland Security agent could be.

"Sheriff? You're putting in some long hours, aren't you?" Timothy Cranston rose from the couch, straightened his wrinkled jacket
on his shoulders, and flashed Zeke a sly smile. "Rogue and I were
just discussing the unseasonably cold weather."

"No, we weren't, we were talking about Zeke." Rogue jerked
her wrist from his grip and moved around him as Timothy chuckled at her revelation.

"Very well, we were talking about you." He shrugged. "She has
a very high opinion of you."

"No, I don't. I think he's a prick," she stated, a tight smile curl ing her lips as Timothy laughed again, his gaze thoughtful as it came back to Zeke.

"Good-bye, Agent Cranston," Zeke stated, his voice harsh.

Putting up with Cranston's bullshit wasn't high on his list of priorities right now. He'd deal with him later; for now, he intended to deal with Rogue. The teasing little minx had flitted around the restaurant, like a flame-haired seductress while he had been there. Half the men in the restaurant had been panting over their meals, the other half were probably home jacking off to visions of lifting that little skirt over her ass and paddling it for driving them crazy. That was definitely what he would have been jacking off to. If he'd had the good sense to go home.

"Well, I can tell when I'm no longer needed." Timothy adjusted the front of his suit jacket over his chest before picking up the overcoat he had laid on the couch beside him. "Good night, my dear." He nodded to Rogue before turning to Zeke. "Later, Sheriff."

"Much later," Zeke assured him.

Timothy smiled again, one of those amused, condescending curls of the lips that never failed to raise Zeke's hackles.

He had issues with the agent, serious ones, that weren't being resolved anytime soon. He'd been working with Timothy Cranston for ten years now to break the Freedom League and its hold in the Kentucky mountains. What had he gained for his efforts? In the past two years, two operations had been conducted in Pulaski County that Zeke had been kept in the dark about.

He didn't appreciate it. And now, six months later, he and Cranston were still at a stalemate over it.

"Soon," Timothy corrected as he shrugged his overcoat on and moved around Zeke to the open door. "Very soon, Sheriff."

The agent at least had the consideration to close the door behind him. Zeke went one better and locked it before turning back to Rogue.

She was no longer leaning against her desk. She had lifted herself onto it, sitting poised on the edge with her shapely, silken legs crossed. Red gold curls cascaded around her like silken flames of temptation.

"And I ask again, what do you want?" she asked archly. "Or did you decide to come by and torture me another night? Keep it up, Zeke, and you may find yourself shackled to a bed somewhere with your own handcuffs."

He snorted at the threat. "I don't think so."

He watched her, simply watched her as the need to touch her grew like a sickness inside him. Staying away from her was impossible. He was learning that. The more he tried, the harder it became. The more he denied himself, the more he ached for what he shouldn't have.

"You deliberately made me crazy earlier," he accused her roughly. "Flipping around that restaurant in that little skirt, daring me to take you."

Her brow arched. "Are you paranoid, Zeke? Maybe you just needed to see it as a dare so you could have an excuse to do something you were dying to do anyway."

"And that would be?" He forced the words past his lips as he stepped closer.

Her tongue, damp and pink, flicked over her lips as her gaze lowered to his thighs, then back to his eyes. "You're dying to have me, aren't you, Zeke?" Her voice lowered, became tempting, seductive. "You want me so damned bad you can't stand it, and you refuse to admit it."

"Oh, I freely admit it." There was no denying it.

Before he could curb the impulse he took the last steps to her, wrapped one hand around the back of her neck, tilted her chin back with his thumb, and lowered his head.

Spicy, consuming pleasure exploded through his senses as her lips parted for him. Hunger beat through his veins, surged to his hardened cock, and had him pulling her thighs apart with his free hand to get closer to her.

The taste of her was liquid hot as she arched against him, a surprised breath of sound barely escaping. Keeping her head tilted back, he devoured her lips, her tongue. He slid his hand up her thigh, touched the wet panel of her panties, and groaned at the heat he found there.

"You're like an addiction." He nipped at her lips as he released her neck, only to drag the hem of her camisole up, over the filmy lace of her bra.

"We'll find you a twelve-step program." She arched against him.

"Twelve steps to complete insanity?" he asked as his lips traveled along her jaw. "Fuck, Rogue. How the hell am I supposed to do my job when all I think about is the taste and feel of you?"

"Take breaks to feed the addiction?" Breathy, sensual, her voice had his body tightening further.

"That would be a hell of a lot of breaks." It was a hell of a good idea.

Rogue tilted her head back as Zeke's lips continued their campaign of complete sensory rapture along her jaw to her ear. Shudders of pleasure raced through her body at each lick of his tongue, each nip of his lips.

It was like being consumed by hunger, by the eroticism of the feel of him against her. The heat, the lightening stroke of rapture. God, she needed more. So much more that she arched closer to him and all but begged for it as the heat continued to build in her pussy, the tension tightening in her clit.

The feel of his calloused palm cupping her breast was enough to steal her breath. The stroke of his thumb over her distended nipple sent pulses of lightning-sharp sensation to attack her womb and her clit.

She was sinking in sensual overload. In the hunger that wrapped around her and sank into her flesh. Nothing mattered but his touch, his kiss. If he thought he was addicted, it was nothing compared to her need for him. She felt as though she were drowning in the pleasure, drowning in the complete abandonment of her body to his.

Sensation jerked along her nerve endings as his fingertips brushed between her thighs, then over the dampness of her panties. Heated and wet, her juices spilled from her shamelessly, preparing her for his possession.

Oh boy, she hoped he possessed her. She was about to explode with need. Tension built inside her, drawing her tight as her knees lifted. Her shoes dropped from her feet as she raked the backs against the desk and propped her bare heels on the edge.

"Damn you," he growled, his head lifting as she leaned back and flashed him a wicked smile.

His fingers pressed against her pussy, rubbing the silk of her panties against her clit as she lifted her hips to him.

"That's so good," she whispered breathlessly.

"It can get better," he promised.

She shuddered at the thought of it getting any better, then cried out in surprise as his lips lowered to the tops of her breasts.

He licked over the swollen rise of flesh above her bra. His teeth raked the sensitive flesh, and his fingers drew patterns of heated ecstasy on the silk between her thighs.

It was too much. Too much sensation. Too much need.

"Zeke, please." Her head fell back on her shoulders as she fought to hold herself up. Palms planted on the top of the desk, her arms trembled with the effort to stay in place.

"What do you need, baby?" His cheek brushed over a hard nipple. "Tell me what you need."

What did she need? She needed so much. She needed to be

touched, everywhere. She needed to sink into his skin and never be without him.

"Tell me, Rogue," he breathed over the hard tip of her nipple. "Tell me what you need."

It was a dare and a challenge.

Rogue lifted her head to stare down at him, the effort it took to keep her eyes open sapping nearly all of her strength.

"Suck my nipple," she demanded, not to be outdone. "Suck it hard and deep, Zeke."

His jaw clenched, his golden brown eyes seemed to flame with heat as his lips parted and a breath later covered one stiff peak and sucked it, lace and all, into the heated cavern of his mouth.

Her hips jerked, thrusting against his fingers as he lashed at her nipple with his tongue. Pleasure detonated through her, striking without warning and stealing her breath as his fingertips grazed the silk material covering her clit.

"Take the bra off," she demanded as she shook beneath the caress. "Please, Zeke. Let me feel everything."

She couldn't take it off herself. If she moved her hands from their braced position she would melt on the table like hot butter.

"Oh baby," he crooned as one hand stroked up her back, then around between her breasts. "All you had to do was tell me how you wanted it."

He was teasing her, burning her alive.

The clip of her bra came free easily. Rogue fought to breathe as she watched him peel the cups back from her breasts, watched as her rosy nipples seemed to lift to him.

"How pretty," he groaned as he tweaked one tight tip with his fingers. "So sweet and hard."

"More," she gasped. "Suck them more."

His head lowered to one nipple as his fingers worked the other. Rogue shook her head as a cry spilled from her lips. It shouldn't be this good. The pleasure shouldn't go so deep that it bordered on pain. It shouldn't dissolve any objection she had.

"Oh yes," she moaned. "Oh God, Zeke. I need you. I need all of you."

She needed him inside her, between her thighs. Her pussy ached, burned. She could feel the desperate emptiness there as she never had before, and the need to be filled rose to desperate heights.

"There, baby." His head lifted as one hand pressed against her stomach. "Lay back for me."

Lay back? Move her arms? She would be lost if she didn't concentrate on holding herself up. She would lose her soul to him, and that couldn't be a good thing.

His dark, knowing chuckle wrapped around her as his hands moved; they caressed down her arms, gripped her wrists, and pulled them free. And Rogue melted.

Like a sensual sacrifice she reclined back along her desk, her arms falling over her head as his lips returned to her breasts. First one, then the other. His mouth sucked at her nipples, pulled them deep into his mouth; his tongue rasped over them, the wet heat of his mouth burned them.

"Damn, you're fucking pretty." His voice was low, sensual, wicked as his head lifted again and he pulled her camisole over her head. "So sweet and hot. Can I taste you, baby? Taste you all over and get drunk on you?"

Oh God, she had never heard anything so sexy in all her life. This wasn't fair. How was she supposed to retain any control when he talked like that? When his lips moved lower as he spoke, spreading a line of kisses along her abdomen to the band of her panties.

"Zeke. Oh God. I need you."

His fingers hooked in the elastic band. She didn't have to worry about him pulling them off her legs. The elastic snapped and his fingers brushed the material aside from the heated, aching folds of her pussy.

That was it. At the rending of the material Rogue swore she lost her mind. Sensation surged and exploded inside her as her hips jerked up and a shattered moan fell from her lips.

She was so turned on she wondered how she could breathe. Pleasure lashed through her system as desperation began to take over. Her arms lifted, her hands moved to his head, her fingers curling into the short strands of hair as she tried to push him lower, between her thighs.

She'd dreamed of this, fantasized about it, ached to know what it would feel like. Her eyes opened as she watched, watched as he kissed his way to the flushed mound, then breathed a heated breath over the sensitive flesh.

Her thighs fell apart at the urging of his broad hands. Breath suspended in her lungs as she watched his tongue lick, slowly, so slowly around her hard, distended clit. His eyes were on her, watching her as she watched him lick. Watching her as her lashes drifted closed and ecstasy took over.

A second later a light sucking kiss had her crying out. Then his tongue became ravenous. Hard hands slid beneath her rear to lift her closer as he licked through the wet slit, circled the opening, then plunged inside in one hard, hungry stroke.

Rogue felt the explosion detonate inside her. She felt her pussy clench and spasm around his tongue, felt her clit implode with rapture, and lost herself in the fiery cataclysm that overtook her.

She was drowning in a pleasure that bordered on pain as he continued to fuck her with his tongue, drawing her juices from her as he groaned into her tender flesh. Each searing sensation seemed to tear something loose in her soul. Each stroke of his tongue fueled an orgasm that didn't seem to want to stop just as his fingers brushing against her clit rocked additional stimulus through her nerve endings until she was near screaming. She wanted to scream. She tried to scream. All that emerged were breathless whimpers and desperate moans as that last shattering wave of pleasure tore through her.

Zeke leaned his head against Rogue's thigh, lust barreling through him until he felt as though he'd shatter from the need to fuck her.

His hands went to his belt. He had to have her. He was tearing at the clasp when the cell phone at his side began to beep imperatively, the tone emitting from it assuring him it was an emergency.

He wasn't on duty, but he couldn't ignore it. There was too much going on, too many things beginning to come to a head for him to ignore the summons.

With a throttled curse he jerked up and tore the phone from its holster.

"What?" he barked into the receiver as he watched Rogue's lashes lift, saw her eyes, the violet color darker, more intense than he had ever seen them as she stared back at him in confusion.

"Zeke, we have a problem at Joe and Jaime's mobile home," Gene stated. "The state police are here and you're needed."

"What's the problem?"

"It's a ball of fire," Gene stated. "It's burning to the ground as we speak. The damned thing exploded like a bomb as I pulled up in the Tahoe after we received a call that there were vandals here. It's the Fourth of July on this mountain."

Zeke felt fury burn inside him and saw the desperation in Rogue's gaze, felt it in his own body.

"I'll be right there," he snapped. "Have the state boys wait on me."

"We're all waiting," Gene promised. "I'd hurry though, because one of the neighbors thinks they saw someone in here just before we showed up. We could have a body."

"I'm on my way." Zeke snapped the phone closed and shoved it back into its holster as Rogue eased up until she was sitting on the desk.

Zeke clenched his teeth as she pulled the bra over her breasts and secured the little clip before pulling the silky top back down and smoothing her skirt over her upper thighs.

"Are you coming back?" She didn't look at him as she asked the question.

"Eventually." Not tonight. If he came back tonight, God only knew how he'd handle the lust tearing through him. He needed time to consider this, time to figure out how he could protect her amid the danger he could feel brewing in the county.

"Eventually," she breathed out as she lifted her head, her lips parting as a caustic smile shaped her lips. "A few hours? A few days? A few years?"

"There are things going on that you don't understand, Rogue," he said, trying to keep his voice low. "Things I have to deal with first."

Her head nodded jerkily. "Fine, deal with your things." She jumped off the desk and stalked to the door as he watched her, fighting the heaviness in his chest and his body's demand that he stay.

She jerked the door open and stared back at him furiously. "Don't come back until you've made up your mind whether or not you can stay long enough to at least supply the wham-bam-thank-you-ma'am that any other woman would get. I don't like being played with, Zeke."

She didn't like being played with, but by God, he didn't like games, either. At the moment, the game he was involved in wasn't one he couldn't step out of.

"Don't push this, Rogue," he warned her gently. "Don't push me where you're concerned. There are things you don't know and don't understand. Until I can fix that, then I don't have a whole hell of a lot to offer."

"Did you hear me asking for anything?" she asked sweetly. The sweet part was a dead giveaway. Rogue was pissed. And she was hurt.

"I'll be back." He strode to the door and stopped in front of her. "And the next time I catch you getting cozy with any other man, no matter who he is, Rogue, there's going to be violence."

He didn't give her a chance to respond. His hand curved around her neck and his lips took hers in a quick, hard kiss before he released her and strode from the office. He was out the back door in seconds and loping to his truck as he fought himself and his desire to walk right back inside where she waited.

She was his weakness. A man in his position couldn't afford a weakness. Especially now. Zeke could feel it beginning to come together. Whoever they were looking for was getting scared. The questions he'd been asking about Joe and Jaime's death had gotten a response. This was the response. Someone was scared the two men had left something, anything, hidden that would reveal what they were doing or why they were killed.

Now, Zeke just had to figure out what it was, without the hope of finding more.

SIX

Zeke walked into his office the next morning, paused, and stared at his visitors before shaking his head with a bemused acceptance that was beginning to grow inside him.

The file in his hand was the coroner's report on the Walker boys. The forensics report was due in any day. But it wasn't looking good. And now, staring back at the four men waiting on him, he could feel his gut burning.

"What the hell do you and your sidekicks want, Cranston?"

Special Agent Timothy Cranston was supposed to be on suspended leave from the Department of Homeland Security. Zeke knew better. Timothy had never been suspended anywhere but on paper. The investigation running now was a time bomb waiting to explode with the same power that had been used on Joe and Jaime Walker's mobile home. And Timothy Cranston was smack in the middle of the whole damned thing.

Short, round, his face more often than not wreathed in a smile that rarely reached his eyes, the agent had been Zeke's nemesis for too many years. Anytime Cranston was around, trouble was sure to be there. And anywhere in Pulaski County that he found the Mackay cousins, he was damned sure to find trouble.

Douglas "Rowdy" Mackay, James "Dawg" Mackay, and their younger cousin, recently married to Homeland Security agent Chaya Dane, Natches Mackay.

Rowdy, Dawg, and Natches Mackay, and Timothy Cranston. Hell, he didn't need this. His own investigation was beginning to come to a head after the years that Cranston had kept him pushed to the sidelines, unaware until too late that Homeland Security was working to take down the Freedom League without him. Cranston and the Mackay cousins had cut off the head, now Zeke was going for the backbone. Alone. He wouldn't be pushed out of this one. Not after all these years, the nightmares, or the evidence Cranston had against him personally.

"When the four of you show up, there's trouble. I don't need trouble this week." He strode across the office to take his seat behind the wide, wood desk that sat in front of the shuttered bank of windows.

Pulling his chair close to the desk, he slapped the file on it and stared back at the four men. The Mackays were tall, muscular, and dark. Rowdy, the middle cousin, was the most clean-cut, the thinker of the group. Dawg, the oldest, was more clean-cut than he had been before his marriage. He was no longer scruffy, but his wild days reflected in his light green eyes and his hard expression. Natches, the youngest, now, he was the wild one of the group. The ringleader of most of the trouble and unapologetic about it.

Dawg and Natches had worked with Cranston for several years. As far as Zeke knew, Rowdy had just been dragged into it lately.

"The Walker boys," Natches drawled. "You have anything yet?"

Zeke leaned back in his chair. "They involved with DHS?" He stared back at the agent. Of course they had been, he knew it and Cranston knew it, but he wasn't so sure the Mackays knew it.

Timothy grinned. A flash of teeth, like a shark, and a sparkle of brown eyes. "Not to my knowledge. They weren't one of my contacts."

Timothy was a consummate liar. Zeke knew the Walkers fed information to DHS because they'd brought the information to him first.

Zeke looked at the Mackays.

"They helped us pull in information on that mission last year," Natches revealed. At least Natches wasn't lying to him. Yet. "Joe and Jaime were always reliable sources of information."

"You think their deaths had something to do with that operation?" Zeke asked. He knew it did, in part. Their murders had been too similar to others over the past twenty years.

He hoped for the Mackays' sakes that it didn't. Zeke was approaching his limit where their complete disregard for the chain of information was concerned. Running ops in his county, without his knowledge, not just once but twice, had pushed his level of endurance to its limit. And Cranston just took the damned cake. That son of a bitch had recruited Zeke ten years before when he had been with the FBI and Zeke had gone looking for an agent he could trust. When he'd chosen Cranston, he'd fucked up. Cranston had begun the investigation without Zeke's knowledge and then had the gall to draw in three other citizens of the county instead of coming to him. Ex-marines known for their wild ways.

The Mackay cousins had spent the past two years on an investigation into stolen missiles and homegrown terrorists that Zeke had been waiting on Cranston to begin taking down. And before that, Rowdy had been too damned quiet about a stalker that had targeted his wife. They hadn't told him shit about their activities; now here they were, wanting to know about his.

They were wild and arrogant, and they made his life hell when they got involved in trouble. He'd hoped marriage would have settled them down.

"We don't believe it should have," Cranston answered as Dawg's lips parted to answer. Dawg flashed the little man a brooding glare. Evidently, Dawg was aware he was lying, too.

"You don't believe?" Zeke kept his gaze on Dawg. "Dawg, you boys are newly married. The three of you have babies on the way. Do you really want to spend a few nights in jail for withholding information on me again?"

Three Mackays glared back at him. "Your jail wouldn't survive it, Zeke," Rowdy stated. "Don't threaten us. Joe and Jaime were friends and their families are close to us. Grandma Walker and their sister, Lisa, and her two boys are pretty much alone now. The twins took care of them. We need to know what happened."

He stared back at Rowdy. Normally, Zeke would have believed him, but several years back, Rowdy had pulled his own bullshit over on Zeke. He hadn't forgotten it. There were times he wasn't sure he had forgiven it. He used to believe he was friends with these men, until he learned how easily they would hide the threats to the county he was duly sworn to protect.

They were here, and they didn't know shit about what he was doing; only Cranston was aware of it, and only because the other man was well aware of who and what Zeke was looking for. While they were here, he may as well get what information he could.

"I don't know what happened yet. Not fully," he lied as he leaned forward and stared back at the cousins. "Did those boys do hard drugs that you knew of?"

They looked at each other in confusion before Rowdy shook

his head firmly. "Joe and Jaime were hell-raisers, but they didn't do the hard stuff."

Well, hell, that didn't help him much where the coroner's report was concerned.

"Do you have the forensics' or coroner's report yet?" Special Agent Timothy Cranston leaned forward in his chair, the wrinkled material of his cheap gray suit jacket shifting loosely on his shoulders.

"Cranston, what's your business in this?" Zeke leaned back in his chair with a brooding look. "If this has anything to do with another operation in my county, then now's the time to give me a heads-up. Otherwise, I'll stop playing nice."

And that was Cranston's only warning. The agent was hiding too much information from him and Zeke was losing patience with him.

Timothy grunted. "You stopped playing nice when your buddies in the Justice Department kicked my ass last year. Now, I'm being nice." His smile was all teeth. "Janey's upset over this. Rogue's her friend and mine. Those twins were her friends, and Janey asked me to see what I could find out. I'd prefer not to pull in my own favors in D.C. at the moment, Sheriff. Might need those favors to get my job back." The lying bastard. "So why don't we all just play nice, and see if we can help each other here."

Which pretty much meant Cranston was involved up to his beady little eyes in Zeke's business. Playing along was easy enough, for the moment.

"Well, hell," he growled, lifted the file, and tossed it closer to the edge of the desk. "Initial report. Joe was pumped on heroin. The city's investigative coroner still has the bodies, but this is the county coroner's initial findings. Joe was pumped, walked in, shot Jaime, then himself."

Natches lifted the file from the desk, sat back, and opened it.

Two cousins and one portly Homeland Security agent read over his shoulder.

"Not possible," Dawg murmured. "Joe didn't do this shit, Zeke. And he wouldn't kill Jaime."

"Dawg, I'm doing my best with what I have here." Zeke sighed. "Forensics hasn't come up with anything yet. No vehicle tracks were found outside the twins' trailer, other than official vehicles that arrived that day. There was rumor of a fight over a girl, but no one knows who the girl was. There's just nothing to stand on here but my gut and your suspicions. That's not going to get me far."

Natches tossed the report back to the desk before breathing out heavily and raking his fingers through his shaggy black hair.

"If we hear anything, we'll let you know." Dawg shook his head at that point. "But I know Joe or Jaime wasn't doing heroin. That's a promise. They weren't exactly upstanding citizens, Zeke, but they didn't do trash, either."

Zeke could only shrug in response. "I need proof, Dawg. You know how it works. I'll wait until forensics and the coroner's investigator finish their reports. But initial calls to each aren't promising. Until then, I'm asking questions and trying to piece this together. If Joe and Jaime were murdered, then someone knew what the hell they were doing, because I can't find so much as a whiff of suspicion. It's that simple." And it was a message to Cranston. Zeke knew who he was after; the agent could stay the hell out of his way if he didn't intend to play fair with Zeke in this little game.

"Damn." Dawg rubbed at the back of his neck in a rough gesture.

Zeke's gut went haywire when he knew things weren't as they seemed. Dawg's and Rowdy's neck itched. Natches just became a time bomb with an assassin rifle. Who the hell knew what Cranston did; Zeke sure as hell couldn't figure him out.

The Mackays weren't happy, Zeke wasn't happy, Cranston was

smiling, and Zeke knew that this was a bad sign. Welcome to Lake Cumberland, he thought caustically. The last few years had been hell, for law enforcement as well as citizens. Pulaski County was a quiet little place, despite the tourism to the lake.

The mountains, vibrant forests, fishing, and hometown atmosphere hadn't made up for the realization that a dark underbelly had been existing for decades beneath their notice. The operations Homeland Security had conducted, using the Mackay cousins as agents, had revealed a festering evil that Zeke had been fighting far longer than the Mackays could ever guess. It had become his own personal battle, the only way to make up for his sins as a child.

"What about the explosion last night?" Natches asked. "Their mobile home went up like fireworks. If it was murder-suicide rather than two homicides, then why would anyone bother to blow the place up?"

Zeke lifted his shoulders in a shrug. "I went over it with the state police and the arson investigator. We didn't find jack. There was a call made here to the office that there were vandals at the place. It went up in flames as Gene pulled into the driveway with the state police. There was no sign of a body." He lifted another file as he glanced at Cranston. "There was a gas stove in the mobile home that the arson investigator believes must have been faulty and caused the explosion."

Zeke didn't believe that for a moment. It was too easy and it was too similar to how he knew the League's exterminator worked. Zeke knew things the Mackays didn't. He knew things Cranston didn't. And he knew this was the work of someone from the homeland terrorist group that had escaped the net Cranston had used to pull the others in.

"I have an idea." Cranston smiled as he leaned forward in his chair. "Right now, whoever you're looking for, if this was a murder, knows you're looking for him. Let him think you're distracted, otherwise occupied."

"Meaning?" Zeke gritted out. Cranston was a cunning bastard, but that didn't mean Zeke liked the games he played.

"I mean, let them think a woman has your attention. Concentrate on something pretty, pretend to be totally focused there, give your killer a chance to mess up rather than watching every move and every word because he's on guard." He shrugged his shoulders as he sat back in the chair. "It couldn't hurt."

"Just use some poor woman as a tool to find a killer?" Zeke snorted. "How did you make special agent, Cranston? Did you cheat on the exam?"

Cranston chuckled at that. "While you're occupied, myself, Alex Jansen, and the Mackays can watch your back. We'll see who's interested, and who's doing what. We can ask the questions needed much easier, and get more."

"Forget it," Zeke gritted out as he saw the mockery in the agent's eyes.

They both knew exactly who he was suggesting Zeke use. And Zeke sure as hell didn't like the excuse his lust was trying to grab with both hands.

"Come on, Zeke," Dawg chided him harshly. "Those were our friends. Let us help with this."

"I don't need your help, Dawg, and I sure as hell don't need to pretend to be focused on a woman to solve this case. But if I learn anything new, I can let you know," Zeke told them with a complete lack of sincerity. "Unlike some agents and kamikaze rednecks, I don't mind a bit of cooperating when the situation warrants it." His smile was all teeth this time. A reminder, a careful warning. He could be a friend, or he could be an enemy. One more operation in his territory without his knowledge, and these men would find themselves on the enemy side. That wasn't a good place to be.

"You're worried about kamikaze rednecks when, according to every gossip source in Somerset, you're consorting with leather-wearing maniacal pixies?" Dawg snorted. "Hell, Zeke, even me and Natches were smart enough not to get mixed up with Rogue Walker."

"She turned you down," Natches reminded him as Zeke tensed. "I was just smarter than to approach her."

All eyes turned to Natches.

"What the hell do you mean by that?" The words slipped past Zeke's lips without control as a core of possessiveness seemed to slam into his chest. He'd be damned if he'd allow her to be insulted by these men.

Natches grinned. "Hell, Zeke, five years ago, you nearly lost your tongue when you met her at that town hall meeting when she arrived as a new schoolteacher. I have a rule, man. Don't mess with a buddy's woman." He rose from his chair, chuckling as Zeke narrowed his eyes on him. " 'Bout time you made a move. Personally, I think she should tell you to go to hell for waiting so long. But that's just me. And Cranston's idea has merit. Grab Rogue with both hands and hold on for dear life. We'll watch your back and do what has to be done."

"No one asked your opinion." Zeke ground the words past clenched teeth.

"Yeah, Chaya reminds me of that often." He laughed as he headed for the door, cousins and one special DHS agent following behind him. "Tell Rogue I said hi when you see her."

They left the office, and left Zeke with a raw, almost blinding sense of need where Rogue was concerned. Son of a bitch, he hadn't had enough of her last night. He'd wanted it to be enough, convinced himself that he wouldn't feel what he knew he was going to feel today.

Lust had slammed into him. Even now, in the cold light of day, his balls were tight, his cock hard. The memory of her lips, like hot satin, the taste of her, equal parts liquor and female, the feel of her body, heated and molding to his, haunted him.

Rubbing his hands over his face, he tried to contain it, to push it back where it belonged, where other things he knew were not in his best interests were locked. Unfortunately, Rogue refused to stay locked away.

There were times he swore he could almost feel the silken warmth of her hair between his fingers as he caressed a fiery curl. He could almost feel her lips against his. He could almost imagine her taste. Almost. It was never enough, and the need to experience it again was making him crazy.

Lucinda and Shane hadn't helped his self-control the other night. Hell, Lucinda and Shane nothing. Damned nosy busybodies in town. Too many people had known he'd gone to her apartment the night before, in plainclothes, and stayed too long. And too many gossips had put two and two together the next morning when it came to that reddened mark beneath her jaw.

Oh hell, he remembered leaving that mark. Remembered tasting her a little too deeply, too roughly. And she had loved it. Her head tilting back, her breath passing her lips in a hard sigh. She had done the same thing last night. Melted for him. Became slick and hot and ready for his touch.

Sweat collected along his spine as he shifted in his chair, trying to find a more comfortable position to accommodate the erect length of his dick. At this rate, he was going to die of a hard-on. It had to be dangerous for a man of his age to stay this hard for so long.

A sharp knock at his door had his attention turning from the need raging through him.

"Yeah," he called out.

The door opened and Gene stepped in slowly.

Well now, wasn't this just what he needed?

He stayed silent and waited as the deputy stepped into the room and closed the door behind him.

"Can I have a minute, Zeke?" Gene asked quietly.

He was dressed in the black-and-gray uniform, his hat clenched in his fingers as he faced Zeke across the room.

"A minute." Zeke nodded.

Gene cleared his throat. "I'm still on schedule. I thought maybe we could talk about the other day. I was out of line."

A frown clenched Gene's weathered forehead as he raked back his dark hair and grimaced heavily. Zeke remained silent.

"I don't have a problem with you, Zeke," he finally said. "I got family issues goin' on, and I guess I was blowing off steam with the Walkers. I'd like to make up for it."

Zeke hadn't filed the report against him, he hadn't initiated a suspension, simply because he hadn't had time. He and Gene had once been friends. Zeke had fought for the position as sheriff, and Gene had come on board as deputy for the same reasons Zeke had. Or so Zeke had once believed. To clean up the county, to find a way to eliminate Dayle Mackay's stranglehold here, and make up for the wrongs their fathers had committed.

He and Gene had promised themselves they would make up for those darker years. Gene was a good deputy, and once, Zeke had known him as a good friend. But Zeke suspected now that Gene's loyalty might not run as deep as he'd once believed it had.

"Everyone deserves justice, Gene." He finally sighed as he watched the other man closely. "Walkers are no different from any-one else. Hell, they weren't involved in that mess last year when some of our leading citizens were. I'd say they were a damned sight better than some around here."

"I agree, Zeke." He nodded. "I went off when I shouldn't have. It won't happen again."

Something had changed in Gene over the years, Zeke thought. He wasn't as compassionate, he wasn't as patient as he had once been. But hell, had he really ever been as diligent as Zeke knew he had wanted Gene to be? He hadn't been, and it was a fault Zeke had acknowledged a while back.

It wasn't as much Gene's fault as it was his own. He should have known better than to put Gene against his own father and the past he had shared with Zeke's father. Gene didn't have the demons Zeke had; he hadn't faced hell and turned his back on it.

"We'll let this one go, Gene," he finally said. "We'll both see if we can't fix things in the future."

"Thanks, Zeke." Gene inhaled in relief as he moved to grip the doorknob. "I'll head out on patrol then."

"Gene." He stopped the other man before he left the office.

Gene turned back, his brown gaze curious.

"You said the Walker boys were fighting over a girl at the bar last week. Any gossip as to who they were fighting over?" It was the one piece of information Zeke hadn't been able to uncover.

Gene lifted his hand and scratched thoughtfully at the side of his nose before shaking his head. "There was no name mentioned, now that I think about it. Just that Rogue had to throw them out because they were fighting, and the fight was over some girl both of them wanted." He frowned slowly. "I didn't hear who the girl was."

Zeke nodded. No one else had heard, either. Just that it was over a girl.

"I'll head out then." Gene opened the door, slid from the room, and closed it behind him, leaving Zeke alone to stare at the coroner's initial report that was lying on the desk.

Joe pumped up on heroin didn't make sense. Joe and Jaime fighting over a girl didn't make sense. Nothing about their deaths added up or pointed him in the right direction to look for evidence. All Zeke had was the fact that it was identical to a method the exterminator used. He knew it was, because his father had told him about it repeatedly when he'd been a teenager. When he, too, had been a part of the Freedom League.

He rubbed at his jaw, sat back in his chair, and visualized the murder scene again. The TV remote and the half a bottle of beer. But the television had been turned off.

There had been no drugs in the house, though Joe and Jaime weren't strangers to a little marijuana. There should have been some.

Jaime hadn't fought, he hadn't even tried to come out of his chair.

Joe had put the gun in his mouth and pulled the trigger within moments of killing his brother.

There were no signs of tears on his face or in his eyes. There were no defensive wounds to indicate he had been murdered. The gun was in his hand, his prints alone marking it.

He closed his eyes and let the scene form in his head. There was something off there. Something more than the lack of evidence for anything illegal, something more than that damned television being turned off, the remote in the exact position it would have been if it had fallen from Jaime's hand.

There had been traces of marijuana in Jaime's system, but heroin in Joe's. The coroner's report showed a single track mark in the arm. Nothing more. He'd shot up only once and killed his brother while under the drug's influence.

Zeke knew it hadn't happened that way.

His eyes opened, his lips compressing as he rose from the desk and jerked his hat from the desk where he'd tossed it.

He wanted to see the scene again, remember the layout of the bodies, and figure this out. The mobile home may have been blown to hell, but the ashes were still there, and Zeke could remember how it had been when he'd found the bodies.

Joe had shot up only once. Just that single time. And that was bullshit. Someone had managed to shoot him up and walk into that mobile home with him. Once there, the unsub had shot Jaime, then killed Joe.

Zeke left the office and headed from the building, walking into the warm April sunshine and ignoring the sharp pang of longing he felt at the sound of a motorcycle purring past the sheriff's department.

He looked, but it wasn't Rogue. Wild hellion curls weren't flowing back from the rider's face and a fun-loving, devil-may-care smile wasn't aimed his way.

Hell, she was working, he knew. It was her afternoon at the restaurant, and if nothing else, Rogue was damned dependable in what she did.

He was the inconsistent one. He'd lusted after her for years and fought against it. He'd kissed her, then pushed her away. He ordered her not to bring another man between them, but he made damned certain he stayed as far away from her as possible. And when that hadn't worked he'd at least tried to give her pleasure and satisfaction before walking away again. Staying away from her was killing him.

And he had to fight himself, daily now, not to go to her, not to take what he knew he could have, what she would willingly give him.

Twenty-six. She was twenty-six years old. Slender, delicate. Pixy wasn't far off when describing her. She barely topped his chest. She was fragile. She wasn't strong-boned; she wasn't mountain stock. Hell, she looked like a good breeze might blow her away, but still, she wasn't skinny. She was slender. Rounded where a woman should be rounded. Curvy and tempting. But too damned fragile, he had to remind himself as he pulled himself into the official Tahoe emblazoned with the Pulaski County sheriff's seal.

He could fuck all night, most nights. He was so damned testos-
terone driven that there were times he cursed it. When men he went
to school with resorted to taking Viagra, Zeke still had the stamina
he had had ten years before. Hell, there were times he wondered if
he hadn't gotten worse as he'd gotten older.

It was a Mayes male trait, his father had once bragged. All
Mayes men had a big dick and lots of fire, his father had been
known to tell anyone who cared to listen.

It was definitely a Mayes trait, and one he wasn't happy with at
the moment. If he had to take a little something to help his flesh get
happy, then it might be better for him and Rogue both. Neither of
them needed the complications that would come from the relationship he feared would evolve.

Because the fire wasn't the only Mayes trait. Zeke loved sex;
he just managed to keep his lusts reined in and tried to turn them
toward women he knew weren't looking for commitment or for
something more than the hard ride he could give them.

Familiarity could breed a greater hunger. His marriage to Shane's
mother had suffered beneath the desires that often tormented Zeke.
Not all women had the hungers or the needs that Zeke knew; he'd
realized that with his wife before her death.

He'd had to hide his needs because of her distaste of them. After
her death, he'd learned there were more women like her than he'd
realized. He was the odd one, the one that needed to put a handle
on his unruly fantasies and needs.

He hadn't thought he was odd when he lived in L.A., when the
friends he'd made there had revealed their own darker desires. He
didn't share his women. What was his was his, but damn, he liked
to push them sexually.

He liked to play, to tempt, to tease a woman's body and watch
her go crazy as she grew wet and wild. He loved seeing a lover with
a black blindfold, his handcuffs circling her wrists, bare flesh be-

tween her thighs, sweet syrup glistening on feminine folds, and the heated flush of her flesh from an intimate spanking.

Or better. Ah, even better. A pretty, shapely ass raised for him, clenched rounded curves straining as he invaded a tender, sensitive little rear.

Perverted, his wife had called him. She'd rage for days if he even tried to touch her there. And God forbid he should mention blindfolding her or spanking her. The insults she'd thrown at him over that one had been nearly as bad the ones that had come when he suggested she shave or wax her pussy.

He was a hard lover. It was a part of him. It was something he'd sworn he wouldn't deny himself after his wife's death, only to learn that more often than not finding a woman who enjoyed the kinkier sex was easier said than done. The women he'd had affairs with liked their missionary position and their gentle loving, which could be good. But it was like having steak morning, noon, and night. Sometimes, a man craved a little variety, a little spice to his meal, or to his sex life.

And Rogue was definitely spice. All the more reason to stay the hell away from her.

Because all he could see was Rogue stretched out on his bed, her pretty violet eyes hidden by a silk blindfold, her hands cuffed, her little rear lifted to him.

She was a baby compared to him. He had no business fantasizing about her, and he had no business touching her. Despite her air of cynical sexuality, there was a glimmer of innocence in her eyes that warned him that the schoolteacher wasn't far below the surface.

The soft-spoken, tentative, shy young woman that had come to teach and had learned the dangers of a small town far faster than she should have. She was still there, and she still looked at him the same way she had looked at him at that town hall meeting. With stars and heat in her eyes.

Rogue. She was definitely wild as the wind and bordering lawless. But that schoolteacher still lurked beneath the surface. Soft, delicate, her smile shy, her violet eyes filled with curious sensuality.

She was like a delicate, sensual little bomb waiting to explode in his hands. In his hands, beneath his body, with his cock buried inside her.

And he couldn't allow it.

He had managed to contain himself over the years. Rumors of his desires had never leaked out because he never gave in to them. He didn't spank his lovers, he didn't handcuff them, and he didn't fuck their asses. He rode them hard and heavy and left them panting and exhausted at the end of the night.

That mark on Rogue's neck had surprised him. He hadn't even marked his wife Elaina's neck. He'd never left a mark on a woman's flesh. Not beard burn and sure as hell not a bite mark. He'd lost control in those few brief seconds that he had held her. Lost control of his need and his hunger. It was time to rein them in now. It was time to forget Rogue and get back to the business of finding a killer. The same killer that had taken his wife's and mother's lives in L.A., and then his father's, here in Kentucky.

The killer that would have no compunction in wiping out Rogue's existence if he thought it would serve his purpose. And if he learned Zeke was searching for him before Zeke managed to identify him, then it would definitely serve his purpose. It would destroy Zeke.

SEVEN

There was very little to be found in the remains of Joe and Jaime's mobile home. Bedsprings, the springs on the couch and chair. Appliances were blackened and melted in spots; the rest was pretty much cinders. Standing at the edge of the burned remains, Zeke could remember what he had seen when he had been there the day he found the twins.

The burned, twisted metal left from the recliner became the chair Jaime had died in. Surprise. There had been an expression of complete surprise frozen on his face. There had been something, someone he hadn't expected with his brother.

Zeke narrowed his eyes as he imagined how it could have played. Joe arriving, possibly high, not exactly himself, with a friend. They step into the house as Jaime stares at his brother in surprise. A second later, he was dead.

Zeke stepped into position, lifted his arm, and pointed his finger as though it were a weapon, imagined it firing, saw in his mind's eye where the bullet may have caught Jaime.

Either the killer was a quick aim, or he was taller than Zeke. Taller, Zeke thought. The killer's arm came up and he fired, dead center between Jaime's eyes before the other man could raise up in his chair.

Joe was high, but he would have been surprised by the shot. Turned a little, just enough. The gun barrel against his head. *Pop.* Zeke imagined the shot, saw where it went, and nodded his head slowly.

"Been a long time since I've seen you do that."

Zeke froze at the sound of Gene's voice behind him. Turning slowly, he found Gene's cruiser parked farther down the graveled road.

Zeke shrugged in answer to Gene's comment. "It's been a while since I've had to do it."

Gene shoved his hands into his uniform pockets and frowned as he stared around the small valley. "Guess you were right about something not being right about those boys' deaths," he stated. "Someone made damned sure that fire was hot enough to wipe that trailer out." He turned and looked at Zeke in confusion. "Why the hell would someone want to kill those two boys?"

Zeke breathed in heavily before turning away and staring out over the valley.

"I figure it had something to do with the girl," he finally answered, and it struck him that he was having to tell too many damned lies lately in an attempt to protect the information he was looking for.

Gene didn't say anything. When Zeke turned back to him the other man was watching him closely.

"You don't tell me stuff anymore, Zeke." He sighed. "We used to share cases like this."

Yeah, they had, until information had begun leaking from the office, until he had lost DHS's support and cooperation. It bit his ass that the Mackays had been involved in investigations that Zeke should have been a part of. He wouldn't have even known why he had been pushed out of it if his contact in Washington hadn't suggested that was the cause last year.

"It's nothing personal, Gene," he told him, though that, too, was a lie. Gene had been a part of the Freedom League along with Zeke when they were younger. Zeke had believed Gene had gotten out after he left, but information he had dug up over the years suggested otherwise.

Gene nodded slowly as though accepting the explanation. "Do you have any idea who the girl is?" Gene finally asked.

Zeke shook his head. "No clue. And that's damned strange in this town."

"No kidding," Gene snorted. "I've asked around myself and haven't gotten any answers. Those boys didn't seem to trust anyone where she was concerned."

Zeke felt a pulse of energy at Gene's statement. If Joe and Jaime didn't trust anyone with their potential lover's identity, then it was because they were afraid of someone. A member of her family. Father, brother, or uncle most likely.

The manner of their deaths was consistent with the exterminator's killing style, or at least one of them. Could the man he was searching for have a daughter? A daughter the boys were messing with?

"Guess they kept her too much of a secret," Zeke said slowly as he turned back to Gene. "She could be our only clue to who killed these boys."

Gene nodded. "Yeah." He ran his hand through his hair before replacing his hat and grimacing. "Too damned bad, too. A man doesn't deserve to die like that."

Zeke nodded to that before making his way along the graveled parking lot back to his Tahoe. "I'm heading back to town then," he told his deputy. "See you tomorrow, Gene."

"Yeah, sure, Zeke," Gene answered pensively. "I'll see you tomorrow."

What the hell was Gene doing following him? Zeke wondered as he pulled away from the wreckage of the mobile home. His deputy hadn't cared to share a murder case with Zeke in a while. He'd taken patrol while Zeke normally worked with the state or Somerset city police himself to solve the crimes committed in the county.

Gene was hiding something, Zeke knew that. He knew the other man, sometimes better than he wanted to. And he knew Gene was keeping an eye on him for someone else. For the remaining members of the League, Zeke suspected.

Despite the knowledge he could feel burning in his gut, he knew if he didn't come up with something soon on this case, then he would have to put it aside, close it, and let it stand as a murder-suicide. And that just pissed him off. There was something about this case that had his nerves on edge every time he thought about it. Something he knew he wasn't seeing, and should.

He'd questioned every associate of the Walker boys that he could think of. He was pushing the coroner to push the investigative coroner, and he was harassing forensics to find something more. The only ones he hadn't questioned yet were Joe and Jaime's younger sister, Lisa, and their grandmother. That he would be taking care of soon.

Turning into the graveled lane that led to the Walker house, Zeke grimaced at the sight of the black Harley parked in the barren drive.

It looked pristine and out of place among the straggling weeds and clumps of grass that surrounded the house and the run-down sedan parked next to it.

The house was in need of several coats of paint, maybe a few new boards on the porch. The home itself was sturdy though. Joe and Jaime had always made certain their grandmother's home was kept in good repair while Lisa oversaw her care.

As he stepped out of the Tahoe the door opened and Lisa, rounded and somber, stepped out on the porch. Grief had ravaged her pretty, pale face. Weariness gave her blue eyes a bruised, haunted look and thinned her lips as she watched him approach.

"Grandmother's awake," she breathed tiredly as he stepped up onto the porch. "She's been demanding that I call you since we got back from Louisville."

Zeke's eyes narrowed. "Is everything okay?"

Lisa shook her head. "You mean other than the gossip that one of her favorite grandsons killed his brother, then himself? God, Zeke, this is killing her faster than the pneumonia is."

Tears sparkled in her eyes as he wrapped his arms around her shoulders for a quick hug and looked inside the house where Rogue was staring back at him silently.

"I need to talk to you, and to your grandmother if she's up to it," he told Lisa. "Are you up to that, Lisa?"

She nodded against his chest before moving back. "Whatever it takes to find whoever did this. Joe wouldn't have killed Jaime. It just wouldn't happen, Zeke. And now even our memories of them are being stripped. What the hell happened to their home?"

Yeah, that was what everyone else was telling him, too. As for the mobile home, he just didn't have the answers he knew she needed.

Lisa turned away and led him into the house. To face Rogue. He stared into violet eyes and damned if he knew what to do. He wanted her in his arms, he wanted to lower his head and kiss those shimmering lips, and at the same time he was aware of the dangers that lurked there.

Zeke Mayes hadn't publicly claimed a woman since his wife had died. He kept his affairs hidden and his desires carefully controlled. And controlling them had never been as hard as it was now.

As he stared at her, the heated wonder in Rogue's gaze seemed to dim when he did nothing. She turned away, her spine stiff beneath the white T-shirt she wore, her hips twitching angrily beneath her jeans as she moved toward the back of the house.

All those long, fiery curls were restrained in a braid that fell below her shoulders. She looked younger than her age, but that did nothing to cool the fire burning in his dick.

"I'll check on Grandma, Lisa, then make coffee. You talk to Zeke," she called back.

Zeke nearly followed her. He almost moved to grab her, to pull her back, and give her what he knew she needed. What he needed. A touch, an affirmation that there was more between them than the simple friendship he had claimed for so long.

"She's not going to wait on you forever," Lisa said behind him, her voice quiet.

Zeke turned and narrowed his eyes on her as her lips curved into a sad little smile.

"That's the hazard of living where everyone knows everyone." She shrugged. "People start seeing things when they see you every day. And Rogue's not nearly as good at hiding what she wants as you are."

He rubbed at the back of his neck, blowing out a hard breath.

"I need to talk to you about Joe and Jaime," he told her, ignoring her advice. "I'm sorry, Lisa, but if I don't get some evidence to the contrary soon, then I'm going to have to rule their deaths as a murder-suicide."

Her lips trembled, but she nodded in acceptance. "I don't know much, Zeke. I know they were seeing some girl. They fought over her at first. Joe was angry with Jaime for a couple days, then . . ." She blushed and shrugged. "You know how they were. When they argued over something like that, they either ended up both doing without it or sharing it."

He moved to the threadbare though clean easy chair as she sat on the matching couch.

"So they were sharing a woman? Do you know who it was?" he asked her.

"I don't know if it had gone that far yet." She shook her head. "And they wouldn't tell me who the girl was. They just said her daddy would have a stroke if he found out. That was a couple of days before you found them." A tear slipped down her cheek.

"You were close to your brothers, Lisa," he stated. "You've always known what they were doing."

"And who they were doing," she said mockingly, bitterly. "But they weren't talking this time. They did that sometimes though, if their lover didn't want anyone to know, then they didn't tell, Zeke. You know how it is around here. Joe and Jaime knew how to keep their secrets, even from me. Most of the time I only found out by accident when they were dating someone together."

"Did they say anything more about the father?" he asked.

"They didn't say anything more, period." She shook her head. "The next day I was at the hospital with Grandma. There was no time to question them, and I was worried about Grandma. I didn't think." Another tear slipped free. "I just didn't think to question them about it."

Another damned dead end and a secret that had killed. The story of his life for too many years to count.

"Were Joe and Jaime involved in anything else?" he asked her then. "Any kind of drugs?"

A flash of anger darkened her eyes. "Joe and Jaime didn't do drugs, Zeke."

"We found evidence of pot in the house, Lisa; could they have been involved with anything stronger?"

"Hell, that's like finding a beer in the house," she exclaimed. "Come on, Zeke, pot's not that big of a deal around here and you know it. Sure, they smoked a little of it, but never a lot. And Joe and Jaime didn't do the hard stuff."

He tightened his jaw for long moments, staring back at her, hating the questions he had to ask.

"Lisa, I need you to think for me, to be very sure. Now's not the time to try to protect Joe and Jaime, not if you want me to figure out what happened to them. Did you ever know of them doing heroin or anything stronger than a little pot?"

She stared back at him as though he were a stranger now. As though he were accusing her brothers of some heinous crime.

"Never, Zeke," she finally answered. "And I would have known. Plain and simple, they didn't have the money or the personalities for that junk. Joe and Jaime liked to play, they liked to have fun, and they didn't consider hardcore drugs as fun."

He nodded at that. Joe and Jaime didn't do hard drugs. That was what everyone said. But someone was trying to make it look as though Joe at least had done something a lot stronger than a little pot.

"Zeke?" He turned to Rogue's melodious voice, his body tightening, his cock giving an eager jerk at the pure, sweet sound that wrapped around his head. "Grandma Walker wants to talk to you. She said you can come in here and discuss her boys with her or you can face her once she's strong enough to get to your office. It's your choice."

He grimaced at that. Callie Walker was hell on wheels when she was pissed off. If she made it to the sheriff's office, it would be an event no one was likely to forget for a while. Callie Walker would flay the hide off a man at twenty paces with a look alone.

He rose from his seat. "I'll talk to her." Turning back to Lisa, he felt a senseless frustrated anger filling him. They were expecting him to fix this. To figure things out and make someone pay. He couldn't make anyone pay without proof, and proof was sadly lacking.

Rogue watched Zeke as he moved into Grandma Walker's room. She could hear his voice, low, deep as he talked to the old woman. It was gentle, soothing. Grandma Walker wouldn't be with them much longer, and she knew it, ached because of it. The death of her two favorite grandsons hadn't helped anything.

She wasn't Rogue's grandmother, though the old woman had all but adopted her. The relationship was distant—she was a cousin to Rogue's father—but Rogue couldn't have loved her more if she had been her own grandmother.

"He's crazy about you," Lisa said softly as Rogue moved into the room. "He couldn't take his eyes off you."

Rogue snorted at that. "Not hardly, Lisa."

Lisa shook her head. "He's always watched you just as hard as you watch him," she said. "He likes to deny it just as hard as you do."

Who said she was denying her part of it?

Rogue let a soft smile tilt her lips as she sat down on the couch and drew Lisa down with her. The other girl was exhausted. She'd been trying to take care of her grandmother and her two twin boys at the same time for months. Divorced and on edge, the pressure was beginning to show on her pretty face.

"How are the boys doing?"

A small sparkle lit Lisa's eyes. She loved her boys. "They're with their dad tonight." She finally sighed. "With Joe and Jaime's deaths and Grandma's illness, I had to beg him to help me with them. There's just not enough hours in the day."

"If you need anything, you'll let me know?" Rogue asked.

"I will," Lisa murmured, but Rogue knew her. Lisa wouldn't tell her if she was starving; Rogue had to guess at it. She had to buy groceries and get someone else to deliver them or face Lisa's anger. She had to slip in when Lisa wasn't around and pay home health for Grandma Walker's medicines and hospital bills. Lisa was proud as hell and she hated taking money from anyone, especially family.

Her head turned as Zeke moved back into the room. She fought her response to him, fought to keep her expression clear of the need and the hunger that burned inside her.

He was dressed in jeans again and his uniform shirt. A black official sheriff's hat perched on his head. His badge was clipped to his belt and he looked so damned sexy it made her mouth water. Her hands itched to touch him, her lips felt swollen, inflamed for his kiss.

Rising to her feet, she watched him expectantly. She wanted him until she was consumed by it, but she also remembered why he was there.

"Had the boys told her anything?" Rogue asked as Lisa stood beside her.

He shook his head, his eagle-fierce gaze going between her and Lisa.

"Nothing," he breathed out roughly. "If forensics or the coroner's investigator doesn't come up with anything, I'm going to have to close this case."

He knew something, she knew he did. She knew that closed little look, that official expression, and she hated it.

"I need to head out," he told them, heading for the door. "If the two of you think of anything, then don't hesitate to let me know."

With a slight little nod of his head he walked to the door. Rogue let him get outside before she gave Lisa a quick good-bye, grabbed her backpack, and followed him.

"Sheriff?" She kept her voice casual, composed.

Show no weakness, she warned herself. No familiarity. Stay distant. Zeke didn't like public displays of anything from women, and she knew it.

He paused by the Tahoe, watching her curiously as she moved toward him.

"We need to talk," she told him, keeping her voice low despite the fact that there were no neighbors.

"About what?" he asked carefully.

"Joe and Jaime." She propped her hands on her hips as she faced him. "What have you really learned?"

His arms went over his chest, his gaze became hooded. "Nothing conclusive," he said.

"What do you have that isn't conclusive?"

His eyes narrowed, his jaw bunched, and for a second she saw lust blaze in his eyes.

He grimaced as he glanced over her shoulder to the house. "Are you busy this afternoon?"

Surprised, Rogue shook her head. "I'm off the rest of the day. Why?"

"Follow me to the house," he stated, opening his door and stepping into the Tahoe. "We'll talk there."

Follow him? To his house?

Rogue knew his farm wasn't far from Grandma Walker's. It was sheltered, private. Hidden. Just as his relationships and his women stayed as hidden as he could manage.

She nodded slowly before moving away. He started the Tahoe as she moved away and was backing out of the drive as she straddled the Harley and started it with a flick of her wrist.

The rumble of power filled her senses, reminding her of Zeke.

Kicking the stand up, she maneuvered the cycle back, turned, and hit the gas as Zeke's vehicle moved ahead of her.

Why his house? she wondered. Her heart was racing in her chest through the drive, her palms sweating. She could feel the wind against her breasts, her nipples peaking in anticipation, and she knew why. It wasn't because they couldn't talk in the Walker driveway; it was because Zeke had no intention of talking.

What were her intentions though? God, she didn't want to become one of his hidden little secrets. One of the women that he kept behind closed doors and never claimed in public. But her body was raging. The memory of his touch, the need for more was building inside her like a volcano ready to explode.

She dreamed about him. She ached for him. She was the biggest fool living if she allowed him to do that to her.

Nothing ventured, nothing gained, another part of her argued. She would never know if she didn't try.

He was going to break her heart, her head warned her, but she was damned if she could stop it from happening. Zeke was her weakness, and she knew it.

She made the turn onto the farm behind him. The graveled road was long and winding, moving through the valley and angling up and around to another smaller, clear valley where the two-story wood-sided house sat beneath the blazing sun. It was surrounded on three sides by forests, and in the back led directly to the backwaters of Lake Cumberland.

A glimmer of water could be seen through the trees; the scent of it surrounded her as Zeke drew the Tahoe into an opened two-car garage and then motioned her in beside him.

The doors slid closed as the engines shut off. Rogue closed her eyes for a second, realizing what he was doing. Hiding her Harley, hiding her presence.

Breathing in deeply, she kicked the stand into place before swinging from the cycle. Pulling the small backpack from her shoulders, she looped it over the bar on the back of the seat, all the while watching as he moved toward her.

His expression was predatory. It was hungry.

"Hiding me, Zeke?" She couldn't keep the question inside as he came abreast of her.

He paused, stared down at her as some shadow of emotion flickered in his eyes.

Zeke couldn't believe he'd allowed his control to slip this far. He never brought a woman to his home. Ever. But he couldn't stand it any longer. Need was eating him alive, the hunger for the taste of her was wearing at his control until he was like a man possessed.

It was get her here, or take her in the damned driveway in clear view of Lisa and her grandmother. Now, wouldn't that just give rise to enough gossip to fuel this county for the next decade?

"Come on." He didn't answer her question. Instead, he gripped her arm and pulled her to the door, only distantly aware of the fact that she hadn't tried to shove his balls to his throat.

Men didn't manhandle Rogue, she didn't allow it. Until him.

"You are so pushing your luck," she warned him as he slammed the garage door behind them and swung around to face her.

"You think I'm not aware of that?" he asked.

He knew damned good and well he was pushing his luck.

"Get ready," he warned her. "I'm about to push further."

Already part of his control was lost. The ability to deny her, to deny the hunger pulsing through him, tempting him. It was shot to damned hell, the edges frayed and broken. But another kind of control kicked in. Instinctive. Dominant.

His fingers curved around her jaw, pushing her head back as a rush of breath parted her lips and her violet eyes darkened, widened.

Did she like it?

Her face flushed as he held her. One hand at her hip, the other controlling her head. His nostrils flared as he drew her scent in. The smell of the mountains rushed around her as the breeze had while she rode. Beneath it was the simple, clean scent of desire and femininity. The smell of the woman that tempted him into his dreams and through every second of reality.

"You're a weakness," he told her, letting his thumb stroke over her jaw as he backed her against the wall.

"Really?" Her breathing was deep, rough. "I'm surprised, Zeke. I thought big, bad sheriff didn't have a weakness?"

"Smart-ass." His gaze dropped to her lips.

Tempting, sweet, her tongue licked over them slowly. Teasingly.

"Now I'm a smart-ass, too," she whispered, her tone sensual, sexually weak.

The sound of her need had his dick throbbing. His balls were tight, the need wrapping around him like manacles as he stared down at her, fighting it, fighting what he knew he was going to do.

"Damn you," he growled.

His head lowered, and she was waiting on him. Waiting for him.

Kittenish little nails dug into his scalp as his lips covered hers and fire erupted through his system. Heat blazed along his nerve endings, dominance and overwhelming sexual starvation erupted through his mind.

She tasted like sunshine. Like spring. She kissed like the hottest caress of the sun, her lips parting beneath his, her tongue meeting his, her body arching like a slender tree before the force of a summer storm.

He was lost. Son of a bitch, he was lost in her and he knew it.

Nothing mattered but more. Kissing her deeper, stronger. Fueling the desire inside her to the depth that his had been fueled. Wiping her mind of everything, anything, but his touch, his taste. Because that was what she did to him. She wiped away the control he prized so highly and revealed the man he kept hidden from the world.

Because Zeke knew he had never kissed another woman like he was kissing Rogue now. It wasn't just hunger, it was dominance. It was the dark central core of his sexuality moving in and claiming, when he had never claimed before.

He controlled the kiss. He held her face in place, fingers on the pressure points of her jaw, keeping her mouth open to him, controlling her ability to wrest that dominance from him. And she was trying. She tempted and she teased, licked at his tongue and tried to suckle it. She moaned when he refused to allow her the upper hand. Her body arched, her nails dug into his scalp, and her hips arched to cushion the hard-on raging beneath his jeans.

Just this kiss, he had told himself once, long ago. If he could just have this kiss, he would be satisfied. But the kiss only pushed him closer to the brink, made that dominant core stronger, more insistent.

He let her suckle his tongue lightly before pulling back. He wanted to see her lips wrapped around his cock like that. He wanted to hear her moaning around the thick, hard crest as he shot his release to her throat.

"You're dangerous." He pulled back, nipped at her lips warningly as she tried to follow his kiss.

"I'm lost." She sighed, fingers trailing to his neck, her nails prickling over his flesh. "Kiss me again, Zeke. One more time."

Her lashes lifted, showing the brilliance of dark, dark violet eyes. Her lips were swollen, her cheeks flushed as her breasts rose and fell roughly.

"Take the shirt off." He released her and stepped back enough to allow her to move. "Let me see you."

Her face flushed deeper, the color tempting him as it washed over her neck and beneath the collar of the T-shirt.

Her tongue ran over her lips. Her hands moved to the low-rise waist of her jeans. The metal button slid free.

His hand caught hers, his gaze narrowing. "Just the shirt, Rogue. Nothing else. Pull it off."

She shivered, her eyes shadowed with wariness and excitement as she pulled the material free and eased it up and over her head.

Zeke felt his jaw tighten as he tried to push back the darker aspects of the man slipping free.

"The braid," he said. "Loosen it."

"You're bossy." Her pouty little grin was filled with challenge and defiance despite the fact that her hands lifted to work her hair free.

He watched her breasts beneath the white skimpy lace of her bra. The material barely covered the hard, pointed flesh of her nipples. The cotton-candy pink tips had his teeth clenching with the need to taste them.

"Good," he crooned as her hair fell around her shoulders and down her back.

His hands lifted to the silken strands, though he kept his gaze on her breasts. "Now take the bra off."

"Take your shirt off first," she whispered. "If you want, Zeke, you can give."

And take his hands from her hair? It wasn't going to happen. He bunched his fingers in the silken strands, lowered his head, and took her lips again. He took her with the kiss. Claimed her. His lips slanted over hers, his tongue working in her mouth until she was moaning and straining closer, her wicked little fingers at the buttons of his shirt, struggling to release them.

She was fire in his arms and he knew it. Controlling her sexuality would never be easy. Hell, he'd never control it; he didn't want to control it. He wanted to harness it. He wanted it to burn out of control while he let the flames twist around him.

A second later, he felt buttons pop as the material of his shirt parted, revealing his chest.

He pulled his head back, ignored her need for more, and stared down at her.

"The bra," he demanded.

He wanted to suck those sweet, hard little tips into his mouth again. He wanted to taste her, feel her shuddering in his arms.

Her hands were trembling, her fingers clumsy as she worked the clasp between her breasts loose and shed the bra.

Hell yeah. This was what he wanted.

"How pretty." One hand moved from her hair to cup a hard, swollen mound and caress it.

"Zeke?" She whispered his name, her voice nervous, uncertain.

And innocent. The innocence was like throwing gas onto a fire. Damn her. Damn his own depravity because he wanted nothing more than to turn that shade of innocence to sexual knowledge.

"Does it feel good?" He let his thumb rub over the sensitive tip. "Should I stop, sweetheart?"

She shook her head, her lashes drifting closed as his head lowered.

"You know what I'm going to do, don't you, Rogue?"

How innocent was she? That question tormented him. Was her experience limited to the event that produced those pictures or had she had more than that couple for a lover?

Not much more, he decided as his lips brushed over the curve of her breast and she shivered beneath the caress.

"Drive me crazy?" she accused him, her voice thick.

He almost chuckled, because that was exactly what he intended to do.

Keeping his gaze locked with hers, his lips parted, his head lowered. He watched her face, insane lust rising inside him as his lips closed over a tight, hard peak.

Rogue cried out. The sound wouldn't stay inside, the need wouldn't abate. When his lips closed over the ultrasensitive flesh of her nipple she felt electricity sizzle from the tight tip to the swollen bud of her clit.

She stared down at him in wonder, watching the way his thick, dark lashes fell against his cheeks. The way his cheeks hollowed, his lips drew on her. The sensations were incredible. Electricity and heat sizzled through her, firing her cells and nerve endings, turning her into a shuddering mass of sensation.

"Zeke." She whimpered his name, she couldn't help it. It was incredible. It was a pleasure that drove all rational thought from her mind and had her shuddering in reaction.

She was on the verge of climax. She could feel the sensations whipping around her clit, pushing her closer. He had one hand in her hair, pulling at the heavy strands. The other was wrapped around her breast, fingers stroking, caressing it, plumping it.

Shudders raced through her. She needed more. So much more. She was so close, just a little bit closer, just a little bit more. Then his teeth gripped the hard tip and exerted just enough pressure to bring her to her tiptoes and send little quakes of near-release tearing through her body.

It was fingers of lightning wrapping around her clit. It was heat. It was a shuddering, vibrating rasp beneath her flesh that had her arching, pressing her sex against his thigh, writhing and exploding in pure white-hot pleasure.

"That was very, very bad, Rogue," he growled. "I wasn't ready for you to come yet."

"Oh my," she panted. "Wasn't that too bad?"

Her lips curled in satisfied pleasure. She wasn't finished by a long shot, but she was definitely vibrating from the pleasure that had spiraled through her. She was weak, almost relaxed, and waiting for more.

"My turn," he growled, and excitement sizzled through her veins as he pulled back, turned her, and leaned against the wall.

Rogue licked her lips, then raked her teeth over the lower curve as he took her hands and pulled them to his belt. His gaze was narrowed, watching, probing. Something warned her that if he ever realized she had never done this before, then she could kiss him good-bye right now.

She wasn't saying a damned thing.

The metal button released, the zipper rasped down. A second later she was swallowing tightly as the dark-crested length of his erection was pulled free.

He palmed the shaft, watched her intently.

Okay. She'd read about this. She'd watched it on some movies she'd rented. She'd dreamed about doing it. She ached to taste him.

She laid her lips against his chest and felt him tighten. One hand returned to her hair, his fingers bunching in it as he pressed her closer, lower.

He tasted hot and male, wild. The short chest hairs tickled her nose, but the taste of his flesh was more than worth it. Feeling him tighten, feeling the power that surged through her as his groan echoed around her.

He enjoyed her touch.

She flattened her hands on his abdomen, slid them down slowly as she moved lower, lower. Her heart was racing in her chest, fear and desire, excitement and uncertainty racing through her.

She wanted him to enjoy her touch. She was terrified he would guess her inexperience.

Remember the movies, she told herself. Those women knew what they were doing. Think, Rogue. Think.

Her lips slid over his abdomen as she gripped his thighs. He was breathing hard, his abs flexing, his thighs tight.

Brushing his hand away from his erection she let her fingers curl around it and moaned at the feeling of silk-covered, heated iron. Blood throbbed along the heavy shaft as a bead of moisture gathered in the small slit on the crest.

She was breathless, mesmerized. Kneeling before him, holding the hard length of his cock in her hand, she felt alive, energized.

Her tongue peeked from between her lips, lapped at the creamy droplet, and her lashes fluttered over her eyes at the salty male taste of him combined with the sensual sound of a male curse of pleasure.

Okay, she was doing okay.

She licked and his hands tightened in her hair. She opened her lips and drew the hard crown between them, sucking it into her mouth, and felt his other hand slide into her hair, holding her in place.

"Damn, Rogue." The sound of his voice was a spark of pleasure along her clit and inside her aching sex. "Ah God. That's good. So fucking good."

She was so fucking good.

She sucked him deeper, rolled her tongue along the sensitive undercrest in an imitation of what she had read, and was rewarded by a savage flexing of the shaft she still held.

Oh God. This was so good. He was here, she was touching him, sucking him, and he was enjoying it. His hips were moving as she sucked, fucking against her mouth with smooth, controlled movements.

Rogue was shaking with anticipation now. Zeke was leaning back against the wall, his thighs were taut, his abdomen flexing, his cock throbbing between her lips as she caressed and licked, sucked and moaned around the rapidly thrusting flesh.

She stroked the shaft with both hands now, needing him. She wanted to taste him, wanted to feel him spilling into her mouth, wanted a part of him that she had never known from any other man.

"Damn. Yeah," he groaned as her lashes lifted, her gaze locking with his.

And it was sexier. It was making her crazy. She could feel herself creaming, saturating her panties with her juices as he held her head tighter.

"Rogue, baby. I'm going to come. Damn." He grimaced, his expression tortured as his breath became rougher. "Pull back."

He pulled at her hair as defiance flashed through her. She wasn't pulling back. This was hers. She had waited, fantasized. She had studied, ached. He wasn't stealing this from her.

"Sweetheart. Damn you. I'm going to come, Rogue. Straight down your damned throat if you don't pull back."

She wasn't pulling back. Her tongue worked beneath the thrusting shaft, her mouth suckled, drawing him deeper between her lips.

"Fuck."

She felt his cock flex. He stilled, then dangerously tightened before a low groan preceded the first hard spurt of semen from the heavy cock head as it sank nearly to her throat.

Oh God. She felt herself shaking, trembling. She was coming. She could feel it. Her thighs tightened as her clit vibrated and throbbed and a lash of heat seared her body as he held her in place, growled her name, and spilled more of the heated, silken release to her mouth.

"Ah fuck," he gasped. "Rogue. Son of a bitch, your mouth."

His groan was followed by a slam. The slam of a door, a moment of surging tension.

"Oh hell." A youthful male voice squeaked. "Oh fuck! Hell!" The door slammed again as Rogue's eyes widened, staring up into Zeke's harsh, granite expression as he stared across the room.

At the door straight across from them. The outside door. The one that would have given a clear view to exactly what the hell was going on. That someone being Zeke's son.

If mortification could kill.

Rogue drew back and stumbled to her feet, her horrified gaze turning to the door, then to Zeke. He was still hard. Sweat sheened his chest and icy fury marked his expression.

"Well." She swallowed. She could still taste him. She still burned for him. "I guess I can forget this going any further, huh?"

His gaze sliced to her silently.

Yeah. That was what she figured.

"Go talk to your son, Zeke." She picked up her clothes from the floor when she really wanted to sink to the tile and sob. "I'll get dressed and head home. Maybe I'll see you again . . . sometime."

She turned away from him. She wanted him to say something, anything. To blame her, to rage, whatever. After all, his teenage son had just caught him getting a blow job in the kitchen. It had to be a major catastrophe in any man's life. It was sure as hell a major catastrophe in her life.

"Go home," he told her, his voice hard despite its very softness. "We'll talk later."

Uh-huh. She just bet they would. Like never.

She glared at his retreating back as she jerked her bra on and hurriedly clipped it. With shaking hands she pulled her shirt over her head and jammed her arms into the proper holes. She held back her tears. She held back her anger.

Until she backed the Harley out of the garage. She hit the gas, spun enough gravel to leave a trench, and raced for the main road.

Fuck him. Fuck it all. She'd had enough.

EIGHT

Shane was slightly in shock. He paced the back deck, ran his fingers through his hair, and mumbled another curse. Hell. Some things a guy didn't need to know about. Sometimes, a guy needed to be a little more careful.

Hell, he'd seen the Harley in the garage; he just hadn't thought. His dad never brought women home. It was just something that never, ever happened. Especially in the middle of the day.

Sheriff Zeke Mayes didn't do "nooners." Shane almost laughed out loud. Hell, he didn't know if he should be mortified or laughing. Because he'd wondered if his dad was some kind of fucking monk or something. At least now he knew that one wasn't happening.

But hell, walking in on him? Him and Rogue Walker?

Shit. He'd had enough fantasies about Rogue himself; he didn't need to see his dad doing her.

His dad was going to kill him. It was that simple. Shane had seen his face. His dad was freaking going to kill him. He flinched at the sound of the door opening behind him and closing softly. He paused, took a deep breath, then turned around.

Yeah, Dad was going to kill him. He was scowling at him, arms crossed over his re-buttoned uniform shirt, his expression forbidding.

"Look, I didn't think." Shane cleared his throat and tried the honesty route. "It just didn't occur to me, you know?"

His dad was damned freaky about his privacy anyway. He was one of the most secretive people Shane knew, especially about his private life.

"Where's your car?" his dad asked carefully.

Shane winced. "At the garage. I had a friend drop me off earlier. It was rattling. You know it had that rattle, Dad. I came home to get it fixed. And there are no classes tomorrow."

He could feel the flush on his face and rubbed at the back of his neck nervously. He wanted to cuss again, but knew better with his dad scowling at him like that.

"Sorry, Dad," he finally muttered.

His father drew in a harsh breath before dropping his arms and stalking to the porch railing. They both listened to the sound of a Harley starting. The low throb of power, then Shane winced as it roared. Oh hell, Rogue was pissed off.

He glanced at his dad and watched his shoulders tighten, the way his jaw bunched as the cycle's motor ripped through the silence of the valley on its journey to the main road.

"She's pissed at me, too?" He sighed.

Zeke shook his head. "She's not pissed at you."

She was hurt. He'd seen that flash of pain in her eyes and hadn't known how to deal with it. Hell, it wasn't every day a man's son walked in while he was getting blown.

"I didn't see anything. Much," Shane ventured hesitantly. "I turned my head. Fast."

Zeke glanced over at him. "You saw enough."

Shane cleared his throat before turning and gripping the railing. He stared out at the lake, his youthful expression still a combination of amazement and shock.

"Yeah. Enough."

Shane rocked against the railing and this time, Zeke didn't chastise him for it.

"It won't happen again," Shane ventured. "I mean, I moved out. I should, like, knock first or something. Not just barrel in when I know you have company."

"That would be a start," Zeke said heavily. Though he doubted there would be more "company." Hell, he'd be lucky if Rogue didn't kick his ass the next time she saw him. And he'd deserve it.

He should have said something. He should have promised to call later. Something. Hell, he'd just shot his cum down her throat and threw her out. He could feel himself cringing inside.

"Sorry, Dad," Shane apologized again, but Zeke could hear the amusement in the boy's voice. He didn't blame him for being amused.

"I'll kick your ass if you ever bring a girl here and let me catch you," he warned Shane, just in case. Sometimes, with a boy that thought he was a man, it was best to lay the ground rules out front and center.

"Uh, yeah. Wouldn't blame you." Shane sounded as horrified as Zeke felt.

Shit. This was his son. There were things a man should never let his son, no matter how old he is, know about, let alone catch a glimpse of. And Rogue. She was gossiped about enough, she didn't need her name tarnished further.

"And this won't be mentioned," he warned Shane. "Especially to your aunt Lucinda."

Horror shaped Shane's face. "Oh my God, you think I'd tell Aunt Big Mouth?" he gasped. "Come on, Dad. I like Rogue. She's cool. Too good for you, but she's cool."

Zeke's brows arched as Shane flushed again.

"Didn't mean it the way it sounded," he muttered.

"Then how did you mean it?" Zeke asked him carefully.

He mumbled.

"Come on, Shane," he ordered. "If you're going to run your mouth, be a man and stand by it."

He had never let Shane shirk his responsibilities or his punishments. If he could run his mouth, then he could back it up.

"I didn't mean to insult you." Shane finally shrugged. "Well, kinda, I did."

Zeke stared back at the boy silently as he turned and faced him. Shane's eyes met his as his brows lowered into a fierce frown. He looked like an adult when he did that. Zeke didn't like admitting Shane was becoming an adult.

"Look, I know Rogue's half crazy over you," Shane said then. "Even when I was in school and you came for those stupid parent-teacher conferences that year, I could see it. She likes you. Maybe too much. And you're all about no ties. She deserves better than that."

Zeke crossed his arms over his chest and faced his son then. He'd be damned if he was going to let his son stand and chastise him over something he didn't know or couldn't understand.

"That's not your call, Shane," he pointed out firmly. "What's between me and Rogue stays there. Understand? I don't need your advice."

Shane looked away for a moment, and Zeke was struck by the maturity his son had achieved in the past year at college. Hell, he'd missed it. Shane's face had lost that youthful fullness. It was becoming more honed, closer to Zeke in looks rather than his mother's father.

Hell, it was a defining moment, Zeke thought, realizing his kid looked like him. And that his kid was berating him over a woman. There was something about that that just clashed in his head.

"I'm not trying to give you advice." Shane turned back to him, eyeing him fiercely now with eyes almost the same color as his own. "I'm telling you, Dad. You break her heart, and you won't be the man I've always respected."

It was all Zeke could do to keep his jaw in place. Hell. When had reality shifted?

In his kitchen with his dick down Rogue's throat, another part of him reminded him.

"Son, you're getting big enough to hit," Zeke warned him, though he knew hitting the boy wasn't in question.

Shane snorted at that. "Yeah, sure, Pop. And you're old enough to know better than to mess with a girl like Rogue without being serious about it. You're older than she is. And you know things she doesn't."

"Things like what?" Zeke gritted out in a snarl. Maybe he should rethink the hitting part.

Shane flushed, then straightened his shoulders and glared back at him. "I'm your son," he snapped. "Don't make me spell crap out. It was bad enough walking in on you like that. I'm a man, not a kid, and I know I'm not always normal in some things. I figure I got it from someone and I'm figuring after hearing tales about Grandpa, that I get it from your side. Okay? So be careful. I like Rogue. She's cool, and she doesn't treat me like a stupid kid. You break her heart and I'm gonna be pissed. That's just all."

With that, Shane turned on his booted heel and slammed back into the house, rattling the door on its hinges as Zeke stared at it in shock.

Fuck, he needed a beer. He needed a beer, a long nap, and then he needed to get his head screwed on straight where Rogue was concerned. She was pissed. Shane was pissed. And Zeke couldn't blame either damned one of them. The question now was damage control.

He rubbed the back of his neck as he grimaced. When he'd been married and pissed his wife off, all he had to do was leave her alone for a while and she forgave him. When Chaya was pissed at Natches, he said the best thing to do was leave her the hell alone. He'd seen various Mackay men moping at the diner when their wives were in a snit. Rogue couldn't be much different, could she?

Hell, it was humiliating to realize how little he knew about this female's quirks. He was thirty-seven years old, he'd been married, and he hadn't exactly been celibate over the years since his wife had died.

But, he reminded himself, neither had he actually had relation-ships. Not that he had one now. Did he? He shook his head. Hell no, he didn't have one now. Rogue wasn't a relationship. But she was definitely going to be a lover. He'd give her a few days, let her get over her mad, then he'd find her.

He nodded to himself. That was all he had to do. Because the next time he found her, he was fucking her. It was that simple. He'd come down her throat today with a force he hadn't known in his entire life. Watching her, seeing her innocence, realizing how she was struggling with the act and trying to hide the fact that she had no idea what she was doing. And still, she'd gone down on him with a sensuality and a hunger that amazed him.

And when he'd filled her mouth, she'd come with him. Not the way she was going to come once he got his lips between her thighs or his cock buried deep inside that hot little pussy he knew would drive him insane. But she had come from the sheer sensuality and excitement, with him. He wasn't about to fight this much longer.

He'd managed to hide the darker core of his sexuality for most of his life; it was second nature now. He'd hide it with Rogue as well. He'd have to, because he knew he had to have her. There was no other option.

He would hide it from Shane, he'd hide it from the county. He knew how to hide his lovers and he knew how to hide his interest.

If something warned him it wasn't going to be that easy with Rogue, then he pushed it aside. Rogue was hotter, more of a temptation, more of a forbidden fruit because of her age, he told himself. It wasn't emotion. Zeke had learned long ago not to let himself get emotionally involved. He wasn't involved now.

Was he?

He wasn't, he decided. Cranston's idea had merit, too. He could have Rogue, he could let the killer think his focus was divided while Cranston and the Mackays asked their questions. Hell, they were going to do it anyway.

And he wouldn't be using her, he assured his guilty conscience. He was dying for her. His attention was divided, it was too focused on his hunger, and he'd end up missing things. This way, he'd at least have a clear head for the investigation.

And he was making excuses. The plain and simple fact was he simply couldn't stay away from her any longer.

Rogue showed up at work the next day even though she didn't want to. She felt raw inside, rejected, used. She felt as though she had been stripped to the bone and had no idea how to heal the wounds; she only knew how to hide them.

She pasted on a smile after a careful application of makeup. Smoky eyes were sensual, and they hid the shadows of emotional catastrophe. Bronzed lipstick made her look seductive.

She wore chocolate ankle-strapped stilettos and a matching slip dress that just barely hid the band of her bronzed stockings. She spent hours straightening her long curls until the mass of red gold strands hung to her hips like a shimmering ribbon. Parted on the side, it framed her face with rakish appeal and gave her a slight ego boost if nothing else.

She didn't ride the Harley into work but had Jonesy drive her in with a promise to pick her up later that night. He was silent, moody, and obviously not exactly happy with her style of dress.

He approved of the leather, no matter how skimpy she got with it. He thought it was tasteful. To Jonesy, silk was a trick and her straight hair was a come-on. Go figure.

She stepped into a full restaurant, took over for Tabitha, and kept a smile on her face. She fielded advances, she laughed at the flirtatious comments, but something inside her felt as though it was breaking.

Okay, so it was pretty bad having your son walk in while you were getting a blow job. She could only imagine how horrifying that was. It was bad enough getting caught, period. He was shocked, needed to yell at Shane a little maybe. She excused that. She was pissed, hurt, but she understood.

She understood all night. She watched the hands of the clock tick by and felt the knowledge that she didn't matter enough to seek out growing heavier inside her.

The dinner crowd moved through, in and out, until the doors were locked and she gave one last peek as she turned the sign to Closed and realized he wasn't going to show up.

Showing up would mean others would see him. It would be an acknowledgment that she was more than just a casual little fuck, she admitted.

But how could she have expected anything less?

Ignoring Janey and Alex's concerned looks, she strode through the restaurant back to the office and started putting receipts together to begin the paperwork for the night.

She often finished up in the office while Alex and Janey went on home. She called Jonesy and told him she would be late. She'd get a cab. He wasn't happy, again. It seemed Rogue had lost the ability to please anyone who mattered to her that day, she thought with a scowl.

Damn men. When had she started caring what any man felt?

The day she'd met Zeke Mayes, she admitted to herself. God, she was such a fool for him. It was insane, completely pathetic actually.

She looked up as the door to the office opened and Janey and Alex stepped inside. She knew that look on her friends' face, and she knew that evidently she hadn't hidden her emotions as effectively as she had hoped. Great, now Janey would have questions. And what Janey knew, Alex would know. What Alex knew, he would probably say something to Zeke about. And well, didn't she just know how private Zeke was?

"Everything okay, Rogue?" Janey asked casually as Alex closed the door behind them.

"Actually, no." Rogue pushed the receipts back as Janey looked at her in surprise. "Sheriff Mayes has no idea who killed Joe and Jaime. Grandma Walker hasn't stopped crying, and Lisa won't let me help." She rubbed at her temples. Those were concerns, and they were heartbreaking, but that wasn't what was digging gouges out of her soul.

"Forensics hasn't come back yet, Rogue," Alex stated. "I've been checking on it, and the coroners haven't finished their tests on the bodies yet. We should know something conclusive soon."

Rogue shook her head. "Grandma won't be with us much longer." Her lower lip trembled despite her battle to keep her emotions in check. Acknowledging that was a bitch. She would have to bury the boys with no one to comfort her, and she knew that soon she would be burying their grandmother the same way.

How had she let this happen? How could she let herself care for a man she couldn't even lean on in her grief?

"Is there anything we can do to help?" Janey moved to the front of the desk and sat down gingerly in one of the chairs.

Her forest green eyes were somber and filled with compassion, but there was an edge of suspicion in them as well. She knew when Rogue was hiding things, when she wasn't talking. That was the risk you took when you let someone become your best friend.

"Yes, there is," she said softly. "Don't ask questions."

It was the closest she could come to admitting anything.

Alex snorted as Janey's lips compressed. "That's not fair, Rogue."

"It's very fair," she told her friend. "I have to deal with family right now, Janey; I don't have the strength to deal with more."

"Aren't you telling the wrong person that?" Janey asked her.

"No." Rogue shook her head, her voice roughening. "I'm telling the one person that should understand I need time right now. And I need a chance to figure things out on my own."

Janey stared back at her for long, silent moments.

"You know we're here," she offered. "For family things or anything else."

She couldn't risk it.

"Rogue?" Alex spoke then. "I can leave the room. Anything you tell Janey would go no further, you know that."

No, she didn't know that. She knew men. She knew they talked and gossiped worse than women. And she knew Janey. Before she knew it, the entire Mackay clan would be privy to Zeke's secrets, and that whole privacy rule he had would be shot to hell and back. Hell, she felt sorry for his former lover now.

"Not a problem, Alex." She smiled tightly. "I just want to get these receipts finished and head home to bed. It's been a damned long day and it doesn't look as though things are going to get any better for a while."

They were likely to get worse. It was normally not a good thing to threaten or attempt to commit bodily harm on an officer of the law, and she knew one she wanted to shoot with his own gun.

Janey sighed. "You're sure there's nothing we can do?"

Rogue looked down at the receipts, then back up to her friend. "I need a few days off actually. The bar is going to hell right now and I need to straighten a few things up."

The bar was the one place she knew Zeke wouldn't enter. He may have that first night to question her, but he wouldn't do it again. Too public, and of course, no one could know he was trying to fuck the little bar whore.

Fucking Nadine Grace and Dayle Mackay. God, she had never hated them as much as she hated them now.

"How many days?" Janey asked carefully, causing Rogue to smile.

"I need at least four days, maybe five," she told her. Long enough to get the need eating her alive out of her system. Long enough that when she returned she wouldn't be watching for him, waiting for him. Long enough to find her balance again and get her heart straightened out. Long enough to avoid prison because of her homicidal tendencies toward one man.

"Five days." Janey nodded. "But you promise you'll be back after that?"

"I'll be back after that," Rogue promised. "I just need to get things squared away. That's all."

She could feel Alex's stare, it was like a laser that cut straight through the lies she was telling.

"Fine. Five days." Janey sighed as she stood up. "You can leave tonight's receipts. I'll harass Natches and make him get them in the morning. He can work for his share of the profit for the next few days. But don't think I don't know what's going on, Rogue."

Rogue's head jerked up to stare back at her. "What's going on?"

Janey leaned forward. "The plague. A plague known as redneck male stupidity. Want to know the cure?"

Uh-oh, Janey's smile was all teeth. It was a Mackay smile and never boded well.

"There's a cure?" she asked warily. She was intrigued now.

Janey's smiled widened.

"Janey," Alex said warningly, which only made Rogue more curious.

Her brow arched as she stared back at her friend. "A girl can never have enough cures for redneck male stupidity. Just in case she runs across it."

Janey leaned closer. "When you get your hands on him, Rogue, and you will get your hands on him, remember one thing. He's rumored to have stamina, but you have something that can bring him to his knees."

"Do tell." Rogue replied mockingly. Oh yeah, she definitely wanted to hear this one.

"The word 'no.'" Janey pulled back, her expression tightening in anger. "Tell him to go to hell and walk away."

"Like you did?" Rogue arched her brow, remembering well just how effective that had been with Alex.

Janey pouted. "That was Alex. He's different."

"Uh-huh." Rogue nodded. "Do tell how different, Janey." Her gaze flickered to Alex. He was looking less than comfortable with the direction of this conversation.

"Yes, sweetheart," he drawled then, his voice silky, curious and warning at the same time. "Do tell us the difference."

Janey's smile was satisfied, sensual, alluring as she gazed at her lover before turning back to Rogue. "His condom broke the first time." She laughed, ducking as Alex reached for her with a laugh.

"I had to have mercy on him. You know, just in case I had to make an honest man of him."

Janey's laughter was filled with happiness as it echoed around the office. Her lover caught her in his arms, lifted her against him, and gave her a kiss that was filled with his smile.

"And on that note." He turned to Rogue. "We'll give you a ride to the bar."

"That's not necessary," Rogue began.

"Well, you could ride with us or with him."

With him? Rogue started back at him with a rising sense of dread.

"Meaning?"

"There's a certain sheriff's Tahoe parked out front, most likely ready to turn away any cabs. My truck is out back." Alex's smile was tight. "We could sneak you right out."

Rogue swallowed tightly. She couldn't face Zeke, not tonight, not yet. If he was waiting outside for her, then she knew exactly what would happen before they managed to get out of the parking lot.

She picked up her purse casually, each move deliberate.

"I appreciate the offer of a ride, Alex," she said as she stood to her feet. "I think I'll take you up on it after all. It's rather cold to wait outside for a cab in this weather."

"Yeah." He nodded. "I thought you'd see it that way."

Zeke was fucking up.

Alex led Janey and a rather silent Rogue to his truck, helped them in, then moved around to the driver's side with a quick look to the side of the street. The sheriff had gotten sneaky over the past weeks as he watched for Rogue to leave. Tonight, he wasn't being sneaky at all, and that was telling.

He grinned as he started the motor and pulled out of the back lot, easing slowly down the street, just to make sure that they were seen. He had no doubt Zeke was watching, and he didn't mind tormenting his friend a little here and there. Hell, sometimes, a man had to be pushed to follow his heart, and Alex didn't mind pushing Zeke any more than Zeke had minded pushing him when it came to Janey.

As they drove past the front parking lot, he timed his good friend, holding back a smile and counting off the seconds until his cell phone rang. He let it ring a time or two before taking it from the clip on his belt and answering with a brief, "Yes?"

"Rogue's with you?" Zeke didn't sound pleased, and Alex considered that encouraging.

"Yes," he answered shortly.

There was a brief silence. "You're taking her back to her apartment?"

"Yes."

"Why?"

It was all Alex could do to keep from laughing. He could hear the sheer frustration in the other man's voice, and he sympathized, he really did.

"It just seemed like the neighborly thing to do," Alex answered. "Is there a problem with it?"

That silence again. He could almost feel Zeke glaring at his back. And he probably was, considering the sheriff's Tahoe had pulled out behind him after he passed the parking lot.

"No problem," Zeke finally answered. "Tell her I'll talk to her soon." And the line disconnected.

Alex's brows arched. Give her a message? Now wasn't that uncharacteristic of their private sheriff?

He closed the phone and glanced to the backseat where Rogue sat silently, watching him.

"Zeke said to tell you he'll talk to you later," he told her. "You two been talking a lot?"

"Or something," she muttered, turning to stare out the window and keeping her lips pressed together firmly.

Alex grinned, looked at Janey, and wagged his brows. This was very interesting. Zeke had never been known to chase after any woman.

"Wonder why he didn't call your cell phone?" he mused after a few minutes. "Seems odd he'd call me."

"Mine might be turned off," she answered.

He almost had to bite his lip to keep from laughing. As though that was going to keep Zeke off her ass. She just had no idea. Once a man like Zeke decided what he wanted, nothing would hold him back. And Alex had a feeling Zeke knew exactly what he wanted.

"Why is he following us?" Janey asked then, her voice smooth, and so genuinely curious as she glanced behind them.

"Maybe I have a taillight out," Alex suggested. "Should I pull over?"

He laughed as Janey pinched his thigh. In the rearview mirror he caught Rogue's glare. Whatever was going on, he was sure he'd hear about it soon. Until then, he'd drop his passenger off and head home to be with his own woman. Zeke would learn what Alex already knew. There was nothing as satisfying as holding your own woman in the still of the night and greeting the next day with her. He had confidence in the sheriff's abilities to figure that out. And if he didn't, well, Alex just might have to help him along a little.

NINE

Spring was in full flush in the mountains, the trees were greening out, the evenings were mildly cool, the days pleasant, and the Bar, better known as the biker haven in the Lake Cumberland area, was hopping.

For a Thursday, it was packed. The winter country tunes were replaced by harder, driving music. Leather and denim rubbed shoulder to shoulder, thigh to thigh, and cycles filled the parking lot along with a heavy share of pickups and SUVs.

Dressed in her customary black leather pants and sleeveless vest, a lacy violet camisole peeking over the top, Rogue surveyed the crowd. Four-inch stiletto-heeled boots gave her barely enough height that if she strained, she could almost see over the writhing mass.

Mainstream hard rock and metal was pounding through the PA system, drinks were flowing, bouncers were alert, and Rogue was in her element. She loved the pulse and pound of the music, the laughter, and sometimes, she even enjoyed the fights.

It had been two nights since she had last seen Zeke, and she had used the time to regroup and reassess the damage she had allowed in her life.

Rogue had remade herself after the debacle four years before. She hadn't let that night destroy her, she hadn't let it beat her. She was bitter at times, but only because she had once believed that Nadine and Dayle had taken away her chance with the man who fascinated her. She no longer believed that was the truth. There had never been a chance, because Rogue knew, even then, the "good girl" image wouldn't have changed anything. And in time, she would have matured and stepped out of that more submissive role anyway.

She had moped the past two days. She had pouted. She had even shed a tear or two and watched outside her apartment window as Zeke drove through the parking lot each night before he went off duty. And she had had a spark of realization.

Rogue didn't hide. She wouldn't be a closet lover, she wasn't going to be one of the women Zeke kept hanging on a string, always worrying, always wondering when or if it would be over on any given night. She wasn't a submissive little lapdog content to wait on the pillows for his attention.

That was her realization. It didn't change the fact that she still dreamed about him, and it didn't change the fact that she still woke wet and wild, reaching for him. But there were other things in life to occupy her.

For the moment, Grandma Walker, Lisa, and Lisa's twin boys were a concern. She had friends, she had family. She had, over the years, become content with her life.

"Hey, Rogue," Jonesy called from behind the bar as she moved through the crowd in front of it. "Get your luscious ass back here and help me."

Jonesy and his assistant 'tender, as he called her, were working frantically to fill orders as customers lined up around the wide bar.

Rogue worked her way to the entrance behind the bar, moving quickly to take orders and fill them. Thursday night wasn't usually this heavy, but the unseasonably warm days and evenings had spring fever in the air. Bikers mingled with farmers and tourists, fishermen and hikers. The Lake Cumberland area had something to tease the imagination and interests of a wide variety of people.

"Hey, beautiful. I wondered where you'd been." Hank Gentry was from Virginia. He and his small group of friends made the trip several times a year from their homes to the lake where they rented one of the available houseboats.

Hank was handsome as hell. Very accountant neat, and biker wild. He liked to say he pretended he was revisiting his twenties when he made his trips.

"Hank, you're early this year." She laughed as she pushed a mug of draft beer his way and turned to pour more for the friends standing behind him. "I see you have your misfits with you," she yelled over her shoulder.

The other four men laughed, obviously pleased that they were being called misfits at forty-something.

"You saving me a dance?" Hank's wide grin met her as she turned back, handed over the beers, and took the cash.

"My dance card is full, sugar." She cast him a wide grin. "Jonesy keeps me leashed to the bar or serving drinks."

Jonesy glowered at her. He'd been doing that for two days now. His temper was getting testy, and she was getting ready to take a bite out of his butt for it.

"When she ain't consorting with undesirables, you can almost get a good night's work out of her," Jonesy snarled, and it wasn't playful.

Hank's green eyes turned back to her in surprise, his brows raised. "Shame on you, Rogue." He wagged his finger at her chidingly. "Consorting with undesirables." He shook his head before glancing around the bar. "You surprise me." He winked, took his beer, and moved off.

"Cut it out, Jonesy," she snapped as she turned to pour another beer. "You don't want to fight with me here."

"You got fight left in you then?" he grunted. "Now that one surprises me. I thought you'd done tucked your tail and turned vanilla on me."

God, there were days she hated men; their PMS was worse than a woman's any day, and less understandable.

"I'm going to turn homicidal if you don't get off my back," she ordered him. "Wait till closing and take up your problems with me then."

She turned away before he could snap back in reply. She'd had just about enough of snarly, snapping males that thought they could order her around or steer her damned life. She'd been steering it fine on her own for over five years now.

"Ronnie's having problems with a couple in B area," he called out as she pushed a handful of beers across the bar. "We got a regular and a tourist having a bit of a problem over a woman."

Jonesy wore a headset radio atop his head that connected him to the other bouncers.

"Get out there with him," Rogue warned him. "Lea and I can handle the bar for a while."

"Kent's on his way," Jonesy informed her as he collected a heavy bat from beneath the bar and exited the bar area on the other side quickly.

"He's been dying to use that bat all week," Lea called out as she worked furiously to mix several drinks and slide them across the bar.

"He's a man. Playing with his bat is the only thing he understands." Rogue laughed back at her, causing Lea to nearly drop a bottle of whisky in her mirth and most of the men around the bar to hoot and yell in agreement.

She toasted the men with a hastily poured shot, tossed it back, and slapped the glass on the bar with a grin at the eager cheers before going back to work.

She was having fun. She liked to have fun. She had always imagined any lover she had she would be able to tease and flirt with, to laugh and share her enjoyment of the atmosphere she had built here. She wasn't going to be ashamed of it. She wasn't going to change who and what she was, and she wouldn't ask Zeke to change his rules, either.

That left things rather at a stalemate. The night wasn't at a stalemate though. She worked the bar before making her rounds through the building again. She watched the waitresses and waiters, made certain everything was running smoothly in between brief hip-shaking dances and laughter. If Zeke were here, she wondered, what would he see? The bar whore she was rumored to be, or the woman she truly was? She refused to question herself as to why it should matter either way. She was who she was. She couldn't be anything less, anything more.

As the night deepened, her frustration with Jonesy only mounted though. He was scowling more often, and each time he spoke to her, he snapped. It was wearing on her nerves, and she knew better than to allow it to continue. He had his moods, and if she put up with them, they would only escalate until he ended up in a fight with someone else. The only way to end it was to confront it, before she ended up with bar damage.

Motioning to Lea and Kent to take over the bar, she moved to Jonesy. "My office," she ordered.

"My ass," he growled, his brown gaze glittering in anger. "I have work to do."

"Not after tonight you won't," she snapped. "My office now, or get your ass out of my bar. And you damned well better remember who owns the place."

She turned on her heel and stalked out of the area toward the back door marked Private. Pushing through, she moved through the short hall, made a sharp turn, and quickly unlocked the door to her office.

She threw it open before Jonesy could barrel into it. He stalked into the room, jerked his white apron off, and wadded it into a ball before throwing it to the floor.

His white T-shirt stretched over the bulging muscles of his tattooed arms. The ham-sized biceps flexed menacingly as he glared back at her.

"Drop the attitude." There was no fear of Jonesy. He was temperamental, tried to be a bully, and fussed like a mother hen gone rabid, but she had never seen him as dangerous.

"Don't tell me to drop the attitude, little girl," he snarled, face flushing as his heavy brows lowered over his dark eyes. "I'm the dumb bastard watching you mope around with those big, pathetic eyes of yours as you watch the door and pray that no-account sheriff makes his way back to mark you. Where the fuck is your head, letting that bastard touch you?"

Rogue drew back in surprise. Evidently Jonesy had seen the reddened mark beneath her jaw as well.

"The mark or the man is none of your damned business, Jonesy," she said, voice tight.

"It's my damned business when I have to listen to the gossip and field the questions," he yelled back, his lips pulling back from his teeth furiously.

"Like I've ever given a damn about gossip," she retorted. "And since when do you give a damn? Hell, Jonesy, they talk about everyone and everything. It's a fact of fucking life and I couldn't give a damn one way or the other."

"Maybe that's your problem!" he said, his voice rising further. "You simply don't give a damn. You didn't give a damn when they made you look like a tramp in those pictures, and now you don't give a damn and spread your fucking legs for that whoremongering sheriff who doesn't have a chance of being good enough for you."

She was going to pull her hair out. Staring back at him incredulously, she fought to figure out what the hell kind of bug had gotten up his ass to make him act this way or to say something so vile.

"Zeke is not a whoremonger," she bit out between clenched teeth.

"Yeah, you'll take up for him, but you don't give a shit when I call you a tramp," he accused roughly, his eyes narrowing as his entire body seemed to quiver with outrage. "Your daddy raised you better than this, girl."

"My daddy raised me to have enough confidence in myself to do whatever the hell I want with whoever the hell I want," she yelled back, nearly shaking in her own anger now. "How dare you think you can take me to task for anything, Jonesy? You don't have that right, and I'll be damned if I'll let you pretend you do."

He was six feet tall to her five feet seven in her highest heels. She was in his face, snarling back at him, overwhelmed by her anger. She hated being told what to do or being taken to task for decisions she made. She was an adult. She knew what the hell she was doing even when she wasn't certain of the way to get there, and she knew she was damned sick and tired of others trying to tell her she was too young, too inexperienced, or evidently raised to do things differently than she was.

Jonesy was still glaring down at her. His breathing was rough, face flushed. At his side, his beefy hands were curled into fists as though it was all he could do to keep from hitting her.

She knew him. She knew his rages, and she knew his affection, but she didn't understand his sudden animosity toward Zeke.

"You used to understand how the world works around here, Rogue," he spat out. "What the hell happened to you?"

The way the world worked around here. Here being Pulaski County, as though it was a separate part of the rest of the world.

"Oh, don't worry, Jonesy, I understand the rules very well, and I intend to break every one I can," she informed him with a tight smile.

Jonesy and his damned rules. Stay with your own kind, he'd always warned her. White trash to white trash, upper-class trash to upper-class trash, and she was somewhere in between and yet somewhere above them all. She could return to Boston and take her place as a society princess there, or she could stick to her own kind here. That being the hard-drinking, motorcycle-riding men and women that made the Bar their home away from home. To Jonesy, she shouldn't look any further for entertainment or for a relationship.

"This ain't about breaking the rules, you little twit," he bit out in disgust.

Her eyes narrowed as she began to shake in fury. "Don't call me a twit, Jonesy."

"Then don't act like one," he sneered. "I've just about had enough of it. That sheriff ain't gonna do nothin' but use you up, just like he does his other women. You're nothing but another notch in his bedpost, and you'll be a small one at that."

Rogue didn't flinch at the accusation, but it hurt. Damn, that one had been below the belt, and she felt vibrations of the pain racing through her. A part of her feared he was right; another part of her was determined to take what she wanted no matter the cost.

"Where I get notched is none of your business though, is it?" she asked him. "Your job is to run that bar out there, not my life. If you can't keep a civil tongue in your head otherwise, then you can get the hell out."

His eyes widened, darkened as anger flushed his face deeper and creased his rough face.

"Get the hell out? I've been here since before your ass was born," he yelled, stepping closer. "You don't tell me to get out, little girl."

"I'm telling you if you don't learn how to keep your insults and your sneers to yourself, then replacing you will be my first priority after I have my bouncers throw your ass to the curb."

Surprise flickered over his face. "I hired those bouncers. Those are my men."

"I sign their paychecks. They'll do as I say or they'll find themselves on the curb with you," she yelled back.

She had always trusted Jonesy; she had never known a moment's fear of him, until that second. Those big hands reached out for her, his fingers curving harshly around her upper arms before he shook her like a rag doll.

"The hell you will." He pushed her back just as suddenly.

Rogue felt her hip hit the corner of the desk, her hair flying around her as she fought to steady herself and retreat far enough that he couldn't grab her again.

She stared at him in shock and in hurt. Jonesy, for all their fights, had never laid a hand on her, had never become threatening.

"That's out of line, Jonesy. You don't want to touch me again."

His lips twisted furiously as he paused, his gaze narrowing on her. "Someone needs to show you your damned place. You've become a disgrace to your daddy, and I'll be damned if I'll put up with it much longer."

He started for her again. Rogue felt her heart racing, a tingle of fear tearing through her as she glimpsed the pure rage that seemed to transform his face. She moved to jump back, only to find herself frozen as Jonesy suddenly swung away from her, his heavy body crashing into the wall from the fist that had been planted in his jaw.

Zeke stood before her, dressed in jeans, a black shirt, and boots, his expression icy, his hawklike gaze burning in fury.

"Get the hell out!" Zeke's voice rang with authority and with pure unbridled power. "Now."

Shit. This wasn't good. How the hell had she managed to let her argument with Jonesy develop into this? If these two men fought, then there would end up being bloodshed.

"Jonesy, get your ass back to the bar," she snapped as Jonesy came slowly to his feet.

Zeke's gaze swung around to her. There was no shock, no surprise on his face, there was no fury. His expression was emotionless, but his eyes burned.

"Did he sneak into the back?" Jonesy sneered. "I bet you this bar he did."

"You don't have this bar to bet with," she told him, her heart was in her throat now as she fought to get him out of the office. "Now get back to work. And don't worry about coming back after tonight until you can get your stupidity under control."

He flashed her a glare filled with animosity. "My stupidity is the least of your worries." It sounded like a warning. "But, hell yeah, I'll get out of your office. You want to play this bastard's whore, then go for it. See who gives a damn when it's all over and you're the one crying in your beer rather than those pathetic little sluts you've consoled over the years."

Ouch.

Rogue ignored Zeke's suddenly penetrating look as Jonesy straightened, threw them both a furious glance, and stalked back out of the office. The opened door slammed behind him with enough force to leave Rogue wincing.

She faced Zeke. Two days. She hadn't seen or heard from him in two days, and she was at the point that she didn't want to see or hear from him.

Men. They made women insane for a reason. They were so damned closed minded and closed in on themselves that it made her crazy. Even her father shared those qualities, to a point.

"You can leave now as well," she told Zeke as his broad shoulders shifted beneath the black shirt.

"You know that's not going to happen." Was his voice deeper than she remembered it or had she just never seen him angry before?

She knew his effect on her hadn't gone away. Her heart was tripping in her chest, excitement filled her, and she swore she could almost taste him in her mouth again. Wild, tangy, and completely sexy. She wanted more of him, and she knew it was the last thing she should allow herself to reach out for.

But she ached for him. Ached for his kiss, his touch. She ached for more than a few hidden little bedroom sessions and the knowledge that just as Jonesy accused, she would be no more than a very small notch on his bedpost.

"One fight a night is enough." She rubbed at her arms, knowing she had more to face tonight than just this overriding need for Zeke's touch.

She had never been frightened of Jonesy as long as she had known him. They had yelled, screamed, thrown things, but he had never shaken her, he had never let his anger spike to the point that he was a threat rather than a friend.

"Let me see your arms." He advanced.

Rogue retreated behind her desk. "My arms are fine."

"Your arms are fucking bruised," he bit out, his expression becoming livid now. "Do you think I don't see those bruises forming even now, Rogue? Do you think I'll stand for it?"

Rogue pressed her lips together in an effort to gain control. She was halfway tempted to bite her tongue just to hold back her own anger.

"I think, quite simply, that it's none of your damned business."
And that was no less than the truth. "You're not my father, my
brother, my lover, or my husband, so I guess you lucked out in the
explanations department, didn't you?"

What stroke of fate had decided that this man had to fascinate
her as no other did? That his kiss, his touch had to torment her,
haunt her? She didn't want this, and she knew he didn't, either. He
had proven that two days ago when he had sent her on her way
without so much as a good-bye kiss, a hug. There had been nothing
to soften the humiliation that had filled her. That still filled her.

Having him here in her office, seeing him, being close to him
was torture. She had fantasized for so many years, dreamed of him
for so long. The knowledge that she couldn't have him, not fully,
sliced through her soul like a dull knife.

"You're fooling yourself," he told her, his voice rough. "We're
going to be lovers, Rogue. We both know it."

She shook her head to that.

God, she was tired of this internal fight within herself. Lately,
it seemed her emotions were never under control, and she blamed
him for that. He had tilted her world on its axis, and she was having a hell of a time straightening it back up.

"I think, Zeke, being lovers would be the worst decision the
two of us could make. You need to turn around and leave. Get back
in your nifty little sheriff's vehicle, and go look up one of your former closet lovers or whoever you keep dangling as a replacement.
Because this isn't going to work."

She wouldn't hide in a closet. She couldn't. Rogue knew that the
one thing she couldn't do was enter into an emotionless relationship with this man.

His lips tilted as she watched him. A half grin, filled with male
confidence and certainty. He stood before her, the epitome of the al-
pha male, and a shiver raced up her spine as he watched her. There

was nothing hidden, nothing latent in that look. It was pure male power and sexual intent.

It was dominant.

Heat flushed through her body as she stepped back. Distance, she needed distance between them before he could follow through with that look.

"Did you really think I was just going to let this go after the other day?" he asked, advancing on her. "You were on your knees, Rogue. You climaxed as I came in your mouth."

"And you pushed me right out the door five seconds later," she reminded him. "You weren't just ashamed that we were caught by your son. You were ashamed of being with me, period."

"I don't broadcast my affairs." His expression tightened as Rogue felt her chest ache.

"Then you won't be having an affair with me," she told him quietly. "Find someone else, Zeke, because I can't afford the broken heart."

She thought he would heed the request. A part of her was certain he would turn and walk right back out of her office and out of her life.

Nothing could have prepared her for how quickly he moved, his hand latching around her wrist, pulling her to him an instant before he threw her over his shoulder and strode from the office.

TEN

"Have you lost your mind?" Furious, outraged, Rogue beat at Zeke's back as he strode from her office and made the turn to the stairs that led to her apartment.

"Let me go, you bastard!" She pinched his ass, ineffective as it was through his heavy jeans.

"Settle down, you little wildcat." The order was followed by a heated slap to her ass, not quite a caress, too hot to be anything but a warning.

Rogue froze. She felt the heat travel from her ass, up her spine, back down, and into places she didn't want to consider. Not as furious as she was. Not in the position she was now in.

"This is insane," she screeched. "Damn you, Zeke, let me go this instant."

A muscular arm held her steady as he reached the landing and pushed open the door to her apartment.

"You need a spanking," he growled. "Leaving your apartment door unlocked like that is dangerous, Rogue."

"As dangerous as giving you the time of day?" She fought her hair, fought a response burning in her stomach that she didn't want to feel.

"As dangerous as getting on your knees and sucking my dick." The door slammed behind him as he spoke.

A second later, she was bouncing on the couch, fighting her hair for precious seconds before she was back on her feet, teetering in the high heels as her arm swung back, her fist clenched, and she let loose with every ounce of strength she possessed toward his face.

Rogue had never hit anyone deliberately. She was an admitted pacifist unless backed into a corner. She could feel the corner at her back now.

His fingers caught her wrist a second before she could make contact.

Zeke stared at her small fist, feeling that ravenous hunger burning through him. She was his weakness, and he couldn't figure out why. She tempted the darkness. She tempted hungers he didn't want to admit to.

Staring down at her, he locked her gaze with his, watching her, seeing the hurt and the anger that darkened her eyes.

"I shouldn't have let you go the other day," he admitted, fighting to tamp back needs he knew he should keep carefully hidden.

"Of course you should have." Disdain and anger filled her voice. "That was the biggest favor you could have done me."

He didn't let her go as she tugged at her wrist. He should, he knew he should. He stared into her furious little face and saw the hurt she was trying to hide. Pain he had dealt her.

"Stop fighting me, Rogue." He caught her other wrist as she slapped at his chest in her bid for freedom. "Settle down, we'll talk about this."

God, he needed her to settle down. Now, before he lost complete control.

"There's something to talk about?" Her eyes narrowed on him, defiance shimmering in those violet eyes. "Sorry, Zeke, but I guess I just don't have much left to say."

She struggled against him again. It wasn't a halfhearted struggle; the little minx was putting some serious effort into breaking his hold. The harder she fought against him, the more he tensed. He could feel that haze of lust burning at the edges of his vision. He hadn't felt it in years, not since leaving L.A., not since he had begun denying those urges and refusing to allow himself lovers that knew how to push those buttons. But never had he had a woman as innocent, as unknowing as Rogue awaken that core of sexuality he possessed.

"Rogue, enough." He heard his own voice deepen, felt his cock hardening painfully, throbbing beneath the confinement of his jeans as his balls drew up violently.

"Kiss off, Sheriff Mayes," she snarled, lifting herself, glaring back at him, her eyes, those beautiful fey eyes watching him in anger and in hunger. He could see the hunger; he could sense it, feel it.

Before she could evade his move he had both her wrists in one hand, his other cupping her jaw. He was going to burn in hell for this and he knew it. He was helpless against it. His control was so damned thin it was all he could do to hold on, but the dominance surging forward was another control. One he reveled in, one he knew he needed to fight even as he let it have hold.

Just for a second, he promised himself. Just for this moment. He wouldn't let it go further. He'd keep from taking her, he'd keep himself from frightening her, from revealing all the dark acts he wanted to commit on that gorgeous little body.

"I'd rather kiss *you*."

He held her arms behind her back, arching her closer, feeling her stomach cushion his cock as she writhed against him, stroking his arousal higher.

Damn, she needed to stay still. Just for a moment.

He held her jaw firmly, stared at her lips, felt her arching against him, and gave in to the need clawing at his mind and at his body.

Zeke knew kissing Rogue again was a damned bad idea. He had come to talk to her, to try to figure out a way to have her and to hold back that part of himself now slipping free.

There was no way to do it, he finally admitted to himself. As his lips covered hers, as he felt her gasp, tighten in his arms, he knew having her would mean breaking every damned rule he had lived his life by for years now.

Not having her wasn't an option. Not when her kiss was like fuel to a fire. Not when touching her became as important as breathing. Not when the very act of possessing her mouth sent a surge of adrenaline racing through him.

Defiance raged in the air around him now. His tongue parted her lips, pressed forward, and felt her furious cry. But he also felt her need. She was shuddering in his arms despite her struggles, fighting not to capitulate, struggling not just against him but against the pleasure that he could have told her there was no way to resist.

This pleasure was addictive. Rogue's kiss. Driven with challenge. Her teeth would have nipped at his tongue if he hadn't controlled the graceful line of her jaw. Instead, her tongue pressed against his, fought against it, and he felt a surge of heat so blistering it burned away the remaining resistance he'd built against his need for it. He wanted her to fight. He wanted her to defy him. He wanted to tie her to his bed and spend hours fucking her into exhaustion. Until there was no defiance, until there was only pleasure. No fear. No anger.

God, he had to rein back, just a little. She was a virgin. She had no idea what he could demand from her. He had to be gentle, he had to make sure she remembered this night with pleasure. The need for that was almost as sharp as the need for her touch. As sharp as the need to hear her screaming his name.

"Damn you," she tried to scream as he lifted his lips and stared down at her swollen lips. "What are you trying to do to me, Zeke?"

"Taste you," he murmured, those pouty lips holding his attention as he allowed his thumb to rake across the lower curve. "I've spent two days remembering the taste of your kiss, the feel of your lips against mine, then wrapped so snug around my cock. I didn't get enough, Rogue. I need more."

Another shudder raked through her body. The tremor was hard, telling. Her thighs relaxed against him despite the anger in her eyes and the refusal he could see hovering on her lips.

"Tell me to leave again and I won't return," he warned her harshly, his lips lowering again to brush hers as he spoke. "Anything is negotiable but that. Tell me to leave, and it will be over before it begins."

Her breathing hitched. Shadows of indecision filled her eyes as she stared back at him.

"Don't do this to me if you expect me to act like your other women in public, Zeke. Pretending we're not touching, that we're nothing to each other. I can't do that. I'm not some whore you're buying and can just walk away from before the sun comes up."

It would be so much easier if that were the case. But he already knew it wasn't. He had known as he stared down at her two days ago, his erection filling her mouth. She had never gone down on a man before. She had never taken his release and she had never known the stinging rejection he'd dealt her moments later. Or the regret that dug into his guts like a knife each time he thought of how he must have hurt her.

He doubted she had ever faced a relationship with a man who demanded as much from a woman as he knew he could demand from her. So much that his first wife had refused to sleep with him for years.

"I don't have relationships," he told her. "I've not had a relationship since I returned here from L.A., Rogue, for a reason."

"Gossip?" she sneered.

He smiled at that. "I never gave a damn what anyone thought. I cared more about making certain I never allowed myself to be caught in a loveless relationship or that no other woman ever paid for my sins as my wife did. If no one knew who I was fucking or thought I cared about who I was fucking, then they were safe."

He watched her gaze flicker then, those beautiful violet eyes watching him intently as he held her hands against the wall.

"You're involved in an investigation," she whispered. "Joe and Jaime were mixed up in something, weren't they?"

He couldn't, he wouldn't discuss this. Not here. Not yet. He shook his head instead. "I don't know what they were involved in, Rogue. But being careful is a part of me. Protecting you will always be a priority with me. You'll have to accept that. There's no other choice."

She stared up at him, her eyes wide, lips parted. "I make my own choices."

"I'm not an easy lover," he told her softly then. "I'm not the type of the man that will watch his woman flirt and laugh with other men, that will allow other men to touch her with anything approaching intimacy, with any semblance of grace. You're a young woman, Rogue. Sweet and flirty and filled with life."

"And I know how to be a woman," she informed him fiercely. "And I know the rules of the game, Zeke. You won't own me any more than I expect to own you."

Zeke felt his stomach flex, his muscles tightening at the look in her eyes. Frustration and heated anger filled her gaze. She was a woman ready to explode in his hands, and how he touched her, how he treated her would decide if she exploded in pleasure, or in rage.

"There will be no other men." He leaned closer, letting her feel the determination, the arousal filling him. He couldn't let her feel his hands shaking, he wouldn't let her feel the adrenaline and need burning inside him. Touching her was like a shock of electricity that sang through his body, leaving every nerve on high alert.

"There are no other men now," she argued back. "You can't change who or what I am. I own a bar. I talk, I laugh, and I dance, and you won't change that."

And he had suspected that. Could he accept it? Could he get past the possessiveness that rose inside him like a sharp-toothed monster waiting to tear into any other man who even thought about touching her?

Zeke stared down at her, unwilling to delve too much into what he knew were deeply imbedded possessive traits. What was his belonged solely to him. He wasn't a man that could or would share the woman he allowed fully into his life.

And to have Rogue, he would have to allow her fully into his life. There was no other answer. Some part of him, a part that clenched his chest and left him aching for her long into the night, warned him that fully in his life was exactly where he wanted her to be.

It was a problem he would have to tackle later. It was a worry that had gnawed at his mind far longer than he wanted to admit. It was one of the concerns that had held him back in the past years, that had kept him from taking what he knew he could convince Rogue to give him.

"I tried to stay away from you." He had to taste her flesh. Zeke lowered his head, his lips pressing beneath her jaw, right there, where the flesh was so tender, where her pulse beat erratically.

He licked at the flesh, felt her shiver. His teeth raked over it, and he needed more. The taste of her was incredible. The sound of her breath catching, the feel of her melting in his arms was addictive.

God, he needed her. The need was like a fever devouring his insides. He ached for her. Ached clear to his soul for something he didn't even know how to name.

Drawing back, his hand framed her neck, not threateningly, possessively.

"You'll belong to me."

Rogue's eyes widened, her heart raced. She had never seen this expression on a man's face, in his eyes. Zeke was staring at her as though his look alone would brand her. The flesh was stretched tight over his cheekbones and lust made his eyes gleam with an intent that had her fighting to breathe.

She couldn't let herself hope, but she couldn't help but hope that she would mean more to him than his other lovers had. How could she let herself believe that? Wasn't she the one who had sat and listened to several of those past lovers cry into their beers over him? Would she be next?

"You don't mean that." Rogue shook her head slowly, hearing it in his voice, seeing the possessiveness in his eyes.

"Do you think I don't mean it, Rogue?"

A shiver raced down her spine as his hand caressed down her throat to her collarbone, and she shivered in reaction. A reaction that was both physical as well as emotional. Fingers and palm flat, he touched her completely; not an inch of his palm didn't touch her.

Swallowing tightly, she felt sensation wash over her. His voice stroking her senses, his hand on her flesh, sensitizing her, reminding her of the pleasure of his kiss, his touch. Reminding her of all the fantasies, the dreams she'd had of this man.

Anticipation and excitement had her shaking. Her heart raced out of control, and she even hoped, though she knew better than to allow herself that commodity. She hoped, maybe, he would care for her, just a little. That the emotions that rose inside her whenever she thought of him, saw him, would be returned in some small measure.

She couldn't resist allowing her head to fall back to the wall as his fingers, his hand, slid to the rise of her breasts, revealed by the violet lace that peeked over the top of the deeply cut vest.

"Leather and lace." The words were grating, rasping from his throat with primitive arousal. "Do you know what that does to a man?"

She licked her lips slowly, aching for more of him. "Maybe it just does it to you."

He shook his head slowly, his fingers flicking the first button of the vest open. "Not just me, baby. Every man that sees you lusts for you. It's in his face, in his eyes. That lace peeking over the leather. It makes a man want to tame you."

The second button slid open. Then the third, second by second the snug material of the butter-soft leather vest loosened until the edges hung open and the lacy camisole was revealed and another part of her resistance fell away.

She wore no bra. Her breasts swelled, her nipples hardening further beneath his gaze as he brushed the edges of the vest aside.

"Last chance," he said, his voice soft, deep. "Tell me to leave, Rogue. If I stay, you don't know the things I'll ask of you."

"Maybe." She swallowed tightly as she fought to breathe. "Maybe you should be the one to make that decision, Zeke. I'm not a child. And never imagine I don't know what I want."

She wanted all of him. She wanted that assurance in his eyes that the wildness rising inside her would be harnessed, would be satiated. She wanted the heat rising inside her quenched. She wanted to experience the wild hunger and need she glimpsed in his eyes.

That hunger poured through her when his lips lowered to hers. They covered hers, his tongue pressing past them as he stole her breath. Nothing had ever made her more aware of the restlessness, the wildness that filled her than this kiss. The feel of his lips stroking over hers, the pleasure cascading through her body, rushing through her veins.

Hard, calloused palms cupped her breasts; confident, knowing fingers raked over her nipples. Pleasure shot from the tender tips to scatter over her nerve endings. Like tiny implosions, a rush of sensation that had her gasping and arching closer to the warmth of his hands. This was incredible. Oh God, how had she waited so long for his touch?

She lifted her hands from her sides, plowed them into the short strands of his hair, and tried to force him to kiss her deeper, harder. Tongues twining, lips melding.

It was incredible. The rush of adrenaline through her veins, the heat that seared her flesh. This was what she dreamed of in the deepest part of the night.

The surge of pleasure that tore from her nipples to her clit, that swelled the little bud between her thighs and set it to throbbing in a hard, hot tempo. Perspiration dampened her flesh and she swore she could feel his touch beneath her skin.

"No." She grabbed his head as his lips lifted. He was going to stop now? Right when she could feel the rising crescendo of pleasure whipping through her pussy, heating it, sending her juices flowing between her thighs?

She found her hands caught in the grip of one of his again. He pressed them back against the wall, over her head, as she forced her lashes open and stared into the dark, taut lines of his expression.

"Damn, you're like dynamite." His free hand slid low on her stomach, then caressed back up, sliding beneath the camisole as she sucked in a hard, moaning breath.

Calloused fingers rasped over her flesh, sending waves of sensation washing through her. The pleasure was almost violent. It was incredible. The way it struck against her nerve endings, caused them to jerk, to press more fully against him as he held her, hands bound, his body pressing her against the wall.

"Look at your face," he whispered. "One of these days I'll take you in front of a mirror where you can see how good it is."

In front of a mirror? She blushed at the thought, and Rogue wasn't prone to blushes. Except with Zeke. Just thinking about him could make her blush.

Her gaze dropped to where his hand cupped her breast over the camisole, lifting it, pressing the swollen mound up until it appeared to want to spill over the edge of the lace.

"I want your nipple in my mouth, Rogue."

Her eyes jerked up, widened, and right there she lost her breath. A gasp left her lips and the moan that fell from them shocked her.

"Do you want your nipple in my mouth, sweetheart?" The hard shiver that raced up her spine shocked her.

"Do I have to beg for it?" she asked, amazed at the sultriness of her voice. "Gee, Zeke, here you've gone all dominant on me just to start asking permission now."

"Smart-ass." His lips quirked into the sexiest little grin, even as his golden brown eyes seemed to flare with heat.

A second later the lacy cup of the camisole was pushed beneath her breast and his head lowered. Hot, firm lips surrounded her nipple. Rasping, ecstatic pleasure surrounded the sensitive tip as she strained against his grip.

She needed to touch him. She was desperate to touch him, to feel him. To feel more of this. To hold his head closer to her breast, to force her throbbing nipple deeper into his mouth. She wanted to feel him sucking her harder, feel his teeth scraping.

"Oh God. Zeke." She felt it. His teeth rasping over the tender tip, sending a flood of sensation racing to her clit and the depths of her pussy.

Her muscles spasmed inside, clenched, and a sense of emptiness overwhelmed her.

She tried not to watch him. Watching his lips tugging at her breast, feeling his tongue curl around the swollen tip triggered sensations that bit into her womb with sharp, erotic teeth as her heart pounded out of control.

But she was still in control. She assured herself she was. Until his lashes lifted, then his knee bent and pressed between her thighs as he lowered his arm and pulled her hips forward.

Oh Lord, have mercy. The butter-soft leather slid over denim, pressing his thigh firmly against the swollen, sensitive flesh of her pussy until she was riding his thigh.

It was exquisite. It was the most pleasure Rogue had ever known in her life, and she was desperate for more. She whimpered at the need, at the pleasure.

She wanted to hold him to her, desperate to feel every sensation, every chaotic emotion raging through her. This was Zeke, and she had waited so long, had dreamed for so long.

"Let me touch you," she moaned, straining against the hold he had on her wrists as his head lifted, his lips raking over the valley between her breasts. He nudged the camisole over her other breast, kissed around the enflamed tip of her nipple, and without answering or giving in to her plea, drew it into his mouth.

There was no such thing as control in Zeke's arms. There was only this. Flashpoints of pleasure that seared her, left her trembling, damp with perspiration, and shaking as his hand slid down her stomach to the low-rise band of her pants.

The snap and zipper were dealt with quickly, efficiently. The edges spread apart as he slid his thigh back and pressed his hand inside.

Rogue froze. Even the breath seemed suspended in her lungs as his fingers inched lower, lower.

She was slick and wet. She could feel it against the crotch of the thong she wore. The swollen inner lips were heated, slick, bare of curls, and awaiting his touch.

His fingers paused just above her clit. His head lifted from her breast with one last lick to her hypersensitive nipple.

"Are you a virgin?"

The question shocked her. It tore through her mind with all the implications of the truth that might cause him to walk away from her.

"Oh really, Zeke," she chided breathlessly, weakly. "I'm a bar owner and a biker chick. Do you really think I'm a virgin?"

Brave last words. She almost snorted at her own daring in lying to him. It wasn't as though he wouldn't find out the truth soon enough if this continued.

The sharp little nip to her lips and the narrowing of his gaze was a warning.

"That was a nice, evasive little answer."

She gasped as he released her wrists, only to swing her up in his arms and stride into the bedroom. Within seconds she was bouncing on the bed, pushing at her hair as it fell over her eyes and feeling his hands at her hips, dragging her pants over her thighs.

He didn't waste time. Evidently, he must have felt as though he had already wasted enough time. Her shoes were slipped from her feet and the pants tossed to the floor before she could protest. If she meant to protest. She was certain she didn't.

Why would she protest? He was staring between her thighs, his expression tight, a muscle ticking in his jaw as he straightened and began unbuttoning his shirt quickly. Just his look was enough to make her breath short and labored, enough to cause her heart to tighten and ache with the emotions racing through her.

And this was more than a casual fuck to him as well. What tomorrow would bring she had no idea, but for now, this meant something to him. Dark emotion shadowed his eyes and tormented desire filled the air around them.

"Take off the vest," he ordered.

There wasn't a request in his voice, it was an order, plain and simple.

It made her shiver. The dominance in his expression, in his voice, it was wild and erotic and called to the wildness Rogue had fought to keep in check inside herself, for so long.

Her fingers fell to the vest as she sat up. It slid easily from her shoulders.

"The camisole." His shirt fell to the floor before he sat down on the edge of the bed to jerk his boots off.

Rogue pulled the camisole off as she fought the disconcerting feeling of being naked in front of him. No one had seen her naked since she was a child. But Zeke was seeing her now.

He rose to his feet, his hands going to the belt that cinched his hips. He unbuckled it quickly, confidently. The snap and zipper on his jeans came next. Then he was shedding them along with the snug boxer briefs he wore. The material slid over his powerful thighs and released the heavy length of his cock to her avid gaze.

She'd had him in her mouth. She'd tasted his release. But she hadn't really *seen* his erection until now. Hard, thick, heavily veined. The crest was dark, flared out, and flushed with an excess of lust with a small drop of pre-cum gracing the tip.

Rogue licked her lips, the remembered taste of his release sizzling her senses.

She was reaching for him when his hands landed on her shoulders. One knee braced on the bed, he pushed her back, loomed over her, his head lowering, his lips taking hers. He took the kiss he wanted. His lips captured hers, held them imprisoned as his tongue slid between them and conquered hers. The kiss was hard, erotic, so sensual that the pleasure of it slammed into her senses, igniting the lust already flaming out of control.

The rasp of his chest hairs against her nipples had her arching close, crying out. Pleasure shouldn't be this extreme. It shouldn't be filled with such wonder and such desperation.

One knee slid between her thighs, pressed high and firm until she was rocking her clit against the heavy muscle of his thigh. And it was so good. It was blazing. Hot. It was so much pleasure, so many sensations that she wondered if she would survive the inferno.

She had waited so long for this. So many years. And now here she was, naked, lying beneath his heavy, muscular body, her hands touching him, her fingertips catching each flex of his hard biceps as his kiss ravaged her senses.

"Now." He pulled back, stared down at her, his gaze hard, brilliant, the color of raw gold as he watched her with predatory awareness. "Now, Rogue, you get to see why I waited. Why I tried like hell to stay away from you. We'll get to see just how brave you are."

ELEVEN

How brave would she have to be? It was a distant thought that raced through her brain. There one second, gone the next as he pulled back from her and reached down for his jeans.

When he returned he tossed a condom on the nightstand and in the next second she saw the flash of handcuffs just before Zeke caught her wrists, pulled them up, and had her secured to one of the found iron pipes that made the headboard of her bed.

Her eyes flashed up to where the cuffs circled her wrists, then back to Zeke in surprise. There was no teasing smile on his face, only pure, dominant lust as he stared down at her.

"Is this supposed to scare me?" She jangled the metal restraints and let a smile shape her lips. "Oh, Sheriff, the fantasies I've had about you and these cuffs."

He didn't grin back. His fingertips ran from between her breasts to the mound of her pussy, his gaze following the path they took before returning to hers.

"Frighten you?" he asked. "No, Rogue, this shouldn't frighten you at all. I'd never hurt you."

The tone of his voice had her heart rate increasing. It was darker, rougher, as though the hunger that glittered in his eyes was at the edge of slipping the leash she could sense he had on it.

She wasn't frightened, but she was wary. Zeke wasn't joking, he was intent, fiercely controlled. Her heart was racing in her chest as his palm flattened on her abdomen and his lips lowered to her neck.

"There's a reason why you don't want me to touch you?" she asked.

"There is," he admitted, his voice rough. "I want you to feel every touch, every sensation. Don't worry about anything else. Just feel."

His teeth raked over her shoulder. Heated pleasure jumped through the nerve endings there and seared her with heat.

"What if I want to touch you, too?" she gasped.

"Too bad." His hands stroked down her side, fingertips pressing, feeling her.

"Not into mutual pleasure, huh?" She breathed in roughly as he parted her thighs, his head lifting, his gaze locking with hers.

"I'm into you, Rogue," he said then. "And very soon, I'm going to be so into you that you won't know where you end and I begin."

A cry fell from her lips as his teeth raked over a nipple, then his lips closed over it. He didn't stop there, he lingered long enough to have her arching, writhing beneath his touch before he went to her other breast, tortured it with pleasure, and stoked the arousal burning inside her higher.

There was something about Zeke's touch that stole her mind. She would have never trusted another man enough to restrain her, she knew she wouldn't. But with Zeke the progression of fantasy to reality seemed natural. It was white-hot flames licking over her body where his tongue touched, but it felt natural.

It was Zeke. Hard, intent. The man she couldn't get out of her head, and he was touching her.

Rogue heard the moan that fell from her lips and would have been surprised by the desperation in it if she had been able to actually think clearly. She couldn't think, she could only feel. Feel what he was doing to her. Feel his hands spreading her thighs, his lips traveling from her breasts along her abdomen, the way his hands pulled her legs apart and he lay between them.

"I've dreamed about tasting you here again." His lips were at her hip bone. A kiss, a little nip that had her arching and crying out at the pleasure.

"So pretty." The backs of his fingers slid along the swollen flesh of her flesh. "Flushed and damp. You're so wet for me, Rogue."

She could feel more of her juices easing from her vagina, coating her inner lips, tormenting her with the need for his touch.

A jerk of reaction tore through her body at the first fiery lick against her clit. A wild cry spilled from her lips as sensation raced along through the tiny bundle of nerves and sent spasms of pleasure clenching her womb.

Her feet dug into the mattress, her eyes opened, and she became lost in the sight of what he was doing to her. Gently, tenderly, his fingers parted the folds. His jaw tightened for long seconds before his lips parted and a breath of air struck the ultrasensitive bud of her clit before his tongue stroked through the slick folds.

Jerking, moaning, Rogue felt a landslide of pleasure begin to explode through her body. She trembled beneath him, anticipation and hunger building inside her as she fought to hold on to some part of herself.

She was losing herself in his touch. She could feel it. Every cell of her body was reaching out for him as her heart opened, her soul melted, and she felt herself melding to him.

"Damn, you taste like candy," he rasped, his voice tight, rough. "So fucking sweet I could drown in you."

But he licked instead. From the fluttering opening of her vagina to the hard throb of her clit. One slow, long lick as she watched, breathless. His tongue hovered over the bundle of nerves then, flickered around it, stroked, and caressed and sent her flying into a maelstrom of complete eroticism.

The pleasure was torrential. It washed over her, through her, built and rose until she was swamped with sensation with each lick. Then his lips pursed as they covered her clit to deliver a gentle, ecstatic little kiss that nearly sent her flying into rapture.

Sensation after sensation slammed through her system. Her womb clenched with it, her sex was drenched in it.

She wanted to close her eyes. She wanted to revel in the pleasure tearing through her. But she wanted to watch. She wanted to stare in his eyes as she was now, and watch as he enjoyed her, tortured her, left her shaking, so close to release she could feel it burning at the edge of her mind.

"Go over, sweetheart," he whispered. "Go over for me."

His lips closed over her clit. He sucked the little bud into his mouth, his tongue caressed around it, over it, flickered against it, and she exploded. Like a catapult, sensation flew inside her, exploded, vibrating through her body with a violence that had her screaming out his name as she arched to him and felt the quaking sensations tear through her.

Rapture. It was ecstasy. It was bright lights in front of her eyes and sparks detonating one explosion after another through her senses. It was feeling him touch her, inside and out. It was knowing she would never be the same after Zeke's possession.

And he didn't stop.

She screamed his name again as his hand slid beneath her rear, clenched, and lifted her until his tongue could plunge inside her. The quick, fierce thrust had her melting, then imploding. Her senses were rioting with the overwhelming pleasure. Perspiration ran from her flesh as her fingers clenched the iron bar her hands were cuffed to.

Shudders tore through her body. The pleasure was torturous, extreme. It singed every nerve ending, sent flames racing across her flesh, and left her wilder than she had been before.

She wanted more.

Opening her eyes she stared back at Zeke as he rose between her thighs, his fingers rolling the condom over the stiff length of his cock.

For a second, she considered telling him it was her first time. She almost allowed the words to pass her lips. But she forced them back. She didn't want gentle and tender. She wanted Zeke as he was now, primal, hungry, his gaze reflecting the wildness she felt tearing through her as well.

"Lift to me." Still sitting on his knees, his hand gripped her hip, pulling her up his thighs until her legs draped at his hips and the heavy width of his cock head pressed against the sensitive folds of her pussy.

"Oh God," she breathed out, feeling the heat and hardness through the latex as the hard crown pressed against her, into her.

Seeing Zeke, muscles tight and bulging, his hands holding her hips as he pressed against her, stole her breath, her senses.

He watched her as though nothing mattered but her—taking her, touching her. The feel of his erection stretching her, pressing deeper fed the wild need burning inside her. She bucked closer. Needing more. She didn't want slow and easy. She wanted to go wild beneath him, yet he restrained her, held her, watched her, and eased in by only the barest inch before pulling back.

"What are you waiting for?" Bucking against him, she fought the restraints at her wrists and glared back at him.

He was trying to kill her. He had to be. He was torturing her past bearing.

But he was just as tortured. Sweat rolled in a thin, damp line down the side of his neck as he stilled, staring down at her, his golden eyes fierce and intent. Desperation hovered in his expression, in the tight lines of his face as hunger glittered in his eyes.

"I need you," she whispered the plea, begging for more. If he stopped now, could she bear it?

"Tell me you're mine," he demanded, his voice dark and low. "Say it, Rogue. Admit it. You're mine."

She shook her head. She couldn't belong to him, she didn't know how to belong to anyone, and she knew he didn't know how.

"Say it, Rogue." He pressed deeper, stretched untried tissue, heated it with his strength and hardness. "Tell me. Mine." The words were a snarl, a growl of ownership as his cock dug in deeper, parted her flesh, and sent a hard, fierce jolt of electric pleasure racing through her.

"Maybe," she gasped desperately. "We can negotiate. I promise, we'll negotiate. Later."

Negotiate? Oh Lord, where had she come up with that one? She stared back at him and might have laughed at his expression if the need wasn't pumping hard and fast through her veins.

She had managed to surprise him. She liked that, loved it. He may have the upper hand on her here in the bed, but she still had the ability to affect him as well.

She jerked at the cuffs again. If only she were free. If only she could touch him, tempt the control that seemed as iron hard as the flesh barely buried inside her.

"Negotiate?" he asked carefully, his eyes narrowing, his hands flexing on her hips. "You want to negotiate on whether or not you belong to me, Rogue?"

"Yes," she promised breathlessly, nodding, trying to thrust against his hold. "Later."

A smile curled at the ends of his lips. It wasn't a comfortable smile.

"Oh, bad baby," his chuckle was dark, knowing. "Negotiate this first."

He slid deeper, pressed inside her slow and easy until the barrier of her virginity drew him to a halt once again.

Mocking amazement widened his eyes as he felt the shield of her virginity. "Why, Rogue, would you have lied to me?"

She shook her head quickly. She hadn't lied. She really hadn't.

"Don't stop, Zeke. Please don't stop."

"You lied to me, sweetheart." He glanced to where his erection was buried no more than an inch inside her. "What if I want to punish you for that?"

"Technicality," she gasped, tightening around the flesh she held captive. "We'll argue later, damn you. Fuck me, Zeke, before I die for it."

She bucked against him again, her hips jerking against his hold enough that she was nearly free, that she felt a hard stab into the fragile barrier. But she felt pleasure as well. Enough that it stole her breath, left her gasping and twisting in his arms in an attempt to experience more, to know where the sensations racing through her were threatening to take her.

Hard, calloused hands held her hips still as he moved against her. Slowly. His cock slipped back, then returned. Slow, easy, shallow thrusts that had adrenaline pumping through her system and hungry flames burning around her.

"Not enough," she cried out, her hands clenched around the bars of the bed. "Not enough, Zeke. Please."

Tears filled her eyes as perspiration dampened her body. She fought against his hold, twisting, surging against him, needing. Oh God, she needed. So bad.

He pulled back again, ignoring her tight, smothered scream. Pausing at the entrance to her pussy, he stilled for a moment, letting her work herself on the crest. Her juices coated the condom-covered flesh as she stared down at where they met.

She pushed closer, gasped, cried out as he buried deeper, then deeper yet as his hips surged forward, his cock tearing past that last veil of innocence.

Rogue stilled. Her eyes flashed to his face from where he was buried inside her. Burning heat and liquid pleasure seemed to enfold her. She felt as though she was drowning in the contradictory sensations as she stared into the hard, savagely honed features of his face.

"I told you," he grimaced. "Mine. Deny it, damn you."

Rogue shook her head. She wouldn't deny it. She wouldn't confirm it. She didn't know what belonging meant, and she was certain he had no idea what it meant to own that part of her.

He could have this. This was exquisite. It was desperate. It was real. This need, this burning hunger, every part of it. This she understood.

"Damn you," he cursed again, pulled back, and buried fully inside her in one hard, long stroke.

He buried into her entire being. Rogue felt a flash stroke of emotion that made no sense as he moved over her. The cuffs fell away from her hands and she was touching him, holding him.

Locking her arms around his shoulders, wrapping her legs around his hips, her head tilted back and a low, drawn-out cry left her lips. He was moving hard and fast inside her now. Once he breached the barrier of her virginity, he didn't let up, he didn't stop.

His fingers tangled in her hair, turned her head, and his lips were on the column of her neck. Hard, fierce kisses, the scrape of his teeth, a nip, and the quick, hard thrusts inside her were the catalyst. The explosion when it came destroyed her. She felt parts of herself dissolving, burning, turning to ash. She couldn't scream, she could barely breathe.

Eyes wide open, staring blankly at the ceiling as a heated kiss was pressed to her neck, and she felt herself free-falling. She was lost to the sensations burning around her, through her. She was lost to Zeke, and she was very much afraid she just might truly belong to him in ways that might end up terrifying her later.

"Ah God!" A harsh exclamation left his lips, his thrusts became harder, ratcheting her release higher until she felt him shudder. Felt his kiss at her neck become more fierce, hotter. Marking her. He had marked her. Again.

Rogue tightened her hold on him, keeping him to her as she clenched through the final tremors of her release, and exhaustion began to claim her.

Her legs slid to the bed, but her arms remained around his neck. She didn't want to let him go. She didn't want to lose him tonight.

"Don't leave yet," she whispered, her voice slurring from the exertion and the pleasure. "Not yet."

"Not yet," he agreed, his lips caressing her ear. "Not even soon."

She wanted to whimper as he pulled back. Instead, she loosened her hold and let him move, watching as he straightened from the bed and headed to the bathroom.

She was surprised when she heard the shower running and disappointed for the few seconds it took before he returned to the bedroom.

"Come on, naughty baby." He picked her up in his arms before she could protest and carried her to the bathroom. "We'll shower and see if you won't let me sleep a few minutes tonight."

She cuddled against his chest rather than protesting that he was the one that was keeping her awake. She didn't want to protest it, she loved it. Craved it. She wondered if she would ever have enough.

Zeke had a feeling he would never have enough of the fiery-haired little hellion he carried to the shower. Placing her on her feet, he crowded her into the glass stall before closing the door and letting the water fall over them.

She stared up at him, her expression slumberous, and he swore his chest clenched in response to it. When had any woman affected him as this one had? He had never showered with one before. He had never soaped a washcloth and cleaned another woman's body as he was washing Rogue's. And she had never been cared for in this fashion.

She was a virgin. Untouched. Untried. Unmolded. Her body would fit his alone now, she would always remember his touch, always know who had been the first.

Damn, pride swelled as hard and thick inside him as his dick swelled between his thighs. She had waited. He didn't want to fool himself into believing that she had waited for him, there lay disaster. There lay a relationship that could end up destroying the balance he had found in his life.

Holding back with her hadn't been easy. He had freed just enough of the dominance inside of him that he could be easy with her now, gentle. But it wasn't enough. He wanted so much more. He wanted her so wild she didn't know her own name. He wanted her screaming out for him. He wanted her swearing she belonged to him, and to him alone.

And once she did, he asked himself, what then? Could he swear himself to her?

As he watched suds slide sensually from the slender line of her back, over the pale, full globes of her ass, the question taunted him. He had promised himself he would never vow his soul to another woman. He had done that with Elaina. With their marriage he had given her parts of himself he hadn't been comfortable letting go of at the time. And over the years, he had learned to regret it.

He couldn't let regret stain whatever was developing between him and Rogue. Ignoring his own needs wouldn't work. As he watched the suds cover her rear, his teeth clenched at the needs that began to fill him again.

He couldn't let her go. Not yet. And he knew whatever this was between them, it would be nothing as it had been with past lovers. He wouldn't be leaving Rogue's bed when dawn broke. He'd be lucky if he managed to get to work on time. Because he was hungry. Because this need clawing at his guts warned him he wouldn't know a measure of satiation for many hours yet.

Pushing her hair farther over her shoulder he laid his lips at her neck, stroked the soapy rag over her ass before hanging it on the shower rack and catching her wrists.

He heard the breathy little catch as he flattened her hands against the shower wall and pressed her legs apart with his foot.

"I want you again." He had to have her again.

Bending his knees, he gripped the stalk of his cock, eased it against the swollen lips of her pussy, and tested her readiness.

He had to clench his teeth to hold back a yell of pleasure. Fuck, she was tight, hot. So damned good. With slow, easy thrusts this time he pushed inside her until she gripped him to the hilt.

Without the condom, the heat of her pussy was electrifying. It sizzled around his cock, caused his balls to tighten with the need for release, and sent a shock wave of pleasure tearing up his spine and back down again.

Have mercy. She was killing him with pleasure. She moved against him, rolling her hips, stroking her slick, hot flesh over his erection, working him in deeper, easing away from him, then teasing him to thrust hard and deep inside her.

Gripping her hips, Zeke held her still, plunged inside her, and lost himself. He couldn't hold back, he couldn't take her slow and easy, not yet. Not until the hunger ripping him to shreds had eased a bit more. He needed her fast and hard, desperate and screaming.

"Zeke!" she screamed, her voice hoarse, fierce. She was coming apart in his arms, clenching around his cock, exploding around him with a force that left him fighting back his release long enough to jerk free of her.

With one hand he pumped the hard flesh until his semen spilled to her back. The other slid up her hip, to her breasts. He rubbed her nipples, cupped a breast, and lowered his head to the shower wall above hers. His emotions felt jumbled, sharp. He couldn't get a handle on them, he could only let them free, let them flow with the same jagged sensations he felt as his semen pumped from his cock.

"Fuck. You make me crazy," he growled, jerking at the pleasure that tore at the fragile bonds of control.

"Not yet," she said, her breathing heavy, almost a gasp as she rubbed her head against his chin. "Give me a day or two, then I'll really show you crazy."

He almost smiled, because he had a feeling it could definitely get worse. It could definitely become addictive. Rogue was his weakness, and he had known it for years. Zeke wasn't certain exactly what he thought about having a weakness. But he knew what he thought about having Rogue. And that might be the part that really worried him.

TWELVE

Rogue had never slept with a man. Hell, she had never slept with anyone, and she hadn't expected to fall asleep after they returned to the bed. But Zeke was as inexhaustible as he was rumored to be with his lovers. As though the same wildness that tortured her filled him as well, and the only way for him to extinguish it was in sex.

Which was fine with Rogue. By the time he had her the third time, she was exhausted and slipped easily into his arms and into sleep, never imagining he would still be there when she awoke the next morning.

She wasn't a dawn kinda girl. The morning sun was high in the sky before wakefulness had begun intruding on the heated, comfortable slumber she was enjoying.

Her pillow wasn't too hard, it wasn't too soft. Evidently she had managed to ball her blankets up in front of her again, something to hold on to through the night, because her arm was resting across something.

Something that moved slow and easy. Something that breathed. It wasn't her blanket.

Memories of the night rushed through her then, flushing her face as she remembered how tirelessly Zeke had taken her, and how she had met each thrust. At times she had been forced to bite her tongue to hold back the pleas for something more. Something . . . just more.

It wasn't that she didn't orgasm. Oh boy, had she orgasmed. Satisfaction had definitely not been a problem. But there was an underlying restlessness she still hadn't managed to figure out.

"Wake up, sleepyhead." Zeke's voice was scratchy, still a little drowsy.

"Not time yet." She almost smiled. "I don't go to work until tonight."

He grunted at that. "Yeah, Janey's still glaring at me and Alex is laughing his ass off because he caught me waiting on you the other night. I should spank you for that, Rogue."

Her buttocks clenched involuntarily at the threat. Okay, so she had well fantasized about Zeke spanking her more than once. One of those erotic little spankings she had read about a time or two. She had a lot of fantasies where Zeke was concerned.

"Hey, you were the one waiting." She rolled to her back and stared up at him, her heart racing as he propped his head on his hand and remained on his side, watching her. "You could have driven me home if you had shown any interest in doing so."

A dark brown brow arched. "I've been showing decided interest of late," he pointed out. "Even my son managed to notice my interest."

Heat built in her face at the reminder of exactly how interested Shane knew his father was now. She rolled back to her stomach and buried her face in her pillow at the reminder.

"Go to work," she mumbled.

He chuckled, his hand settling on her back beneath the sheet, his fingers rubbing at her hip.

"Shower with me." She felt his lips at her ear, a tender kiss that reminded her of the aches she could feel in the tender parts of her body.

The thought of showering with him definitely aroused her interest though. As well as other things. She felt herself growing damp, felt her clit awakening and tingling at the thought.

"Shower only." He nipped at her ear before she could turn to face him. "Other activities can wait until tonight."

She stared back at him, seeing the amused curl of his lips, the warmth in his eyes. He was sexy like this, playful and seductive. His short hair wasn't long enough to really get mussed, but it wasn't as perfectly in place as it was when he'd arrived at her office the night before.

"Maybe I don't want to wait until tonight." She let her hand settle on his chest before allowing it to slide down, caressing along his abdomen and moving lower.

"Minx." He caught her hand. "We'll play later. This morning, we have to talk."

"About what?" She was more interested in exploring his manly body now that she had it in her bed.

"Your bartender."

Rogue stilled. The steely quality of his voice assured her that playtime wasn't going to happen right now. Evidently Zeke was no more pleased with Jonesy this morning than he had been the night before.

"I'll handle Jonesy." She shrugged. "I've been dealing with him for several years now, Zeke. I don't need your help."

"I didn't ask you if you needed my help." His voice hardened. "I said we're going to discuss this. The discussion will involve how quickly you'll be firing him."

Rogue flipped the sheet off her and rolled to the edge of the bed before standing, fully nude, and stalking to the chair across the room that held her robe.

"Get your shower; I'll fix your coffee," she told him, ignoring the anger that wanted to flash hot and wild inside her.

"Coffee won't settle this, Rogue," he warned her. "Your bartender wasn't just disrespectful last night, he was threatening."

"And you know nothing about him." She turned as she belted her robe snugly. "I'm not firing Jonesy, and I'll warn you right up front, Zeke, I don't take orders worth shit, so you may as well stop right now."

He was sprawled in her bed as though he had slept there for years rather than hours. She had always wondered what it would be like to awaken beside Zeke; she hadn't expected this.

"The next time he threatens you, he may not live to regret it," he warned her as he rose from the bed, naked and aroused, his cock standing out proudly from his body.

The sight of it had her mouth watering, her pussy dampening. No man as arrogant as Zeke should look so damned good while he was pissing a woman off.

"I'll make sure you're not around the next time then." She smiled back at him with brittle mockery. "I know how to get along with Jonesy, Zeke. This isn't something I need you to take care of for me."

A scowl creased his face, and even that made him look damned hot. Hell, she shouldn't have to deal with an irate Zeke while she was still remembering the touch of his hands and his possession from the night before.

"Do you need me to take care of anything for you?" he growled.

Her gaze dropped and she let a teasing smile shape her lips. She could think of several things he could take of. His scowl only deepened, his lips set in a firm line, and he turned and stalked to the bathroom as she stared at him in surprise.

Damn, Zeke might be pissed off, she thought in amazement. She had never seen Zeke pissed off. It tempted her to stalk right into that bathroom behind him and join him in the shower.

Unfortunately, having never seen Zeke pissed off, she fought herself, wary of pushing him further. There was a glimmer of warning in his eyes before he turned away. A look that had her tummy jumping in excitement even as she decided to tread very carefully for a while.

He was right about one thing though. She was going to have to deal with Jonesy. What had happened last night hadn't really frightened her, but it had concerned her. Jonesy had been uncharacteristically angry with her. It wasn't like him to lose his temper to that degree over so little.

Shaking her head, she left the bedroom and headed for the kitchen. She put on a pot of coffee, put some packaged Danishes she had bought at the store the day before on the small kitchen table.

Zeke had to force himself away from her. The farthest he could get was the shower. It was that or push her against the wall and plow into her with all the frustrated lust building inside him. Except that was the only thing she seemed to think he was capable of doing for her. Fucking her. Son of a bitch, he could feel karma biting his ass now.

For years, he had wanted nothing from his lovers but sex. Now, it was all he could do to keep from demanding more than that from Rogue. It was a situation he was going to have to fix.

Would that give her a whole new insight into the man she wanted as a lover? The one and only time he had let his emotions and his control free and had taken Elaina as he had taken Rogue last night, she had cried for hours. He'd felt like the lowest form of a man to walk the face of the earth for months afterward.

It hadn't mattered that her body had responded. It hadn't mattered that she had found her release in the act. At least to her it hadn't mattered. She had raged that he had treated her like a whore he had bought for the night, and that he had broken her heart with the act.

Shame had been like a burning demon inside him. It had sliced into his soul and left him fighting to bury the hungers that tormented him.

He had never allowed himself to give in to that impulse with her again. Hell, he hadn't even been aware of the hang-ups he'd had regarding sex and relationships until Rogue.

But, after Elaina's death, he had promised himself he would never get involved again. It had been his fault that she had died. His investigation that had been compromised and had backlashed onto his wife. He had sworn he would never let it happen again. And now, it was doing just that. It was happening again. He was letting another woman get under his skin and in his heart.

Bracing his hands on the wall, he let the warm water cascade over his head and fought the need to stalk back into that damned bedroom and just take her. To draw those heated cries from her lips, to feel the fragile muscles of her pussy clenching around his dick as he drove into her. To possess her. God, he wanted all of her. Not just her body, but all those fierce emotions burning in her eyes. He ached for it, but he knew the price of taking it. It was a price he didn't think he could pay again.

The need had never been this hard to control. And he knew what it would lead to. Once he released his control to give in to one impulse, another would slam into him. Taking her against the wall, wild and uncontrolled, was nothing compared to the things he wanted to do to her. The ways he wanted to take her.

Ways that only the most experienced and jaded of lovers had ever accepted.

Hell, he'd never stressed over having sex with a woman before. He just fucked all night long when the need burned inside him and pushed back the desires he had restrained for so long.

He'd never given a lover all of himself, so those desires had never tormented him for long.

How much of himself was he giving Rogue though? Because for the first time since he had moved back to Kentucky, those needs were slicing into him like the sharpest blade. And for Zeke, that was damned unfamiliar and uncomfortable territory. He wasn't certain if he wanted to give a woman that much of himself. He'd been self-contained for too long. He'd restrained too much of himself for too many years; realizing how much was slipping free was enough to send a spark of sensation racing up his spine.

It also had the power to leave his cock fully erect and throbbing as well. He was harder than he had been the night before, so damned eager to fuck her again that he could barely force himself to remain in the shower.

God, he wanted her. Right here, right now. However he could have her. He wanted her in his arms, he wanted her warmth and he wanted the taste of her, her heat and softness surrounding him so damned bad he could almost feel her against his flesh.

He ached for her.

She was so damned young though, and so innocent. The innocence was killing him. That dark lust inside him was pushing him, urging him to replace the innocence in her eyes with all the feminine knowledge of the pleasure he could give her. The extremities of passion. The dark lines between pleasure and pain that could fill her with sensations she couldn't imagine.

It wasn't quite BDSM. What he needed didn't cross those lines. It was a driven lust. A dark infusion of extreme pleasure and control-shattering hunger. It was hearing her scream his name because she needed to come so badly she was shaking apart from the tension. It was watching her eyes as he took her as she pleasured herself, or as he fucked that sweet little ass and filled her with a pleasure/pain that left her screaming.

It was leaving control behind and taking her against the wall, on a table, or better yet, his back deck while nature looked on. It was doing all the things with her that he had never allowed himself to do with a woman when he was involved in a relationship with them. It was being who and what he was when he had never allowed himself to do that with any other woman. And now, pulling back from Rogue was next to impossible.

Gritting his teeth, he grabbed the washcloth he had hung on the inside rack, soaped it, and put himself to showering rather than driving himself insane over a problem he couldn't fix at the moment.

He had enough to keep him busy; he didn't need to add to his problems. He had a meeting with the coroner and with Alex later in the afternoon, and his own reports to file. He didn't need the additional headache of wondering if his lover was too innocent for the dominant sex his tastes ran to.

He wanted to own her. That was his problem. Own her emotions, her heated response, and the fiery depths of her heart. And owning those parts of Rogue would never be easy. She would steal his soul. And the thought of that was enough to leave him stumbling amid his own emotions. It was enough to assure him he was getting in deep, perhaps too deep, and that walking away later may be next to impossible.

Rogue was pouring her first cup of coffee when Zeke strode from the bedroom, fully dressed in clean clothes. The sight of that official uniform conforming to his body sent a shiver up her spine. It wasn't just the effect of the clothes on his hard body, but the effect his masculine expression had on her insides. It made her heart pound, made her flesh feel too sensitive.

Her brow arched at the uniform he was wearing. "You came prepared."

"I keep an extra uniform in the Tahoe. I went down earlier and got it." He shrugged as he moved for the coffee cup. "I have to be on duty in an hour. Are you working at the restaurant this evening?"

She shook her head. "I have two more days off from the restaurant. I have some things to clear away here."

"Things like Jonesy?" he pressed.

Jonesy worried her, but she wouldn't tell Zeke that. There was something in the other man's attitude last night that warned her that her bartender was close to stepping over the line. He wanted Rogue away from Zeke, and she couldn't figure out why.

"I told you, Zeke, Jonesy is my business," she warned him as she stared into his fierce, demanding gaze.

He was staring back at her as though he could force her to do as he wanted with nothing more than his eyes. And she had to admit, she almost wished she could give in to him. But she knew Jonesy, loved him like a brother. He had helped her when Nadine Grace and Dayle Mackay had tried to destroy her life. He had taught her how to fight; he had taught her how to be who she had always been meant to be.

"Zeke, keep your nose out of my business," she warned him as his gaze flickered with a dangerous glitter. She didn't doubt he was planning to confront Jonesy himself. "I know how to handle things fine all by my little lonesome."

Rogue almost laughed at the frustration and the hint of arousal in his expression. Her defiance was turning him on. She loved it.

"I'm sure you do." He appeared to agree. Somehow she doubted he was as agreeable as he sounded. He looked damned pissed.

She watched him suspiciously.

"Poke your nose in my business and I'll get pissed," she warned him. "I'm not very nice when I'm pissed, Zeke."

He snorted at that. "Yeah, I'm the one your casualties run crying to," he reminded her. "How many attempted lawsuits have you had this year so far for wrecking men in your bar?"

She almost blushed. She was a bit prone to using her knee rather than cool reason. But in her own defense, cool reason didn't always work when a man was filled with drink and bravado.

"Not a single one this year I'll have you know." She glared back at him. "And if their mothers had taught them how to behave, then I wouldn't have to spank them, now would I?"

His lips almost twitched into a smile. She could see him holding back his amusement, but it was there. She would have been offended if she didn't often find it funny herself.

He lifted his cup to his lips and sipped at the coffee; as he lowered it, the phone at his side rang imperatively. Rogue's gaze jerked to his hip, then to his thighs as she felt her breath tighten. Damn, he really was aroused, and the pants of his uniform did nothing to hide it.

Frowning, Zeke pulled the cell phone from its hip holster, checked the number, then flipped it open with a terse, "Hello."

Something was wrong. Rogue felt it the moment his expression went hard, emotionless. His gaze became flat, distant, and something dangerous flashed in his eyes as he listened to whatever was being said.

"Secure the scene, I'm on my way," he ordered.

His frown deepened. "I don't give a damn what you think, Gene," he snapped. "Secure the fucking scene and try not to compromise it any more than you can help."

Danger seemed to radiate from him. Somehow his body seemed harder now, almost more muscular, definitely ready for action.

Rogue watched as he flipped the phone closed, his gaze locking on hers as she felt her heart begin to race in her chest.

"What's wrong?" she asked.

He moved to her, staring down at her with those hard, furious brown eyes.

"It's Grandmother Walker, Rogue," he said, his voice incredibly gentle as he reached out for her. "Lisa found her this morning. She's dead."

Grandmother Walker, it appeared, had known her granddaughter was gone from the house on an errand, freed herself from her oxygen tank, moved from the bed, and attempted to take a bath. It appeared she had slipped while getting into the tub, fallen, and hit her head before sinking into the water.

Zeke watched as the coroner loaded the body into the official vehicle and drove away. Forensics had dusted the house, but Zeke doubted they would find anything. There was nothing there to point to foul play, but still, the back of his neck was itching.

Rogue was with Lisa and Janey in Lisa's small living room, attempting to comfort her. Lisa had taken her boys to their father again that morning. While she was gone, her grandmother had died.

He shook his head as he moved back into the house, silent, watchful as Gene talked to the forensics team as they packed up.

His deputy hadn't agreed with the forensic team's involvement, but this time, it had been Alex's call. The Walker home was within the Somerset city limits and Grandmother Walker had been a friend of Janey Mackay as well as Chief Alex Jansen.

The detective Alex had sent was a good one. Robert Leeson was no one's fool. With his dark hair and suspicious eyes, he was a damned fine detective. He'd already talked to Lisa, collected the information he needed, and promised to keep Zeke apprised of anything they found.

Rogue and Janey had taken Lisa to her home after the detective had questioned her. She had been in shock, grieving, and confused. Her grandmother didn't even like baths, Lisa had stated. She showered. She couldn't imagine how or why the old woman would have decided to try to take a bath. Grandmother Walker had been ill, weak, but she hadn't been delusional or incapable of making a rational decision. The old woman had been stubborn as hell, but she wasn't stupid. So why had she decided to disconnect her oxygen and attempt to take a bath before her granddaughter returned?

First the Walker twins and now their grandmother. The back of his neck was itching like hell.

Zeke moved back to the small bedroom, stared around it slowly with narrowed eyes, and tried to figure out the knife edge of warning prodding at his guts.

There was no evidence of foul play, nothing to suggest that murder had been committed, other than the fact that Zeke's stomach was rioting and his neck was itching.

"Zeke, I'm heading out unless you need me to stay longer."

Zeke turned to see Gene watching him somberly.

"Go ahead." Zeke nodded. "I'll catch up with you."

"I'll leave my report on your desk before I go off duty." Gene nodded. "Too damned bad about old lady Walker. She was a good woman."

"Yeah, she was." Zeke sighed as he turned and stared around the room.

Hell. Just like Joe and Jaime, this didn't look right; it didn't *feel* right.

Behind him, Gene sighed heavily and asked, "Did you know Lisa had life insurance on her brothers and grandmother?"

Zeke turned around slowly. "Where did you hear that?"

"She took out the insurance here in town," Gene answered him. "Aubry Riley's agency. It's not a huge amount, but there'll still be cash left over from the burials."

"When did you find this out?"

"Yesterday evening Aubry came in after you left the office. He was telling me about the policies on the brothers then, and mentioned the one on the grandmother. Joe and Jaime took out their policies. They had survivorship on theirs. In the event of both their deaths though, Lisa was beneficiary. She's also the beneficiary on the policy her grandmother took out 'bout twenty years ago, after her husband's death."

Zeke rubbed at the back of his neck. "I'll talk to Lisa and see if she'll turn over the policies."

Would Lisa have killed her brothers and grandmother for the insurance? Zeke had seen it happen before.

"I'll head out then," Gene told him. "See you later, Zeke."

Zeke rubbed at his jaw as he turned back to the bedroom and focused his gaze on the oxygen tank, its lines hanging forlornly to the pillows of the bed.

Lisa didn't kill her brothers. She didn't kill her grandmother. Zeke could feel it, despite the evidence of the insurance policies and the attempts to make it look as though each death had an explanation. Someone had killed with such perfect precision that not even a trace of an intruder had been left behind.

As he stared around the room the cell phone at his belt beeped demandingly.

"Sheriff Mayes," he answered.

"Sheriff?" Lisa Walker's voice came through the line, timid, husky with tears. "I wanted to ask. Grandma mentioned calling you last night; she said she might have known who the girl was that Joe and Jaime were seeing. I wondered if you would tell me who it was?"

Click. He felt it now. Like a piece of the puzzle falling into place.

"She didn't call me, Lisa," he said calmly. "She didn't tell you who the girl was?"

Lisa sighed. "She said she wanted to talk to you first, to be sure about something before she said anything more. You know how Grandma was about gossip."

She had hated gossip. She didn't gossip, and she didn't hesitate to berate anyone who came to her with idle talk. This time, Zeke wished she had gone back on those principles.

"She didn't mention anything?" he asked.

"She said Joe had come to see her a few days before he was killed. He was laughing, said he and Jaime had a date Saturday night. Grandma was giving him hell over it and Joe told her that sharing what they loved was better than fighting over it and neither of them having it. It was the first time he'd ever mentioned love in regard to a woman, she said. When she asked who it was, she said he wouldn't give her name, but he said something that made her suspect who it might be. She wouldn't tell me what he said."

She hadn't tried to call him, Zeke knew, but she might have called the office.

"I'm sorry, Sheriff." She sighed. "I should have pushed her."

"Don't worry about it, Lisa," he said. "If you can though, could you bring the insurance policies you had on your grandma and brothers into my office? I'll need to go over this to make sure everything's taken care of on my end."

"I can bring them in tomorrow." There was no hesitation in her voice or her attitude. "I need to get that taken care of anyway for the funerals." Her voice broke.

"Yes, you do, Lisa." He sighed. "I'll see you tomorrow whenever you're ready. Just give me a call and let me know when you're coming in."

"I will. Good-bye, Sheriff." She disconnected and Zeke folded the phone before placing it back in its holster and moving for the front door.

Lisa didn't kill her family for the insurance. Zeke had a feeling whoever had killed Joe and Jaime had done so because of a woman they were sharing, and now their grandmother was dead because she suspected who it was. Now Zeke had to figure out who it was before anyone else died.

THIRTEEN

Jonesy was back behind the long counter serving drinks when Rogue stepped into the bar that evening. A scowl was etched into his face as he glared at her, but his brown eyes weren't filled with fury. She thanked God for that, because she didn't have the nerves to deal with another of his snits. He had never become rough with her in all the years she had known him, but she admitted he had spooked her a little the night before.

She gave him a sharp nod but kept her gaze cool before moving around the dance floor and checking with the bouncers. She'd just spent the evening on the phone with her parents and grandparents to let them know about Grandmother Walker's death.

Her father had been saddened, but Rogue knew he wouldn't grieve for the woman he had once known. He worried more about her and the rash of Walker deaths now than he did anything else. He had begged, bribed, and ordered her to return to Boston. She had declined sweetly. At least as sweetly as possible as they screamed and yelled at each other over the phone.

It was how she got along with her father. Calvin Walker wasn't the most diplomatic of men. Tact wasn't a word in his vocabulary outside a courtroom. And Rogue admitted, she was too much like her father some days rather than her soft-spoken Bostonian mother.

It had put her in the perfect mood to make a meeting that a friend had called for after her discussion with her father though.

Timothy Cranston wasn't really a friend, she corrected herself. More of a friendly adversary. He didn't seem to really like anyone except Janey Mackay and Alex Jansen. He more often seemed to only tolerate others. The Homeland Security suspended agent was a thorn in everyone else's side. But Rogue liked him. He was snarly and grouchy and rarely seemed to smile when it was appropriate. When he did smile, he tended to cause others to shudder in wariness.

Rogue didn't shudder; privately, she was usually laughing at others' reactions. Until now. Now she felt that little shiver of wariness herself.

She made her rounds of the bar, stopped, talked, and laughed with the customers. She bumped hips with the accountant from Virginia, shimmied around the mechanic that worked for Natches Mackay, and flashed a smile at Deputy Gene Maynard as he lifted his hand in hello from the bar.

Jonesy was still scowling, but he was serving beer as he was supposed to be and keeping his hands to himself. She contented herself with that for the moment, though she knew she was going to have to discuss the night before with him.

Breathing out tiredly at the thought, she caught sight of Agent Cranston at a back table, hidden in a corner just off to the side of the pool tables that were set up in the large open room back from the dance floor.

He was nursing a beer; he wasn't really drinking it. His expression was composed, almost innocent. God, she wished she could perfect that expression herself. She had been trying for years and hadn't quite managed it.

Maybe it had something to do with the ill-fitting wrinkled suit or the thin hair falling over his brow. She knew there was something both compassionate and dangerous that lurked in his eyes. Something that warned a person not to consider crossing him, and yet invited trust. He was an odd little man, that was for damned sure.

"Cranston, you're going to make me nervous if you keep lurking in corners in my bar," she told him as she moved into the other side of the booth and motioned one of the waitresses for a beer.

He smiled pleasantly. "I live to make people nervous. Keeps them from conspiring against me."

"Ah, so that's your secret." She grinned back. "So what makes you believe you need to keep me from conspiring against you?"

He grunted at that. "I wouldn't think that for a moment. You're too honest to conspire, Ms. Walker. You'd just kick my balls into my throat and laugh at my anguish if you wanted to strike out at me."

She smiled back at him approvingly. "I do so enjoy an intelligent man, Agent Cranston."

His smile was smoother this time, more manipulating as he lifted his beer and sipped before asking. "So, is Sheriff Mayes as intelligent?"

What an interesting question.

Rogue leaned back in her seat as the waitress approached and set the chilled bottle of beer on the table in front of her. She continued to regard the agent as she sipped her own drink and wondered where the question had originated from.

"Sheriff Mayes is very intelligent," she finally answered him. "From what I understand, he's a master of making certain the family jewels are well protected."

A wide smile creased Timothy's lips. "Ah, how very elusive your answer is. Tell me." He tilted his head to the side as he regarded her. "Is it true you're sleeping with him?"

"Is it true that it's none of your business?" She opened her eyes wide and appeared a bit surprised that she had let the words pass her lips. "Forgive me, Agent Cranston, I'm sure that was the bitch in me speaking. I try to contain her as often as possible."

He tipped his beer toward her in acknowledgment of her not-too-subtle hint that he had crossed the line.

"You're a strong woman," he said as he leaned back in his seat and regarded her intently. "I've heard there are bets being placed that you'll be the first woman the sheriff has publicly claimed since his wife's death."

"And that's about as much your business as whether or not I'm sleeping with him," she pointed out. "Why don't you tell me what the hell you want, Agent Cranston, and let me get back to work."

His lips quirked at her demand. "I'm just a curious man, Rogue," he finally stated. "And one that worries about supposedly unconnected threads. Did you know your cousins supplied information to Homeland Security in the operation that busted Nadine Grace and Dayle Mackay's little homegrown terrorist group?"

Rogue stared back at him in surprise. "No," she said faintly. "I didn't know that."

But it shouldn't have surprised her. Lazy and a little shiftless the boys might have been, but all in all, they'd had a patriotic streak a mile wide. Jaime and Joe both had attempted to join the Army when they turned eighteen, but a lung defect that they had shared had kept them out of the service.

Cranston nodded as he leaned forward again and braced his arms on the table and asked, "Do you think Joe killed Jaime, then himself?"

"There's no evidence to suggest otherwise as far as I know," she stated.

"And within days of their deaths their grandmother slips and falls attempting to take a bath?" he questioned. "Is that coincidence?"

"Why do you care? Fine, you think Joe and Jaime were upstanding citizens for helping you once. That doesn't explain why you're going out of your way now, Agent Cranston, or what makes you think I have any information you could use. So why don't you get to the point while I still have some patience left."

"My point." He sighed. "My point is that I'm worried now. Maybe we get didn't everyone Dayle was working with last year. The organization we disbanded didn't have lists of names to guide us to their members. We've been shooting in the dark in rounding them up. I want to make sure all the loose ends have been tied."

That made more sense. Rogue had a feeling Agent Cranston wasn't the benevolent sort; having it confirmed at least eased some of the suspicion rising inside her, though it didn't touch the tension knotting her shoulders.

"I'm the wrong person to ask then," she told him. "The last I heard, Sheriff Mayes was investigating that case, not me."

His gaze flickered as another smile threatened to curl his lips.

"So he is." He nodded. "But men like to share things in the dark with their lovers. And you were related to the twins and their grandmother. I was hoping you could tell me more than he has."

She leaned forward, eyes narrowed as her gaze locked with his.

"If you want information, Agent Cranston, then go to the source. I've never seen you as a man that likes to pussyfoot around anything; don't start playing that game now. And while you're at it, stop with the little innuendoes concerning your suspicions about my relationship with the sheriff. It's not your business, nor is it anyone else's. Now, if you have no further questions, I have a bar to run."

She rose to her feet, turned, and stepped into a hard male chest that blocked her way.

Damn her temper. Her eyes shot up to stare into Zeke's annoyed brown eyes as he stared over her head at the agent. If she had been paying more attention, she might have suspected he was there. She realized he must have been there for at least the latter part of the conversation because the agent's eyes had continually flicked over her shoulder as Cranston fought a smile.

"What are you doing here?" Pushing back from him she tried to still her heart rate, tried to still her hopes.

As Cranston had said, Zeke had never publicly claimed a woman. Had he come here for her or for more information?

His gaze flicked to hers. "Why shouldn't I be here?"

Great, he was in one of his uncommunicative moods. Answering a question with another question, his gaze flat and hard, his expression honed and savage. She had a feeling he wasn't there to put his handcuffs to use again. At least, not in the way she would have preferred. Guess that answered the question of whether or not he was there to see her.

"I'll just let the two of you have your little male-bonding time then." She smiled back at him tightly. "If you wouldn't mind though, before you leave, I'd like to know what you've learned about Grandmother Walker. If you can find the time for me, that is."

His brow arched. She hated the arrogance in that smooth, practiced shift of his expression.

"I didn't come to talk to the rabid little leprechaun," he told her, referring to the nickname the Mackays had given the agent. "I came to see you."

She was certain she didn't hide her surprise.

"Really?" She couldn't contain her surprise, either. "Why?"

His gaze heated, moved over her face, touched upon the smooth tops of her breasts that rose above the bodice of the bustier that she had paired with a thin violet silk blouse, a leather skirt that almost showed too much, and over-the-knee black leather boots.

The look in his eyes had heat flooding to her cheeks. For a second she could feel the handcuffs around her wrists again, his hard hands on her thighs as he held her legs apart, and the touch of his tongue at her clit.

Wet heat flooded her pussy, her clit swelled, and her nipples pressed demandingly against the lace of her bra.

"Good-bye, Cranston." Zeke's voice was deeper, rougher as he settled his hand at the small of her back and he moved to her side. "Tell the Mackays I said hello."

The hand at her back prodded her to move ahead of him. Surprised, uncertain, Rogue allowed herself to be led toward the bar's exit before she turned to him with a frown.

"I can't just leave, Zeke." She hadn't spent enough time there as it was. Working at the restaurant to help Janey out and then struggling to put in enough hours at the bar to keep it running smoothly had her stretched pretty thin for the past six months.

"Jonesy's still here," he growled. "Leave a message with one of your bouncers that you'll check back in later. We need to talk."

The chill in his tone had her spine tingling with warning. Looking around, she caught sight of Ronnie, one of the older bouncers, and waved him to her.

"Let Jonesy know I'll be out of the bar for a while," she told him. "I don't know when I'll be back, but I want him in my office tomorrow at noon."

Ronnie nodded his dark head quickly, though his hazel eyes were suspicious as he glanced at Zeke. "I'll let him know, Miss Walker."

Zeke caught her hand then, twined his fingers with hers, and led her out into the night. The feel of his hand holding hers did things to her that she didn't want to delve too deeply into. She felt a band of emotion tightening around her heart and a fragile flame of hope burning within her.

He had come to the bar for her. He had taken her out of the bar while damned near every customer in the building had watched them.

"You can be arrogant, you know," she told him as the hollow sound of her heels clicked against the paved parking lot.

"Really?" he drawled. "And here I thought I was being amazingly considerate. After all, I didn't throw you over my shoulder this time."

Her stomach tightened, her breasts felt fuller, swollen and sensitive at the implication in his tone.

"I can't just go running off whenever you're in the mood to drag me out of the bar, Zeke," she couldn't help but to argue. "Do I interrupt your day like this?"

"Just on a regular basis," he grunted as she caught sight of the big red pickup he drove parked at the edge of the lot.

"In your dreams," she retorted. "Tomorrow, I'm showing up at your office, locking the door, and interrupting you. You'll see what I mean."

"You'll see what my desk feels like against your naked back," he said, his voice rougher as he pulled her around and pressed her against his truck. "Damn you, Rogue, one damned taste of you and you're like a fucking narcotic I can't get enough of."

His head lowered, his lips shocked hers, parted them, and made room for his tongue to slip past.

Holding on to him now was all that mattered. Her fingers gripped his head, her lips moved beneath his, her heart raced in her chest.

What was it about him? What made her crave him to the point that nothing mattered but his kiss, his touch? She had missed him, she'd ached for him. She hadn't realized how much she needed the comfort of his touch until he was there, holding her, his hands on her ass, lifting her against his chest as her arms wrapped around his neck.

"Zeke," she whispered his name, desperation clawing at her as his lips moved from hers to her neck. They caressed as his evening beard scraped against the flesh just under her jaw.

His teeth nipped at her, his tongue licked.

"I need you." She let her tongue flicker over his ear as her legs bent to grip his thighs, her skirt lifting, her sex cushioning the heavy impression of his cock beneath his jeans.

"Damn you." His fingers threaded in her hair, tugged, and sent heated fingers of sensation to curl over her scalp as he pulled her head back.

His lips met hers again. His kiss was hungry, devouring. It worked over her lips as his tongue stroked past them, thrusting against hers before retreating, only to return again.

It was a hungry, desperate kiss. It was a kiss that fed the hope inside her, a hope that had been so fragile she had refused to even acknowledge it. A hope this need he had for her was more than physical. That emotion fueled him just as much as lust. That he might care for her. That he might need her in the ways she needed him.

Admitting she was falling in love with him wasn't easy. Letting herself acknowledge that she no longer had control over those emotions was frightening.

Almost as frightening as realizing she had no control over her response to him. She was losing herself in his touch, in his kiss, in his hunger for her. Losing herself to the point that he could take her right there, under the lights that blazed overhead, against the warm metal of his pickup truck, and she wouldn't offer the first protest. She would revel in the pleasure and the heat he filled her with instead.

"You're stealing my mind," he groaned as his lips lifted. She tried to follow, tried to retain the hunger and need she could feel pouring out of him.

"I haven't given you permission to stop," she whimpered. "Come back here."

She received a rough chuckle in reply, but still he steadied her back on her feet before shifting away from her.

Damn him. She wanted more than one of his little tease-fests.

"Come on, get in." He opened the passenger side door and lifted her into the seat before she could attempt to navigate the running board that ran down the side of the cab.

"Where am I going?" Her lips quirked as she stared back at him, amazed once again that somehow, there was something developing between them. She wasn't certain what it was, but it was something. Something more than sex, but perhaps something less than emotion.

"For a ride." He reached out, touched her cheek with his fingertips, and caressed the line of her jaw with his thumb. "We need to talk."

He backed away before she could reply, shifted her legs into the truck, then closed the door, all without saying another word.

Rogue blew out a hard breath as she watched him move around the front of the truck. Hard-bodied, graceful in that predatory kind of way, dressed in jeans, a dark cotton shirt, and boots. Damn, he made her mouth water. He made her heart ache.

He made her realize all the dreams she had never known she

had. Dreams of being more to him perhaps than just his current little pillow mate.

Which was amazingly funny actually. It wasn't as though he had so much as taken her out to a burger joint, let alone anything resembling something as public as a date. God forbid he would do anything so juvenile at his age.

"That look on your face is scary," he told her as he opened his door and lifted himself into the driver's seat before turning his head to stare at her as he pushed the key into the ignition and started the motor.

"Scary?" she asked with a smile. "How do you define scary, Sheriff Mayes?"

He grunted at that. "Equal parts feminine charm and sheer calculation. I saw that same look on your face before you broke Bobby Joe Wingate's nose last year at the local fair."

She *had* broken Bobby Joe's nose. "There was no proof I broke his nose," she still reminded him. "He buried his face in the cement; I didn't put it there."

"No, it was your cute little fist that plowed into it though," he chuckled as he pulled out of the parking lot. "I was there, remember? I heard the crunch."

"And here you didn't arrest me?"

Bobby Joe Wingate liked to tease and torment those much younger than himself. The twenty-three-year-old college dropout had been picking on a thirteen-year-old child whose father had been arrested on suspicion of terrorism.

The child had been unaware of the reason for her father's arrest until Bobby Joe had begun spouting accusations at her and her uncle. Rogue had hit before she had thought. And as Zeke said, he had been there. He had come up as Bobby Joe had hit the cement, jerked him up, and rushed him away from the crowd before someone had ended up dead. Likely Bobby Joe, because if he had tried to strike back at Rogue, the six bikers with her would have ripped his head off and used his guts to strangle him.

"The girl's uncle found me and told me what was going on," he said. "If you hadn't hit him, I would have. I hit harder."

Rogue let a smile curl her lips at that. Yeah, Zeke could hit harder. She'd had the supreme pleasure of seeing him do just that a time or two when he had been called to the bar when things became a little too rough during a conflict or two between customers and bouncers.

"So, you took me out tonight to discuss Bobby Joe Wingate?"

He was driving through town, his eyes on the traffic as he headed toward the heavily forested city limits. Out of town. She watched as the city lights disappeared and the headlights of the truck picked up the black ribbon of the road winding through the mountain.

"Bobby Joe wasn't high on my list of discussion topics," he finally admitted as he signaled and turned from the main road onto a county road that led deeper into the mountains.

"Then what is high on your list of priorities?" she asked, smoothing her hand over the short length of her skirt as they drove deeper into the mountains.

"You."

That effectively shut her up, for the moment.

Zeke pulled the pickup into a clearing next to the lake several minutes later. The rays of a full moon glistened across the water as it lapped at the large rocks that had been set along the bank.

He stared out the windshield, too aware of Rogue sitting in the seat beside him, too aware of all the things he wanted from her.

"So I'm topping your list of priorities tonight, huh?" she finally asked. "I have to admit, Zeke, I'm a little surprised. I haven't been your priority before now."

Her voice just did things to him. It was smooth, melodic; it was a breath of summer heat and a reminder of the sweet sound of her cries as she came around him. It made him fucking hard. It made him want to fuck her, right there, right then.

"You've been my priority longer than you can imagine." He continued to stare out at the water, scowling at the truth of that statement.

"Really?" Suspicion filled her voice. "Damn, you sure had me fooled, Zeke. I guess all those rejections were just your way of making a pass?"

He glanced over at her. "Smart-ass."

Flashing that wicked smile of hers, she brushed back the long red gold curls that fell over her shoulder and turned more fully to him as she released her seat belt.

She crossed one leg over the other, those damned erotic boots making him crazy with the thought of them wrapped around his back. The leather cupped her knees, skimmed down her legs, and enfolded her feet until the four-inch heels drew his gaze.

Four-inch heels. Thin, stiletto heels.

The toe of her boot tapped against the floor of the truck and she stared back at him, obviously expectantly. The part that worried him was that she wasn't responding to the teasing little name he had called her.

She was watching him with those odd eyes of hers, a pure violet, not quite blue, not quite purple. Eyes that threatened to mesmerize him. Threatened to strip his control and make him forget exactly why he had brought her here.

It wasn't to enjoy how the moonlight made her eyes appear more violet, or how her skin glistened in the shimmering rays. Hell. He was turning fucking poetic. Son of a bitch, he wanted to fuck her until his balls felt on fire from the need. There, that wasn't the least bit poetic.

Shit.

He was reaching for her. He wasn't even aware he was reaching for her until his hand was curving around her neck.

Control. He'd always known control, he'd always known his own sense of self and how to rein in the needs, the hungers that tempted him.

Until Rogue.

"I don't want to hurt you." His hand flexed against her nape, his fingertips stroking the soft flesh he found there.

"Hurt me?" Her head tilted, her neck curving into his grip as that smile tempted him. "Are you afraid of breaking my heart, Zeke?" There was a hint of amusement in her voice now. "Or your own?"

His hand tightened on her nape.

"I want you to leave Somerset." His voice was harder than he had intended, a strange, burning anger rising inside him as she stared back at him, composed, her lips tilted into that mocking grin as her eyes gleamed with anger.

"You want me to leave Somerset." Her neck flexed beneath his hold as a light, scoffing little laugh left her lips. "Now why doesn't that surprise me? What's wrong, Zeke, can't the big, bad sheriff handle the hard-on he's packing in his jeans for the town whore?" She leaned closer. "Or is that the problem? It's just for the town whore?"

Fury flashed through him. "Call yourself that again, Rogue, and I might show you exactly why I keep trying to protect you. You don't want to push that limit."

Her smile was as old as time itself, as knowing as pure erotic sin.

He sat still as she moved. As she slid over him like satin silk, those leather legs straddling his thighs, the damp heat of her pussy settling over the denim-covered length of his tortured cock.

"I'd say *bwok-bwok*, but I think you need a more direct approach." She breathed against his lips. "I have no fear, Sheriff, because you know what I know?"

His hands slid to her hips; his fingers pressed into the leather-covered flesh.

"What do you think you know?"

"I know," she crooned, "the big, bad sheriff is all talk and no action. Sheriff Mayes, you're chicken. One big hard-on-packing coward when it comes to something more than a quick little fuck in the dark. You don't have the guts to give more of yourself than that, and we both know it."

FOURTEEN

A hard-on-packing coward!

His hand slid to her neck, then into her hair. His fingers fisted into the curls and the dominance inside him broke loose. He lost control, and for the first time in his life he didn't even attempt to pull it back or attempt to soften it.

A hard smile pulled at his lips instead.

"Remember, Rogue, you made the dare."

"It wasn't a dare. It's the truth," she charged relentlessly. "What's wrong, Zeke, afraid I don't tame as easily as your other women?"

He hoped to hell she didn't, because he was damned if tame was what he wanted.

Her head tipped back as he pulled at her hair, a firm tug that tilted her chin and placed her lips in the perfect position for his kiss.

Fighting his needs had never been so hard.

"Taming you isn't what I had in mind," he growled, his head lowering, his body tight as he fought not to take what he wanted.

"Taming me is impossible." She nipped his lips; she broke his control.

He couldn't fight it, hungers hidden for so many years and the force of his lust slammed inside him, rocking him to his core.

The taste of her lips beneath his was imperative at this point. Silken soft and meeting him hunger for hunger, Rogue lifted against him, her arms wrapping around his neck, her fingers digging into his scalp.

This was what he craved.

His hand fisted in her hair to pull her head back further, his senses gloried in her moan as her kiss became hotter, wilder.

Hell, he hadn't fucked in a vehicle since he was sixteen years old, but the thought of not touching her for the length of time it would take to get to his home, or her apartment, was abhorrent.

Taking the edge off the lust thundering through his veins was imperative.

Touching as much of her as possible was an addiction, an instinct that he couldn't deny any longer.

Shoving her skirt to her hips, his hands gripped her ass, moving her, forcing her to ride the hard ridge of his cock as it pressed against her hot pussy.

He knew her taste. He knew the tight grip of her around his cock. He knew he would never get enough of her.

Rogue clenched her thighs around Zeke's, heard her own fragile cry as it echoed around her. Nothing mattered but Zeke's touch.

Arching her back, she pressed closer to his body, feeling his erection press tighter between her thighs. The blood was thundering through her veins as she rubbed her clit against his denim-covered cock. The tight knot of nerves was agonizingly sensitive, radiating with sensation.

"Beautiful girl," he growled as his lips pulled back before he nipped at her lips. "Beautiful, sweet Rogue."

Rough, dark with lust, his voice stroked over her senses and left her shuddering with the needs rising inside her. His hands gripped the bare flesh of her rear, guided her movements as she rocked over him.

She needed more. Needed him inside her, stretching her, filling her.

"Patience, baby," he crooned, his teeth raking over her neck as she panted for breath.

If he didn't do something soon, if he didn't ease the agony rising inside her, then she was going to end up screaming in need.

She wasn't used to this yet. The hunger and the need. It was unfamiliar, it was lightning sizzling across her flesh and striking at the tight bud of her clit.

"Patience isn't my name," she groaned, her hands gripping the edges of his shirt and pulling.

Buttons flew, popped out of their moorings, and the material parted, revealing the warm, hair-spattered planes of his broad chest.

This was what she needed. Arching her back Rogue pressed her hands into his chest, feeling the muscles tighten, flex.

She was drunk on him. The taste of him on her lips, his hard body against hers, it was more intoxicating than whisky.

"There, sweetheart." His voice wrapped around her, another caress, a stroke of sound that had her shivering as his fingertips stroked the cleft of her butt.

Oh God, how was she supposed to ever deny herself this? She needed him. She needed this. The only way a woman could ever hold this man. With her body. She would worry about holding his heart later, for now, nothing mattered but his touch.

His fingers gripped the cheeks of her ass, parted them farther, and sent a shard of sensation tugging at the forbidden entrance to her lower body. She could feel the juices easing from her pussy as she writhed against him, trying to press closer to his erection.

"I need you," she cried breathlessly, struggling as his hands moved from her ass to her hips. "Now, Zeke. Take me now."

A low, wicked chuckle met her demand, and a second later she felt his palm caress over her bare ass before it lifted, then fell in a heated little slap that sent heated pleasure tearing through her.

Her clit throbbed, her pussy clenched in need.

"More," she demanded.

She wanted to feel it again.

Zeke tensed against her.

"Like that, do you, baby?" His hand fell again, the heat burned hotter.

Her hips rolled, thighs clenched. Tipping her head back, she fought to breathe as his hand landed again, then again, stroking the burn beginning to bloom in her ass.

"What are you doing to me?" She couldn't catch her breath; she couldn't fight against the lust that continued to build inside her.

No, it wasn't just lust. It was something deeper, something hotter.

"Everything." One hand tangled in her hair holding her in place as his lips descended again, stealing hers.

He didn't ask for the kiss; he owned it, just as he owned her response. His tongue slid inside, stroking against hers, thrusting between her lips as his hips lifted, pressing his cock tighter against her sex. His hips rolled, thrust. His tongue stroked and plunged as he moved, turning her as he lifted his own body and bearing her down along the bench seat, coming over her, surrounding her.

It was wicked and erotic. Moonlight spilled into the cab of the truck as she felt her panties being ripped away from her body.

A second later the corset she wore over the silk blouse fell away and the buttons were released on the blouse. The edges spread away from her breasts.

Rogue stared up at Zeke, her breathing hard and heavy. His expression was savagely hewn. The flesh was stretched tight over his cheekbones as his gaze took in the hard rise and fall of her breasts.

As he watched the hard-tipped mounds, his hands went to his belt. Rogue swallowed tightly as the belt was undone, then the snap and the zipper.

"I didn't bring a condom." He finally grimaced as he eased the heavy length of his cock free of his jeans.

She stared at the heavily veined flesh. The crest was dark and flushed, a sheen of moisture glistening on it as his big hand stroked the erect flesh.

"You don't need a condom." She was protected. And she wanted him like this. She wanted him bare and hot, intimate.

"This is dangerous, baby." His eyes roved over her possessively, finally falling to her legs. They were splayed over this thighs as he knelt on one knee before her, his other foot braced on the floor of the truck. "I haven't taken a woman, until you, without a condom since my marriage."

Rogue licked her lips nervously. Not since his marriage. He hadn't been like this with another woman. The thought sent a surge of hope, of possessiveness tearing through her when she had promised herself she wouldn't let either emotion take root inside her.

"That's okay, I didn't mind being your first." She grinned back at him as her palms pressed against his hard abdomen, then slid lower. "Don't be nervous, Sheriff, I promise it won't hurt."

His surprised chuckle had her smile widening as she fought to breathe through the pleasure wrapping around her.

The smile faltered though as his hand suddenly cupped the heated, slick flesh between her thighs. Her back arched. She trembled as his fingertips parted the swollen folds and found the convulsing entrance to her sex.

"Damn, you're so wet," he groaned, a flush mantling his cheekbones.

Electric, destructive. Sensation tore through her body, arching her to him as one finger pierced her, pressed inside, and stroked the tender tissue flexing around his finger.

"Oh God, Zeke, don't tease me," she cried, her hips twisting against the penetration.

Erotic, blazing heat consumed her.

"I'm not going to tease you," he crooned. "I'm going to fuck you, Rogue. Is that what you want, sweetheart? My cock stretching that sweet pussy?"

"Duh!" she breathed out hoarsely. "God, Zeke, you're killing me."

A tight smile curled his lips as he pulled his finger back, then pressed back, hard and deep as the pad of his palm ground against her clit.

Oh hell, she was going to come apart. She could feel the shudders racing through her, destroying any control she might have thought to have as she felt her juices spilling around his finger.

He pulled back again, retreating fully from her before returning, this time with two fingers. The added sensation had her hand gripping his wrist as she stared up at him, her lips parting as pleasure surged through her.

"Damn, I love watching your face while I touch you," he breathed out, his voice tight. "Are you ready to come for me, sweetheart?"

Pulsing, ecstatic tremors raced over her flesh as his fingers thrust inside her, twisted, stroked, and sent curling, lightning-sharp spikes of pleasure tearing through her.

She ached, she burned.

"Please." Her head thrashed against the leather seat. "Zeke, please, I can't stand this."

It was too much; it wasn't enough. Her pussy clenched on his fingers, her clit throbbed. Sensation swirled and struck with brutal pleasure, and more of her silken juices spilled onto Zeke's fingers as her chest tightened at the emotions tearing through her.

Staring into his eyes, she watched him grimace, watched his gaze become heavy, his expression twisting with emotions she couldn't decipher. But she saw the pleasure in his eyes. She saw the desperate lust, and she saw a painful need that struck an answering chord inside her.

There was a restlessness in his eyes, a flame that wouldn't be doused. She knew, because she felt it in her own soul.

"Are you going to fuck me or tease me to death, Sheriff?" she drawled breathlessly, teasingly as she let a hand stroke over his as he gripped the thick stalk of his erection.

Her fingers trailed lower, her thumb caressing over the ultra-sensitive head of his cock, and she smiled as it flexed beneath her touch.

"Touch yourself." His voice hardened. "Stroke your clit. I want to feel you coming against my fingers."

Her lashes drifted over her eyes as weakening need and pleasure surged hard and fast inside her.

Memories, she reminded herself as her other hand moved slowly, touching her stomach first, then trailing to the sensitive mound of her pussy.

"Yeah," he breathed out, his voice rasping in his throat. "Let me watch you, Rogue. Show me how you pleasure yourself when you think of me."

"So certain I'm thinking of you?" she questioned a second before her breath caught.

His fingers pushed inside her, thrusting hard and deep as her fingers glanced over her clit.

"I know you think of me," he stated harshly. "I know, Rogue, because I think of you. When I'm alone in my bed jacking off, it's your face I see, your touch I feel."

Her sex spasmed, her womb clenched, the surge of sensation like a punch of pleasure to her system. The explicit words were sexier, more erotic than she had ever imagined they would be.

"Damn, look how sweet," he crooned as she stroked her clit. "You make my mouth water for a taste of your sweet pussy, Rogue. You make me ache for it."

"Then take it." Her thumb stroked over the head of his cock as she felt a small bead of dampness form there. "Take me, Zeke. Don't you know I belong to you?"

She couldn't hide from him. She couldn't stop the words from spilling from her lips. She did belong to him. Just as in her heart, he belonged to her as well.

"Damn you." He came over her, his big body blotting out the light of the moon.

His lips caught one tight, hard nipple between them and sucked it into his mouth as he tucked the head of his cock against her entrance. One hand gripped her hip, the other brushed her fingers away before he caught her wrist and drew it over her head.

Holding her hand to the seat he pushed his other hand beneath her rear, lifted her, and surged inside.

Heat slammed through her vagina. A stroke of pure, carnal sensation burned through her body as she arched her back and cried out his name.

She was stretching for him; brutal pleasure was whipping through the nerve endings just under the flesh that surrounded the thick flesh he had pushed into her.

Pulling back, he paused, his tongue lashing at her nipple before he heaved inside her, pushing deeper, stretching her farther.

Rogue felt the fingers of her free hand latch onto the side of the seat, nails digging into the leather as she wrapped her legs around his back and lifted closer. She wanted all of him inside her. She wanted to hold him there for eternity and never know a moment that he didn't fill her.

She wanted him just like this, out of control, surging inside her hard and fast, his breath as broken and choppy as her own. It was different than it had been last night. This time, it was stronger, the passion and the hunger ran deeper, more imperative than it had that first time.

It was what she needed. What she wanted. Rougher, harder, a man taking his woman. Making her his.

"Hold on to me," he snarled, lifting his head from her breast, his brown eyes glittering with desperate, raging hunger before his head lowered to the other nipple. "Hold me, Rogue."

His lips covered the tight peak, sucked it in, sending pulses of ecstatic pleasure racing from her nipple to her clit and beyond. Flames were burning across her flesh; her chest was tight, not just with the pleasure, but with something that went much deeper, that tied her emotions into knots and assured her there was no escaping this need for a man that seemed to almost regret his hunger for her.

"Hold me, Rogue." It was an order, it wasn't a request.

Hold him. She needed to hold him. He released her wrist as she loosened her fingers from the seat. Both arms wrapped around him as he slid one hand beneath her rear, his fingers tucking into the cleft there to find the ultrasensitive little portal they hid.

Rogue was flying on sensation. Breath suspended, every muscle tight, clenching in pleasure as he began to fuck her with deep, hard strokes.

His fingers caressed her rear entrance. He drew the moisture from her pussy back, rubbed against the sensitive opening, and sent her senses spinning.

His hips moved faster, harder. His fingers caressed, pressed, eased the nerve endings at her rear, and then pressed inside her, opening her, stretching her as she felt the world explode and dissolve around her.

The orgasm, when it hit, was like a cataclysm. It raced through her, shattered her with sensation and then with emotion as he cried her name, buried his face in her neck, and began to ejaculate, hot and fierce inside the tight grip of her body.

She felt him, the pulse and throb of his erection, the wet heat of his release, and the fierce kiss he laid at the bend of her shoulder.

She felt him holding her, felt him surrounding her, his arms tight, his muscles clenched, his erection jerking inside her.

He had lost control. She sensed it, she felt it. His dominant, possessive touch, the muted groan of her name, the violent tension that radiated through his body as he spilled his release. It hadn't been like that the first time. It hadn't been wild and untamed, it had been focused and controlled.

Rogue decided she was going to have to see about breaking his control a little more often.

Zeke pulled the truck into the parking lot at the back of the bar and cut the ignition silently. He was aware of Rogue watching him, the frown at her brow and the tension that had been steadily rising between them since he had fixed their clothes earlier and left the lake.

He'd taken her there to talk, not to fuck. But she was like a drug; once he touched her, he had to have more. The more he had, the more he wanted. It was a vicious cycle that threatened to destroy his mind.

"Do you want to tell me why you're acting like a jackass, Zeke?" she finally asked curiously. "Or do I have to start guessing?"

He almost smiled. Damn her, she wasn't supposed to make him laugh.

"What would you guess?" He looked over at her, realizing he was genuinely curious as to what her answer would be.

Fiery, mussed ringlets of hair fell over her shoulder as her violet eyes went over him slowly. She was silent, thoughtful for long moments.

"A lousy marriage would be too easy." She finally sighed. "You're mysterious, secretive. I'm betting even your wife didn't know the real you."

He shouldn't have been surprised by her insight.

"She didn't want to know the real me," he finally said wryly. "Women want the fantasy, Rogue. It's what my wife wanted, it's what my lovers have wanted."

"If you say it's what I want, then I might have to hit you, Zeke." Her eyes narrowed on him. "I didn't wait five years to lose my virginity to you so you could give me some kind of song and dance about how you can't be whatever the hell it is you think I want. So save it."

"Why did you wait five years to lose your virginity to me?" He'd kept that question silent, but now, Zeke found, he needed the answer to it. "You could have any lover you wanted, Rogue. Why wait?"

"Because I'm a fool?" She stared back at him, her eyes flashing with a glimmer of anger. "Why did you wait five years to take my virginity, Zeke?"

"Hell, there's a question." He gave his head a quick jerk. "Because I knew you were trouble the first second I set eyes on you. All prim and proper in your schoolteacher clothes, your pretty lips unsmiling, but those eyes." He chuckled. "You snuck a peck at my crotch right there in the middle of that damned town hall meeting."

She didn't deny it. "You have some fine-looking goods, Sheriff." She laughed. "But it doesn't answer my question."

"Just as you didn't answer mine," he pointed out.

She shrugged at that as she turned her head away for long moments. "Call it instinct," she finally said, turning back to look at him. "I knew you could satisfy me. Your turn."

Oh, there was more. She thought she was in love with him. Zeke could see it in her eyes. He wondered how long it would take her to realize that love was no more than a carefully contrived deception.

But she wanted answers, and they were answers he knew would hurt her.

"You're temptation," he finally answered her. "Young, wild, sweet. Every dirty old man's fantasy."

She seemed to flinch. "Oh, so I'm your midlife crisis? I wonder what that makes Janey to Alex. You are so full of crap, Zeke."

He snorted at that. "Alex doesn't come with the same baggage I come with, Rogue," he told her, shaking his head. "You're young, and you're innocent."

"And you want to tie me down and fuck my ass until I'm screaming for mercy," she drawled. "You want me blindfolded, spanked, and insane from wanting you. You want to get nasty with me, Sheriff, and you're terrified of losing all that perfect control of yours."

He snapped his teeth together, his hands clenched the steering wheel, and he fought to keep the vision of those acts out of his head. If he didn't think about them, they wouldn't torment him nearly as much.

She leaned closer. "You want to get rough and wild with me, Zeke. So bad it's like a hunger."

"Are you finished yet?" He kept his expression hard, unemotional. He'd managed to keep his control for years now, he wasn't going to let go now.

She stared back at him for long moments before something resembling resignation flashed in her eyes. "Yes, I'm finished now," she finally said. "Don't bother seeing me upstairs. I know the way." She reached for the door handle.

"Rogue. I didn't take you out to fuck you tonight. I need to talk to you."

"We've been talking." Her eyes were filled with shadows now, with pain. "What more is there to say?"

"This investigation into the twins' deaths, and their grandmother's," he stated. "I called Lisa this evening and convinced her to go stay with her aunt in Louisville. I want you to leave town for a while as well. Until I figure out what the hell is going on. Until it's safe."

She was still, silent. Zeke stared back at her, watching as what he said sank into that quick little mind of hers.

"You think someone is killing Walkers?" she asked.

"I think Joe and Jaime were messing with the wrong girl," he told her. "I believe their grandmother was killed because she might have known who that girl was. Joe and Jaime kept her a secret for the most part, but Grandmother Walker thought she might have known who the girl was. She told Lisa she was trying to contact me to tell me who it was, but she died before she could get ahold of me. You and Lisa were close to the twins. Someone could be afraid you might remember who the girl was as well."

Someone could kill her. Zeke hadn't forgotten what it felt like six months ago, staring down at her unconscious form in a hospital bed after she had been attacked over something someone was afraid she knew. He couldn't imagine it happening again, or worse, finding her dead.

"So you want me to leave town for my own good?" she questioned him carefully.

"Go home to Boston," he told her. "You weren't meant to put up with the bullshit you've put up with here. See what it feels like to be Caitlyn Walker again rather than the rebel Rogue. I have a feeling you might like it more than you think you will."

"So, you think I should just walk away? Just forget about my home, my bar, and my friends?"

"You're home is a trashy little apartment over a bar full of thieves and drunks," he ground out between clenched teeth. "Your friends consist of Janey Mackay and her family, and it took you years to let down your guard enough to accept them as friends."

"What about you?" she whispered. "We were friends once."

"We were never friends, Rogue," he snapped. "I was the one man that didn't stand up and beg for a treat whenever you were near. I was a challenge. Now we've both had our fun, it's time to face reality. You're in danger here. Fucking go home before it's too late to realize where you belong and you're dead."

Rogue stared back at him for long, silent moments. No tears filled her eyes, no pain creased her face. Bitterness flashed in her violet gaze though as she seemed to straighten her shoulders and stared back at him relentlessly.

"Wow, quite a little speech," she said softly. "And here I thought all that 'you're mine' crap you were spouting the other night actually meant something." Her smile was filled with mocking bitterness. "Oh well, my bad for believing in it, huh?" She gripped the door handle and opened the door slowly. "Go to hell, Sheriff Mayes."

She jumped out of the truck before he could reach out and grab her. The door slammed closed, and she crossed the short distance to the back door, unlocked it, and disappeared. Zeke sat staring at it as he rubbed at his chest, wondering at the deep, painful ache he could feel there.

He inhaled, clenched his teeth, then started the truck and backed out.

He'd taken her without a condom. He'd claimed her, despite his own best intentions. He'd so fucked this up he didn't know which way to turn at the moment. He knew he had to get her out of town. He had to get her away from the danger that could be stalking her, even now. He couldn't risk a repeat of the past. His soul couldn't handle it again.

Shaking his head, he drew his cell phone from his hip, flipped it open, and punched in the speed dial he had set earlier that day.

He waited and when a deep male voice answered the call he said, "Cal, it's time to do something. You need to get your daughter home."

Calvin Walker was silent for long moments. "Why?" he finally asked.

"Because, if you don't, she could end up dead."

FIFTEEN

The ringing of the telephone brought Rogue out of a restless sleep. Her eyes cracked open as she glared at the shades on the window. It had to be too early for her to be awake. There was barely any light between the cracks of the shades.

She reached for the phone, fumbled, dropped it on the floor, and cursed before scrambling for it and rolling back in the bed as she flipped it open.

"You could die for waking me up this early."

She knew who it was. Only one person dared to call her so early and to have the temerity to laugh in her ear about it.

"Now, baby sister, getting grumpy with me wouldn't be nice when I just finished doing you a favor of major proportions."

Amusement filled John Calvin Walker Jr.'s voice.

She almost grinned at the sound of it. But she knew better. If he was calling, then she was in trouble.

"What is Daddy mad over this time?" She yawned. "Tell him he can't cut off my allowance simply because I never use it anyway."

John laughed again. "I believe he may have canceled a delivery Mother had arranged for you. Something about silk, lace, and feel-good girly stuff?"

She sat up in the bed. "The French collection? Mom was supposed to have sent that a week ago."

"Well, it appears she may have been a bit late sending it." She could almost see John's violet eyes gleaming with amusement as a smile curled at the corners of his lips.

"Why would Daddy cancel my delivery?" she asked, frowning. "He sent the stuff he bought in Saudi last month."

John chuckled. "Well, sweet sister, it could be due to a very important phone call he received last night from the son of an enemy he used to have in Somerset. Seems this certain gentleman called Father and confirmed his suspicions that Walkers are being killed." John's voice hardened. "The family jet is prepping to leave this morning. ETA at Louisville is for noon. Have your ass there and be waiting for it."

Rogue breathed in slowly. Patience, she reminded herself. Without it, her father and John would win before the battle began. They were overprotective, forceful, and though her father loved her and tried to allow her to live her life as she pleased, he was still her father.

There was nothing Rogue hated more than being tattled on. When she was a little girl her older brother and sister had always tattled on her. Her teachers tattled, her babysitter had tattled. Rogue had always found a way to get into trouble. And her father had always given the pretense to her mother that he was disciplining her.

Calvin Walker had been born to be a father. He had taken the time to get to know his children from infancy. He knew the best way to deal with their weaknesses and how to draw out their strengths.

But he was, at the very soul of the man, a protective father.

"Tell Daddy he can ignore the sheriff. Whatever Joe and Jaime were involved in, I'm not a part of it."

"And you know how well Father is going to listen," John pointed out with chilling logic. "Get your butt on that plane, Rogue. It's time to come home."

"But I am home, John." She sighed. "I'm not leaving Somerset. If Daddy wants to come visit, then he's more than welcome to do so. Hell, the whole family can come visit, but I'll warn you right up front, contrary to what Zeke Mayes believes, I am more than capable of watching out for my own butt here."

"So we're to just sit here and wait until we get that phone call that lets us know you're dead?" John was becoming angry. His voice was cold, quiet. He was a lot like Calvin Walker in that regard. The angrier he got, the icier he became.

"No, you're to accept that I'm a big girl now and I don't need to run to the bosom of my family every time some paranoid sheriff gets a wild hair up his ass."

"You know, Rogue, six months ago we stood over your hospital bed after some bastard tried to bash your head in. I'd prefer not to do that again, if you don't mind."

"I don't mind in the least," she said in exasperation. "This is ridiculous, John. Don't make me hang up on you. I'm not returning to Boston. This is my home and I'm old enough to decide for myself whether I stay or go."

"I should bash you over the head myself and drag your ass home," he snapped. "From what Father says, Zeke Mayes isn't some paranoid fool, Rogue. He was worried enough to call Father; that means there's something to worry about."

"Yeah, he's real damned worried someone might touch that frozen heart of his." She swung her legs out of the bed, fury erupting inside her. "Let me tell you what Zeke's problem is, John. He can't stand to keep his hands off me, so he had to make certain Daddy hauls me home for his own piece of mind. Now I really don't give a damn if either of them are resting easy at night. I'm an adult; I'll decide for myself when to tuck my tail and run, if you don't mind."

Her voice was rising. She was so furious she could barely stand it. How dare Zeke call her father and upset him this way? How dare her father sic her brother on her rather than calling himself?

That was just like Daddy. He knew if he called himself that Rogue would go ballistic. Rather than facing her anger, he called John. Because John would rather fight with her as to breathe some days.

Yes, sibling rivalry was still alive and well.

"Rogue, don't make me get on that jet and come after you," John warned her.

"John, don't make me call Daddy and fight with him over this. You know it will only end up coming back to slap you on the ass. I'm his favorite, remember?"

"You're his favorite because you're as crazy as he is," John accused. "You can fight it out with him here. I'd suggest you pack."

"I'd suggest you take a flying leap," she raged back at him. "Good-bye, John."

"Rogue, don't you hang up on me."

She hung up the phone, then turned it off. Rogue inhaled slowly, deeply. If she didn't get a handle on the hurt and the anger churning through her, then she was going to explode. Exploding wasn't a good thing. She never failed to hurt herself more than she did anyone else whenever she lost control of her temper.

Damn Zeke, she thought as she stalked to the shower. Damned tattletale. He should have never called her father and gotten him involved like this. She knew her family. She could expect every damned one of them to descend on her like a plague of locusts now. She'd be lucky if her grandparents didn't fly in with the rest of the brood.

She shuddered at the thought. She loved her grandparents, she really did. But they were dangerous. Forget the upper-crust Bostonian reserve they used like a shield. Her grandparents were wicked. And they didn't take prisoners or show mercy.

She was going to kill Zeke. She was going to string him up and make him scream for mercy. Oh, he had seriously underestimated her.

An hour later, showered, dressed, and ready to rumble, she pushed into the main section of the bar and behind the long teak counter where Jonesy was checking liquor. He straightened from his stooped position and glared back at her.

They hadn't talked much since the night Zeke had caught him trying to throw her across the room, and Rogue was saddened by the fact that the friendship she had once believed they had was disintegrating.

"You working that damned restaurant today?" Jonesy barked. "It's a sad day when a Walker is more concerned with other folks' businesses than they are with their own."

Rogue ignored the comment as she moved around him to the register and collected the receipts from the past night's sales.

"We gotta put orders in today," he snapped. "Or do you care?"

"Then put the orders in," she told him. "You know how to do it."

"It's your business," he sneered. "You do it."

"I could always fire you. Again. And hire someone who will do it." She shrugged.

She hated to admit that she preferred working with Janey over working at the Bar. The Bar had saved her at one time; it had helped to remake her at a time when she had been smarting from the loss of her teaching job and the humiliation of the pictures that had hit the Internet.

Over the years the bikers that had helped her survive had slowly drifted away. A few had died, others had found lives, until there was just her and Jonesy. And now, Jonesy was drifting away as well.

Maybe it was time to admit what she had sensed all along. The bar wasn't a permanent part of her life. It was a way to piss folks off and a means of survival. It wasn't what she enjoyed doing though.

"There were comments made about you sneaking off with that sheriff last night," he spat back at her. "Folks are gossiping over it. It's going to hurt business."

She rolled her eyes as she shoved the receipts into a large enve lope to go over later.

"My private life is just that, Jonesy," she informed him. "If folks don't like it, then they can find another bar to go to."

She was wary around him now. She kept him in her peripheral vision and made certain she had room to run if she needed it. She should have ordered him out of the bar the night he had thrown her across her office. Where would he go though? Rogue knew him; she knew he had nothing but the bar and the little house he owned a few miles away.

Jonesy didn't have family, with the exception of a daughter that rarely spoke to him, and the only friends he had worked at the bar. He was always snarly and grouchy, but lately, he had been extreme, tense, and hard for anyone to get along with.

"Lea quit last night," he informed her.

Somehow, that didn't surprise Rogue.

"Then hire someone else," she told him as she looked over the liquor that lined the wall and the shelves beneath the bar.

"It ain't that easy," he ground out between clenched teeth.

Rogue straightened and stared back at him suspiciously as he towered over her.

"What would make it easier, Jonesy, is if you didn't scare your bartenders away," she told him. "You're like a rabid junkyard dog and the employees get tired of taking it."

She should have done something about him before now. She'd always convinced herself that Jonesy was just like that. It was a gruff exterior, and it didn't mean anything. But now, she was beginning to wonder if it didn't go deeper.

"Pussy-faced employees are what they are," he snapped. "None of 'em have a lick of sense. I told you to let me take care of hiring them, but you have to just stick your nose in it, don't you? You tell me to take care of hiring, then you turn around and get all nosy and bossy. What good does it to do me to even consider anyone?"

"Jonesy, what the hell is your problem?" She swung around on him, anger beginning to beat harshly inside her. "What makes you think you can tell me how to run my life or my bar? And what in the hell made you think you could manhandle me the way you did the other night? Are you losing your damned mind?"

He stared back at her in surprise now, his face flushing before he turned away and ran his hand over his bald head.

"I didn't mean to get rough with you," he snarled, his back to her. "It was an accident, and I shouldn't have touched you."

An apology from Jonesy?

"Then why did you?"

He turned slowly, his expression fierce as he stared back at her. "You don't listen anymore, Rogue. You're tramping yourself out to that sheriff knowing damned good and well he won't stick around no longer than it takes for him to get his rocks off. Just like Joe and Jaime. I told you they were bad news. Always in here bumming beer and sucking up to you. You were going to give them part of the bar, weren't you? I heard you talking about it."

That had been her plan. Joe and Jaime had loved the bar; Rogue had known she was growing discontented with it. But she wanted it to remain in Walker hands.

"Joe and Jaime loved the bar, Jonesy," she said, a sense of sadness enveloping her. "They helped me a lot here."

"They got in your damned way and conspired to take this damned bar from both of us," he snarled, his beefy arms crossing over his heavy chest. "They were good for nothing, Rogue. You just couldn't see it. Just like that damned sheriff. He'll get you killed as dead as he got his wife killed."

Rogue stared back at him in surprise.

"Zeke had nothing to do with his wife's death," she shot back furiously. "She was killed in a car accident while he was still in L.A."

A flash of cunning glittered in his gaze for a second.

"Well, there's a piece of gossip you didn't know," he chuckled coldly. "No, little girl. Zeke Mayes's wife was murdered because he was sloppy. He was working an investigation in L.A. into the bondage scene. Good ole married detective Mayes was bopping pain whores and one of them found out who he was and what he was doing. His wife died and his son almost died. He was the reason she died, just like he's going to be the reason you die."

Pain whores. It was a term Rogue had heard used for women who liked sexual pain. Whips, chains, multiple sexual partners, cutting, the list went on and on.

"Where did you hear this trash, Jonesy?" she asked in disgust. "Zeke is not into giving pain, and I doubt very seriously if he did anything to cause his wife's death, no matter why or how she died. And you need to stop this now, before I call Alex Jansen and have you escorted off my property."

"Gonna fire me, are you?" He snorted, dropped his arms from his chest, and moved farther back along the counter. "Check it out yourself. Ain't many people that know what happened, but I was here when he came back with that kid of his, and I was here before his old man died. His daddy blubbered the whole story into his beer one night, whining like a little girl 'cause his boy was a failure."

Jonesy didn't lie. He was mouthy, he was pissy, but he wasn't a liar. He believed what he was saying. Rogue refused to accept it. Zeke's wife might have died because of his involvement in an investigation, but it wasn't because he had failed. She knew him too well for that. His steely control wouldn't have allowed for such a failure.

"Jonesy, don't make me fire you." She faced him, shoulders squared, fury beginning to build inside her. "Don't push our friendship any further."

"In other words, don't tell you the truth about that jackass you're fucking?" he sneered.

"If that's how you want to see it," she replied coldly, "then that's exactly what I mean. Because the next time this trash comes out of your mouth, you'll be out of here."

With that she turned away from him and began making the order list for the liquor. An hour later she was in the kitchen in the back getting the order list the cook had left last night before moving to her office to make the necessary orders.

She still had her own financials to go through and get in shape for monthly taxes, and those for the Mackay restaurant were waiting for her to complete as well.

She had a full day ahead of her, and one little side trip to make to the sheriff's office before she headed to the restaurant. Zeke, like Jonesy, would find out just exactly how much she thought of tattlers. Which was nil. Zero. And she was getting fed up to her back teeth with autocratic, arrogant men. It was time to do something about both of them.

That evening Zeke ran his fingers over his short hair and stared at the reports the county and city coroners had submitted. The county coroner, Jay Adams, sat in the visitor's chair on the other side of the desk, his lined face creased into a worried scowl as Zeke read the report.

Long minutes later Zeke lifted his head and pinned the other man with his eyes. "You sure about this, Jay?" he asked quietly.

"Gene and I both ran the same tests and came back with the same conclusions, Zeke. I don't know who killed those boys, but they were unconscious before the shots were fired. Both boys were pumped full of heroin, not just Joe. Evidence shows they were nearly dead before those shots were fired. I don't know what you have going on here, but I'm ruling it a double murder and I'm using those grounds to justify holding their grandmother's body for an autopsy as well."

Zeke rubbed his hand over his jaw and shifted through the reports before blowing out a heavy breath.

"Why?" He lifted his gaze back to Jay. "Why go to these lengths to hide a murder?"

Jay shrugged. "Hell, it looked like a murder-suicide, Zeke. Chances were, we'd never have run these tests this in depth. Even with your suspicions I wouldn't have normally justified it myself. It was a damned slow week though, so what the hell. Whoever did this, they almost pulled it off. We had to look for this." He waved his hand to the report. "It didn't come easy."

Zeke stared down at the file and he knew, knew in the pit of his stomach, that the Walkers had been killed by the Freedom League's killer. The why of it was driving him crazy. There were no answers to be found, no way to tie Joe or Jaime to any one particular woman, or to pinpoint if this was simply a League hit and the woman was an incidental.

"The Walkers were rumored to be courting one particular woman," Zeke said. "They told their grandmother they had a date with her that weekend. The day of that particular date they're killed. According to their sister, their grandmother was trying to contact me in regard to that girl's identity. She never called, but she ends up dead the same day."

"Sounds like you're looking for a very smart little girl, or a really pissed off husband or lover." Jay shrugged as he rose to his feet. "If you learn anything let me know. Until then, you have our reports and your evidence to continue the investigation. Good luck on that."

"Thanks, Jay." He nodded as Jay turned and left the room.

He shook his head as he closed the files and slid them into the drawer at the side of his desk. It was time to figure out exactly what had happened to those boys.

Zeke had questioned everyone he could think of that were close to the Walker boys. He knew they were supplying DHS with information, but Zeke knew Cranston and the Mackays. Unless the Walker boys had let that information slip, then no one else had known it. And from everything he'd learned, Joe and Jaime hadn't talked. But their grandmother must have.

Running his fingers over his hair, he tried to narrow down the choices of who Callie Walker would have chosen to talk to. Lisa hadn't had any answers for him there, and Zeke wasn't coming up with his own.

The only thing he was certain of was that this had to do with the Freedom League and the killer that seemed to shadow his life. The same killer that could threaten the one woman Zeke had promised himself he would always protect.

Rogue wasn't going to leave town, even for her own good. He'd accepted that sometime in the middle of the night as he stared up at the ceiling, his dick pole stiff, his balls tormented with need.

She was just that damned stubborn that she would stay come hell or high water. Or death.

He rubbed his hands over his face as he considered the fact that he may have even made an error in judgment in calling her father. But at the time, nothing had mattered but her protection. Someone was killing Walkers, and she could be next. This investigation into Joe and Jaime's deaths could possibly bring that danger closer to her door. Just as his mother's association with his father and the League had brought death to Zeke's life in L.A. His mother had died when flames had engulfed her small house, but the coroner's report had stated she had been dead long before the fire started.

Elaina had died in a car wreck when her car has sped into traffic on a busy interstate, straight into an oncoming semi. She had been drugged, not with heroin but with a toxic mix of narcotics that she wouldn't have survived even if she had managed to live through the wreck.

On the day of Elaina's death he'd received a short, printed note. *We protect our own.*

It was the League's motto. He'd known the minute he read it that his wife had died because of his past, because of his hidden investigation into certain members of that League once he made detective.

He'd thought he was being so careful, that there wasn't a chance that anyone could have known what he was doing. And he'd been wrong. He hadn't protected his family as he should have, and now Rogue was being drawn into the same fire.

It was time to call Cranston, he thought. He'd protect Rogue, and Cranston and the Mackays could help with this investigation. He couldn't risk her. God help him if he allowed anything to happen to his Rogue.

And he knew, the danger was drawing closer.

Zeke could feel it, that sixth sense, that awareness that the killer wasn't going to stop; he would only get cockier. Whoever it was had a taste for murder and for giving pain.

A light knock on his door had his head lifting; a second later it opened and Gene stepped in.

"I'm heading out on patrol," Gene told him, a light frown on his brow. "I just saw the coroner leave. Do we have the report on the Walkers?"

"Both boys were murdered," Zeke answered as he waved Gene into the room.

The deputy stepped in and closed the door behind him, scowling.

"Well, hell," he breathed out roughly. "I'm damned sorry for what I said now, Zeke. It's hard to believe someone wanted to kill those boys."

"Well, someone wanted to and they accomplished it." Zeke rubbed the back of his neck tiredly. "The part that confuses the hell out of me is how they pulled it off this slick. It would take experience and balls to make that look as close to a murder-suicide as this one did."

Gene plopped down in the chair in front of his desk as he gazed back at him thoughtfully. Zeke hated the suspicion that roiled in his gut now, the feeling that Gene was somehow a part of this.

"Experience would be the hard part," Gene said. "We don't have a lot of folks that I know of that would have that except our new chief, the Mackay boys, and that DHS agent that seems to be loitering around the Mackays, Agent Cranston."

Zeke shook his head. "No motive and out of character. Whoever did this, it has to do with the woman the Walker boys were sniffing after." That and their work with DHS. Zeke kept that to himself. If Gene was involved in this, then he didn't need to know that Zeke suspected him of it.

"How so?" Gene grunted. "Hell, those boys always had a woman they were sniffing after."

"Lisa said their grandmother was trying to contact me the day she died, to tell me who she thought the girl might be." Zeke leaned back in his chair and shook his head slowly. "She didn't call here or my cell phone. I have a feeling what she did was call someone else. The wrong someone else."

Gene stared back at him in amazement. "Hell," he finally breathed out. "She was confrontational as hell; she would have done that."

And if Gene was involved in this, then he was a better actor than Zeke had given him credit for.

"I have a request in with the job for a subpoena of her phone records; maybe I'll figure something out there." Zeke tapped his fingers against the arm of his chair. "The way she died is sitting about as well as the way her grandsons died. She didn't decide to take a bath on her own."

"Then we have a triple homicide and no clear suspect." Gene grimaced. "Hell, you'd think we'd get a break after that bullshit with the Mackays and those terrorists last year. What do you need me to do, Zeke?"

"Keep your ears open, see if you can get a name. I have a few more people to question." Top of his list was Rogue's bartender Jonesy.

Jonesy had a daughter that had been in town until the day before. Angie Jones was only eighteen, pretty from what Zeke had heard. Her name hadn't been linked to the Walkers, but it was an angle he couldn't overlook. Gene had a daughter as well, one in her early twenties, but she was married and living in Louisville.

"I'll do that." Gene nodded, rising to his feet. "And the missus told me to let you know you're invited to dinner next weekend. Willa and her new husband will be in from Louisville for a visit and they were asking about you."

Zeke shook his head. "I can't make it next weekend, Gene. Shane's supposed to be home and I try to spend some time with him when he's in," he said apologetically, though Zeke didn't regret that he couldn't.

"Yeah." Gene sighed. "I figured. Anyway." He nodded sharply. "I'll see you tomorrow then. I best head home or the missus is likely to have my hide for dinner. Evenin', Zeke."

"See you tomorrow, Gene." He nodded back as Gene left the office, then rubbed at the back of his neck while rising from his chair.

Picking up the coroner's report, he moved to the file cabinet, filed it, then locked the tall, gray metal cabinet and glanced at the clock.

Tonight was Rogue's early night at the restaurant. She would have taken care of paperwork rather than working as the hostess.

Hell. He'd fucked up last night, it was that simple. He was so desperate to get her out of the line of fire and just egotistical enough to think he could make her mad enough, or worse, hurt her enough, to send her running for home.

He should have known better. He had known better; that was the reason he had called her father, because he had known in his gut that wasn't going to work. Rogue wouldn't run, not from anything. She hadn't run from Nadine Grace and Dayle Mackay when they'd threatened her with those pictures, and she hadn't run from her assailant six months before. She wasn't going to run now.

And she definitely wouldn't run when he showed up at the bar tomorrow afternoon to question Jonesy. She'd stick right to the other man's side and glare at Zeke the whole damned time. He'd get hard, horny, and once questioning was over he'd be trying to carry her to her bedroom. If she didn't try to kill him first.

SIXTEEN

It was Ladies' Night at the Bar. This was the reason Rogue made certain she was on-site from seven that evening until after closing. Ladies' Night, spring and summer, was often the wildest night of the week. Saturdays could run a good close second, but the majority of her bouncers were on duty every Friday and Saturday evening. Wednesday was a bit lacking in that area, as most of her bouncers had second jobs through the week.

She kept meaning to hire more bouncers for Wednesdays, but so far she had been able to handle it with her skeleton crew. She had four bouncers on duty along with Jonesy, and the assistant bartender Kent.

The bar was filled close to capacity. The band was belting out country dance tunes and ballads, and the alcohol was flowing freely. A large majority of the regulars were there as well as a surprising number of tourists in town to enjoy the unseasonably warm weather and the many attractions to be had in Lake Cumberland.

As the day had progressed, Rogue's frustration had only grown. Her father had called. Ten minutes later her mother had called. After that, her grandparents and her sister. John hadn't called back, and that worried her more than anything.

Her father no longer suspected that Walkers were being killed; Zeke had confirmed his fears and now Calvin Walker was determined to get his daughter home.

Damn them all. She had been manipulated from the moment she stepped foot into this damned town. By one person or another she had been jerked around until she felt like a fucking rubber band.

She stared around the bar, realizing what it had come to represent, the escape from reality that it had been for all these years. She had raced here after her life had fallen apart, and she had molded herself into a woman that others feared. Men and women alike. She had surrounded herself with men who were ready to fight at a moment's notice, and they had taught her how to fight.

How to use her fists. How to use her knees. How to be the rogue that didn't care what others thought or what they expected from her.

The problem was, she did care. She had always cared. And she was only now realizing it.

"Rogue, dance with me, baby." An arm snaked around her waist, pulling her against a strong male body. Dressed in camouflage and smelling like week-old sweat.

Rogue wrinkled her nose and pushed away with a forced laugh. "Get a shower, Bubba," she called back to him. "Soon."

It was typical. A few feet away a hand reached out to her, laughter, most of it drunken or forced, echoed around her as the customer requested a dance. A smile and polite refusal, and a stronger dislike for where she was.

She was here when she wanted to be back at the restaurant. Where she could make certain Janey or Alex or, God forbid, Natches wasn't messing with her accounting file or the reservation layout. Where she could dress in something other than denim or leather.

Where Rogue was more than the bar whore she had always allowed everyone to believe.

Damn her pride. It ran wide and deep inside her, that was for damned sure. Four years she had spent here, rubbing it in Nadine Grace's and Dayle Mackay's faces that they couldn't run her out of town. Rubbing it in Zeke's face that he couldn't ignore her.

For what? A few one-night stands? A few hours that in the end had left her feeling stark and hollow inside. And hurt. Damn, she hated feeling hurt. It was her weakness. Make her angry and she'd explode and just get it out of her system. Hurt her and it was like her brain short-circuited. She didn't care for people as a rule, didn't give them the chance to hurt her because she couldn't handle that kind of pain. Emotional pain. Rejection. Fuck, she hated rejection.

"Rogue, get your ass behind this bar for me," Jonesy called out as he lifted his bat from under the counter. "Jason's got trouble near the door."

Rogue jumped and jerked the bat out of his grip before he could stop her.

"You man the bar," she yelled back, adrenaline jangling through her nervous system. "I'll take care of the trouble."

She turned and moved away, slapped the bat in one hand, and grinned. She hadn't had a good rousing fight all year long. That was all she needed to get over this. She could just get mad, get it out of her system, and then get on with her business. She could clear the emotional bullshit out of her head, then get on with getting over Zeke.

"Dammit, Rogue!" She heard Jonesy cursing behind her and flashed him a smile over her shoulder before flipping her hair back and heading for the confrontation evolving close to the bar's entrance.

She didn't intend to use the bat. She had never used the bat. She'd used her knee only when she had to, but the times she'd been forced into it had been noted and most men tread warily around her now.

Moving quickly through the crowd, she pushed her way into the circle of customers that surrounded the two men. Billy Joe Wingate and Luke Taylor. Two rawboned country boys with a little too much drink and a whole lot of anger.

"Don't tell me what to do, fucker!" Billy Joe spat back at the bouncer behind him and sidestepped his grip. "I ain't goin' no damned where. Not till this son of a bitch apologizes." Billy Joe slammed his palms into Luke's wide chest, sending the other man back several spaces and bouncing against a female customer who slammed into the man behind her.

Oh fight.

"Whoa there. Whoa there." Rogue jumped between Luke and the woman's escort, her hands gripping each end of the bat and pressing it hard into the man's chest. "Hold back. We have it. Jason, get these boys out of here."

She glanced over her shoulder to see Jason and another bouncer struggling with Billy Joe and Luke.

"Take it outside, dammit," she yelled over the din as the bouncers dragged the two men to the door. She turned around quickly to the man she was holding back. "Keep your ass in here," she yelled, pressing against his chest with the bat for emphasis. "Don't make me have to take your head off, too."

She pushed away and swung around toward the door where Jason and the other bouncer were struggling with the two young men. Both combatants were a little too drunk and a little too full of adrenaline and anger.

"I said I ain't leaving here," Billy Joe yelled out, his hazel eyes wild with anger as he glared at Luke. "Not till you make him apologize."

"I ain't apologizing, you stupid little fucker," Luke screamed back at him. "You want to go dumb over a little bar whore, then you better get used to the truth."

"She ain't no whore."

Rogue was rushing to the door when Billy Joe managed to tear loose from Jason and throw a wild punch at Luke. Rogue chose that moment to push between them and went flying when that fist crashed into her cheekbone.

Stars exploded in front of her eyes as a vicious curse ripped from her throat. Turning, her foot kicked out and up, caught Billy Joe in the chest and knocked him back by maybe a foot. Dammit.

Her face felt shattered. She stumbled after the first instinctive reaction and nearly went to her knees as she shook her head and used the bat against the floor to catch herself.

Dammit. She said enough. She wasn't here to get a ham-sized fist in her face.

"Get him out of here!" She turned, yelling at Jason as the pain reverberated through her head. Hell, her eyes were going to pop out of their sockets.

Fury surged inside her, hot and deep as she slammed the bat into Billy Joe's chest, gripping both ends, trying to hold him back as he jerked out of Jason's hold again. Her boots slid on the wood floor as a chorus of curses and accusations began to ring around her head.

"Billy Joe, enough!" she yelled.

Billy Joe gripped her shoulders, snarled down at her, then drew his fist back, and as far as she was concerned, enough was enough.

Her knee swung up and connected between his heavy thighs as

his fist landed at the side of her head. His eyes went wide, a high-pitched whine filling the air as silence suddenly echoed around her, and Billy Joe Wingate went to his knees, his hands now clapped between his thighs.

Rogue's head was ringing, she swore there were spots in front of her eyes, and she was thanking God that Billy Joe had pulled his punch at the last second.

"Get them the fuck out of my bar!" she yelled at Jason as he gripped the younger man beneath the arms and began dragging him out the door.

The other bouncer, Timmy, was pushing Luke out and Rogue followed with the bat. Adrenaline and anger were pumping inside her. Her head hurt, her eyes hurt, and she was more furious with herself that she had allowed it to happen than she was at Billy Joe for throwing the first punch.

She stalked into the cool air of the night, glaring at the two men as the bouncers tossed them to the blacktop pavement. And of course they came up fighting, fists flying.

Hard hands gripped her shoulders and jerked her around, and she swore she saw Jonesy's face blur for a precious second.

"Have you lost your damned mind?" he screamed in her face, his expression twisted in fury, his eyes burning with it as he shook her roughly. "Look what the hell they did to your damned face. Damn you. You've fucking lost your mind."

He shook her until her head lobbed on her shoulders, back and forth, and she grew dizzy from the effort it took to retain consciousness. Just as she thought she was going to lose it, an enraged yell sounded behind her. She was jerked away from Jonesy, stumbled, and fell against another hard body.

Helping hands supported her as curses rained around her. Shaking her head, Rogue blinked desperately and fought to make out what was going on around her. When she finally managed to clear her gaze she saw Jonesy laid out on his stomach, Zeke straddling as he locked cuffs around his wrists.

Jonesy was still and silent, but he wasn't unconscious. He was staring back at her, his gaze filled with resignation and hurt. The kind of hurt fed by betrayal and steeped in emotion.

"What the hell are you doing?" She jerked away from the hands holding her, pushed back her hair, and stomped over to Zeke as he rose from Jonesy's back. "Let him go. Now."

"The hell I will! Have you seen your damned face yet, Rogue? What the hell happened here?"

"He didn't hit me." Her hand connected weakly with his chest. "It was those damned yahoos the bouncers are holding for you. Now let him the hell go."

"He was shaking you," he yelled into her face, his hands gripping her arms, and she could feel the bruises Jonesy had already left there.

"Yeah, well, what the hell are you getting ready to do?"

Rogue stared up at him, seeing the rage in his brown eyes, the tension in his hard, lean body. Zeke was ready to kill. A muscle ticked along his jaw and his lips were a flat line of anger as he scowled back at her.

"I warned you," he growled. "The next time he laid his hands on you—"

"Get over yourself!" she yelled back at him. "I can't have public rights with you, then I'll be damned if you can have protective ones with me. Now let him go."

She was in his face, almost nose to nose as his head lowered and he glared down at her. She could feel a heavy breeze whipping around them, feel the attention of the onlookers locked on them.

"Let him go, Gene." Zeke's lips pulled back from his teeth in a snarl.

"Let him go?" Gene questioned in amazement. "He was about to break her damned neck, Sheriff."

"Now." The order was an animalistic growl that sent a tremor racing up Rogue's spine. "Get the two that started this shit in lockup and dry them out. Take statements."

"Uhh, sure, Sheriff," Gene cleared his throat. "You're off duty, it's my call anyway."

"You're damned right I'm off duty." Zeke's fingers slid into her hair, clenched, and pulled her head back as his arm went around her back, jerking her to him. "And by God, I know how to take advantage of it."

His lips landed on hers in a kiss so fiery, so filled with hunger that she was left gasping. As quickly as it had begun, it was over. His head lifted, eyes narrowed, he stared back at her intently.

"In public," he snarled. "Now let's go, you're going to the hospital."

He swung her up in his arms before she could protest and amid the surprised gazes of customers, Jonesy, and Rogue was certain she glimpsed a Mackay or two, he carried her to the pickup he had used the night before. His personal vehicle. The one he had taken her in.

He swung the door open, then pushed her inside, one hand at her rear as he pressed her along the bench seat.

"Buckle up," he bit out angrily, his voice rough.

"I'm not going to the damned hospital. You try to make me and I promise you'll regret it." She buckled up before turning to him and eating him with her eyes. "You damned tattletale. I'm not going anywhere with you."

"Tattletale?" He twisted the key in the ignition and reversed out of the parking lot with a squeal of tires. "Since when am I a damned tattletale?"

"Since you called *Daddy* on me," she sneered. "Oh really, Zeke, did you think that worrying my father would save your ass? Like hell. I'm going to kick your ass."

She was enraged, furious, and the object of every frustration she had ever had was sitting in the truck beside her.

"And why the hell am I in your truck?" Her hand slapped the dashboard furiously as she turned and stared back at him.

"Because evidently it's where you damned well belong," he yelled back at her, his voice rough. "For God's sake, Rogue, why couldn't you just go back to Boston?"

That stopped her. Rogue narrowed her eyes on him, taking in the way his hands were clenched on the steering wheel, the hard set of his lips, the gleam of anger in his gaze when he glanced back at her. She could feel the blood thundering through her veins now, excitement and arousal pounding in her nerve endings.

"Why is it so damned important to you that I go back to Boston?" she argued. "Come on, Zeke, I have nothing to do with Joe and Jaime's death. Why the hell do you want me in Boston so bad unless it's because you can't keep that frozen heart of yours in cold storage as long as I'm here?"

His jaw tensed and his foot became heavier on the gas as they sped, she assumed, to his farm.

Zeke pressed his lips tightly together and reined in the anger pulsing through him. All he could see flashing through his mind was Rogue, shaking in Jonesy's grip, her head bouncing on her shoulders as her bartender shook the shit out of her.

There were bruises on her arms from the bastard's fingers, there were bruises on her face, courtesy of a fist he had heard about while he was cuffing Jonesy. One of those bastards had hit her, not once, but twice. There was a dark area close to her temple; her cheek was beginning to swell.

"It wasn't my heart I was worried about protecting," he ground out between his teeth. "Did it ever enter that stubborn little brain of yours that maybe I was trying to protect you?"

Silence continued to fill the cab of the truck as Zeke took the turn that led back to his farm. Hell, he should have rushed her to the emergency room, not to his farm, despite her objections.

"I don't need your protection." Her voice shook and he could hear the pain that resonated inside it. "I don't need anything from you, Zeke. I'm sick of your hot and cold attitude, and I'm really damned sick of only seeing you whenever you need to fuck."

He shot her a furious glare. Only when he needed to fuck? He made more rounds of that damned bar and the Mackay restaurant a day than he did any other business. He waited for her, watched for her, and damn her, all he did was think about her, and she thought he was just there for the sex?

"I didn't need to fuck tonight," he stated with an edge of disgust. "I was more concerned with getting you away from that damned bar crowd before you ended up with your head bashed in. For God's sake, Rogue, you waded into a bar fight between two men more than twice your size."

"For God's sake, Zeke," she drawled mockingly. "It just so happens it was *my bar*." She screamed the last two words at him. "You had no right to pull me out of there, and you sure as hell had no right to handcuff Jonesy."

"He's lucky I didn't kill him." Rage nearly consumed him at the remembered sight of Jonesy shaking her like a rag doll. "That's the second time that bastard thought he could manhandle you."

"And it's the second time that you jumped to the wrong conclusion," she accused him. "I think you do it deliberately."

Zeke wiped his hand down his face before clenching the steering wheel in a death grip. Just a few more minutes, he told himself. He'd be at the farm, when he should be taking her to the hospital, in the house, and then he could turn her over his knee and paddle her ass for daring to allow herself to be in such a situation.

Damned stubborn woman. She refused medical care but wouldn't care a damned bit to jump into the middle of another fucking barroom brawl.

"I don't just jump to the wrong conclusions," he said carefully, attempting to throttle his anger. "And Jonesy won't get away with this, Rogue. I'll have my own little talk with him."

Her eyes widened in alarm. In real alarm, there was no mockery in her gaze as she stared back at him now. "You're going to get into a fight with him because he shook me a little bit? Good God, Zeke, this is ridiculous."

"Not nearly as ridiculous as the knots you have me tied into." Zeke knew she was breaking through barriers he hadn't even realized were weakened by her. Hell, he'd just kissed her in front of a Wednesday night crowd at the bar and hauled her into his truck before reports had even been gathered. How many state and federal mandates had he broken with that one?

"Oh yeah, Zeke, you're really tied in knots over me," she snorted sarcastically. "So tied up that I'm continually trying to figure out exactly where I stand with you. It's like trying to catch the wind."

He heard the hurt in her voice and he didn't blame her for it. He was trying too hard to make certain she didn't end up in danger that her emotions were being sacrificed. That wasn't what he wanted. He wanted her safe, and until he identified the man the League sent in to do their dirty work, then she wouldn't be safe until she was out of Pulaski County.

"I'm not that damned hard to figure out," he finally protested with an edge of disgust. "Hell, Rogue, wanting you out of the county until this investigation is over doesn't mean I'm trying to deny anything that's between us. It simply means I'm trying to protect you."

He made the turn onto the graveled road that led to his farm and prayed that Shane hadn't come home for the night.

"Oh yeah, that's why you just left last night rather than coming upstairs with me," she pointed out.

"I didn't come upstairs with you because we were too angry with each other for what we both know would have happened. I won't fuck you while I'm angry with you, Rogue. We have things to settle between us. I wanted those things settled first."

"Things like me leaving town?" she argued. "You can forget that one, Zeke. It's not going to happen."

Yeah, he'd already pretty much figured that one out. Blowing out a deep breath he tried to consider an alternative way to make certain she didn't end up hurt, or worse, dead. Hell, he'd already lost his wife to an investigation; he didn't want to lose Rogue to another one.

"We'll discuss other options," he said as he pulled into the driveway and shut off the ignition before turning to face her. "I won't let you risk yourself though, I want that made clear here and now. Until this is over, you can't work the bar, you can't travel alone. Not until I figure out what's going on."

Rogue's expression was stark as the outside lights reflected off her pale flesh.

"You've learned something more," she whispered.

Zeke breathed out heavily. "Joe and Jaime were murdered, Rogue, and I suspect their grandmother was as well. If she was, that means you are in danger. Whoever started this isn't finished, and I have a bad feeling about it. Whoever it is will end up coming after you."

Her lips parted, vulnerable, silken soft as her tongue licked over them, leaving a glistening sheen of dampness that could have tempted a saint.

A hint of fear flashed in her eyes, and he hadn't wanted to see that. He wanted her wild, angry, laughing, or mocking, but never hurt or frightened. And seeing it made Zeke want to kill.

SEVENTEEN

Rogue sat on the couch, an ice bag on the side of her face. The bruising really wasn't that bad, but she could see why Zeke would have been a tad upset. It sure as hell didn't look pretty.

She had changed out of the leather pants and silky camisole top she had worn at the bar and into one of Zeke's white shirts. The material enveloped her in his scent, in a sense of warmth.

With her legs curled beneath her she watched as he made a small fire in the fireplace across from her. He had changed his uniform for jeans, though he wasn't wearing a shirt or shoes.

He hadn't said much after they entered the house, and Rogue didn't know what to say at this point. She had called the bar while Zeke showered to learn that Jonesy had been released and was still running the bar. At least she didn't have to worry about him.

She was going to have to make a decision about the bar though.

She knew Natches was looking to sell his share in the Mackay restaurant if she decided she wanted to buy him out. It was something to think about. Hell, it was something she had been thinking about for months.

"How does your face feel?" Zeke straightened from the fireplace, turned, and moved toward her.

He didn't walk, he stalked. Dark, heavy muscle flexed in his arms, chest, and powerful abdomen. His jeans lay low on his hips and beneath them, she could tell he was still heavily aroused.

"My face is fine." She let the ice pack drop to the coffee table in front of her before leaning back against the couch cushions as he sat down beside her.

His fingers curled along her jaw to turn her face to where he could get a better look.

"You should have gone to the hospital," he said, his voice dark, rough.

"I've had worse." She shrugged. "The absolute worst hit I ever had was given by a woman. She was with a small biker club a couple of years ago. She gave me a concussion with her fist. That wasn't fun." She smiled back at him and gave him a wicked little wink. "Come on, Zeke, stop glaring at me, I'm fine."

"Yeah, you're fine. For now." He shook his head as he released her jaw. "What about the next time, Rogue?"

"Well, I'll deal with the next time when it comes around," she told him quietly, then asked hesitantly, "Are you worried because of what happened to your wife?"

Rogue watched as all emotion cleared from his face with her question.

"What did you hear about my wife?" he finally asked.

It was a good thing she wasn't frightened of big men like her sister was, or cared who she pissed off.

"I heard your wife died during an investigation you were conducting in L.A. You were posing as a SWAT member interested in the BDSM lifestyle to expose another member that was involved in drugs. It's amazing the information you can get if you dig enough." And evidently, she had dug just enough.

Zeke felt his jaw clench. Hell, his entire body tightened with furious tension. He'd been able to cover up most of the talk his father had instigated when he first arrived home. The rumors his father had started had only one purpose in mind. To protect the League, because he had known damned good and well who had killed Zeke's wife. And it wasn't anything Zeke had done.

"My wife died because of an investigation," he agreed. "But it wasn't the investigation I was involved with in L.A. It had to do with something more personal."

He let her see his eyes and what was reflected in them. Shame welled inside him, and that same fury that had followed him for so many years.

"Meaning?" She watched him intently for long seconds.

"Meaning, what happened to Elaina had more to do with the reason my mother left with me for L.A." Staring into the fire he fought to hold the full truth back from her. She deserved to know everything; unfortunately, Zeke couldn't tell her everything.

"That was a long time ago," she whispered.

Zeke nodded. "Long ago and far away, I'd hoped. It followed us though when Mom decided to threaten Dad with something she knew. She was killed first. When I began investigating things myself, Elaina was killed and I was warned off the investigation." His jaw tightened with the memories. "I had Shane to think of. I backed off then. When I returned here, I started checking into it again. I've been tracking the same man ever since. A man that killed for the Freedom League. The same group Dayle and Nadine were a part of."

He heard her hard, indrawn breath and glanced back at her.

"Dad was a part of the League," he told her then. "And I think it goes without saying that this stays between the two of us."

Her violet eyes flashed with anger. "You can be an asshole, Zeke," she accused him. "Of course it stays between us."

He almost grinned at her vehemence. "I figured it would." He had known it would.

"So you blame yourself for your mother and wife's death?"

Violet eyes darkened. Zeke could see the conflicting emotions that raged in her eyes and felt his heart clench. There was no recrimination in her gaze, only acceptance and trust. He shook his head at the sight of it.

"Damn, you're too trusting," he said mockingly. "I was the reason for it, Rogue. I fucked up, it's that simple. Somehow, I managed to ask the wrong question of the wrong person. They found out what I was doing and they struck back. The head of the League is behind bars now, but that killer is still out there. I don't have proof yet, but I know in my gut that he killed Joe and Jaime, and I suspect he killed Callie Walker. There are too many similarities to their murders and the murders that man has committed over the years."

"Then this has something to do with what happened last year as well? When the Mackays and Cranston arrested the homeland terrorists?" she said. "I'd wondered. I knew Joe and Jaime were close with the Mackays, but I wasn't certain if they were supplying them with information or not. Jonesy and I wondered about it, but they never said anything and I didn't ask. But I knew they had connections to some of the suspects. They worked for Dayle for a while, and they were friends with several of the men arrested."

"And Jonesy isn't to know anything else," he warned her. "Not until I know for certain who is who and talks where."

"Don't piss me off, Zeke. I know how to keep my mouth shut," she warned him.

"And I know how to protect you now," he promised her. "I won't let you get hurt by this, Rogue."

"But we're responsible for ourselves, Zeke." She sighed. "If I was frightened by someone who showed up at my door, then I'd take the necessary steps to protect myself. That would be common sense, wouldn't you think?"

He wondered if any other woman would have thought of that. He wished he had thought of it then, perhaps so many things would have been different. But it wasn't different, and Rogue shouldn't have to protect herself.

"No," he said gently as he let the backs of his fingers caress over her bruised cheek. "It would be my place to protect you."

And that was how Elaina had felt. It was his place to make certain she was protected so she could enjoy her life as she pleased.

"Look, stud, I don't need you to protect li'l ole me," she informed him testily. "I've been doing just fine for the past five years, and I'm quite certain I'll continue doing so on my own. It's not your place to pave my way with bubble wrap, okay?"

No, it wasn't okay, because Zeke knew she had no idea what they could be facing. Death could come around any corner, and she wouldn't be prepared for it. And if the killer's trend continued, then eventually, Rogue would be targeted, if she wasn't already. She was close to Joe, Jaime, and their grandmother. She was also close to him.

"It's my place to take care of you." He cupped the back of her neck, holding her head in place as he relished the feel of her silken flesh against his fingertips and the way she seemed to push closer to his touch.

Her violet gaze was dark with emotion as he held her in place.

"You just keep thinking that, Zeke," she said mockingly. "And I'll even let you believe it, when it suits me."

He almost laughed. Damn her, she shouldn't have the ability

to make him laugh when he was facing more emotional upheaval than he had ever known in his life.

"Brat." His head lowered, his lips whispered over hers.

"Stud," she drawled as her lips parted and she pressed closer.

Zeke started with small, sipping kisses. His lips tugged at her lower one, his tongue stroked over it as he felt her hands against his bare chest. Her fingers stretched out, touched tentatively, then curled against the hair-roughened flesh of his chest. Delicate nails rasped over his flesh, and a small, feminine moan left her lips as his settled more firmly over them.

She was sweet and hot and as addictive as hell. Damn, he'd missed her in the bed last night, ached for her. She was like a ray of sunshine, and she hadn't spilled into his life all day. That was uncalled for, he decided. He had to have a taste of her, morning, noon, and night.

What the hell made him think he could do without her? he wondered as he pulled her closer and groaned at the taste of her kiss. There was no way in hell he could bear for her to leave his life, not when he was just beginning to learn what having her meant. Not when he was learning, with each new touch, her effect on his own sexuality.

He wanted to cherish this kiss, he wanted to make it last for an eternity, but she went to his head faster than moonshine. She made him drunk on his own lust, made him crazy to have her in so many ways. In every way possible.

Rogue trembled from the sheer power of Zeke's kiss. She leaned in closer to him, let her fingertips rake over the hard, muscular line of his chest and let herself drown in the pleasure building inside her.

There was a different element to his touch this time. His hands were just as firm, his kiss just as hot, but each touch, each fractured breath of sound seemed more intense now, sharper, darker.

Her hands smoothed from his chest to his shoulders, her fingers gripping the hard muscles there as she felt the clamoring sensations bombarding her now. His kiss was hungrier, rougher. Sensation rioted through her as his tongue plunged past her lips and found her own. She tasted him, reveled in him. His taste was completely male, rife with lust, with passion. It seared her lips, it seared her mind, and left her reaching, pressing tighter against him, desperate for more.

Her arms twined around his neck, her fingers gripping the back of his head as she fought to get closer, always closer.

"There you go, baby," he growled against her lips as she came to her knees and straddled his powerful thighs. "So sweet."

A cry tore from her lips as her head tipped back on her shoulders; the feel of his hands sliding beneath the long shirt to cup her ass held her enthralled. It felt so damned good. The way his calloused hands cupped the curve of her butt and flexed into the muscle there. His fingertips rotated, caressed, pulled against the twin globes and sent a spike of heated pleasure burning into the hidden entrance there.

Writhing against him she could feel her breath panting from her lips, the tips of her breasts pressing into the material of the shirt as she rubbed against his chest like a cat.

"Damn, there you go, darlin'," he crooned. "Go wild for me, Rogue. Let me feel you lose yourself, baby."

She had lost herself with his first kiss. She lost herself in the sensations pouring over her and the heart-melting emotions she couldn't escape, no matter how hard she tried.

Loving Zeke Mayes could be a dead-end street. It could be the most painful lesson of her entire life. She knew it, and she was walking into it with her eyes wide open.

Well, figuratively wide open. At the moment they were closed. Her hips churned against him, broken cries falling from her lips as she pressed against the hard ridge of his cock with desperate strokes of her silk-covered pussy. Her clit was swollen, throbbing in need. Her vagina was spilling its slick dampness, and she had no will to fight it.

"Sweet Rogue." His hands slid over her ass, along her sides, then cupped the swollen mounds of her breasts. Calloused thumbs flicked over her engorged nipples and sent a flurry of sensation to strike at her clit.

She wanted it to last forever. She wanted the flames racing over her flesh to hold her spellbound for life. She didn't want it to end. She didn't want to chance ever losing this pleasure or this man.

"Hold on to me, Rogue."

He was lifting her, rising to his feet as she wrapped her legs around his hips and cried out at the feel of the hard ridge of his cock pressing tighter against her humid flesh.

"This is so good," she moaned as he walked. "Oh God, Zeke, its damned wicked."

Each step was agony, it was desire in its rawest form.

"You haven't seen wicked yet," he promised her as he mounted the stairs, his hands moving to her ass again, cupping the cheeks and holding her to him as he moved up the steps.

Each step raked fiery sensations across her clit and drove fragmented arcs of sensation throughout her body.

It should be illegal to give this much pleasure, she thought. There should be a law against warping a woman's mind until nothing mattered but one man's touch.

As he carried her, she made it a mission to ensure that he was just as crazed from her touch. Her lips moved over the side of his neck as she ignored his groan for mercy. Her teeth raked over his pulse, then her lips settled at the base of his neck, parted, and she drew a small bite of tough skin into her mouth for a sizzling little nip.

She had carried his brand more than once; now he could carry hers.

She was surprised as one hand jerked from her butt. His palm covered the back of her head and a strangled groan left his lips as he seemed to stumble against the wall.

Rogue tightened her legs around his hips and kept her lips at his neck. She licked, nipped, and suckled delicately at the masculine flesh as she heard him curse, then whisper her name as though on a prayer.

"I should spank you for what you do to me." His voice was dark and rough as he moved into a bedroom.

"Promises, promises," she murmured.

A second later Rogue felt her back meet the mattress, though she refused to release the hold she had on him. Her hips lifted and she ground herself against his erection. A gasp of agonized need left her throat at the pure sensual pleasure that raged from the action.

"Get this damned shirt off." He forced her arms down as he leaned back and ripped buttons and all.

"You like tearing my clothes," she gasped.

"I want you naked. Naked and ready for me. Besides, it's my shirt," he reminded her, his gaze going over her breasts as they rose and fell with each desperate breath she tried to take.

Evidently, he didn't care if she breathed or not. His head lowered and Rogue watched, suspended, held in a vortex of pleasure as his lips descended, parted, and sucked a tight, hard nipple into the hot, damp cavern of his mouth.

Arching, she cried out at the pleasure. It whipped its way across her nerve endings, sent jagged forks of heat racing across her flesh.

Tightening her legs around his hips, she lifted closer to the erection throbbing beneath his jeans and dug her nails into his scalp as he ground against her.

There was nothing like being held against him, feeling his touch, losing herself in the pleasure. He caressed each nipple, sucked it deliciously, and reduced her to begging for his possession.

"Not yet," he growled long moments later as he pulled her legs from around his waist.

His fingers hooked in the elastic band of her panties as he pulled back from her and stripped the fragile material from her legs before dropping it to the floor.

Anticipation and sexual awareness sizzled in the air now. Rogue felt perspiration dampening her flesh, sizzling over her skin as he straightened at the side of the bed and lowered his hands to the band of his jeans.

He disposed of his jeans quickly, efficiently, and within seconds stood before her, naked and aroused. Rogue could feel anticipation like a physical caress as he watched her, his eyes narrowed, one hand gripping the stalk of his cock as his expression tightened with hunger.

"Spread your legs for me," he ordered, his voice rough.

Rogue spread her legs slowly, watching him as excitement flooded her body. In that moment she realized how much he meant to her, and it terrified her. She should have run from him; she should have pushed him out of her life rather than giving him the opportunity to hurt her more.

But she couldn't run. She couldn't say no. Because she needed him more than she had ever wanted to admit.

"Have mercy," he growled, his gaze centered between her thighs as he moved between her legs, his broad shoulders pushing them farther apart as he stretched out below her. "Sweet, sweet Rogue. You'll be the death of me."

She didn't have time to argue the statement. Rogue's head tilted back on a strangled cry as his lips lowered to the wet flesh between her thighs. Hot and voracious, he consumed her from the first lick.

His tongue swirled around her clit, licked at the overly sensitive folds and sent her flying into a pleasure she couldn't deny if she wanted to.

The rush of pleasure was intoxicating. Her legs fell farther apart as her fingernails dug into his scalp. The sensations were overwhelming, thundering through her veins. Nothing mattered but holding him to her, feeling him, touching him.

"Zeke, please," she whispered as the pleasure began to build and tighten between her thighs.

"Oh, you please me very much," he promised before his lips pursed over her clit and gave her a sucking little kiss.

Her hips arched as excruciating pleasure tore through her from the caress.

"Easy, baby," he crooned as he lifted his head. "Just feel good for me."

His lips returned, another kiss, the feel of his fingers easing through her juices, moving lower, lower, then touching, caressing the entrance to her rear.

Sensation whipped through her; it drove white-hot spikes of pleasure through her clit, her womb. Heat whipped through her, bonded her to him.

His fingers were as wicked as his mouth. He drew her dampness from her pussy back to the tiny entrance of her rear. He stroked, he massaged, then one broad finger slid inside her, stretching the opening and sending flares of heat racing through her.

She wanted more. Needed more. She could feel her mind dissolving as she cried out, arched, and drove his finger deeper only to cry out in protest as he retreated.

"Turn over, Rogue."

He didn't give her time to turn. Before she could catch her breath he rose between her thighs, gripped her hips, and turned her to her stomach.

Rogue felt the hands at her hips pulling her to her knees.

His hand smoothed over her rear, then landed in a series of small, heated taps that had her shuddering, shaking from need as he used the fingers of his other hand to lubricate and stretch her rear.

She was panting for breath, feeling the burning stretch of his fingers, the tension in the air, the hunger that seemed to sear every inch of her flesh.

She was crying out his name, lost in sensation, lost in the pure dominance of what he was doing. The significance of the act swirled through her head. A sense of submission, of bonding wove silk-covered chains through her psyche.

When she felt the broad head of his cock against the opening she stilled, barely able to breathe now and definitely unable to protest.

"Are you mine, Rogue?" His hand smoothed over her rear before he used both hands to part the cheeks of her.

"Are you mine?" Her voice was strangled, the need to own as much of him as he owned of her tearing inside her.

"Always yours now, Rogue." His voice was heavy as he held her still and pressed inside her. "All of me, Rogue. Take all of me."

"Oh God, Zeke." Her back arched as burning pleasure tore through her. Her rear parted beneath the pressure as jagged lightning-hot sensations began to race through the nerve endings there.

She thought the pleasure couldn't become more brutal. She thought she had experienced everything she could know about the extremity of sensation.

When the broad head popped inside the tender entrance, Zeke paused. She was lost in the flames of that small penetration when she felt another one.

"Zeke!" She tried to scream his name, but the breathless sound was more of a weak plea.

She felt the vibration of the vibrator tuck against the entrance to her pussy. Felt his wrist moving against her thigh as he impaled her slowly with it.

"There, baby," he crooned behind her as the toy slid slowly inside her, parting her, working every nerve ending with an insidious, buzzing caress.

When it was lodged fully inside her she thought she was going insane from the pleasure. The vibration of the toy inside her set mini-explosions off inside her nerve endings. Her pussy flexed around it, her rear tightened around the intrusion easing inside it. She was a singular mass of sensation and she was drowning in the pleasure-pain filling her.

"Easy," Zeke groaned behind her.

Easy? She didn't want easy. She wanted it all.

"Here, baby." He grabbed her arm, eased it down until her hand was between her thighs. "Hold it inside you."

Rogue whimpered at the demand as her fingers curled around the heavy base. He pressed her hand forward, pushing the toy fully inside her until the thick, rough extension that rose from the base began to massage her clit.

She lost her mind, her senses. Sensation tore through her as Zeke began to move behind her. His hands gripped her hips; his cock surged into her ass as he began to fuck her with long, even strokes. She was filled, stretched, burning, and aware of each and every stroke against nerve endings that were too sensitive to bear the pleasure for long.

Her pussy was filled, stretched tight with the buzzing toy. Her ass was on fire from the heavy strokes he was pounding into her now. She could feel every pulsing throb of his erection, each thick vein that ran the length of it.

Her head dug into the mattress as his hands tightened on her hips, and she felt the pleasure begin to build to critical mass inside her.

Every bone and muscle in her body began to tighten. She lost control of her senses, of her body. Fiery flames raced over her flesh and exploded in her womb as a long, agonized wail left her mouth.

Shock waves of destructive ecstasy flamed out of control and tore through her sensitive flesh as pinpoints of sensation ruptured inside her.

She screamed his name, the muscles of her rear tightened, trying to lock his erection inside her. Her pussy clenched on the vibrator, tightened. Her clit exploded in a cataclysm of sensation that raced to her pussy, her womb, and every point beyond as she heard him cry out her name.

He thrust inside her hard and deep, his hands tightened on her, the hard muscles of his thighs pressed into the backs of her legs, and within seconds she felt his release.

The feel of each shockingly heated spurt of semen inside her threw her higher, harder into the maelstrom of rapture.

She was flying through space and time, locked in a pleasure so intense she wondered if her heart could bear it.

Her back arched, her nails dug into the blankets, and finally, with one last powerful explosion inside her, she was flung into a place where only heat and pleasure resided. Where she knew nothing, felt nothing but the sensation coursing through her.

She was left shaking, trembling in exhaustion when it was finished. She had collapsed to the bed. Zeke covered her, still buried inside her, his lips at her neck, his groans still filling her ears.

His hands still gripped her hips, his lips were pressed into her neck, his kiss as fierce as the hold he had on her.

"God, yes," he groaned. "Ah God, Rogue."

His voice was tormented, breathless. Behind her, his chest rose and fell harshly against her back as her flesh spasmed in pleasure around his cock and the erotic toy still pressed inside her.

At least the vibrator wasn't buzzing any longer. At some point he must have turned it off. Damned good thing he had, because she doubted she had the mental capacity to do it.

But she had emotional capacity. Her heart, her soul, and she knew she had just given both to Zeke.

EIGHTEEN

She was going to destroy him. That was the singular thought in his head as Zeke carefully covered Rogue with a blanket after she slipped into an exhausted slumber. She slept as deeply as a child, curled up in the center of the bed. Red gold lashes feathered her cheeks, her pink lips free of lipstick, her face free of makeup, she looked like some innocent little fairy come to tempt his mind to insanity.

She was doing a damned good job of making him crazy, too. Because he knew he wouldn't let her go after tonight. She was his, and now she was going to have to deal with the man she had tempted from the darkness.

She could handle him, of that Zeke was certain. The problem was would she want to handle him once she learned the ground rules?

Checking to make certain she was sleeping deeply after their shower, he cleaned the vibrator he had placed in the drawer of his bedside table after she had been at the house the last time and returned it and the tube of lubricating gel into the drawer.

He had known it would come to this. He had known that when he got her in his bed, where that loss of control would lead to.

After kissing her brow gently, he dressed and left the house. It was still dark, though dawn wasn't far away. Which meant he didn't have much time to do what he needed to do.

He was in control now, but he hadn't maintained his control earlier. He had known the moment he bared her pretty ass to his gaze that he was severely out of control. Thank God that she hadn't realized the line he had been riding. But he had known. He had known and he hadn't been able to pull himself back from the brink.

It had been all he could do not to spank her as he wanted to, and that was only because he had been so desperate to test her sexual submission to him.

She was innocent, as of days ago, a virgin. She wouldn't have known the implications of what he was doing to her, and she shouldn't have accepted it so easily. There should have been a measure of fear, of wariness from her. He had expected to have to ease her, gentle her. Instead, she had lifted that pert little butt right up to him and invited him to do his worst.

He wiped his hand over his face as he started the truck's engine and reversed out of the driveway. She had taken a part of him that night that he didn't think he would ever be able to give a woman. She had stolen his heart when he had believed he didn't have a heart to steal.

It wasn't just the sex or her submission to it. It wasn't any one thing, Zeke realized. It was the realization at the moment he had taken her that she didn't just belong to him, but he belonged to her. Because in all the years that he had known of the dark sexual core he possessed, he had never known a woman like Rogue.

She was adventurous, wild as the wind, but steady, honorable. She was a woman that would love a man with every ounce of her heart, and he knew she loved him. It had been in her eyes, in her sighs, in every response she had given to every touch he had bestowed.

She was his, and protecting her was his right, ensuring that she was never, ever harmed was his privilege. Making certain he never lost her because of the job that meant so much to him was imperative.

That part would be harder than what he was setting out to do tonight. Tonight, he would make certain one particular man understood that he was never to lay his hands on her again.

Keeping control when he had driven up on the scene had nearly been impossible. Giving in to her demands that he release Jonesy had been even harder. But he had realized something about Rogue a long time ago. She would lay down her own life for a friend; she had proved that when she had defended Shane and lost her own reputation. He wasn't going to risk such a confrontation, especially in public, over Jonesy.

No, he would take care of Jonesy privately, just between the two of them while Rogue slept.

It didn't take more than a half hour to arrive at the Bar. It was close to four in the morning now, but Jonesy's truck was still in the parking lot, as Zeke knew it would be.

The bartender was usually in the bar until daylight, leaving just as the sun peeked over the horizon and didn't return until just before the evening shift. His assistant bartenders along with Rogue opened the bar at five every evening except Sunday.

He pulled his truck into the front lot and shut off the engine before leaving the vehicle. The front door was locked until Zeke strode up to it and pounded on the heavy panel.

He didn't have to wait long before it was pushed open and Jonesy stepped outside, his expression wary. Bald and heavily muscled, Jonesy was a bull of a man that most men were uncertain of antagonizing.

Zeke intended to do more than antagonize him.

"Change your mind about arrestin' me?" Jonesy's broad face twisted into a sneer as he faced Zeke, his heavy fists clenching. "Ain't you scared Rogue might cry a little bit if you do?"

A hard laugh left the bartender's throat at the statement. As though the thought of Rogue crying amused him. It sent a spurt of pure undiluted rage building inside him.

"Whether or not Rogue sheds tears over you isn't what concerns me, Jonesy," Zeke drawled. "The bruises you left on her arm tonight does."

For a moment there was a flicker of regret in the bartender's eyes. It was gone just as quickly and replaced with a hateful sneer.

"She don't ever listen to reason," he bit out furiously. "That girl waded right into that fight as though it was her business who was slingin' fists. Better a bruise on the arm from me than a snapped neck from someone else."

Like hell.

Zeke didn't intend to stand around arguing with the other man; he had come here for a reason.

"This makes the second time you've laid your hand on what belongs to me," Zeke state softly. "You don't touch what's mine, Jonesy, not for any reason. No way, no how."

"Last I heard no man had papers on that girl," Jonesy grunted. "I been watching out for her for four years now. Where the hell were you when she needed someone at her back? You were whorin', Sheriff. Sleeping with tramps and trash while I was watching after

Rogue. Now you think you can waltz right in here and treat her like you treat your flybys? Not while I can still talk some sense into her."

"Like one of my flybys?" Zeke's eyes narrowed.

"Yeah, your fly-by-night little whores that you keep hanging on a string. You know, Sheriff, the ones you hide in the day and fuck at night? Or was I wrong about Rogue? Maybe hangin' with that Walker trash has rubbed off on her after all."

That was it. Zeke saw the haze of red that descended over his eyes. Before he could hold back the impulse, adrenaline surged through his veins. His fist flew, collided with Jonesy's rock-hard jaw, and sent the other man careening into the side of the building.

Jonesy was a bull of a man. The hit that took him by surprise wasn't the only one it would take to make him realize who was the top dog in Rogue's life. Zeke would rather kill him, hell, he'd rather lock him up and see him suffer, but he knew Rogue would never stand for it.

That meant going at it man to man.

The fight that ensued was one of the hardest fistfights Zeke had been in, possibly in his life. Jonesy's fists were like hams and slammed into flesh like bricks. Zeke's kidneys took a bruising and if Zeke wasn't mistaken, Jonesy may have lost a tooth.

"You bastard!" Jonesy cursed when his fist missed Zeke's jaw.

A second later a strangled, "Fuck you!" tore from Jonesy's lips as Zeke kicked him back against the cement wall of the bar.

Jonesy's nose was bleeding, his lips were split, there was a cut beneath his eye, and he was holding his stomach where Zeke had landed a hard kick only moments before.

Jonesy surged away from the wall. This time, his broad fist connected with Zeke's jaw, throwing him back as stars exploded before his eyes for precious seconds. It gave Jonesy the opening he needed to slam another fist into his kidneys and another hard right to his jaw.

Zeke buried his fist in Jonesy's gut, threw him back, slammed his fist into his stomach again, his jaw, and another to his kidneys.

The bartender went to his knees, coughing, wheezing as he held his stomach.

"Touch her again, and next time, you'll spend time behind bars," Zeke warned him, his own breathing rough, tearing in his chest as he dragged Jonesy up by the torn collar of his shirt and threw him back up against the wall. "Do you understand me, Jonesy?"

"I didn't hurt her," Jonesy coughed roughly. "I wouldn't hurt Rogue."

"Do you understand me?" He slammed Jonesy's head against the wall. "Answer me, damn you."

"I wouldn't hurt her."

"I said you don't touch her again. Ever," Zeke snarled.

"I don't know about you, Zeke, but I think he understands now."

Zeke froze at the sound of Rogue's voice behind him. He could feel his stomach tighten now with a sense of dread. Hell, she was supposed to be at home asleep.

"We're fucked," Jonesy wheezed out a whisper, his eyes widening as he stared back at Zeke. "Shit. Damn. She's gonna de-ball us."

"Let him go, Zeke." Her voice was soft, the enunciation of each word carefully precise.

Zeke eased his grip on Jonesy's shirt, grimaced, and once again met Jonesy's gaze.

"Stay out of this," he warned the bartender softly.

"Way out." Jonesy nodded quickly. "So far out I'm just a memory."

This was bad and Zeke knew it. He clenched his teeth, exhaled, then turned to face the wrath of Rogue.

A cab was pulling out of the parking lot behind her. She stood there, dressed in the leather skirt she had worn the night before and his white shirt. The shirt hung below the skirt and made the black platform heels look even more wicked than they had before.

"You're supposed to be at the house," he said, keeping his voice firm, even. "I left you there for a reason."

She looked around him where the entrance door to the bar slammed closed behind Jonesy. Jonesy was running like a rat off a sinking ship.

"So you could beat up my friend?" Anger glittered in her eyes and flushed her face as she moved slowly toward him, each step slow and careful.

Wild, waist-length red gold curls swirled around her in the early dawn light. Violet eyes glittered with fury in her pale face.

She looked like an enraged fairy intent on murder and mayhem. And it was his ass she was intent on murdering.

"So I could come to an understanding with your friend," he told her, wiping his mouth with his arm as he moved, striding toward her and gripping her arm in a firm hold.

"Let me go!" She jerked at his hold, her expression twisting with fury. "Don't even try to touch me."

"Upstairs." Zeke hardened his voice as he pulled her to the door Jonesy had gone through earlier. "Now. I'm not going to fight with you in the parking lot."

"Why not, you fought Jonesy in the parking lot," she screamed back at him, trying to kick out at him as he pulled her to the entrance. "You can damned well fight me here."

"Jonesy is a whole other matter, Rogue." Zeke tamped down the frustration rising inside him. He kept his control firmly in place. The situation with Jonesy was resolved as far as he was concerned.

Man to man. He had a feeling Jonesy wouldn't forget the consequences of manhandling Rogue again.

Zeke would have preferred to see the bastard fired, but until Rogue was fed up with the other man's attitude, the only thing Zeke could do was keep a close eye on the situation. And an even closer eye on Rogue. If she didn't end up killing him before the day was over.

"You've gone too far this time, Zeke," she cried out as he kept his fingers locked around her wrist and all but dragged her through the bar. "This was none of your business."

"That's where you're wrong. When another man dares to lay a hand on my woman, it's very much my damned business," he growled.

He wouldn't have it. Possessive tendencies aside, Zeke wouldn't have stood for any man to handle a woman as Jonesy had Rogue, at any time. Jonesy wasn't behind bars simply because of Rogue's interference. Any other man would have been cooling his heels in the detention center.

"And who says I'm your woman?" she snarled back at him as they moved through the private door and took the turn to the stairs and her apartment above. "I don't remember giving you permission to go Neanderthal on me."

"Sure you did," he drawled as they reached the landing and he tested the doorknob.

Son of a bitch, she'd left the door unlocked again. He turned and stared down at her. "What did I tell you about locking your door up here?"

"Excuse me, Zeke, but I was unaware I'd be spending the night elsewhere," she snapped.

He shook his head at the apparent lack of judgment she had used.

Rogue wanted to smack the condescension from his face. She

would have to get her wrist back first. She tugged at it again as he pushed the door open slowly and checked out the living area of the large apartment.

Hell, he should have brought his weapon with him.

"You are being so overprotective, Zeke. Have I mentioned how much I hate being protected?"

Rogue watched as Zeke moved away from her. She crossed her arms over her breasts as she glared at him hatefully.

How dare he start a fight with her bartender, over her? It was her fight; she didn't need his big male fists taking care of her business for her.

"I don't care how much you hate it," he stated as he moved through the living and kitchen area and entered her bedroom.

"You don't care how much I hate it?" She gaped at his back as it disappeared through the doorway before she moved quickly to catch up with him. "What the hell are you doing searching my apartment, and what do you mean, you don't care how much I hate it?"

He paused as he stepped out of the bathroom and stared back at her with those predatory, determined eyes of his. That look, so dominant and forceful, should have had her rage hitting to peak rather than sparking memories of the time they had spent in his bed throughout the night and the forceful sexuality he had displayed.

"I mean, it's too damned late to jump out of the game." His voice was forceful, dark. "I warned you, you were getting into something you might not be able to handle, Rogue. Now you'll just have to learn how to deal with it. What Jonesy did was out of line and you refused to fire him, so I took care of it."

"By beating him half to death? By letting him beat on you?"

Blood marred his chin and jaw, his shirt was torn, and he was going to have a black eye. Rogue had had to curl her fingers into fists when she had first seen the damage. They had stayed curled, waiting on an opportunity to add her own bruise to his hard, stubborn expression.

His lip was swelling and she was betting his ribs were already bruising. Not that he looked or acted as though he had so much as a scratch. His shoulders were straight and arrogance was stamped thick and clear on his expression.

"It's a male thing." He shrugged.

"It's a male thing? A male thing?" Incredulity filled her as she stared back at him. "You went completely Neanderthal because it was a male thing?"

"You wouldn't take care of the situation and fire his ass, thereby eliminating the risk of him further abusing you, so I took care of it."

"You took care of it?" She blinked back at him. She couldn't believe the utter audacity it took for him to say such a thing. "Is this how you take care of domestic squabbles, too, Zeke? Just beat the hell out of any man that doesn't do as you think he should?"

"I'm on duty then." His smile was tight. "I wasn't on duty this morning. What's more, the fact that you're my woman changes those rules. I took care of what's mine."

"Oh my God," she gasped. "You've lost your mind."

She stared back at him, amazed, bemused as he stalked slowly toward her. There was something about the move and shift of his body now. An aura of sex and danger that seemed to fill the room and surround her as she backed away from him. "You did not buy me. You don't own me. You are a crazy man."

He smiled, a slow arrogant curl of his lips. "I bet your panties are wet, Rogue. I bet you're so damned turned on right now that a good hard breath would get you off."

He was so right.

"You've lost your mind," she accused him as her back met the wall.

"Your pussy is hot and wet," he growled. "Come on, Rogue, tell me it's not."

She shook her head, wishing she could ignore the weakness in her knees, the tingling between her thighs.

"You're bloody, bruised, and arrogant," she snapped back. "That is not a turn-on, Zeke."

"Liar." Black velvet and sex, his voice was rasping, primal. It sent a heat wave crashing through her body.

Rogue swallowed tightly. The wall was at her back; Zeke was a wall barely pressing against her breasts. Her nipples hardened, sensitized as his chest brushed against her, stimulating them further as his hands braced against the wall, bracketing her in.

"What is your problem?" She wished her voice didn't sound so weak. She wished she kept the anger burning rather than the arousal, but it was the arousal, the hunger, spurred by the complete dominance he was displaying, that took precedence.

"My problem?" His eyes narrowed, dark brown lashes shielding his thoughts, his emotions as he moved one hand from the wall beside her and brushed his knuckles down the exposed line of her throat. "My problem is a hard-on that only you can satisfy. My problem is the fact that I tried, Rogue, to stay away from you. I tried to warn you that you were dealing with something you might not be prepared to handle. But did you listen?" He brushed a whispery kiss beside her lips and nearly stole her breath with the caress.

What the hell was wrong with her? She would have slammed her knee into the balls of any other man who dared to attempt to dominate her. She didn't consider herself submissive, but right now, she felt so feminine, so much weaker than Zeke, and yet so much a part of him, that she didn't know what else to call it.

Were women somehow programmed to at least sexual submis-

sion? Was it a part of their genetic makeup, the need to be conquered sexually, to be protected?

"This is crazy," she gasped as his lips slid from the corner of
hers and moved to her jawline.

Her head rested back against the wall and tilted to the side
to expose the sensitive underside of her jaw. Weakening pleasure
flowed through her body. It thundered in her veins, raced over her
nerve endings, then centered in her pussy where it turned into a
blazing ache.

"This is because of your wife," she breathed out roughly. "You
lost her. You think you have to protect me. I won't have it."

"This isn't about anyone but you." He nipped her jawline. "Just
me and you, Rogue."

She shook her head desperately as his lips slid along her neck,
spreading fire along her flesh as she fought to find the strength to
tear away from him.

"You gave yourself to me." His teeth raked over her collarbone.

"My body," she protested.

"Your heart." His voice rumbled as he forged a path to the
valley of her breasts, brushing aside the cotton material of
the shirt, and lifted one hand to palm a swollen mound of her
breast.

Sensation was building inside her again. She had just had him,
no more than a few hours ago, yet her body was weakening, softening, needing him.

And he was right, she had given him her heart.

"I didn't give you my freedom," she panted, trying to find some
fragile threat of independence. Surely there was some lingering
shred of independence inside her somewhere?

His head lifted as he gripped the sides of the shirt and tore it
apart. Buttons were scattering as his lips stole hers in a kiss that

she was certain fried any ability she could have had to speak, let alone think.

His tongue delved between her lips, tangled with hers, and the taste of him went to her head with the same force as a narcotic. He was inside her, so much a part of her that she didn't know how to fight him.

Her arms wrapped around his neck as she gave in to the kiss. A part of her knew he was right. Jonesy had a temper that she had always pampered and had to watch out for. He only really respected men willing to put up their fists.

It grated on her pride. But pride was a weak ideal when Zeke seemed to wrap around her. When he was kissing her as though he were drowning in her. Despite the split lip and the bruises she knew must be marring his body, still his lips slanted over hers as his broad hands cupped her rear and lifted her to him.

"Tell me you belong to me." He nipped her lips, then licked the heat of the rough caress away. "Now, Rogue. Tell me you're mine."

She shook her head as his head lifted and he stared down at her with predatory intent.

"But you are." His lips slid to her ear. "Mine to hold, to protect."

But was she his to love? The thought whispered through her mind, then evaporated as he turned her, his hands smoothing up her arms and flattening her palms against the wall.

"Zeke."

"It's okay, baby." Her hair was swept to the side, his lips tasting her neck, spreading heated kisses along the sensitive column as his hands cupped her breasts.

He palmed the sensitive mounds; his fingers rubbed over her nipples before he encased them in two fingers, working them gently. Waves of incredible pleasure began washing through her.

Rogue tipped her head back against his chest, a moan parting her lips.

"You burn me alive," he whispered against her ear as he moved one hand from her breasts.

She could feel him behind her, working his jeans loose, releasing the heavy length of his erection, and she whimpered in longing.

"I have a bed," she panted, though the thought of moving at the moment wasn't high on her list of priorities.

"Who needs a bed? Fuck, Rogue, I don't think I can wait that long."

She felt his knees dip as his arm slid around her hips, lifting her and holding her in place as he pressed her legs apart with his foot.

"Damn, gotta love those high heels," he groaned as she felt the head of his cock press against her, hot and iron hard.

Dizzying weakness flooded her, pleasure overcame any objections she could have even thought to have as she felt the slow, stretching impalement of her pussy. A strangled cry left her throat, heat flushed her, inside and out.

It was a damned good thing he was holding her, because she would have melted to the floor otherwise. Violent pleasure tore through her as his erection worked inside her. Slow, torturously so as her slick juices flowed around him.

"I can't stand it," she panted. Because it was too good. Because there was something about this position, about having him behind her, controlling her responses, her movements, that made her feel more fragile, more feminine than ever before.

"Should I stop, Rogue?" He paused, buried to the hilt inside her now, throbbing and thick, filling her and stealing her senses with a pleasure she couldn't fight. "Tell me to stop, Rogue, and I will."

Her fingers curled into fists against the wall as she felt perspiration gathering along her body. Her skirt was pushed to her hips, his shirt slid over her shoulders and hung at the bend of her arms.

It was decadent, wicked. The position, her half-clothed state, and the feel of him inside her added to the sensations rioting through her.

How could she ever live without him now? How could she survive without the feel of him taking her, possessing her?

"Don't stop." Her lashes drifted closed as she allowed her head to rest against his shoulder. "Please, Zeke. Don't stop."

He moved. A slow, gliding retreat, then a hard, fierce thrust that had her back arching and a strangling cry falling from her lips.

He gripped her hips with both hands now, holding her in place, holding her up as he began fucking her with hard, even strokes.

Rogue became lost in the pleasure, in the lightning-swift explosions of heat that began to race through her system. The slap of his flesh against hers, the scent and sound of sex surrounding her, his harsh breathing at her ear. It combined to begin that sharp, desperate rise to release that was both ecstatic and torturous.

She moved against him, thrusting back into each hard lunge of his cock inside her as she felt the pleasure tightening inside her, racing through her.

"Zeke, oh God. Don't stop," she whimpered, then cried out as his thrusts became harder, wilder.

She felt his control shatter. She felt it in the slam of his erection inside her, the stroke of the hard flesh over brutally sensitive nerve endings. She felt it in the grip of his hands at her waist and heard his hard, rasping male groan as she felt the pleasure explode inside her.

She tried to scream his name but all that emerged was a breathless cry as she felt her vaginal muscles clench around him as her womb convulsed with her release. Sensation upon sensation detonated inside her, until she was shaking, sobbing, aware of nothing but Zeke, his touch, his heat as ecstatic pleasure surrounded her. She felt his release spurting inside her, liquid hot and consuming.

She heard his groan as he buried his face at her neck and his hands flexed against her hips.

She was aware of nothing but the man and the pleasure. Brilliant pulses of heat were like electroshocks tearing through, shuddering through her body, leaving her breathless and weak as Zeke supported her, holding her between the wall and his body as he groaned her name and shuddered behind her.

Standing there, her legs rubbery, the pulses of pleasure still echoing through her, Rogue felt more than just the pleasure. She felt the emotion. She heard it in his rough groan at her ear, in the hard, desperate caresses of his lips against her neck. She felt his possession. She felt marked, on the inside, by a man she still wasn't certain how to read or how to predict.

But in those moments, his cock still buried inside her, his hands hard on her hips, his lips against her neck, she knew one thing. Zeke was right. She belonged irrevocably to him.

Which left one all-important question. What would she do if or when he decided to move on?

The sun was high overhead when Zeke slipped from Rogue's bed and moved into the kitchen with his cell phone. Flipping it open he pressed speed dial and waited for the call to go through.

"Sheriff." Cranston sounded wide awake, while Zeke admitted his ass was starting to drag from a lack of sleep.

"You're a bastard, Cranston." He sighed. "You've pushed me out of the investigations you've conducted here, and now I'm fucked. I need your help."

"I didn't push you out, Zeke," Cranston answered. "I used you as effectively as I've used the other tools I've had at my disposal. That's my job. Too many eyes were watching you and a killer was just waiting on an excuse to take you or your son, or both, out. I couldn't afford that."

"Yeah, you did it out of the kindness of your heart," Zeke snorted.

"I don't have a heart," Cranston assured him. "But I do try to look at long-term goals rather than short term. Long term, you're more useful to me alive rather than dead. Long term was, I knew the exterminator was out there and focused on you. If we didn't catch him in the first investigation, then I needed you in place. You're in place, he's killing again, and he's trying to get your attention with these murders, otherwise he would have changed his style enough to throw you off his scent. Now tell me what you need."

Zeke's lips thinned at the thought of how effectively Cranston really had used him.

"Are you covering my back?"

"Me and three Mackays," Cranston admitted. "No one else. We're keeping this operation small and on a need-to-know basis. Chief Jansen has been informed of what's going on, but he's holding back for the present. Are you with the Walker girl?"

"I'm distracted," he stated, knowing it was the damned truth. "I want this taken care of this time. Shane's out of state, he left on a school trip a few days ago, so he's safe for the next week. I want that bastard caught."

Silence filled the line for long moments. "A week will be cutting it close," he finally said.

"A week," Zeke stated. "He'll use Shane against me if he gets scared I'm getting too close. I'll continue the investigation from my end while keeping Rogue safe. You and the Mackays do whatever mumbo jumbo you do and let's get this taken care of."

"And if it's Maynard?" Cranston finally asked. "I know he's your lead suspect, Zeke. Are you looking beyond him?"

"I suspect everyone but Rogue," Zeke said softly, aware that this was the first time he had crossed any possibility off his list.

"Now let's do it. I'll play the distracted lover, you help me find a killer."

"It's good to be working with you again, Sheriff," Cranston replied a little gleefully. "Damned good."

Zeke just wished he felt as happy about the situation. As he glanced back at Rogue's closed bedroom door, he knew it could all backfire on him though. He could lose her. And the thought of that had a dull ache centering in his chest and reminding him that for the first time in over ten years, he had a weakness other than his son.

For the first time in his life, he was afraid he might truly be falling in love.

NINETEEN

Zeke entered his office two days later to find the coroner Jay Adams's report on Callie Walker's death. Joe and Jaime's grandmother hadn't died accidently. The blow she had received on the head had been delivered by a blunt object rather than the side of the bathtub as it had been made to appear.

The blow could have been fatal in time, but the cause of death had been drowning as she lay in the bathtub.

He read the report before breathing out roughly and shaking his head. The coroner had released the bodies for burial, and Lisa Walker had been notified.

He rubbed his hand over his head before taking the file and locking it in the file cabinet. Joe and Jaime, and then their grandmother. A woman tied them together and Zeke was no closer to figuring out who that woman was than he had been the day of the twins' deaths, just as he, Cranston, or the Mackays were no closer to finding the killer.

He'd questioned everyone he could think of to question. Even the Mackays had come up blank on the woman's identity. That didn't make sense. Pulaski County wasn't that large. It thrived on gossip as any small county did. Zeke bet he knew every lover, potential lover, or wannabe lover that Joe and Jaime could have had in their sexual lives. All but one. The one that had led to their deaths.

Or had she been the one to commit the murders?

The twins' phone records had revealed very little. They had no cell phones, so there were no records to trace there. There was just nothing left to go on except his gut-deep certainty that all three murders were linked.

At this point, there wasn't much more he could do without any leads. Lisa Walker had called earlier, informing him that she would be returning home unless he was close to an arrest. She had things to take care of, and her sons' father wanted the boys back in town. Lisa still had family here, too, her job, a life. She couldn't stay away indefinitely.

That was an additional worry. Whoever had killed the twins and their grandmother, Callie Walker, wouldn't hesitate to kill again. He had a feeling the murderer might have even enjoyed the elaborate game that had been made of the deaths, just as Cranston had suggested.

A knock at his office door had him moving from the file cabinet back to his desk as the door opened and his secretary peeked in.

"Zeke, you have a visitor." Kendal Birchfield arched her expressive brows as her blue eyes twinkled with amusement. "Mr. John Calvin Walker Jr. requests a few moments of your time."

Zeke's brows arched. John Calvin Walker Jr. It couldn't be anyone other than Calvin Walker's son.

Zeke grinned as he took his seat. "I have a few minutes, Kendal. Show him in."

Kendal winked back at him playfully before closing the door. A few seconds later it opened it again and Mr. John Calvin Walker Jr. entered the room.

Zeke wasn't certain what he was expecting in the form of Rogue's brother. A polished Bostonian lawyer, perhaps. John Walker was known as a lawyer with teeth. He was picky about the cases he took, but the ones he took he rarely lost. Zeke's contacts in D.C. had placed the younger man as an up-and-coming political force to be watched.

It wasn't the first impression Zeke had of him though. John Walker was dressed in jeans, a rumpled white cotton shirt, and well-worn boots. Zeke would have pegged him for a California surfer boy.

"Sheriff Mayes." Violet blue eyes were set behind thick blond lashes in a sun-darkened face. Overly long white blond hair fell almost to his shoulders and framed hard, slashing features.

The boy looked a lot like the father had when he was younger, except Calvin Walker had sported red hair rather than blond and had been broader, more muscular, where John Walker was leaner.

His handshake was firm and hinted at strength. His gaze was cool and determined, and Zeke understood why his contacts in D.C. foresaw a political future for this young man. Zeke saw something that perhaps they didn't though. He saw a decided lack of true deception in the other man's eyes.

"What can I do for you, Mr. Walker?" Zeke held his hand out to the visitor's chair in front of his desk as he took his own seat.

John Walker sat, though he slouched with lazy negligence.

"So, you're the sheriff sleeping with my baby sister." John's smile was tight and hard. "I was wondering what had Jonesy so worked up about you. I understand now."

Zeke leaned back in his chair and arched his brow. "Last I heard Rogue was over twenty-one."

John's eyes narrowed. "Caitlyn," he corrected softly. "And she may be over twenty-one, but you, Sheriff Mayes, are nearly old enough to be her father."

Zeke stared back at him implacably, refusing to be drawn into whatever fight the younger Walker thought he was getting ready to start.

"Your sister is Rogue in these parts, Mr. Walker," he said evenly. "I haven't known a man yet that called her Caitlyn that didn't end up on his knees with his hands covering his balls. She has a wicked knee. And you're exaggerating the age difference by quite a bit."

John's grin was slow and filled with amusement this time. "Little witch. She always did know how to go for the weak spots." His smile dropped just as quick. "That doesn't tell me why a man your age is taking advantage of my sister. Or a man of your past."

Zeke stayed still. He stared back at Rogue's brother coldly, sensing what was coming. This younger Walker was no man's fool; he would have run a check on Zeke the minute he knew his name, and the information he could have found would have worried any brother.

"You have quite a reputation in L.A.," the other man stated. "The detective who took down one of the most corrupt underground BDSM communities in the nation? After your wife's death, you became quite enmeshed in the community before your investigation and the subsequent arrests were made, didn't you?"

Zeke propped his elbows on the arms of his chair and steepled his fingers as he stared back at John Walker.

"The investigation had nothing to do with the BDSM aspects of that community," he stated. "I was there to find a killer and a drug dealer, Mr. Walker. And the lifestyle itself has nothing to do with my relationship with your sister."

John's gaze sharpened. "Strange, I hear you don't have relationships."

"Strange," Zeke drawled. "I hear that who your sister sleeps with or how she lives her life really isn't any of your damned business. If that's why you're here, then perhaps you should head back home."

"Or perhaps I should just ask my sister about it," John suggested.

Zeke leaned forward, his arms bracing on his desk. "Mr. Walker, before this goes any further let me warn you right now, I won't brook any interference in my relationship with Rogue. You don't want to make an enemy of me, and that's something your contacts should have warned you of. You might think you see a dumb hick sheriff sitting in front of you, but let me assure you, Mr. Walker, this dumb hick knows how to hold on to what belongs to him."

Thick lashes narrowed over violet eyes as John stared back at him. "Are parking lot brawls a requirement of holding on to your woman in this town?" he asked. "I stopped by Jonesy's before coming here. His face is a little worse for wear and yours isn't much better, even two days later. What did Caitlyn think of your beating up on the man that protected her for four years?"

"What did you think of the reason he received that beating?" Zeke's smile was cold. "Or didn't you ask him why it happened?"

"He said he was protesting your treatment of Caitlyn," John said softly. "Are you denying it?"

Jonesy had lied. Zeke had to admit that surprised him. He hadn't thought the bartender would bother to lie.

"What happened will stay between me and Jonesy." He finally shrugged. "If you have any questions or objections, then I imagine you'll take them up with Rogue."

"With Caitlyn," John stated again.

"How old are you, Mr. Walker?" Zeke asked then. "Twelve? I

think by now you're well aware of the name your sister prefers, as well as the one that suits her best. If you can't stop with the immature comments, then you can leave my office now."

Silence filled the room as John stared back at him with eyes that were like chips of violet ice. Finally, the younger man straightened in his chair and his expression smoothed out.

"Joe and Jaime Walker, and their grandmother, Callie Walker, were murdered, weren't they?"

The change of subject didn't surprise Zeke. Whatever answers John had been looking for about his sister had evidently been answered. The air of confrontational disrespect had evaporated and clear, icy purpose filled those violet eyes. This was a man on a mission, and his mission was identifying and eliminating the threat to his sister.

"Where do you get your information from?" Zeke asked rather than answering.

John's lips titled. "Let's say I have my sources as I'm certain you have your own, Sheriff. Joe, Jaime, and their grandmother were important to Caitlyn. But even more, they were close to her. I'd like to know if her life is in danger as well."

"I don't know." Zeke leaned forward and watched the younger man intently. "At this moment, I don't believe it is, but I'm taking precautions just in case."

"By sleeping with her?" There was a spark of anger in his eyes now.

"By taking precautions," he repeated coolly.

John grimaced heavily.

"I'm going to assume you didn't stop and see your sister before you arrived here," Zeke said, more than certain that was the case.

John grinned wryly. "My balls are still intact. What do you think?"

"I think your sister must have known how to use that knee

of hers before she ever made an appearance in Somerset." Zeke grinned.

"Let's just say I've experienced her wrath more than once. But in all fairness, I'm the one that first taught her the maneuver. A girl has to know how to protect herself."

Zeke inclined his head in agreement. "And sometimes, a fist is needed rather than a knee," he told the brother as he thought about his fight with Jonesy.

"Then essentially, you have no idea who killed Joe, Jaime, and their grandmother, Callie?"

Zeke shook his head. "All I know is that a woman ties them together. Joe and Jaime were involved with a woman together; they were due to meet with her the night they died. A few days ago, their grandmother told Lisa she thought she might know who the girl was. She was supposed to call me. She was found dead the next day. It looked as though she had slipped in the bathtub, hit her head, and drowned. The coroner's report says otherwise. Callie Walker was murdered, just as her grandsons were."

John reached up and rubbed one finger over his lower lip thoughtfully as Zeke stared back at him.

"Rogue was attacked six months ago because of something someone thought she knew," he mused quietly. "She was hospitalized for over a week, Sheriff Mayes."

"I'm well aware of that, Mr. Walker," Zeke stated quietly. "I intend to make certain it doesn't happen again."

"As am I." John stood to his feet then. The deliberate slouchiness he had displayed when he first entered the office was no longer apparent. The younger man moved with unconscious grace and predatory awareness now.

"John."

John turned back as he reached the door, his expression brooding.

"Yes, Sheriff?"

"I don't need civilian interference in this. This is my investigation. Don't forget that."

His lips quirked. "I'm here, Sheriff, to see after my sister's welfare."

"As long as you stay out of my investigation," he agreed. "And my relationship with your sister."

John arched an eyebrow. "You're not her husband, and that's the only relationship I'm required to stay out of where my sister is concerned. Perhaps that's something you'd do well to remember."

John opened the door, stepped out of the office, and with a click of the latch left Zeke alone with that final thought. It was a thought that should have filled him with a sense of dread. That was his normal feeling whenever marriage was mentioned. Strangely, the dread wasn't there now.

He shook his head at the thought of that, grabbed up his hat before strapping on his weapon and heading for the door.

"Kendal, radio Gene and inform him I'm heading out. I'd like to meet up with him at the diner in town before he takes over the evening shift," he told his secretary.

"Gene called in while you were meeting with Mr. Walker. He had to take the rest of the day off to take his wife to the doctor in Louisville."

"Alicia all right?" he asked.

Kendal nodded. "It was a checkup, but she wanted Gene to go in with her. I think they're going to visit with their daughter Willa while they're there."

Zeke nodded at that. "I'll head on out then."

"Sheriff, you had a call from Teddy Winfred. He asked that you stop by his place when you can."

Zeke stopped and turned back to her. "Teddy lives on the road that leads to the Walker twins' place, doesn't he?"

Kendal's expression sobered. "About two miles."

"I'll head out there now."

"Sheriff," she called him back as he started to head to the door.

"Yeah?" He turned to her again, seeing the worry in her blue eyes.

"He asked me to make certain no one knew that he asked you to come to the house. And he asked that you keep it to yourself."

"Did you tell anyone he called?"

She tilted her head and stared back at him in disbelief. "Not hardly," she said mockingly. "I didn't even tell Gene when he called in."

"I'll head on out there then." He nodded. "Let the deputy on duty tonight know that I'm on call if he needs me."

"Will do, Boss." Kendal flashed him a smile as he left the outer office and moved quickly along the hallway to the exit.

Minutes later he was in the Tahoe heading out of town toward the Winfred place. Teddy Winfred was eighty if he was a day. He didn't venture out of his mobile home often and he didn't like visitors. He'd damned near run Gene off with his cane when the deputy dropped by to question him after the Walker twins' bodies had been found. He was also a close friend with Callie Walker.

Heading out to the Winfred place had put his plans to drop by Rogue's apartment on hold though. The past two days had been hectic, for himself as well as Rogue as she worked at the restaurant well past closing. He'd picked her up after work and returned to her apartment with her where he stayed the night, but there was still an edge of tension between them that he hadn't had time to deal with yet.

The appearance of her brother wasn't going to help matters. He had a feeling John Walker was going to be more trouble than he was worth and definitely more than Zeke wanted to put up with at the moment.

If he was anything like his father, Calvin Walker, then he could become a hazard if he stayed in Somerset long. Calvin Walker had been a hellion when he was younger, more often in trouble than not, simply because he hadn't known when to keep his nose out of others' business. It hadn't surprised Zeke at all that Walker had become a lawyer, and one in Boston nonetheless. Zeke bet he kept all the feathers ruffled there.

He grinned at the thought of it. He remembered Calvin, though the other man was a good decade and a half older than Zeke was. He also remembered how much his father and Gene's had hated the other man.

James Maynard had been Thad Mayes's deputy for several years when Thad had held the sheriff's office. The two men had made it a point to harass Calvin as often as possible. They considered it a game, a way to feel superior. Thad hadn't always run his office with any sense of justice. Unlike Zeke, he had seen it as a means to power, a way to keep others beneath him, and a way to ensure that he was accepted in the upper-class level of the county at the time.

Thad's dreams hadn't been Zeke's, but his father had drawn him into the dark underbelly of that life anyway. He wasn't the county's sheriff; he'd been Dayle Mackay's sheriff, and what Dayle wanted, Dayle got. When Dayle had ordered Thad to prove Zeke's loyalty to the League, Thad had done it in a way that had destroyed the boy Zeke had once been.

Blood stained his hands. It wasn't innocent blood, but it was still murder. It was still a nightmare for the fourteen-year-old child he had been at the time. And it still held the potential to destroy him.

It had left a legacy that Zeke was still sometimes forced to fight. Through those years, Gene had always been a phone call away. A friend that knew the darkness and shared it with Zeke. For a while, Zeke had been certain that Gene had gotten out of the League. Recently though, Zeke had been forced to wonder if that were indeed true.

There were times Zeke wondered if Gene would ever be fully out from under his father's thumb. There had been a time when Zeke had thought Gene was his own man; now, he wasn't so sure of it.

Thoughts of Gene brought Jonesy to mind. Danny Jones was another wild card, and one who had been a part of Thad Mayes's inner group of friends at one time. Danny "Jonesy" Jones had slipped out of that group when he had defended Calvin Walker against Thad Mayes and James Maynard. That had finished Jonesy's friendship with Zeke's and Gene's fathers.

That information had come through the investigation the previous year. It was in the files his contact in Washington had finally gotten for him. Jonesy had once been rumored to be in the selection process for the League when he had learned what it was and how it would affect his friendships and his life. He'd chosen the friendships and had been targeted by Thad several times because of it.

It wasn't surprising that when Rogue had found herself in trouble after arriving in Somerset, Jonesy had stepped in. And now that Rogue was involved with Zeke, Jonesy felt threatened, both personally and for Rogue. That didn't excuse his treatment of her, and Zeke would never forget how Jonesy had bruised Rogue's delicate arms. He didn't trust the other man; there was something about his temper that bothered Zeke. It wasn't just anger that drove Jonesy. There was something more. Something that had Zeke's nerves on edge.

He pushed those thoughts to the back of his mind to consider later as he pulled into Teddy Winfred's driveway.

The white single-wide mobile home sat peacefully within a small clearing surrounded by oak, pine, and dogwood trees. The yard was neatly cut, and old Teddy's late-model Ford pickup was parked next to the mobile home.

Zeke parked the Tahoe, turned off the ignition, then moved from the truck and strode up the graveled driveway to the front door.

The door opened as he stepped onto the faded porch, and a grizzled Teddy Winfred met him with a wide smile on his wrinkled face. Teddy still possessed most of his natural teeth and didn't mind bragging on them with his wide smiles.

"Teddy." Zeke shook his hand. "Kendal said you called and asked me to drop by."

"Come in. Come in." Teddy's smile flashed again as his faded hazel eyes sparkled with humor as he led the way into the scrupulously neat little home.

A threadbare couch and recliner sat in the living room, facing a wide-screen television. Zeke knew Teddy's sons, one a minister in the county, the other a store owner, made certain their father was well taken care of. It was one of their biggest gripes that their father refused to give up his independence and move in with one of them.

"How are you doing, Teddy?" Zeke removed his hat as he took the seat Teddy waved to.

"I'm doing good, Zeke. Real good." Teddy nodded his bald head before wiping a hand over it. "I heard about Callie, how she died and all. I got to thinking about those grandsons of hers and them dying. There's word going around, you know, that they were murdered. That concerned me some."

Zeke sat forward in the chair and watched the old man.

"Why did that concern you, Teddy?"

"Well, Zeke." He rubbed his gnarled hands together before clasping them slowly. "Callie called me that morning. The morning she drowned." His hazel eyes darkened with sadness. "She said she thought her grandsons had been murdered because of some girl they were seeing. She asked me if I knew who it was."

"Why would you know who it was, Teddy?" Zeke asked.

Teddy sighed. "I always know when folks come and go up this road. And Joe and Jaime, they did a lot of fishing here behind the house in the creek. Sometimes, they'd be drinking and talking and their voices carried real good here."

Zeke nodded encouragingly. "Did you hear something before they died?"

"Well, see, that's the problem." Teddy scratched his head thoughtfully. "I heard them the night before they were killed. They were drunk as skunks out back, laughing and cutting up. I opened the back door so I could hear better." He grinned unapologetically. "Old folks like to live vicariously through young, dumb kids like that, you know."

"I can imagine, Teddy." Zeke chuckled. "What did you hear Joe and Jaime talking about?"

"Well, they were talking about a girl. Joe said he was getting serious about her, and Jaime laughed, said if Joe was serious, then he would get serious, too." Teddy shook his head. "Those two got into some wild games with the girls, you know?"

"I know." Zeke nodded again.

Teddy shook his head and breathed out roughly. "I told Callie what I'd heard and she said she was going to call you. But when I got hold of her granddaughter the other day, she said she thought maybe Callie hadn't had a chance to talk to you."

"Callie didn't have time to talk to me, Teddy," he affirmed. "I wasn't aware she was trying to contact me until after her death."

Teddy's eyes glittered with moisture then. "She was killed, wasn't she, Sheriff? Because she was trying to figure out who killed those grandsons of hers."

"I don't know, Teddy. Until I find out who the boys were seeing and if she had anything to do with it, then I can't say," Zeke stated.

Teddy breathed out slowly before rubbing the side of his wrinkled face.

"What else did you hear the boys say that night, Teddy?" Zeke asked.

"Just between me and you, Zeke?" Teddy asked. "Callie was going to talk to you and she ended up drowning in her bathtub. I don't want to drown in my bathtub."

"I can understand that, Teddy." He nodded. "This stays just between the two of us."

Teddy nodded again. "I didn't hear much, and that was what I told Callie. They were talking about being serious about this girl, and Joe said they'd have to be real careful for a while, because her daddy would kill them if he found out. They seemed to talk like they might be a little worried about that. Then Jaime said he had a way to take care of it. That he knew how to keep her daddy quiet. He told Joe he had information, that he knew that her daddy was a part of those men they were looking for last summer and that her daddy wouldn't want anyone to know just how deep he was in that group. Now, I took it at first as just talk; you know how young boys get, and Joe and Jaime could be a little paranoid sometimes about stuff. But when I told Callie what was said, she went real quiet for a long time. And she says, 'That was what I was afraid of, Teddy. That was what I was afraid of.' And she hung the phone up then. Next I heard, she was dead."

The girl's father was a part of what happened last summer. Joe and Jaime had given the Mackay cousins and DHS information then that led to uncovering the identities of several citizens involved in the Freedom League.

"That's all she said? She didn't give you a name, Teddy?"

Teddy shook his head. "She didn't say a name, Zeke. She hung up and that was the last time I talked to her."

Zeke stared back at Teddy thoughtfully.

"And you think Callie figured out who it was from that information?" he asked.

Teddy sighed. "I just know what she said and how she said it. And I knew Callie. She knew something. And I think that something got her killed."

Zeke was pretty damned certain it had. He considered the information Teddy had given him. There wasn't a name to go on, but there was definitely information here that Timothy Cranston needed to know.

The suspended Homeland Security special agent could have information there that Zeke could use. Zeke knew there were files that the DHS agent had on suspected homeland terrorists, though Zeke hadn't been given the privilege of going through those files.

"Did you hear anything else, Teddy?" Zeke asked.

Teddy shook his head. "Nothing about the girl they were seeing. They started talking about being thrown out of their cousin's bar. Said Rogue had a mean knee." Teddy's gaze lightened with a hint of laughter then. "Jonesy taught her how to use that knee, I hear. Jonesy used to be a hell of a fighter."

"That's what I've heard." Zeke nodded, moving to rise to his feet.

"You know your dad and Jonesy used to be good friends," Teddy said.

"I know that." Zeke nodded.

"Yeah." Teddy rubbed his hands together slowly. "Jonesy, James, and Thad, they were all real tight at one time. Until your dad started hooking up with that Dayle Mackay. Jonesy never could get along with Dayle, you know?"

"I didn't know that, Teddy."

Teddy nodded. "Your dad was a good man when he was younger, until he hooked up with Dayle." Teddy grimaced soberly. "He changed. But I guess all men change when they grow older in some ways. Some for the better, some for the worse, huh?"

"So it would seem, Teddy," Zeke answered. "So it would seem."

Teddy nodded again before wiping his hand over his jaw. "You had a good mother though. She loved you like crazy. She was always taking those pictures of you and your dad. Everywhere she went she took pictures. Memories, she called them." He grinned at that. "She used to say they were her memories, and when she was old they would serve her good. I saw her once when I was hunting, taking pictures in the mountains by herself. Your daddy and some friends were fishing out by the old cabin he kept. She didn't see me. She was taking pictures of your dad and you, I guess. There were a lot of folks there. She liked her pictures."

Zeke tensed. Memories flashed in his mind, comments his mother used to make, arguments she'd had with his dad. And one odd comment that stuck in his brain and shot adrenaline through his body.

His mother and her damned pictures. Her insurance, she had told his father when Zeke had been twelve, maybe thirteen. It was her insurance and if Thad was smart he'd save his own insurance. And he knew where his mother had hid her insurance. Son of a bitch, all these years, time spent investigating, searching, and the proof he needed could have been right under his nose all this time.

TWENTY

Rogue watched her brother warily as he prowled the living and kitchen area of her spacious apartment. He made the walls shrink in the once-airy rooms. Pacing like a caged tiger, she wouldn't have been surprised if he had started growling at her.

"You know, Mom and Dad are not going to be pleased." He threw her a fulminating glare as he turned and faced her from the other side of the couch. "Why the hell do you think I showed up? Dad is within days of arriving, Caitlyn. He's not happy over this situation."

"He'll have to live with it." She shrugged. "It's no more his business than it is yours."

She didn't need family interference right now. She'd managed to keep her father off her back for the past five years by putting up with Jonesy, which she had considered the lesser of two evils. Now, she had her brother here looking for all the world like a younger version of her father, albeit with blond hair rather than her father's red gold.

"Dad is not just going to live with it, Cait," he warned her.

"Rogue," she corrected him. She'd lost count of the times she had corrected him. He just threw her another glare, just as he had each time she had reminded him before.

"Look, just come back to Boston for a few weeks." He crossed his arms over his chest and stared back at her as though that look alone would get him his way.

Rogue almost smiled. Why was it that men thought all they had to do was cross their arms over their chests and stare back at a woman with determined eyes to get their way? It didn't work on her.

"And do what?" She grinned. "Are you going to take me out with you at night and make certain I'm entertained?"

His expression didn't change.

"Of course you aren't," she answered her own question with a mocking edge of humor. "And Mom and Dad have their things to do. That leaves poor little Rogue sitting in the corner to stare at the walls."

"Caitlyn," he growled her name. "Your name is Caitlyn. Son of a bitch, you've had four years, Cait. You've had plenty of time to get back at the bastards that hurt you. Now it's time to come home."

She stared at him in surprise, and she admitted a bit of anger. She would have thought that her brother would have known better than to believe she had stayed in Somerset for such a paltry reason.

"You think the only reason I stay here is because I want to get back at someone?" She felt like pulling at her hair. She hated dealing with her brother, or her father, when they got something into their head. They didn't let up until they got their way, and Rogue wasn't of the mind to give in to them.

"That's exactly why you stay," he bit out harshly. "Tell me what else you have. Family? Friends? You didn't even make friends outside the damned bar until last year."

"So? I have friends now." She shrugged as she adjusted the hem of her T-shirt over the band of her jeans. "I have a business, a job, and a sheriff." She winked suggestively as she watched him flush angrily. She hadn't said the word lover, it hovered there in the air between them, infuriating his brotherly sensibilities.

"Caitlyn . . ."

"Rogue," she injected softly. She was getting tired of reminding him.

He grimaced. "Even I know Sheriff Mayes's reputation with women. He's not a relationship kind of guy and you know it. He's going to break your heart."

Rogue pushed her hands into her back pockets and gave him a tight smile, warning herself to keep her mouth shut. She didn't want to fight with her brother. It had been too long since she had seen him. She'd let him bitch a little, then maybe take him down to the bar and let him have a drink or two. Maybe a beer would chill him out a little.

"You're not even listening to me, are you?" he accused her, a hint of anger entering his voice.

"Should I be?" Rogue arched her brows as she pulled her hands from her pockets and turned away from him to grab her apartment keys and cell phone from the kitchen table. "Let's go down to the bar. I need to check a few things out and you need a beer."

"I don't need a damned beer." His violet gaze hardened as he stared back at her. "I'll help you pack instead."

Her lips quirked. "You can come downstairs for a beer, or you can find yourself a hotel room for the night first. But packing isn't something we'll do."

His lips thinned. "You have a spare bedroom here; why should I have to find a hotel room?"

"Because you aren't staying here," she informed him as she moved for the door.

"Because your sheriff stays here?" he forced out between clenched teeth.

"Pretty much." She shrugged mockingly. "I prefer not to have my brother in the next room while I'm sleeping with my lover. It just smacks of tacky."

His hands plowed through his hair. Anger marked his face and glittered in his eyes as she strolled past him.

"Come on, John." Opening the door, she stared back at him warningly. "I'm not in the mood to fight with you, and you don't want to push it. Let's go downstairs and have a beer and chill out. You can go back home tomorrow and tell Daddy I'm just as stubborn as I ever was and you can go on about your business."

"You think all it takes is telling Dad that you're being stubborn, don't you, Rogue?"

"That's all it took before." She moved for the stairs. "I'm a big girl, John. I really can make these decisions all by myself."

She heard him follow behind her, the door closing before she started down the stairs. Music drifted up the stairs, clashing and wild as a popular classic rock tune thundered out onto the dance floor and beyond.

"You like to think you're a big girl," he snorted behind her. "A half-pint wishing is more like it."

She grinned at the comment. A half-pint wishing, that was one of her father's ways of telling her she was too small and delicate to do the things she normally did. It was usually in reference to another fight she had been involved in, or when she went nose to nose with Jonesy over something he ended up tattling over.

Pushing through the door that led to the main customer area of the bar, she let a grin tilt her lips. It was going to be hard at first to step away from the home she had taken over four years ago. The bar had been her rebellion, and she had done a damned good job of rebelling in it. Maybe she had grown up a bit over the years though. The bar wasn't as important as it had been, or maybe she was tired of rebelling. Either way, she knew her time there was limited.

Moving behind the long counter, she drew her brother a draft beer before pulling a chilled bottle of her favorite brand from beneath the counter. Her gaze went over the bartenders' activity, from Jonesy at the register as he made a point to ignore her, to Kent as he filled orders quickly and efficiently.

"You know, you should move to Somerset." She grinned at her brother's look of horror. "Just think, you could escape that stuffy lifestyle you've adopted for yourself and have some real fun. I'd even let you take over the bar."

She leaned a hip against the counter as she stared out over the dance floor before swinging her gaze back to her brother.

"You're joking." He grimaced as he glared at her.

"Not in the least," she assured him, raising her voice to be heard over the din. "I like working with Janey, John. I want to spend more time at the restaurant rather than here. You'd do well here."

Come to think of it, her brother would fit in here, she thought. He'd been discontent for years at her father's law firm. Where her sister seemed to fit in fine, John and her father clashed constantly.

"You've lost your mind." He turned his back on her as though she weren't worth listening to any longer.

Rogue grinned; she knew her brother, and he wasn't as disinterested as he wanted to pretend. His body was tense, a frown was brewing at his forehead—proof that he was at least considering her suggestion.

Shaking her head at him she finished her beer before disposing of the bottle and making her rounds of the bar.

She greeted regulars, chatted with visitors, and picked out tourists from among those just passing through on their way to other locations. She laughed and made certain the waitresses kept the drinks flowing. And through it all she kept her eye on the door, watching for one figure, one man.

"Hey, Rogue."

She turned at the pat on her shoulder.

"Gene, how are you doing?" She shot the deputy a quick smile as he looked around the bar.

"Seen Zeke this evening yet?" he asked as he looked around the bar, his ruddy face creasing into a frown.

"Not yet." She kept her smile relaxed, kept the worry out of her expression. "He usually shows up before the night's over."

"I thought you'd be at the restaurant tonight?"

She looked around the bar as she shook her head. "I've had some things to take care of, so I took tonight off."

"Things like your brother?" His grin was slow and easy. "Talk is already making rounds that another Boston Walker is in town. I hear he's a hell of a lawyer."

Gene's voice lifted to carry over the music, making it loud enough for those standing and sitting around them to hear their conversation clearly. Rogue was aware of the interest they were generating; it would have been impossible to miss.

"John is definitely one hell of a lawyer. If you'd like to chat with him, he's over at the bar." She nodded toward John's location. "If you'll excuse me, I have a few things I need to check on."

"Of course," he answered. "I might just do that, Rogue. Tell Zeke I was looking for him before he left the office. He's not answering his cell phone, but I left a few messages."

"I'll let him know you're looking for him," she promised as she moved away. "Night, Gene."

If she saw him. She checked her watch. It was going on nine and she hadn't seen him yet. That was unusual, and she admitted, it bothered her.

After making a full round of the bar she slipped back through the door next to the counter, managing to evade detection by her brother or Gene. She moved up the stairs, pulled the key to the apartment from her jeans, and unlocked the door before slipping inside.

The apartment was dark. She never left it dark. She always left lights on, simply because she hated fumbling for the switch.

Moving to back out, a surprised yelp left her lips as a hard hand gripped her wrist, pulled her in as the door was pushed closed, before she found herself flat against the wall behind her.

She would have screamed if a part of her hadn't instantly recognized the man that pressed against her. Her lips, parted on instinct, rather than blasting out in furious sound, let a moan slip by as hard male lips pressed into them, and a ravenous tongue licked over them.

Rogue let her arms wind around a muscular male neck. She arched into the hands that slid beneath her T-shirt and caressed her up her back. Her lips returned the fiery kiss that blazed over her lips.

She tasted him, felt him, smelled him. Her senses became filled with him as he lifted her against his harder body, his thigh sliding between hers as his hands moved her to ride the hard muscle.

Heated, pulsating pleasure erupted through her pussy. Instantly, her clit became swollen, her juices began to spill. Her breasts swelled beneath her bra and her nipples tightened. Every cell of her body went on high alert at the touch and the taste of this one man.

Her lips closed on his tongue, hers met it, stroked, licked. A soft cry filled the air, throttled as their lips held it back. Her body was instantly electrified, responsive, needy. She needed and wondered at her response to him. At the sheer pleasure, the sense of anticipation that filled her as his hard hands held her hips, his heavy thigh muscle grinding between her thighs.

Blood thundered through her veins now; her flesh became sensitive, her body weak with arousal. It was like this. Each time he touched her, each time he was near, she was ready for him, waiting for him.

"John is here," she gasped as his lips moved from hers and arrowed down her neck. One hand pulled at the neckline of her T-shirt, pulling it back from her collarbone as he devoured flesh there.

His tongue stroked over the sensitive skin as she breathed in harshly, her head falling back to give him greater access as heated sensation raced through her.

"He's not up here," he growled before raking his teeth over the upper swell of her breast. "I checked."

"He has a key," she moaned, her nails digging into the muscles of his shoulder, feeling naked flesh.

He must have taken off his shirt before she entered the room. He still wore jeans, she assumed he still had his boots on. But his back and chest were bare, heated and hard.

"He's always interrupting things that he shouldn't." She nearly lost her breath as his hands pushed her shirt over the swell of her breasts. "God, Zeke, you make me crazy like this."

When he was hard and demanding, determined to take what he wanted. It made her blood pressure soar, made heat erupt throughout her body as her pussy clenched in need.

She ached for him. She'd ached for him all day, watched for him, needed him.

"I want you crazy," he breathed over the valley of her breasts.

"Crazy and wild. Come on, Rogue, show me how wild you can be."

How wild she could be? She was weak, arching to him as he pushed aside the lace of her bra and licked over her nipple.

"Wild?" she moaned. "Damn, Zeke, I can barely breathe."

His chuckle was dark and sexy against the tight tip of her breast as his lips covered it, sucked it into his mouth, and sent her senses spinning.

The lash of his tongue against her nipple sent fire rippling through her nervous system. Each hard draw at the tender tip sent a spark of reaction straight to her womb, stealing her breath and leaving her gasping at the pleasure.

Her world was on fire with pleasure. Pinpoints of light sparkled behind her closed lids, and nothing existed, nothing was real but this touch, this man that held her against him with a strength, a power that she hadn't sensed in him before.

"Where is the little bastard?" he finally groaned as his head lifted from her breast.

"Who?" she lifted to him, desperate for more.

"Your brother." His cheek rubbed against her breast, the dark rasp of a shadow of a beard sending a shudder through her body.

"Oh. Downstairs, with Gene. Your deputy left you a message on your cell phone." She finally remembered. "You can answer him later. Much later."

She felt him tense against her. Every muscle in his lean, corded frame seemed to tighten to steely hardness.

"Definitely much later," he agreed, though he was drawing away from her now, pulling back before reaching beside her to flip the lights on.

Rogue blinked at the sudden bright light, staring up at him as he slowly released her before jerking his shirt from the back of the couch and pulling it over his head.

"What?" She watched him with a frown as he pushed his arms through their holes and pulled the shirt over his lean abs.

"Grab a jacket." He turned back to her, his expression hard. "I had Alex drop me off here; we'll take your cycle back to my place."

Rogue tilted her head to the side as she watched him curiously now.

"Are we slipping away, Zeke?" she asked him.

"Not for the reasons you might be thinking," he grunted. "This has nothing to do with caring who sees me with you. There's just a few things I'm avoiding right now."

That was strange enough; she couldn't imagine Zeke avoiding anything that needed to be taken care of or anyone causing him any problems.

"You'll explain why later, right?"

He nodded slowly. "Later. I promise."

Licking her lips nervously, Rogue moved to the closet where she pulled her leather riding jacket free, then lifted the keys to the Harley from the small peg inside the closet.

"Here you go." She tossed him the keys after closing the closet door and turning back to him. "Sorry, there's no secret door to slip out of. You're going to have to take your chances going down the stairs, I guess. Unless you want to climb out the back window and shimmy down the drainpipe or something."

He glanced toward the bedroom window as Rogue's gaze narrowed.

"Explanations would be nice," she finally told him.

He nodded slowly. "Explanations will have to come later though. Let's go."

He grabbed his own leather jacket from the couch; she hadn't even noticed it until then.

Shrugging it on, he opened the door, looked down the stairs, then led her from the room before locking the door behind them.

Rogue stayed silent, though the questions were beginning to build in her mind. She followed him down the stairs, then the short hall to the back door. They slipped from the bar as silently as he had obviously slipped inside, and he led her straight to the covered carport behind the bar where she kept her Harley parked.

He straddled the cycle quickly and inserted the key as Rogue swung onto the padded back hump. The throb of the cycle's engines between her thighs was always an exhilarating, almost sexual sensation that gave her a reckless little thrill.

She pulled on the helmet Zeke handed her as he pulled on the extra that he had taken from a hook just inside the carport. Within seconds, the kickstand was up and he was backing the motorcycle from the covered shelter before turning the handlebars and accelerating from the back lot.

The small graveled drive that led from the back lot across a rough meadow exited at a small country road that broke off from the interstate. Zeke turned onto the small country lane before revving the engine and speeding away from the bar.

Resting her hands on his tight waist, Rogue rode behind him silently. She could feel the tension burning in him, feel the need, for whatever reason, to get her away from the bar.

She wondered if his absence that day had anything to do with his tension now. According to his secretary when she'd called earlier, he had an appointment out of town and Kendal hadn't known when he would be back. Now, he'd had Alex drop him off at the bar and they were escaping on her cycle rather than in his Tahoe?

She couldn't bitch about escaping with him though. There was something incredibly fulfilling about riding free behind him, his warmth buffeting the cool night air as she held on to him.

She'd never enjoyed riding behind anyone else. She'd always loved the control of wielding the cycle's power herself. But somehow, with Zeke, it seemed natural, right. The feeling was almost as powerful as lying in his arms after the explosive orgasm he gave her.

The night sped by, the wind chilly but not cutting. There was a hint of warmth to the air, the certainty of the land that summer's heat was heading its way. In front of her, the certainty of her lover's heat seemed to wrap around her, enclose her as he navigated the darkened back roads toward his home.

The drive wasn't long, no more than half an hour, but the cell phone at her side had activated twice, and she had a feeling she knew who it was.

Her brother. Or Jonesy. They couldn't know she was with Zeke, but they would guess that she was heading to see him at the least.

Why, she wondered, was John so intent that she leave Somerset and return to Boston? What drove not just Jonesy but her brother to such lengths to supposedly save her from Zeke? It bothered her, first Jonesy, then John. Both were pissed at the thought of her being with Zeke and she couldn't figure out why.

The broken heart was her risk to take, and the risk was one she wouldn't miss out on, not now, not after waiting this long for the chance to steal his heart.

But was she stealing his heart, or was she fooling herself? She'd been throwing herself at him for years; had he just finally taken what was offered, or did it mean anything to him?

She had to let herself believe that it meant something, at least for now.

Clenching her eyes closed for precious seconds, she held on to the hope, the prayer, that more would come of this than a broken heart.

Her eyes opened as he made the turn onto the side road that led into his farm. The night seemed darker, the stars blotted out by the thick covering of pine that reached into the night sky. She felt isolated from the rest of the world, as though she and Zeke were riding into a place where nothing else could touch them, where nothing existed but the two of them.

When he broke from the heavy tree cover it was to make the short ride to his home. He pulled the motorcycle up to the garage doors, stopped, and kicked down the stand before swinging off, leaving the engine throbbing as he moved to open the garage doors.

Rogue slid into the seat he vacated, relishing the heavy heat he left, kicked up the stand, and pulled the cycle into the garage before cutting the motor and pulling off her helmet and hanging it on the end of one of the handlebars as she watched Zeke move toward her.

The cell phone at her hip beeped imperatively.

Pulling it free, she checked the number, before lifting her gaze back to Zeke.

"Jonesy and John are getting rather impatient," she told him.

"Do you usually check in with them?" he asked her.

Rogue shook her head before flipping the phone open and bringing it to her ear.

"I'm busy," she told her bartender. "What's the problem?"

"Where the hell are you? John is going crazy trying to hunt you down and he's making me crazy," Jonesy growled. "Why can't you just let someone know when the hell you're riding off into the night?"

Her lips thinned at the controlled anger in his tone.

"Where is John?"

"Hang on, you can talk to the little bastard yourself," he snapped.

The muted sound of the band, conversation, and general good times could be heard through the phone for long seconds as Rogue threw her leg over the cycle's seat and waited impatiently as Zeke paced to the end of the garage before turning back, leaning against the wall, and crossing his arms over his chest as he watched her.

"Where the fuck are you?" John snarled into the phone. "I've called every damned number you've ever given me trying to find you."

"Since when do I have to inform you of where I'm going or what I'm doing?" she asked quietly, aware of the sound of the bar fading in the background of the phone.

"Since I suspect you ran off with that damned sheriff you insist on sleeping with," he retorted harshly. "Get your ass back here, we need to talk."

"Is the bar on fire?" she finally asked sweetly.

"Don't fuck with me, Rogue." His voice was grating and harsh. "No, the damned bar isn't on fire, no one is bleeding, dead, or hospitalized, and you aren't in danger of a lawsuit. What you are in danger of is the fact that Dad will be on the first flight out here if I make the call I'm getting ready to make."

Anger threatened to explode through her. Zeke was watching her with those cool, predatory eyes of his, as though he knew something she didn't and he was just waiting on the explosion.

John was exploding, Jonesy was acting damned strange, and for some reason, Gene, Zeke's primary deputy, couldn't get a call through to him. Zeke wasn't even wearing his cell phone.

"I'm not fourteen," she said softly. "Nor does Daddy make the rules I live by any longer. Make all the calls you want to. But be warned, John, cause me too much trouble and I'll leave you lying on the floor with your balls choking you. Understand me?"

She flipped the phone closed before he could answer, then turned it off, all the while her gaze locked with Zeke's.

"I assume explanations will be forthcoming," she said.

"You can assume." He shrugged. "Doesn't mean I have the answers." He shifted away from the wall and headed for the door. "Let's go inside, Rogue. I'll give you what I have. At this point, that's about the best I can do."

His voice was heavy, laden with something bitter that clenched at Rogue's chest and left her aching. It left her frightened.

TWENTY-ONE

Zeke could feel the anger brewing inside him. It was a dark, eternal core that had begun years ago, when he first realized how diseased his father had become. When, as a fourteen-year-old kid, Zeke had made his first kill.

Disgust stirred, thick and oily, in the pit of his stomach, its acrid taste burning his tongue at the memories he rarely allowed himself to revisit. His nervousness, the complete fear that had washed over him when he'd picked up the handgun lying on a small table. The shock and surprise in his victim's face when he'd turned, aimed, and pulled the trigger.

Because his father had told him the man they were meeting would try to kill them and would then kill Zeke's mother. That they had no choice but to be waiting on him, and the only way to surprise him was if Zeke took the shot.

Fourteen fucking years old. So damned dumb loyal to his father that he hadn't known his ass from a hole in the ground. All he knew was that his father said he was in trouble, that someone was going to try to kill all of them. As men, it was their place to protect his mother. They were the head of the house, the protectors, the defenders. And Zeke had bought into it until the second he fired that gun and saw the other man's eyes, heard his last gasping breath as he whispered, "Why?"

It played out in his nightmares sometimes, it lurked in the back of his mind when he was awake, and a part of Zeke had never forgotten that second of insight, as death glazed another man's eyes, that he would never be the same again.

Because of his father. Because he had idolized the man who had raised him, because he had trusted him, believed in him. Because he had been a stupid, dumb kid that the father he loved had manipulated.

Zeke remembered a time when Thad Mayes had been a good man. When his father's brown eyes had been clear with laughter and good humor. Until he had taken a devil's bargain. A bargain that had destroyed his marriage, his relationship with his son, and, Zeke suspected, had eventually taken his life.

Opening the door into the house, he stood aside as Rogue moved toward him slowly, her violet gaze dark with worry, her expression pensive.

The need to touch her was almost overwhelming. The need to sink inside her and forget the horrors of the past was a hunger he could barely deny himself. The need to hold her in his arms, to feel her warmth. It went beyond hunger, it was a compulsion now, an addiction. He needed her touch until he could barely function for it at times.

But under that fierce need was too much rage. It was dark and boiling inside him, demanding action. It was like a demon nipping at his soul, destroying his control.

The anger rode him too deep to allow for touch. It was too much a part of him tonight, rising from his soul until it threatened to push through the very pores of his flesh.

"What's going on, Zeke?"

He shook his head and held his hand out to her. "Come inside; this isn't the place to talk."

Staying away from her would have been the best decision. If he'd had the strength. God knew, he didn't have that strength. He'd had to fight every second for the past five years to remain aloof, to keep from taking her, until the battle had been lost.

She had come to him innocent, sweet, and pure. Her illusion of sexual experience and wild disposition was just that, an illusion. It had taken him a while to see through it, to realize certain things about his tempestuous Rogue.

She was sugar sweet on the inside; that hard outer core was so fragile that it defied understanding. She was too gentle, she was too much of everything that he didn't deserve, should never have. And his soul had claimed her despite his best intentions. The dark, ragged core of his being had reached out to her and been comforted by her when Zeke knew he didn't deserve that comfort.

She licked her lips and his body clenched in longing. She took a deep breath, lifting her breasts against her T-shirt, and his hands ached to cup the firm mounds.

She was young, precious. Could she understand the man he was, the man that had been years in the making?

But she took his hand. Her fingers accepted his as they twined them through hers. Tiny, fragile, so fucking tender. Her hands were like silk and his dwarfed them.

"A lot of people have been looking for you today," she told him softly as he drew her into the house. "I assume John found you?"

"John found me." He nodded as he led her inside, then closed and locked the door behind them.

He set the security alarm, just to be safe. He had no fear of his son walking in on them tonight; he'd made certain Shane was safe in Louisville and that Lucinda kept him there. It wasn't the fear of his son seeing something he shouldn't that rode Zeke now. It was the fear of being caught off guard before he could finish what he started.

"Gene's looking for you," she told him then. "He was at the bar."

"I know." And he didn't want to talk about Gene, not yet. They'd been through hell together as boys, and Zeke thought the bond that had developed then would see them through their adult years. He had been more wrong than he could have ever imagined.

"So you're avoiding him?" she asked as he led her through the darkened house.

He didn't turn on the lights as he led her through the kitchen to the basement door. It was opened, the light below was still on, lighting the stairs as he led her down them.

"I'm avoiding him," he agreed.

"Zeke." She paused halfway down the steps, tugging at his hand.

Zeke turned back to her. There was no fear in her eyes, but there was a hint of worry.

"The answers I have are down here," he told her, his jaw clenching at the truth of his life, a truth he may not be able to hide for much longer.

His father had begun this legacy, and now Zeke was going to have to finish it. Finishing it would mean revealing the truth of the past, the truth of what he had nearly become and the boundaries crossed by men he had once respected.

Dayle Mackay had started this decades ago. With his brother and a few military friends they had destroyed more lives than Zeke wanted to contemplate.

Zeke had worked ten years to uncover the proof of what Dayle was, and in a few short months the Mackay cousins had managed to do what he had fought to do for a decade. But that was okay. He'd let them do it; he had known what they were doing, and he had stood back and watched it unfold as he had been ordered to do. Homeland Security had ripped through Somerset like a plague. Men he hadn't known were involved had been uncovered as homeland terrorists working for a future destruction of the government as the nation knew it.

He'd helped gather the evidence last year, and he'd kept his own secrets.

Until now.

"I was born in Somerset," he told her as he led her into the basement.

Boxes upon boxes of a life he hadn't wanted to remember were opened now, their contents spilling along the floor and the tables he had used to stack them on.

"I knew that." Her fingers were stiff in his hold as she stared around the basement.

"I left when I was fourteen. I was twenty-seven before I came back."

He glanced at her as she nodded slowly, her violet gaze locked on him.

"I came back, because I thought surely, with Thad Mayes's death, it couldn't be as bad as it was when I was a kid. And if it was, I had a plan."

Bitterness welled inside him.

"To become sheriff," she stated.

He nodded at that. "To become sheriff. To clean out the filth I knew lurked just below the surface of one of the most beautiful areas in the world. I'd make it safe, I thought."

"You have made it safe, Zeke," she ventured softly.

Zeke shook his head as he released her hand. "No, the Mackay cousins and DHS made it safe. I worked for ten years to gather the evidence I needed, and I was blocked at every turn. I couldn't figure out how it was happening for years."

He moved away from her then. "It took an old man's careless comment to remind me of a few things, and then it fell into place."

He turned back to her and breathed out harshly.

"I'm not leaving town," she said then. "I can see it in your face, Zeke. You're going to ask me to leave again."

He shook his head to that. "It's too late for any of us to escape this fucking mess."

He turned and faced the contents of the boxes he'd emptied.

"Mom was like a pack rat." He sighed. "She had so much junk she had to rent a storage unit for it. When she died and the house burned around her, I just packed all these boxes away after I retrieved them, thinking I'd go through them someday. See what she had kept. I didn't expect she had everything I had ever searched for. Once I found some of it, it wasn't that hard to know where to look for the rest of it."

There were pictures, there were journals he'd never known his mother kept. Dozens of journals, each day of her life from the day she married Thad Mayes recorded. She had never told him about the journals and he had never known she kept one. After the divorce she never took pictures, so Zeke hadn't remembered the camera she had carried with her during her marriage to Thad Mayes.

He'd forgotten most of his life as a child, because remembering always brought him back to the scent of blood in the air, and the betrayal of a father he had adored.

"What were you looking for?" she asked.

"Proof," he answered, turning back to her. "Proof that Dayle Mackay, Nadine Grace, and several of Kentucky's highest ranking political figures were involved in treason. I knew." He shook his head as he moved to the pictures. "I've always known, I just couldn't prove it."

"Dayle and Nadine are gone," she whispered. "They're dead, Zeke."

"They're dead, but their legacy lives on."

"Zeke, you're scaring me."

There was a hint of fear in her voice, in her gaze as he turned back to her, and he knew that the time for the truth was now or never.

"Thirty years ago, there were three friends," he told her. "They were as close as brothers."

He laid out the three individual pictures. Thad Mayes, Gene's father, James Maynard, and Danny Jones.

"These friends hunted together, they partied together, and like the Mackays did for a time, they fucked together." His lips quirked bitterly at the little gasp that fell from her lips.

"Then, along came a woman." He pulled another picture free, that of Nadine Grace, then Nadine Mackay.

There was a series of pictures then. Depraved, sexual acts the three men were involved in with the woman that had been photographed. He glanced at Rogue's face and saw in her eyes the same disgust he felt each time he had looked at those pictures after finding them. He had no idea who had taken them, or why. But they were the reason his mother had died.

"Then, Nadine Mackay set her eyes on another man." He drew a picture of a young John Calvin Walker free.

He looked like his son, John. This picture showed Cal Walker in front of the Bar, a bright smile on his face as he shook Danny Jones's hand.

"Now, he and Danny 'Jonesy' Jones were good friends. But I don't think he knew what Jonesy was involved in with his other friends. Until this woman showed up."

Rogue's mother, Brianna Evansworth.

"Zeke," she whispered. "Don't destroy me."

He turned back to her and saw the fear and desperation in her face.

Zeke shook his head. "Your father loved her the moment he saw her." He turned back to the pictures. "Do you know why your father left Somerset?"

She shook her head slowly, her eyes filling with tears.

"Because Dayle Mackay wanted her," he stated. "Dayle wanted the Evansworth money that backed her, and he asked his three friends, Thad, James, and Jonesy, to help him."

It was all recorded in his mother's journal. Years of sexual excess and photos that Dayle Mackay had sent to Thad Mayes when he'd tried to deny the other man anything that he wanted.

"Jonesy refused. That's why his leg is messed up. Not from that motorcycle wreck, though that didn't help it. He was shot in the leg by his good friend Thad Mayes when it was learned he had warned Cal Walker that Dayle Mackay was going to try to take the woman he loved. Dayle thought a woman could be trained like a dog. Chain it up, starve it, abuse it, and it will come to heel."

Sickness welled inside him.

"Cal and Brianna left for Boston," he said. "Jonesy stayed, his friendship with Thad and James supposedly severed. But Somerset was his home. He eventually married and had a daughter. Thad divorced and his wife and son moved away, and James's son, Gene, slowly separated himself from his father. They weren't happy times for that little group, were they?" He glanced back at her.

"Except for my father."

"Except for your father," he agreed.

"We flash to the present now," he said. "Joe and Jaime. They were in love with a girl." He turned to her, his chest heavy as she stared back at him. "A very young girl, and they were going to share her. And this is where things get dicey. This is where the sins of the father come back to haunt them."

He ran his hands over his face wearily. "This is where the sons have to pay the price for their fathers' crimes maybe."

"You know the woman they were seeing?"

He nodded. "I think I know who she was. And I know why the boys and their grandmother died."

He slid a picture free. Gene, when he was younger, a teenager. It came from a stack of pictures that showed his friend throughout his life, until Thad Mayes's death actually. Because Thad believed in insurance. He had sent his ex-wife pictures for years.

He fanned the pictures over the table as Rogue moved forward. She stared down at them as he did, that same black fury growing inside him as her hand lifted to his arm and her fingers tightened there.

"Oh God," she whispered when she came to the pictures that incriminated the man he had once thought of as a brother. The picture of Gene, his father, and Thad as they stood together with another couple, all dressed in camo gear, rifles held easily in their arms. The couple they stood with was Dayle Mackay and Nadine Grace.

"They were a part of the Freedom League," she whispered as she stared at the pictures. "Even Gene."

It wasn't hard to miss. The FL was emblazoned on the shoulders of their camo gear, but even more incriminating were the bound bodies in front of them. The dead bodies of two state police officers that had gone missing ten years ago.

It was an unsolved case, one that Zeke had been investigating himself for years. All this time, and the proof was under his nose.

"Goddammit, all this time." He swung away from her, the fury erupting inside him. "I had the proof all this time. That son of a bitch father of mine was sending Mom sealed envelopes of pictures and she never even opened them. Boxes of information, of proof. She kept them in boxes in a frigging rental unit in Los Angeles and never even opened them."

Because she had known what they were. He'd read parts of her journals, bits and pieces. No one would have suspected Thad Mayes of sending his ex-wife anything so incriminating. She hadn't been a part of the League—it was the reason for their divorce—but still, she had kept his secrets, kept his evidence against himself and the men he had banded together with.

Just in case, she had written in her journal. He had asked her to take anything he sent her and place it, unopened, in a safe place. He'd collect it later, he had promised. He had never collected it.

A few months before her death she had written in that last journal that Thad was going to make life easier for her. Zeke was grown and on his own, and it was time she enjoyed her life. She'd threatened to turn the pictures over to the authorities. Pictures she had taken while she had been with him, pictures of the men that had formed the Freedom League. She'd had no idea the proof she had actually held in that damned rental unit. Proof far more incriminating than what she'd had herself.

She'd stored that journal away, the last one she had written in before she was killed. A year later, Thad Mayes had died in another inferno that had burned his body and any evidence he may have kept himself. That had been mere months after the picture of the two dead state police officers had been taken.

"Joe and Jaime were seeing Gene's youngest daughter, Cammi," Rogue said faintly. "That's what this is all about, isn't it?"

Zeke felt as though the tension was going to break him apart. His muscles, his bones, were tight with the fury racing through him.

"She had to have been the girl they were seeing. Joe and Jaime knew Gene was a part of the Freedom League," he said harshly.

"They knew, and they didn't say anything because of Cammi. Because they were in love with her. But someone overheard a conversation they had. One where Jaime stated that Gene was a part of what happened last year with the Mackays. That he'd use it against her father if he caused them too much trouble. They died because of what they knew, and that's why Callie Walker died as well. Because Gene had to keep his part in this a secret." His fists clenched at his side. "Because he was still a part of the League."

"Do you have proof?"

Zeke shook his head. "All I have is proof that he was part of the League, and the deaths of those officers."

"What are you going to do, Zeke?" she asked. "Gene is at the bar looking for you. He said he'd been trying to contact you all day. He has to be suspicious."

"I've faxed the pictures to Agent Cranston," he told her as he turned to her. "I want you to stay here, Rogue, where you'll be safe. No one will know you're here. The bar could be torched with you in it. They don't care to kill innocent bystanders. I'm meeting the Mackay cousins and Agent Cranston in town in an hour. We'll take care of this tonight. All of it."

He'd been busy. The moment Teddy Winfred's information had clicked in his brain Zeke had come home to search for the pictures he had himself from his youth. In searching for them, he'd found the boxes of sealed, mailed envelopes his mother had kept. The information in her journals had shocked him, enraged him. It had taken most of the day to find everything, and there were still more to go through. But he had what he needed.

"What about Cammi?" she asked. "She's not part of this, Zeke."

He stared at her in surprise. Cammi had never been kind to Rogue. She had sneered at her, insulted her countless times over the years, but still Rogue was thinking of her. And, as Rogue stated,

Cammi was innocent of everything but wanting the wrong men. He hoped.

"We'll watch out for Cammi," he promised her. "I want your promise that you'll stay here, keep your phone off, stay out of contact."

He held her gaze, willing, determined that she would do exactly as he wanted her to do. He couldn't give her promises yet, he couldn't let himself believe in promises yet, not until this was finished.

"What aren't you telling me?" She asked the question he hoped she wouldn't. "How are you involved in this, Zeke?"

He leaned against the old desk, crossed his arms over his chest, and watched her carefully.

"Look at those pictures again," he told her softly. "The earlier ones, Rogue. I was fourteen before Mom divorced that bastard. The League is generational, baby. I was a part of it before we went to Los Angeles. Before I even understood what it meant, I was there. I hunted with them, I listened to their plans, and I let myself be convinced I was right, they were right. This is why I came back, to see it finished. The Mackays cut off the head of the organization, but the body's still alive. It can reform if it's not finished. This will finish it. My mother and my wife were killed as a warning. Gene has to know how close I am to revealing his part in this. I can't risk you. I'd die if I lost you."

"There's more." She shook her head, those flaming curls whispering around her shoulders and down her back as she stared back at him from the most beautiful eyes in the world.

He'd tried to hide from what he felt for her. From the time he first saw her, until now. As though a veil lifted from his soul, Zeke saw what he didn't want to see. Emotions fueled by needs. The knowledge that this one woman had been created for him. She could be his greatest strength or his greatest weakness in the hands of his enemies.

"You've played everyone," she finally said softly. "You've suspected all this, all along. Didn't you?"

He barely managed to hide his surprise.

"I'm not sure I know what you're talking about." He forced himself away from the table, paced to the other side of the room, then turned back to her.

"You suspected Gene was a part of the League and that Joe and Jaime had somehow been killed because of the group."

She hadn't moved, but her gaze followed him, thoughtful, partially angry.

"What part did I play in this, Zeke?" she asked him as she waved her hand toward the scattered papers and pictures. "How did sleeping with me help you to get where you were trying to go?"

His jaw clenched. Hell, he was hoping she wouldn't see that, because while that's what it may have begun as, it wasn't finishing that way.

"They were watching me," he finally said softly. "They were focused on my investigation of Joe and Jaime's death. They weren't watching DHS or the Mackay boys. Cranston was never suspended from duty, officially. The Mackays were never off the case. Gene's been watching you for years, simply because you were Calvin's daughter and because Jonesy tried to protect you. He wondered what you knew, what Jonesy knew. I let them focus on that while the others did their job."

Rogue felt the pain explode in her chest as Zeke stared back at her. The lack of emotion in his voice, in his eyes, cut her to the quick.

"It was all some elaborate ruse then?" she whispered. "It was never about us, was it, Zeke?"

"I couldn't afford for it to be about us, Rogue," he said softly as he turned away from her again. "Not yet."

He wasn't turning away because he couldn't bear to see her hurt, she saw. He was turning away to collect the weapons that lay on the other side of the room. His gun belt and weapon, which he strapped on efficiently. The rifle he collected from the side of the wall.

"You're an intelligent woman," he said, his tone so precise, so cool she felt flayed by the very lack of emotion in it. "Stay here where you're safe. Stay off the phone. I'll let you know when it's finished."

She fought back her tears and her anger. She tried to swallow and felt as though she would choke from the tightness in her throat.

"John," she whispered. "What about my brother?"

God, John had been right all along. This wasn't about love, it wasn't about anything Zeke might want from her emotionally. It was about a very elaborate deception. It was all about his job, nothing more.

"Natches has John out of the way," he promised her. "He's safe. You're safe. Now let me clean up my town and undo the damage Thad Mayes did to this county without leaving any more scars on my conscience."

Scars on his conscience. He was protecting her so he wouldn't feel any guilt if she ended up hurt. It was no more than that. She wanted to go to her knees from the pain; instead, she managed to hold her head upright and even managed to nod.

"By all means." She forced a tight smile to her face; she even managed not to shed a tear. "I'm sure I can find something to do here while you're out saving the world." She waved her hand negligently back at him. "Have fun, Sheriff Mayes."

Be safe, Zeke. She whispered the words silently as he turned and headed for the stairs.

She wouldn't cry yet, she promised herself. She wasn't going to let herself shed more tears for another betrayal. She'd shed enough, she'd lost enough dreams. She wouldn't lose her pride as well.

His foot rested on the first step before he paused. His back was still to her when he said, "I didn't want things to be this way."

Lips trembling, she had to force back the cry welling in her soul. She hated him. Oh God, she hated him! She hated him just as much as she loved him.

"But they are," she said, barely holding back the pain now. "We'll talk later, Zeke. You have a job to do. Right?"

He nodded, his head still turned away. "I have a job to do."

With that, he moved quickly up the stairs and left her alone with a basement filled with his memories, his life. Pictures and boxes of mementos. Sand in a bottle. Seashells. A framed picture of his wedding day. Shane's first photo as a newborn. And stacks of pictures from Zeke's childhood.

She turned and stared around the basement, willing her heart not to shatter into the pieces she knew it had already shattered into. She could feel the jagged wound in her soul and the ache that seemed never ending.

Pressing her hand into her stomach she pushed back the sob locked in her throat and took a deep, hard breath. Her knees were shaking, her hands trembling, and damn Zeke Mayes to hell, there were tears on her face.

Her breathing hitched as she wrapped her arms across her breasts and turned away from the pictures, the story he had told her. There were gaps, there was something missing. Something he hadn't told her.

Rogue turned back and stalked to the table, scrambling for the pictures, searching for answers. There had to be answers here. There was more to this than he had told her. There was something in his eyes that assured her of that before he left. There were demons that haunted him, dark places that festered in his soul. Parts of him that she had sensed and yet had never known.

There were secrets.

She pushed aside the first piles of pictures, went through the others. She stacked them in neat, orderly rows as she moved through them.

There were Zeke's baby pictures. Pictures of him with his mother and father as a toddler, pictures as he grew and became a teenager.

The majority of the pictures after his teen years were those with his father. In each progression there was a hardness to Thad Mayes's once-handsome face. A cold reptilian chill began showing in his eyes.

There were pictures that raised the hair on the back of her neck. Pictures of Thad Mayes, James Maynard, and Dayle Mackay participating in sex acts that would have brought shame to the most hedonistic of men. But there were no more pictures of Zeke.

"He burned them all, you know."

Rogue jerked around, fear strangling her as she saw a panel slide open to reveal a gap in the cement wall of the basement, and watched as Jonesy stepped through it.

Eyes round, terror surging through her, she watched as he moved into the basement and looked around slowly, his expression heavy and filled with regret as his gaze came back to hers.

"Jonesy," she whispered, a sob finally tearing from her throat.

"We were always the best of friends," he said softly. "Me, Thad, and James. Your daddy didn't change that. There were just some things that I was too young to understand then."

He stepped fully into the room and then she saw the handgun he held at his side. The one he lifted slowly and aimed toward her.

"John's dead," he said. "I took care of him and that Mackay bastard before I came here for you and the sheriff."

She shook her head; her hands clenched desperately around the rim of the table beside her as she lowered her head and shuddered from the pain. Not Jonesy. Oh God, she couldn't bear it. She loved him like an uncle. He'd saved her when she needed him. He'd been her friend.

"Why?" she sobbed, her head lifting as fury began to pour inside her. "Why, Jonesy?"

He shook his head. "The bastard burned the pictures of his boy while he obviously saved all the others. Thad was a fool. I warned him that little son of a bitch would end up turning up and taking a bite out of our asses. He always was a foolish little prick."

"Why?" she demanded again. "Why are you here? Why are you involved in this?"

He tilted his head and watched her almost curiously.

"Because, despite your sheriff's beliefs, the head of the serpent was never cut off, sweetheart. Mackay didn't have the temperament to be the head of anything. He took orders. He was a soldier that became a liability. He was a disease. The head is alive and breathing." He smiled, a cold, hard curve to his lips. "And Zeke might run, but he can't hide from the truth. He's a part of it. He'll always be a part of it."

TWENTY-TWO

She was hurting. Zeke swore he could feel her hurt
as he left the house and forced himself into the Tahoe he had hidden in the back drive. The vehicle was hidden there, beneath a
dense covering of trees where it wouldn't be detected, along an
old dirt farm road his father had used when his parents had lived
in this house.

His father had moved into another house closer to town after Zeke and his mother had left. The farm had been pretty much
abandoned for years, until Zeke returned.

It was the hardest thing Zeke had ever done, forcing himself
into the vehicle before starting the engine and pulling out of the
drive. He headed back toward the Bar when everything inside him
was urging him to return to the house, to explain, to tell her why
this had to be done and the ghosts he had to exorcise from his own
past.

His mother hadn't left his father simply because of his adulterous activities. Nothing was ever that simple with his mother. She had divorced Thad Mayes because he had finally crossed a line that was unacceptable to her. He had tricked his son into committing a crime that she knew would haunt him for the rest of his life.

At the age of fourteen, Zeke had shot and killed a man. It didn't matter that he had killed another of the League's members, one that his father wanted rid of. It didn't matter that the man was a deviant with the sexual tastes of the criminally insane. The fact was, Zeke had killed him. He had lifted his father's handgun from the table, turned, and shot the bastard in the heart, just as his father had taught him during target practice.

The old hunting cabin where the murder had taken place was gone now; someone had burned it to the ground after Zeke and his mother left town. Zeke often wondered if his father had destroyed it. If he'd ever regretted that night and fought to get rid of the memories as well.

Zeke still had nightmares. He still remembered his father's pride, how he had lifted the slain man's head in one hand and smiled back at the camera James Maynard had wielded, as though the death were a triumph.

Zeke had become ill. He'd thrown up for days. For weeks he'd been unable to sleep, until he finally told his mother what had happened. It was then that she had packed their bags and escaped with him to Los Angeles, along with many of the pictures she knew his father had.

Her insurance, she had called it. And Thad Mayes had sent her more insurance over the years. He'd been confident she wouldn't talk; she knew the price of talking. Everyone who talked died. Proof didn't matter, but she'd had enough to keep her safe.

Now Zeke was breaking that unwritten law of keeping silent. He had talked. Years ago he had talked to Timothy Cranston when the plans to trap the homeland terrorist group were first being hatched.

He hadn't known the Mackays would be brought in on it. He hadn't known he would be pushed out of the investigation once it started. He hadn't known about the pictures his mother had amassed. But he knew now. DHS knew now. They knew everything, even his own crime.

He'd stayed as far away from her as possible until it wasn't possible any longer, he told himself. But he hadn't used her to the extent she believed. Taking her to his bed had been something he'd been unable to fight. But still, it had played into the job he had set for himself. That of trapping the last members of the League.

He needed Gene's attention focused on him while Cranston and the Mackay cousins worked their magic to finish the investigation they'd started years before.

It would come to a head tonight. They had the Walkers' killers; they had the information on the last of the members of the League in this area as well as others. They had pictures; they had his mother's journals, all of which would be turned over to Cranston the second they met up. And tonight Gene would be at the bar with the last members of the homeland terrorist organization that would finally be rooted from his county forever.

It was almost over. More than twenty years of hell, and Zeke would see the end of it tonight. When the sun broke in the morning, the weight of a lifetime of guilt would be lifted from his shoulders, and he would have the satisfaction of knowing he had finished it.

And tonight, Zeke had broken Rogue's heart. He'd seen it in her eyes and he'd been helpless to stop it, just as he'd been helpless to stay away from her. He'd grasped at the excuse to forget his own principles and take her to his bed. He'd known what he was doing even as he'd done it, and he'd prayed they'd both survive it.

He had known he was going to hurt her, but he hadn't expected to feel that pain as though it were a part of him as well. He hadn't expected to hurt with her for everything he knew they may not have.

Not that Zeke was willing to let her go yet. He knew to the bottom of his soul if he survived this night, he'd do his best to heal her heart and claim it again. But if he didn't return, if he couldn't come back to her for whatever reason, then he'd know she wouldn't wait. The pain would ease with the anger, and her hatred would protect him from her loyalty.

Turning onto the back road that led to Rogue's bar, Zeke tightened his hands on the wheel of the Tahoe and felt the muscles in his jaw flex at the thought of claiming her, free and clear, knowing there might be a real future, rather than just the here and now, or the hope of a future.

This had been hanging over his head for too long. The risk of discovery before the remaining members of the League were identified. The risk that the men he was searching for would realize just how deep he was into this rather than watching from the sidelines as it had appeared.

At this point, nothing mattered but finishing this and getting back to Rogue to explain, to beg for forgiveness. To touch her. To know he had the right to touch her as he needed to. God help him, as he needed to.

The need to touch her, to taste her one last time had been nearly overwhelming. If he had though, he'd have not made it out of the house without possessing her, without telling her the truth. Without loving her.

"I'll be back, Rogue," he whispered, and he wished he had said it before he left.

He made the final turn toward the bar when the world exploded around him.

Zeke slammed on the brakes as a ball of fire erupted into the night where Rogue's bar had been. Debris and flames tore through the darkness as vehicles were racing out of the parking lot.

It rained fire. The ground shook with a secondary explosion, spurring Zeke to slam his foot on the gas as he flipped the sirens on.

The Mackay cousins and Rogue's brother were in that bar. They were waiting in the office, watching through the security cameras as Gene met with the other members of the League that were still free at the bar. He'd been meeting them right beneath Zeke's nose. So confident. Damn him. He'd taken Zeke's trust for granted, had taken his loyalty for granted.

All these years he had trusted Gene with the truth. He'd discussed each move he'd made with the other man; he'd let him in on every step he'd taken. And he'd been betrayed. He'd hoped he was wrong. Prayed he was wrong. He had never imagined the depths of Gene's guilt though.

That betrayal was like acid on his tongue as the Tahoe screamed into the bar's parking lot. The vehicle slid to a stop, rocking from the force applied to the brakes as Zeke caught sight of Dawg dragging Natches and John across the parking lot.

He jumped from the vehicle, racing toward them.

"Cranston and Rowdy. Where are they?" he screamed as he gripped Dawg's shoulders, holding him in place.

Dawg's face was pale, blood streaked, his green eyes wild. "Inside. Goddammit, they're inside."

Everything inside Zeke began to congeal in complete rage. Turning on his heel, he ran for the bar. Pushing through the hysterical guests pouring from the main entrance to stagger into the smoky haze inside as he searched for the other two men.

"Cranston!" he screamed out the agent's name.

"I have him."

Zeke turned, staring in shock as Gene stumbled through the smoky haze.

He and Rowdy supported Cranston's half-conscious form. Gene's blond hair was singed, soot covered his face. A gash along his forehead seeped blood and Rowdy didn't look much better.

"Let's get the hell out of here." Zeke took Rowdy's weight as he swayed and nearly went to his knees. "Son of a bitch, their wives will kill me."

"No shit," Gene snarled furiously, his blue eyes enraged. "If I don't end up killing every friggin' damned one of you myself. Motherfuckers. This is what I get for trusting a slimy damned Homeland Security agent and my best fucking friend."

Confusion and rage clouded Zeke's mind. With his hands full of Rowdy's nearly unconscious form, he couldn't slug Gene. He followed him instead, finally having to duck and sling Rowdy's weight over his shoulder to rush him from the bar as another explosion shook it.

Too damned much liquor. It was going off like mini-bombs as the fire began to race through the entire building.

"Thank God. Son of a bitch. Son of a bitch." Dawg raced toward them, his green eyes demented in his haggard face. "Is he alive?"

Dawg jerked Rowdy from Zeke as Gene collapsed on the grass, far enough away from the bar for safety, and let Timothy Cranston's weight slide to the ground.

"What the hell happened here?" Zeke jerked Dawg around, glaring down at him as sirens began to fill the air.

"We fucked up, that's what the hell happened," Dawg screamed. "You were watching the wrong man. Fucking Cranston, I'm killing the son of a bitch this time. He had us watch Gene when Gene was working with him all along. He wasn't the man we were searching for."

Dawg was out of control. Thick, heavy veins pulsed in his neck as his green eyes glowed with a rage that warned Zeke that the other man wouldn't think before killing.

"What the hell are you talking about? You were watching the wrong man?"

"Because I'm not your goddamned killer, you fucking moron." Gene stumbled to his feet, swaying before righting himself. "And Cranston knew it. The dirty bastard, I've been working with him since the day those two state police offers were killed. Yeah, the fucking pictures you found?" he sneered in Zeke's face. "I didn't kill those men, Zeke."

"You were there!"

"I was there, and my whole fucking family was at risk if I made the first fucking wrong move!" Gene screamed. "My family, Zeke. My wife. My kids. I contacted someone I knew in DHS after the bodies were taken away. The morbid motherfucker had me watching you."

Shock resounded through Zeke with a tidal wave force as he stared back at Gene. Cranston was a manipulating bastard, there was no doubt of that. From the moment he had hit town with the supposed excuse of having been suspended, Zeke had known he was playing games. Hell, Zeke had been helping him play those games, and he'd never suspected he was being hung out to dry like every other agent that ever worked for Cranston was hung out.

"He had me watching you," Zeke rasped.

"And the killer got away." Dawg pushed between the two men. "Your killer is Jonesy, Zeke. He slipped out of the bar after taking a baseball bat to Natches and Walker. He's gone."

Zeke stared back at him, fighting to process the information bombarding him now.

He turned to Gene, the suspicions tearing through him now were destructive. Cranston had known all along. Like Zeke, he had no proof of his suspicions, unlike Zeke, he hadn't been chasing shadows. Cranston had had them all chasing shadows as he focused on Jonesy.

"Did you know it was Jonesy?" Zeke rasped back at Gene.

Gene shook his head furiously. "Jonesy wasn't part of the League, Zeke."

"Are you sure?" Zeke grabbed him by his shirt collar and jerked him closer. "Think, Gene. Did he know about the house? My house?"

Did Jonesy know about the secret tunnel into the basement, or the entrance to it?

Gene's eyes widened. "God. You hid her at the house. God, no, Zeke."

"Did he know about the house?" Zeke shook him roughly. "Did he know about the tunnel into the basement?"

It was the only way to get to her without setting off the alarms that would have instantly rang Zeke's phone. It was the only way anyone could get to Rogue.

"Zeke, it was his idea," Gene rasped. "Dad told me about it. Jonesy helped plan the construction of that tunnel years before your father ever built the house."

"It wasn't supposed to be like this." Jonesy's voice was saddened, filled with regret, but Rogue also saw the maniacal glimmer of determination in his eyes as he slowly closed the panel to the hidden tunnel.

He stared around the room, his expression resolved, but also heavy. As though two men resided inside him, but the one that held the gun was now dominant.

"It wasn't supposed to be like what, Jonesy?" She stared at the gun incredulously. "Like a man betraying everyone who loves him?"

She knew the moment she saw the gun that Gene wasn't the only man that had betrayed a friend. Of course it had been in the pictures as well. Those scattered across Zeke's desk. The three men, Thad Mayes, James Maynard, and Jonesy. The friendship they had forged as young men hadn't been broken. The friendship that had aided Dayle Mackay and Nadine Grace in their treasonous activities had never disintegrated. It had remained strong, regardless of what others thought. A bond such as the three had shared would have been nearly impossible to break completely.

"I'm not betraying a friend." He locked gazes with her, anger shadowing his eyes. "A friend would have listened when I warned her to steer clear of trouble. Your daddy listened. He took his woman and he left town, like I told him to do. Unfortunately, he didn't come back and collect his daughter as I've warned him to do in the past five years. For some reason, Cal thought the threat was gone because Thad, Dayle, and Nadine were gone." He shook his head with a mocking little grunt. "He didn't consider James a threat, and he thought Gene's loyalty would stay with Zeke. He's not as smart as he used to be, Rogue. Or maybe he really just doesn't care what happens to his troublemaking daughter."

That wasn't the case. Her father had screamed, harassed, and threatened her for five years in an attempt to get her back to Boston. His last-ditch effort was sending in John.

Her breathing hitched harshly. Oh God, John.

"Where's John?" she whispered, his claim that he had killed her brother ricocheting through her mind. "What have you done, Jonesy?"

"Same thing I did to Thad." He sighed. "That baseball bat I keep at the bar has a lot of blood staining it, Rogue. Now it has your brother's and Natches Mackay's as well. Right now, they're burning in the flames of hell. I set an explosion in the bar. It's gone, little girl. Gone along with your brother, Timothy Cranston, and those bastard Mackay cousins."

"No." Her head shook in disbelief. "You wouldn't hurt John. Jonesy, please. You didn't hurt John."

Where was the man her father had said he would trust his life to? The man Rogue had trusted her life to?

Jonesy shook his head, regret filling his eyes though the gun never wavered. "I told you to stay away from Zeke Mayes, Rogue. He's been trying to identify the remaining members of the League for six months now. Hell, we knew all along that he was working for DHS to take us down. Gene kept us informed there. The League has to survive. Our plans will go through. The future is more important than friendship or blood, girl." His voice rose as anger filled it. His expression creased in fury as his hand tightened around the gun.

Rogue could feel the deadly intent that washed through the room now. Jonesy was going to kill her. She could see it in his eyes, in his face. The man she had thought she had known didn't exist. Nothing existed behind the eyes she had once thought she could read except anger and murderous determination.

Betrayal was a rancid taste in her mouth as she fought to swallow past the tightness in her throat. Rogue wanted to howl with the pain now. She could feel the sharp wounds burying inside her soul, digging into her with merciless agony.

Tears were locked in her throat and in her eyes as she stared back at Jonesy, from his powerful shoulders to the insanity glittering in his eyes. It could only be insanity. There could be nothing sane about what he was doing. He had killed John and Natches.

John lit up the world with his games and his laughter. He was cynical, sometimes he was bitter, but he had loved her, made her laugh.

And Natches, with his crooked grin and his complete devotion to his wife and unborn child. He liked to joke that his wife would be the one to kill him eventually. Instead, it had been Jonesy. A trusted friend.

She couldn't believe either of them were dead. John and Natches both were tough; they were strong. Jonesy might have hurt them, but she refused to believe they weren't alive any longer.

Especially John. The brother who had taught her how to fight, the one that hid frogs in her drawers when she was a child, yet had bloodied his friend's nose when she was younger for frightening her. He had protected her. He loved her. She couldn't lose him.

"Yeah, it's a hard thing, realizing it's your fault your brother's dead. Your friends." A flash of regret clouded his eyes for long seconds. "It wasn't easy to dispose of John, I want you to know that. But it wasn't near as hard as killing Thad Mayes was. We were like brothers. But he was a weakness to the League. All that picture taking him and James Maynard had done. He threatened us with those pictures, you know? He wanted out. Wanted to go to L.A. to be with that bastard son of his." Jonesy snorted at that. "He grew weak in his old age. Then that stupid wife of his trying to blackmail us and his dumb kid asking the wrong questions. We took care of Thad's wife, and Zeke's, too. And we took care of Thad. Thought Zeke got the message, loud and clear. When he came back here, I was gonna let it go. He was nice and quiet, wasn't making any waves that I knew of."

"And Joe and Jaime?" she whispered, her fingers tightening into fists as she stared back at him. "You killed them, too, didn't you?"

He smiled at that. "They trusted me. Joe came to me, said he knew Gene was a part of the League. He wanted to use that information to make Gene back off where that girl of his was concerned. They were stupid, Rogue, and that grandmother of theirs wasn't any smarter. The stupid bitch even called me, asking about Gene." He shook his head at that. "So I killed her, too. And no one suspected. You know she cried when I picked her up out of that bed and told her what I was going to do. Cried tears and begged me not to."

And he had enjoyed it. Rogue saw it in his face. Jonesy had enjoyed killing Callie Walker. The same way he would enjoy killing her, she realized.

"How do you think you're going to get away with this, Jonesy?" Her voice was filled with tears, tears she refused to shed. She wouldn't give him the satisfaction of begging or crying. She wouldn't let him enjoy what he was getting ready to do to that extent. "Zeke will know Gene didn't do this. You've killed too many people."

"And anyone who would have talked is dead by now." He shrugged. "I rigged the main gas tank to explode at the bar. It would have taken out most of the building, especially the back section where Gene was meeting with the few members left in town. I got John and Natches, and Cranston along with the other two Mackay cousins aren't a threat if they managed to survive it. The League will reform without the weak bastards that were cowering in their homes praying not to get arrested. I'll rebuild the League here, and one day, it will be more glorious than ever before."

That damned League. The Freedom League. The group of military and ex-military fanatics that thought they could wage a revolution and take control of the government. Rogue would have laughed if the situation weren't so desperate right now.

"Homeland Security broke the League, Jonesy," she reminded him. "All but a few stragglers are in prison or dead. Your generals are gone. The money is gone. How can you rebuild after that?"

She had to think, she had to keep him talking, give herself a chance to get away from him. She couldn't let him kill her; she couldn't let him hurt anyone else that she loved.

"Rebuilding is never hard." He shrugged his broad shoulders at her question. "You just need the right men in place. I have those connections. I know how to do it."

"You're a bartender," she rasped. "In Kentucky, Jonesy. This isn't a major metropolis. What connections could you have?"

He chuckled at her question. "Poor Rogue. I know it has to be hard to die, sweetheart. I promise, I'll make sure it doesn't hurt." He lifted the gun.

"Look at the pictures, Jonesy. Zeke already knows you're involved." She threw her hand out to the table where the pictures were scattered. "Thad Mayes wasn't stupid. He sent Zeke's mother pictures. He doesn't even have all of them here," she lied. "He went after the others. Don't you think Thad would have protected himself, even from you?"

He paused, his eyes narrowing as it flickered to the table and the pictures. "I burned those pictures," he seemed to wheeze.

"He made copies," she warned him. "Lots of copies, Jonesy. He sent them to Zeke's mother, and you know he sent them other places. He knew you would betray him, Jonesy. Zeke's going to know when he finds them all. He'll know you blew up the bar. You're missing now. He'll notice you're missing."

He shook his head slowly. "I covered my ass. Everyone but you heard me say I had to leave this evening. I wasn't supposed to be there."

"He'll know, Jonesy. He knows you were calling me before I arrived here. He'll figure it out, especially when he finds the other pictures."

It was a desperate lie, but it was logical to her. Thad had sent Zeke's mother pictures; he could have sent other copies elsewhere.

"There are no pictures in there of me." But indecision flickered in his gaze.

Rogue forced a mocking smile to her lips. "But there are, Jonesy. There are several." She moved back and waved her hand toward the hundreds of pictures scattered over the table. "Just look. He has all he needs to take you down just as the others were taken down."

She wouldn't have much time. Rogue fought to keep the thunder of her heart from her ears and to keep panic from setting in. She couldn't think about John or Natches; she couldn't let herself sink into the well of despair waiting on her.

She was logical. She could find a way out of this. She searched the room through her peripheral vision and tried to find a means of escape as she backed away from the table, allowing Jonesy to move closer to it.

The basement was cluttered with years of old furniture, clothes, and boxes. There were lamps propped against old tables, a hunting rifle in the other corner, a two-by-four piece of lumber stretched along the back of the couch.

She wished she had a weapon. She should have thought and made Zeke leave one with her. He'd left her here, thinking she was protected, and she had believed she would be. No, she'd been too shocked to think, too hurt to use her brain rather than her emotions.

The best-laid plans, she thought sarcastically. Zeke had known about the tunnel. He had thought she would be safe, and if by chance she wasn't, then he had given her a place to hide. He couldn't have known that anyone else knew about the tunnel, especially Jonesy, because he didn't trust Jonesy to begin with.

"Crazy fucker," Jonesy muttered as he riffled through a stack of pictures. "He was always taking these damned pictures. For posterity, he said, and Dayle always laughed and said he had a hold on Thad, that he could keep him in line." He grimaced tightly as one of the more sexual pictures caught his eye. "He said he didn't develop the pictures, and Dayle believed him."

"But you knew better," she said. "Didn't you, Jonesy?"

Jonesy grinned. "I knew better. I knew when he left he'd take those negatives with him. I knew he'd betray us for that little bastard of his and the grandson Zeke wouldn't let him see. Damn, Zeke hated his old man, ya know?"

"I didn't know," she lied again.

Jonesy nodded as a thoughtful look crossed his face. He picked up a picture of him, as a much younger man, with Thad and James Maynard. Zeke and Gene were in the pictures. They were just boys, dressed in camo with wide grins on their faces.

"I guess I'll have to get rid of James now." He sighed. "And Gene. That will suck. Though James is still cowarding like a little girl on his farm. He won't even go to any of the meetings anymore. He doesn't want to rebuild what we lost, says he's too old," he sneered then. "If he's too old to fight, then he's too old to live, wouldn't you say?"

Rogue backed against the couch as his attention turned back to the pictures. Her fingers curled around the six-foot length of two-by-four that lay on the back of it.

She wasn't far from him, less than six feet. If she could get a good swing in before he could bring the gun back up, then she might have a chance. That was all she needed, a fighting chance. She refused to stand here like a sacrificial lamb on the altar of his insanity. Freedom League, her ass. Those bastards needed to die anyway. They were all as damned crazy as Jonesy, otherwise they would have never gotten mixed up in such a crazy scheme as taking over the nation.

"He seems smart to me," she said faintly as her fingers tightened on the wood. "Smarter than you."

When he turned back to her, she moved. The two-by-four swung for his head before he could react. His arm came up, but not quick enough. He'd taught her what John hadn't about fighting. He'd taught her how to disarm, how to kick effectively, but more, he'd taught her how to counter a defensive move.

She was short, weak, he'd always said, so he'd taught her to be effective rather than powerful. Using the momentum of her body, her shoulders, she slammed the wood into his shoulder, causing the gun to drop as she kicked out.

The heel of her boot caught his chin as she punched back with the end of the two-by-four into his head. Blood sprayed around her before she dropped the wood and ran for the stairs.

Forget the tunnel, she had no idea where it went. Jonesy was bigger than her, faster; she needed corners and furniture to hide behind, not a tunnel to run through.

She raced up the stairs cursing her boots even as she gloried in the blood they had shed. She slammed open the basement door as the blast behind her sent a bullet tearing through the wood inches above her head.

Ducking, she slammed the door closed, locked it, then threw a kitchen chair against it before racing to the back door and into the night.

It was dark and foggy as hell as the mist from the lake shrouded the house and the forest surrounding it. The night oozed a heavy blanket of thick fog, so thick it felt smothering as she stumbled around the house and ducked behind the border of evergreen hedges planted around it.

A quick glance at the bike had a sob choking her. The tires were flat. There wasn't a chance of escaping on it. For the moment, all she had were the hedges.

It was minimal covering, but it was dark, her clothes were dark. Blinking back her tears, she prayed for a chance.

TWENTY-THREE

Breathing in slow and deep, Rogue tried to force back the panic threatening to rise inside her now that she had escaped the house. Surely it wouldn't be too hard to hide here for a while. Maybe Jonesy would just leave.

She flinched at the sound of the kitchen door slamming closed.

The night suddenly seemed malevolent and frightening. Fear congealed inside her as a shiver raced up her spine and she strained to see through the thick fog to the land around her.

"Scary, isn't it, little girl?" Jonesy's voice was almost conversational as he spoke into the night. "The nights get real dark here in the mountains without the city lights to brighten them. Fog rolls in, and you can't see what's behind you, or what's in front of you. It's real easy to get lost, or to fall over a cliff. Or even worse, fall in the lake. The water is mighty cold this time of the year, Rogue."

She shivered at the thought of how cold.

Eyes wide, the breath laboring in her chest, she fought to stay in place rather than to sprint through the night.

"Do you know the direction of the road out of here?" he called out to her. "Have you been here enough times that you'll be able to stay on the gravel rather than the rocky ground and know where you are?"

She was smarter than that. She knew the difference between a graveled road and rocky ground.

Jonesy chuckled again. "Come on, Rogue. At least I'll kill you quick. The night will make you suffer."

God, how could she and her father have been so wrong about him? He wasn't a friend, he was a monster.

Kneeling behind the thick, heavy hedge, Rogue felt the first tear fall. The night was cold, wet. For the briefest moment she remembered the feel of Zeke's arms, the warmth of his body. A sob lodged in her throat at the need for that warmth.

She had seen the pain in his eyes earlier when he had realized Gene had betrayed him. Rogue felt that pain echoing inside her. In one night she had lost the man she loved, a friend, and possibly her brother.

"Rogue." Jonesy's hiss was filled with amusement as he drew closer to the hedge. "I know this land, this farm. I know every inch of it and of this house. I wonder if I can guess where you're hiding."

Her eyes widened at the sound of his voice, so much nearer now. Struggling to move silently, she edged along the side of the house, careful not to brush against the hedges.

Jonesy was a hunter. Her father had told her about the hunting trips they had taken together and how Jonesy seemed to have almost a second sense of where his prey would hide, which way it would go.

She wasn't an animal, she told herself, but was there really any difference between a human and an animal that knew it was hunted?

Her heart racing out of control, the blood thundering through her veins, Rogue decided there wasn't much difference. There was an awareness of death hovering, the tingle of hope, the defiance to live. She had to live. She'd be damned if she would let Jonesy hurt her family further.

"You didn't ask me how I managed to fool your father and everyone else all these years." Insidious and filled with hated confidence, Jonesy's voice threaded through the night again, closer than was comfortable.

"Should I tell you?" he asked her.

Yeah, keep talking, asshole, so I know exactly where you are.

His laughter was low, cruel. "Your father is so grateful to me for warning him of Dayle Mackay's plans regarding your mother that he doesn't mind a bit to send me a nice fat check every Christmas. He had no idea it was all a very nicely laid plan to get him the hell out of Somerset. See, your father was a troublemaker and your mother was just too damned high profile to just kill. But it worked out, Rogue. Your father proved to be a nice little resource. Why, the law firm he's established has even defended several of our members and cleared their good names of the evil acts they committed. He's a fine man," he drawled mockingly. "Too bad his daughter isn't as smart."

Yeah, too bad his daughter didn't fire you when she had the chance. Too bad she didn't just shoot you.

Rogue slid around the back of the house, her eyes straining to see past the fog as she fought to figure out which way to go, where the best place to hide would be.

"I know where you are, Rogue," he sang through the night. "Just around the corner, just around the bend. Searching for warmth before your life is set to end."

A poet he wasn't. But he had a point. She was just around the corner. Unfortunately, she didn't know a damned thing about Zeke's home other than the fact that the back deck should be within feet of her.

Moving carefully, fighting to stay silent, she managed to find the porch rails. Gripping the wood tightly, she climbed over the banister before hunkering down and feeling her way across the boards.

Would he expect her to be on the porch?

She followed the rails, found the opening that led back out into the yard, and paused there. Her nails dug into the wood as she listened and fought to hear above the racing of her heart. She couldn't hear Jonesy. Could he hear her? Her heart was like thunder in her ears, her breathing raspy. Fear was an acrid taste in her mouth now as her stomach clenched with panic.

The night itself whispered with dread. The breeze coming off the lake was a hiss of deadly intent. The shift of branches, the creak of the trees. Which was nature, which was a killer waiting to strike?

The fog danced slowly around her, shifting and thickening, thinning and moving through the night with hollow grace. Shadows twisted within the dense mist, came together, then drifted apart, giving her no hint to who was near and who wasn't.

How could a man of Jonesy's size move so silently? Surely she would have heard something.

Biting her lip, she remained in place, stiff, still, waiting. Watching. Praying. If only Zeke would get to her in time.

"He has to be bat-shit crazy to think he could get away with this, Zeke." Alex sat beside him in the Tahoe as Zeke cut the lights to the truck and made the turn onto the graveled road leading to his house. "He's a hunter, a fighter. He's had military training. Dishonorable discharge for striking an officer though his fellow officers testified that the officer struck first. If nothing else, he's a tough son of a bitch. If he has Rogue, getting her out won't be easy."

"Rogue will be watching for me." He had to believe that. She wasn't weak; she wasn't stupid. She would know he was coming for her, no matter how angry she had been when he left.

"Listen to me, none of these men that were in the League are operating with a full deck here," Alex warned him as he slid ammo into the rifle he carried.

He wore a night-vision device on his head; a handgun was strapped to his thigh. Dressed in camo with a matching cap covering his hair, the chief of Somerset's police department looked like the Special Forces soldier he had been six months prior.

Zeke eased the Tahoe over, aware of the other men in the backseat and back cargo area. They'd loaded up after dragging on gear they'd packed in their own vehicles. The Mackay boys believed in "just in case." They kept everything they needed on hand just in case something went from sugar to shit in a heartbeat.

Dawg, Natches, patched but still bleeding, Rowdy, limping but still walking, Cranston, a little worse for wear, but he was in one piece. And Gene. His deputy carried a sniper rifle similar to Alex's and his expression was as cold and forbidding as Alex knew his own was.

Shutting off the engine, he pulled his weapon from its holster, checked it, then shoved it back in place before taking the extra clips from Alex and shoving them in the large pocket of the dark camo jacket he wore.

"We're a quarter mile from the house," he said. "Natches, Rowdy, and Cranston will take the tunnel entrance, Alex, Dawg, and Gene and I will take the two entrances to the house." He stared at Gene through the rearview mirror. "You're with me."

Gene nodded, his eyes meeting Zeke's, his expression tight with controlled anger. They were going to have to deal with each other, and with Cranston when this was over. But for now, nothing mattered but Rogue.

"Maynard, give me that sniper rifle. He's had time to get here; that means one of us has to be in place to take him out at a moment's notice," Natches informed them, his voice rough, dark with the threat of violence as Gene handed him the sniper rifle.

Trusting no one, Natches began breaking it apart quickly and effectively. Within seconds he had it down, checked, and clicking everything back into place as Dawg stored ammo in the pockets of his own jacket.

"She's alive," Zeke stated. "That's all that matters."

He was aware of the looks the other men were giving each other.

"If she were dead, the house would be in flames." He nodded to the silent shadows ahead. There was no sign of light, no glow of a fire. "Jonesy wouldn't leave any evidence. He's been too careful so far; he would continue to be."

"Unless he took her out of the house," Cranston suggested.

Zeke ignored him.

"He wouldn't take her out of the house," Gene said. "Jonesy would make it look like a suicide or he'd set fire to the place. Dad told me once that the League had a silent exterminator. He never said who it was, but my money's on Danny Jones."

So was Zeke's.

"Let's move."

They exited the vehicle silently and moved quickly along the graveled road with the night-vision devices in place. The murky green visual displayed in front of his eyes gave Zeke a moment's pause. He rarely used night vision. But now, with the fog from the lake thickening around the mountains and hampering regular sight, Zeke thanked God for them.

With Alex, Dawg, and Gene at his back he set a fast pace toward the house. He could feel the prickling of danger now, the awareness that time was running out.

He had to get to her. God help him, he couldn't let her be hurt, or worse, taken from him forever. At that moment, nothing mattered but Rogue. Thoughts of her twisted through his head, rage and regret and blinding pain twisted and tangled together until rage bloomed from his inability to change the danger she was in.

He shouldn't have left her. He shouldn't have hurt her. He should have taken more time, explained more, made things clear. He should have assured her he was coming back for her, and that they would deal with the future then. He should have told her he loved her.

Rogue could feel the danger, it washed over her skin with an oily sensation and left her shuddering to the point that she had to lock her teeth together to keep them from chattering and giving her away.

She couldn't hear Jonesy anymore. How could a man so big move so quietly? Or was he moving? He could be doing as she was, waiting, watching.

Her muscles were cramping with her efforts to remain completely still. A tear spilled from her eyes, tickled her chin, but she refused to wipe it away.

Where was Zeke? He had to be coming. He had to be close. He wouldn't let her be hurt. She was only going to be able to do so much to save herself here. It wasn't as though she carried a gun or had even borrowed one of his. And she sure as hell wasn't strong enough for a fight against Jonesy.

Damn him. She hoped he knew he was fired now. The bastard had burned her bar? Blown it up? How could he blow up her bar?

Son of a bitch.

God, she was scared.

She clenched her teeth tighter and hoped she was out of sight. Of course in this fog, he could be standing beside her and she wouldn't know it.

A shudder worked over her as the dew began to seep into her thin T-shirt. The cool moisture became freezing after a while, and she didn't like the cold.

She wanted to be in Zeke's arms. She wanted him to hold her, wanted to be warm again against his naked flesh. She wanted a chance to kick him for using her.

She couldn't believe he had played her so easily. Rogue wasn't easy to play. At least, she hadn't thought she was.

She bit her lip as she heard a shuffle of sound. Was it wind or was it death coming closer? She was dead if Jonesy found her, and she knew it.

Another shift, it could be the breeze or the sound of a footfall against the grass.

She fought the need to run, to scream.

"Bitch! There you are!"

She screamed as cruel fingers gripped her hair and jerked her up, then over the railing. She slammed to the ground, her hands jerking to her head, nails digging into his flesh as he cursed.

"You sorry whore!"

Agony screeched through her nervous system as he jerked her up by her hair. A hard fist glanced the side of her head, momentarily rattling her before she could kick back with the heels of her boots.

Wiggling, scratching, she fought to be free as he jerked her around by the hair, his other hand moving.

The gun. He had a gun.

Her screams pierced the night as she released his arm to grip the one she knew held the gun. He shook her as her hands reached for him, causing her to fall against him. The feel of the gun at his waist had her reaching desperately for it.

His hands knocked hers aside as she felt it, as it was almost in her grasp. The blow numbed her wrists as she felt the weapon knock to the ground.

"You fucking bitch!" he yelled into the night, his fist cracking against her cheek as she struggled in his grip.

Stars exploded in front of her eyes as an edge of darkness began to seep through her mind. Rogue felt herself wavering, knees weakening as she began to fall.

He shook her and she barely felt the pain in her head until her knees collapsed and the force of her weight threatened to tear her hair from the roots.

"Where's the fucking gun, bitch?" he screamed in her ear. "I'm going to beat the fucking hell out of you before I put a bullet between your eyes."

It was dark, so dark. Rogue felt herself falling, felt the strength leaving her limbs.

Suddenly she was free. She went to the ground with enough force to bruise her knees. The moment of freedom seemed to pump the strength back into her. Not a lot, just enough to scramble away before turning on her back and kicking out.

She caught him in the knees with the sharp tips of her heels, slamming them into his kneecaps and feeling a surge of triumph at his squall of pain as he stumbled backward.

Turning, she fought to crawl quickly from him. Her nails tore against the hard-packed dirt. Her hair fell over her face, blinding her further.

It was already so dark she didn't worry about the hair. The curls tangled around her arms, her face; rocks dug into her knees and palms.

She had to be close to escape. Close enough to get to her feet and run. She paused only long enough to try to jump to her feet. As her toes dug into the ground, harsh hands wrapped around her ankles and jerked her back.

The rending of fabric where her jeans ripped at the knees infuriated her. Why that would piss her off she didn't know, but a growl clawed from her throat as she tried to kick out at him again.

"I wanted to be nice about this." His voice was demented, monstrous. "I would have been nice."

The gun was in her face.

Rogue stilled. She felt the barrel pressing into her cheek, looked up, and through the fog saw the demon wielding it.

"There's a nice way to murder someone?" she cried out. "Is that what you told Joe and Jaime, that you'd be nice? Is that what you told their grandmother?"

"No," he sneered. "I told them to burn in hell. And that's where you'll burn, too."

His finger tightened on the trigger.

Rogue's scream pierced the night, spurring Zeke through the night as he raced to find her. The night-vision device he wore painted the world in a hazy green, but it was a clear picture of where he was going.

The house was just ahead of them. Gene was at his back, Alex off to his left, while Dawg took the right.

He couldn't seem to run fast enough, he couldn't get enough speed to his legs; adrenaline wasn't coursing fast enough through his body.

Desperation filled his mind as pain seemed to sear his soul. He was too late. He was going to be too late to save her. He was going to lose her. The only woman who had ever touched his heart, and he was going to lose her if he didn't hurry.

Her screams were digging into his head now. Piercing, filled with fury and pain. As he reached the house he jerked his gun from its holster, gripped it with both hands, and tore around the side of the house.

God, he had to run faster.

It seemed to take forever to reach the corner of the house and move around to the back deck. The fog was so damned thick he didn't know how Jonesy had navigated through it. But Zeke could see. He could see everything in slow motion. The gun in her face; Jonesy's finger tightening on the trigger.

"No!" he screamed out in fury as he lifted his gun, then watched as Jonesy jerked at the same moment and the back of his head exploded out into the night.

Zeke didn't pause to think, he didn't give himself time to worry about shooters that might not be friendly. As Jonesy toppled over Rogue's fallen form, he jerked the other man off, threw him back to the ground, and lifted Rogue into his arms.

Keeping his body hunched he raced up the deck steps, threw his shoulder into the door of the house, felt the locks give, and fell inside the house with her. His body covered hers as he rolled her across the floor, forced to ignore her cries until he could get her safely on the other side of the room, behind the couch.

"Rogue. Baby." Propping her against the couch he let his hands race over, his gaze searching her body for wounds or broken bones. "Rogue, talk to me."

"Son of a bitch," she gasped, her bruised face swelling, her violet eyes filled with rage.

Zeke watched her in shock until her hand cracked against his face. The stinging slap wasn't gentle. It slammed into his cheek with enough force that he knew he'd be carrying the imprint of her hand for hours. In the next second, his ever-strong, impossibly stubborn Rogue collapsed into his arms in tears.

"I have you, baby." He buried his head in her hair, a shudder working through his body at how close she had come to dying. "It's okay, baby. I have you."

Rogue never cried. She wasn't a whiner. She didn't complain. She was sobbing in his arms, holding on to him with desperate hands and trying to burrow into his chest.

And God help him, he didn't blame her. Tightening his arms around her, he held her to him, rocked her, and closed his eyes as he fought the overload of fear and remorse that struck his system.

He shouldn't have left her. He should have never left her, believing she would be safe. He should have considered Jonesy, but instead he had relied on the loyalty the other man had always appeared to show her. Zeke knew he should have known better. It was his mistake, and it was one Rogue had nearly paid for.

"Damn, he's in trouble," Rowdy's low voice whispered across the room in a tone of amazement and male concern. "I've never heard of her crying. I bet she cuts his dick off for him."

"Shut up, Rowdy," Dawg growled.

"Yeah, shut up, Rowdy." From Cranston, his voice low and filled with regret.

Zeke lifted his head and stared back at the agent.

"I have to take you in, Zeke." He sighed. "This has to be wrapped up."

His arms contracted around Rogue. God, he'd known it was coming. He'd known all along that the sins of the past could never be buried or even forgotten by the DHS agent that knew the truth.

"God, Cranston, give him a day or two at least," Rowdy protested. "You mean-hearted, slimy bastard. Someone's going to end up killing you."

Zeke heard sirens wailing in the distance then. Reinforcements that would have been too late if Natches hadn't managed to get in place with that sniper rifle. Zeke knew it had to have been Natches, because he was the only one missing at the moment.

"Zeke knew our deal," Cranston stated. "We need the information, those pictures, and his testimony. This wraps it up, boys. The pictures he sent earlier had faces of men we don't have in custody, and he remembers them. This fucking group is gone. It's damned history and I'll do whatever it takes to wrap it up for good." Because this group had destroyed his family, had killed his wife, his daughter, and his grandchild. Because destroying them was all Cranston knew and he would stop at nothing to see it finished.

It finished here, just as he said.

"No matter who you have to destroy?" Rowdy asked.

"No matter who's destroyed," Cranston affirmed. "No matter what it takes."

Zeke held Rogue closer, already feeling the chill inside his soul because he knew he would have to let her go, walk away again, and walking away would destroy him more than the truth of his past ever could.

Pressing his lips to her ear he whispered. "You fill me. Remember that, Rogue. For the first time in my life, I knew what love was supposed to be."

Her head shook against his chest as another sob tore from her throat. Her arms were like silken bands of steel around his neck, and God knew he didn't know if he had the strength to force her to release him.

"I didn't use you." He kissed the top of her head, her forehead. "I was helpless against you. Know that, Caitlyn Rogue. I couldn't have walked away for anything. Even my own life."

TWENTY-FOUR

But he did walk away.

A week later Rogue stood in the parking lot of what had once been the Bar and stared at the debris with a sense of . . . relief.

She'd lost everything she owned except the Harley, but she was thankful she had a reason to walk away from it now. An era had come to an end. The Bar was gone, the dangerous Dayle Mackay and his rabid revolutionists were gone. Jonesy was gone.

She shoved her hands into the pockets of her pants and let her gaze wander over the blackened remains of lumber where the walls had toppled in.

"So what now?" Her father's arm went around her shoulders as his tall, sturdy body gave her a place to lean.

She shrugged at his question. "I bought out Natches Mackay. I guess I'm part owner in a restaurant now."

Her father gave a heavy sigh as she looked up into the strong features of his still-handsome face.

"I want you to come home," he told her as her mother, Brianna Walker, moved to her other side. "Damned house is too quiet. With your sister married and gone, and damned John won't even stay the night. The nest is too empty."

She grinned at that. "Sorry, Dad. This is home."

Somerset was home. Lake Cumberland was home.

All she had left to do was to get over one arrogant, too-sexy sheriff and her life would even out. One day she might even sleep through the night without crying.

"What about Zeke?" her mother asked as though reading her thoughts. "He called again last night."

He had called every night for the past three nights. She refused to answer the phone; she refused to talk to him. He was back on the job now, the crime that had been committed when he was a child had never been mentioned, and for that, she was glad. His father had betrayed him, tried to destroy him and his future. No man should have to pay for that.

"I don't want to talk about Zeke." She didn't want to cry again. The pain was like a festering wound inside her soul that refused to heal.

He had used her. He may not have suspected Jonesy of being the killer he was seeking, but he hadn't been honest with her, either. He hadn't told her he was fucking her so the killer would believe he was distracted by her and not giving his attention to tracking him. He hadn't told her that the only reason he had come to her bed was to further the goal of capturing that killer.

I was helpless against you. Know that, Caitlyn Rogue. I couldn't have walked away for anything. Even my own life.

He had whispered those words before he had left with Cranston. But he had still left. He had walked away from her without a backward glance to help Cranston round up the final straggling members of the organization he had fought to bring down.

James Maynard had been arrested, though he was now free on bond due to his cooperation with the Department of Homeland Security and the Justice Department. Gene Maynard, she had learned, had been helping DHS all along.

There had been other arrests in Louisville as well as Frankfort, and according to Alex Jansen, the Freedom League was now nothing more than a very bad memory.

"Just come home for a while," her father tried again. "A month."

She shook her head again as a smile touched her lips. He kept trying; she had to give him credit for that.

"I'm ready to go back to the apartment now, Daddy. It should be repaired enough," she told him as she turned into his embrace and hugged him quickly. "Just take me home now."

There was a small moment of silence. Her parents were sharing that look, she thought. The one they shared whenever they didn't know what to do with the children they had raised.

"Fine." Her father finally sighed heavily. "But if you're not coming home, then I'm hanging around awhile. Dawg Mackay offered us the use of his houseboat now that's he's moved into the house he built. I think we'll take him up on that."

She almost winced. God, would Lake Cumberland survive her parents? Even for a few days? Surely they wouldn't stay any longer than that.

"You should go home, Daddy," she began to argue the decision.

"Caitlyn, your father said we're staying. The decision has been made." She was using her best "mommy" voice. The one that all three of her strong-willed children understood clearly. That was the final word. Period.

"Fine, but you know he's just going to cause trouble while he's here," she informed her mother as they made their way back to the limo they had ridden in from the airport in Louisville. "He's a trouble magnet, Mom. Him and John. John's already causing trouble and he hasn't been here two weeks yet."

"I'm certain we'll all survive," her mother stated. "We'll take you home, then go check out Mr. Mackay's houseboat. It looked simply charming when we drove around the docks earlier. Did you know your father used to have a boat on the lake as well? When he was much younger."

"No." Rogue looked at her askance. "And I'm sure I don't want to know about it, either. Don't gross me out with your tales of dating Daddy. Please."

Her mother laughed as they sat back in the limo and the vehicle pulled away.

Rogue gazed back at the charred remains of the Bar and wondered about this turn in her life. She was twenty-six years old, and she had just lost the only man she could have ever imagined loving. The knowledge that he had walked away from her that night, claiming to have used her, pushing her back to be protected like a little china doll while he went off to fight the bad guys, still had the power to hurt.

It wasn't that he had left her there. He had believed she would be safe, she could forgive him for that. No, she was angry, she was hurt, because he hadn't left with so much as a "see you later." She could have died believing he had felt nothing for her.

It was the betrayal that hurt. When he needed her he hadn't wanted to accept that she would be there for him. He hadn't told her the full details of what he was doing and why he was doing it. He hadn't shared his feelings for her. He had just left her there. He could have died, been arrested for whatever, and gone from her life, and she wouldn't have known she was any more important to him than the grass under his feet.

Because he had lied to her. He had let her think he was simply using her, when she had known, known to the bottom of her soul that he cared.

"Rogue?" her mother spoke her name softly. "When you're young it's very easy to let pride get in the way of what's most important in your life. Don't make that mistake."

She turned away from her mother's compassionate gaze and swallowed tightly. Was it just pride?

"He lied to me," she whispered. "He left me, denying he cared anything for me."

"And if he hadn't come back?" her father asked. "If he'd died, Rogue? He was looking out for you."

She fought the tears that would have fallen. "He just left."

"And perhaps he had no other choice," her mother said gently as the limo turned into Somerset and headed for the old town center where her new apartment was located. "Men aren't always as logical as they think they are. Sometimes, Rogue, it's up to the women who love them to point that out to them."

"And sometimes it takes a good swift kick," her father drawled in amusement. "Your mother has delivered a few of those over the years."

She stared out the window, her throat tight with unshed tears as she fought the pain that never seemed to ease, the chill that she swore went clear to her soul.

God, she missed Zeke. She ached for him.

"Rogue." Her mother touched her arm gently as the limo pulled into the back lot of the restaurant. "Perhaps you should just talk to him."

She saw the Tahoe then, the sheriff's emblem emblazoned on the door as it opened and Zeke stepped out.

He was dressed in jeans again, that damned badge hanging on his belt. He wore boots and a gray cotton shirt. The sun blazed around him, making his eyes appear more golden, his expression more imposing as the car drew to a stop.

"Just talk to him, Rogue," her father suggested gently then. "It doesn't hurt to talk."

The chauffeur opened the door and she stepped out slowly, aware of the door closing behind her and seconds later the vehicle pulling away.

Zeke leaned against the front of the Tahoe, his arms crossing over his chest, his expression imposing.

"Took you long enough," he growled, his voice dark, deep. His face was almost haggard. He looked as bad as she felt, as though the world had crashed in upon him as well.

She pulled her keys from her pocket, turned, and moved for the steps of the apartment.

Was he following her? She could feel him behind her, watching her. She felt like a rabbit beneath the regard of a hungry wolf.

She saw him as she turned up the steps. He was behind her. Far enough away that she could tell he was deliberately keeping distance between them.

"Is the investigation over?" she asked as she shoved the key into the door and stepped inside.

"It's over. They rounded the final members up the night after Jonesy was killed. They have all the evidence they need to lock them up for a damned long time."

Rogue nodded. "From what I've been hearing they didn't have much of a chance for success anyway. A bunch of crazy old men looking for a war."

"That about sums it up." His voice was clipped, cool as he stepped into the apartment behind her and closed the door. "But these crazy old coots were smarter than you'd think. And more dangerous."

She nodded. Yeah, she'd heard that, too. They'd killed a lot of good men and women and been responsible for even more deaths over the past thirty years.

"How's Gene doing?" she asked.

Zeke blew out a hard breath. "It's been hard on him. He didn't even know Cammi was seeing the Walker boys. It shook him up, realizing she was hiding it from him. Makes sense why she ran off to her sisters after they were killed though. She was devastated."

"She loved them?" Rogue turned and stared at him from where she stood in the living room.

"She cared a hell of a lot anyway." He shook his head, his expression heavy. "She wasn't aware anyone was looking for her. She thought Joe had killed Jaime and then himself, because of her. Gene's taking care of her though. That's the important part."

That was the important part, Rogue agreed. Like her father had tried to take care of her, and she had refused to allow it. Her family had gathered around her, giving advice, offering their support, and nothing helped the pain; no one could ease it.

She stared back at Zeke now and swallowed at the lump of pain in her throat. It had been so long since she had felt his arms around her. So many nights she had cried into her pillow, aching, hurting.

"Do you hate me, Rogue?" he asked then, standing before her, tall and so very arrogant, as though he were daring her to strike out at him. As though he expected it.

"Would you hate me?" she asked him.

She had wondered over the past week if she was right or wrong in how she felt. Should she punish him, or should she simply love him?

He grimaced heavily. "I'd paddle your damned ass if you pulled something like that on me," he finally admitted. "But son of a bitch if I would let you go, Rogue. There wouldn't have been a night that I wasn't trying to get into your bed anyway."

"I can't paddle your ass," she said, her voice thickening with the emotion clogging it. "What am I supposed to do, Zeke, wait until the next time you're worried for me, scared I'll be hurt, and you do it again? How do I know when you're committed to me rather than your fears of losing someone?"

His jaw clenched furiously. "You sound like Shane now. He hasn't spoken to me since he found out what had been going on the past ten years. He's pouting in Louisville like a child because I didn't tell him before he left on that trip what was going on."

"Because you could have died while he was gone," she snapped. "Because he loves you, Zeke. How do you think it makes us feel? To know you'd push us away so damned easily?"

"That I'd protect you?" he growled back. "I'd hope you'd understand how important you are to me. God, Rogue, do you think I wanted to die knowing if I had told you how I felt that you would have grieved worse? Or if I was arrested and charged for a murder I committed as a child, do you think I wanted you to hold on to me when I didn't have a future to give you?"

"And that's acceptable?" she cried. "Fine, Zeke, let's turn the table. Would you accept it?"

"Fuck no!" he yelled back. "You're mine, damn you. No matter what."

"My God, listen to you." She was in his face, almost nose to nose, anger beating a ragged tattoo in her veins. "Listen to how arrogant you are! Why should I accept it? Why shouldn't you belong to me, too, Zeke? Do you think for one damned minute I'll only take you when you're safe? God, what is that, a weekend out of the fucking year?"

His eyes narrowed. "You'll take me, period, every damned day of the year," he snarled back. "Fine, I was a fucking fool. I was stupid. I was a dumb-fuck hick that loved his woman enough to want to protect her. So shoot me."

"Give me the gun." Hands on hips, arousal and anger firing in her blood, she yelled the words back at him.

It flooded her now. The long nights without him, the anger that he would stay away from her without telling her he loved her. That he would wait until she was angry, until she wanted to kick him, before admitting it.

"You little hellion." Amazement darkened his gaze and filled his face. "You stubborn little witch. You won't even say you love me, will you?"

"Why should I?" A pout formed on her lips as she whirled away from him. "Why should I tell you anything?"

If she thought he was going to let her get away that easily, she was wrong. She had hoped she was wrong. Prayed she was.

Before she could take the first step he wrapped an arm around her waist, picked her up, then strode through the apartment. Straight to her bedroom and to the bed.

"You will say it," he promised her, his voice filled with arousal and demand now. "Before you get out of this bed, I promise you, you'll say it."

Rogue swiped the hair from her face, leaned up on her elbows, and watched him undress. He tore at his clothes. Buttons ripped from his shirt, his boots were tossed to the floor, his jeans, underwear, and shocks taken off in one swipe. When he stood before her, all dark flesh and raging arousal, Rogue swore she lost her breath.

His cock was furiously engorged, the wide crest flushed dark and throbbing as his fingers circled the thick shaft and pumped it with several slow, erotic strokes.

"Undress," he ordered, his voice rough, his eyes dark.

"You're getting awful bossy," she murmured, though she rose from the bed as she watched him carefully.

She didn't just tear her clothes off. She bent her knee and pulled off first one shoe, then the other and let them drop to the floor.

Next, with slow, exacting movements her hands gripped the hem of her light sweater and she pulled it over her head, finally shaking her hair free as his groan whispered to her.

His expression was intent now, his face flushed. Golden brown eyes seemed darker, more predatory as her fingers went to the snap of her jeans.

The metal closure came free easily, the zipper rasped open, and seconds later she was pushing the denim from her legs and standing before him in nothing but the wicked black lace of her thong and bra. As he watched, her hands lifted and she cupped the swollen mounds of her breasts before flicking open the plastic clip of the bra.

"God, I'll have a stroke before you get those panties off," he groaned hoarsely. "Could you try to hurry, baby? Control isn't something I have a lot of right now."

She smiled. Let him suffer then. He deserved to suffer for what he'd done to her. Just a little bit.

"I should worry about your control?" she asked, her voice soft, deliberately sensual. "Really, Zeke. I've suffered a week now. Where have you been?"

His eyes narrowed. "You wouldn't even talk to me when I called, Rogue."

She shrugged. "Maybe I didn't want a phone between us, Zeke. Maybe I wanted *you*. And *you* weren't here."

She shivered as she let her fingertips trail down her stomach and imagined the touch of his fingers against her. Calloused, rough, warm.

"You are treading a very thin line, sweetheart," he rasped.

"Are you going to handcuff me, Sheriff?" Her fingers dipped beneath the elastic of her thong, her breath catching as her fingertips grazed her clit.

The look on his face was sexy as hell. Dark and primal. She

wondered how long it would take him to break that incredible control of his.

"Damn, you're gorgeous," he breathed out as she trailed her fingers back to her breasts and whispered a touch over her nipples.

"Am I really?" She smiled back at him. "I'm a little short."

"That's what they make those damned high heels for," he breathed roughly. "Rogue, sweetheart, we're reaching critical here." His hand tightened on his cock. "Take the panties off, baby."

"You take them off."

It was a dare. It was a challenge. And she should have known better. She would have if it hadn't produced exactly the reaction she wanted.

He was across the distance in two short steps. His fingers curled under the band of the thong and pulled. The material ripped away from her with a hiss of a sound. One arm went around her back and he lifted her, dragging one leg over his hip as he turned to the bed.

The heavy crest of his cock was poised at the entrance to her pussy, pressing against her as he laid her back along the bed, spread her legs wide, and lowered his gaze to watch.

It was so damned sexy it should be illegal. Rogue watched, too. Watched as the bare folds of her sex parted and the blunt, dark head of his erection began to press inside her.

Heat seared her from the inside out. Pleasure whipped through her body, centered at the point of penetration, and then sizzled over her flesh. Her clit throbbed, and she swore if he didn't hurry she was going to orgasm before he was even seated fully inside her.

She was desperate, on fire. Her hand pushed down her abdomen again and her fingers found the straining nub of her clit as Zeke jerked against her.

"God, that's fucking sexy," he groaned as she touched herself.

His hips shifted and a cry left her lips as he sank deeper inside her. The erotic stretching was sheer bliss. The little bite of a burn, the stroke of rapture. Rogue's back arched with the sensations, her head dug into the mattress.

"There, baby," he breathed out, his voice rough, the muscles in his abdomen flexing as she watched him pull back. "Ah God. You're so sweet. So tight and hot."

Her finger raced over her clit as he began to move inside her. Deep, heavy thrusts that had her hips writhing as she masturbated to the swift tempo he was creating.

It was exquisite, heated. Bliss.

"More," she begged, watching as his cock pulled free, glistened with her juices, then shoved inside again with a hard, hungry stroke.

Rogue could feel the sensations gathering inside her, the tight knot of heat in her womb, the throb of her clit, the racing of her blood, and the ache in her nipples. They were growing, signaling the approach of her orgasm as she tried to push that steady ascension faster. She wanted it now. She wanted to explode in his arms, wanted to scream his name.

It was more than just the pleasure, more than just her approaching orgasm. Zeke was here in her arms, in her bed. She stared up at him, memorizing the arousal-heavy planes and angles of his face, the perspiration building on his corded, muscular shoulders.

Arching in his arms, she felt the warning thunder in her veins, the burst of almost violent sensation as his hips twisted against her, thrusting heavily, stroking, building the pleasure inside her, and she wondered if she could survive. If she'd live through the cataclysm racing for her.

She saw it as it exploded. Blinding lights, the pulse and throb of her vagina around the heavy thrusts inside it. The stretching burn, the need, the desire, and finally the blinding, soul-shattering explosion that had her screaming his name, twisting in his arms, and melting in completion.

"Zeke. Oh God, Zeke. I love you. I love you."

He couldn't leave her again. She couldn't bear it. She couldn't stand to see him walk away, to see him face danger alone, not knowing she loved him, not knowing that when he came back, she would be there. No matter what.

Her hands jerked to his face, clasped it as he jerked above her in his own release. Their eyes met, melded.

"I love you," she cried huskily. "Don't you know, Zeke? Whether you loved me or not, I'd die for you."

His golden brown eyes flared with heat. His expression twisted in pain, in remorse.

"I love you until I can't breathe for needing you." His voice was jerky, panting. "God, Rogue. I live for you."

He shuddered against her; the feel of his release spilling inside her, the press of his body against her, it was completion. It was where she was meant to be.

This was the dream. It went past the little deceptions he had played upon her, it went past the anger and the hurt pride. It overrode their fears. Here. In Zeke's arms, Caitlyn Rogue found a home.

EPILOGUE

One year later

It was the party of the year as far as the Mackay
Marina and its inhabitants were concerned as the owners of the
marina hosted the reception for the Pulaski County sheriff that
finally tied the knot with the rogue that stole his heart.

The bride was exquisite in an off-white medieval gown. The
groom was debonair in his black tux. The best man, Somerset's
chief of police, Alex Jansen, stood with the matron of honor, his
wife, Janey Mackay Jansen.

The tables that had been set up beneath the canopy erected just
for the event were filled. But the main attraction, even for the bride
and groom, were the three exquisite Mackay daughters that had
been born to the Mackay cousins in the past year.

All girls. Their daddies held them close and glared at the guests
who laughed, because they couldn't believe the notorious Mackay
cousins had all gotten payback quite so good.

"Yeah, those girls are going to be wilder than the wind," one guest remarked. "Can't you just see Natches at fifty, hobbling on his cane to keep up with that girl of his?"

His daughter, with a head full of thick black hair tipped with gold and curious green eyes, stared up at her daddy with a spark of mischief already.

"What about that Dawg," another guest ventured. "A daughter. Oh man. I can't wait to see the shenanigans those girls get into."

Dawg growled.

"Bet me ole Rowdy's girl ain't the wildest," another guest dared. "He was always the quiet one of the bunch. You know he was the ringleader."

The guests laughed, looked at three perfect little girls with black hair and green eyes, and felt a smidgen of compassion for the former bad boys of the county.

Three Mackay girls. Cousins. Gorgeous and already confident of their place in the world.

Yeah, give it another twenty years and the Mackays would be the talk of the town again. The Mackays, and the friends that backed them. The Nauti Boys would one day become the Nauti Girls.